CHAPTER ONE

FOOLISHLY, I blinked several times. My eyes weren't playing tricks on me. No matter how many times I opened them, praying to see something else—anything else—the image didn't change.

Scarlet hair with black streaks flowed past her shoulders, framing the neckline of the tight, short, black lace dress she wore. Her heavily lined misty gray eyes searched for any sign of the person she was supposed to meet.

There was no doubt it was Erin. She stood at the back of the Shell station in one of the parking spaces, leaning against the driver's-side door of her black sedan.

Thankfully, we were in one of the vampires' standard black Suburbans and not Griffin's Navigator, or she probably would've recognized us.

In the back of the Suburban, Killian tightened his arm around my shoulders, nudging me closer to his side. Tingles jolted between us as our fated-mate bond sprang to life. Between that and his sandalwood scent, my head grew dizzy, but now wasn't the time.

We were more at war than we'd known.

Killian's angular jaw clenched as his mocha-brown irises darkened, and he ran a free hand through his short cappuccino hair. He gritted out, "That's why she let Tom live?" Tom was the late wolf shifter alpha who, along with his pack, had tried to kill many of us several times as part of his conspiracy to betray our kind to humans and gain revenge on my mother, who'd broken up with him many years ago when she'd met my father, her fated mate.

Leaning over his center aisle seat toward Sierra, Torak narrowed his dark green eyes. The dark ends of his long ponytail fell over his shoulder. "Who is this person, and which one is she? Several people are standing outside their cars at the gas station."

Torak was one of our new allies and the alpha of his own pack. We'd recently met him and his stepsister, Sadie, a fae-wolf shifter mated to Donovan, the alpha of another pack that included his best friend, Axel, and Axel's mate, Roxy. With them had come other unique allies we were getting to know.

Glancing over the headrest of the front passenger seat, Sterlyn addressed him, her iridescent purple irises reflecting the light from outside. "The woman with red and black hair is the priestess of the Shadow City witch coven and a fellow city council member with Griffin and me. She should be an ally, but there's only one reason she'd be here, since she almost never leaves the city." Sterlyn pulled her light silver hair behind her shoulders as she glanced out of Griffin's driver's side window.

"She's the person we're supposed to meet." Griffin's hands tightened on the steering wheel, causing his knuckles to whiten. He kept his attention on the road and drove past the station. The air from the vents blew against his face, but his golden brown hair contained so much gel

RUTHLESS MOON

SHADOW CITY: SILVER MATE

JEN L. GREY

that it didn't budge. "And obviously, she's working against us."

Making a fist, Sierra growled, "With all the shit she's pulled over the years, does that really surprise you?" Her light gray irises darkened to slate, and she tugged at the end of her ponytail, wrapping the sandy-blonde strands around her fingers. "Now I feel bad that I ever gave Deissy the official 'bitch' title. I take it back. It officially goes to Erin."

I'd met Deissy, and she hadn't seemed *that* bad. Surely Sierra had to mean someone else.

"Sierra, please. Deissy's part of our pack," Killian rasped, and closed his eyes. "There's a reason she stays far away from us, including me, her alpha."

Torak raised his hand. "I hate to interject and...uh...ruin the moment here about Deissy, but I still don't understand why someone from your city is here."

"Damn it, Sexy Dummy." Sierra's head snapped toward him. "It's not *my city*." She raised a finger like a sword and sliced the air between them. "I may live on the outskirts of Shadow City in the Ridge, but that *place* is not my home, nor would I ever want it to be."

Though the situation was dire, the corners of my mouth tipped upward. Leave it to Sierra to tell us exactly what she thought and how she felt.

"Sierra," Killian warned.

I placed a hand on his chest to calm him and myself. Erin working with the humans who had kidnapped and experimented on wolf shifters was worse than Tom doing the same. She was a witch who could track people down, and she had secrets she would kill to keep.

"Erin has always been working against us. She has influence in the city, especially as a representative of the witches on the council, and she's worked with people who didn't have the city's best interests at heart before." Sterlyn rubbed her temples. "I'd hoped that with Azbogah's death, Shadow City being revealed to the world, and humans coming after us, we might finally be able to trust her somewhat. Clearly, I was wrong."

"No clue who Azbogah is...er...was, but I get the gist." Torak leaned back in his seat. "So, since she knows all of you, it's a good thing I came along."

Though I was new to the group, I'd seen Erin for the first time after we'd rescued my grandparents' pack from those humans. She'd shown up as Tom and his pack had been attacking us during the escape. She had implied that she and her coven were going to kill Tom's people. I'd met her personally when she'd visited our pack neighborhood after we'd learned that Tom's pack was still alive. Erin had vowed that she'd spared him so she could learn who was kidnapping packs, but now it seemed she'd been helping Tom find another pack to betray to the humans experimenting on wolf shifters. She must be in communication with the humans. Otherwise, how would she know to be here?

Griffin frowned and turned in at a Dunkin' Donuts a few blocks down.

I understood how he felt. We barely knew Torak, Sadie, and their other pack members, and though we were beginning to trust them—especially after fighting beside them during the most recent battle against Tom's pack—trust took time to build.

Are you really going to let him meet with Erin? Sierra linked with Killian and me. *We* just *met him, and he tried to shoot us.*

She was holding a grudge, and we'd already discussed why he'd done that. Given the situation, I'd remind her one last time. *He didn't know who we were, and we pulled up in standard, government-issued black Suburbans. When Sadie told him not to shoot, he put the gun down.*

Semantics, she retorted.

Glancing at Killian, I was momentarily distracted by his long eyelashes and full lips. Even in a dreadful situation, he stole my breath.

For the love of the gods. Killian rolled his eyes. *Let it go, Sierra. None of us wants him to meet with her, but he's right. Our hands are tied. She'll recognize the rest of us.*

So? Sierra spun in her seat to glare at Killian, then spoke out loud, "Why don't we confront her? We shouldn't have to hide."

I bit my cheek so I wouldn't answer. This was something Killian needed to address as her alpha.

"I can say with complete confidence that every single one of us here wants to march over and confront Erin." Killian released his hold on me and straightened. "But she'll have an excuse, and all we'll do is give her an advantage over us again. If we want to get ahead of her for once, we have to pretend we're in the dark."

I placed my hand on Sierra's arm to comfort her. "Egan and Jade have had plenty of time to get far enough away from everyone." Egan and Jade were two dragon shifters with whom we'd also recently allied. "And if Torak drives off without us, we can call Rosemary, Lowe, April, or PawPaw for help. They're with Sadie, helping everyone bury the dead. There's not much risk in Torak going. We can find him if he betrays us."

Torak shook his head. "And I thought Jade had trust issues." He reached forward and grabbed the shirt Egan had provided for Erin's location spell. It was supposed to belong to someone from a wolf pack whose location "Tom" was betraying to the humans. Egan and Jade were flying far away so that whenever Erin performed the location spell, Egan would be nowhere near the site where we'd fought and killed Tom.

Torak ripped the shirt in half and handed one part to Sierra. "There. You now have a way to find Egan via your witch friends if I do something shady."

Her face fell, but she took the piece of fabric from him, her fingers brushing his. She linked, *He needs to stay in the vehicle. He needs to stay safe.* Her eyes widened, and she slapped her free hand over her mouth.

Head jerking back, Killian furrowed his brows.

Sierra's reaction reminded me of when I hadn't understood my connection to Killian. I didn't envy those unsettling emotions, and I hoped she figured them out. Now that Killian and I were settled with each other, our relationship was better than everything before.

Torak's hand dropped, and the corners of his eyes tightened. His attention flicked among Killian, me, and Sierra, then lingered on her. He asked, "Are you okay?" His tone held an edge.

"No," she snapped, and dropped her hands. "I mean, yeah. We're *fine.*" She hung her head and linked, *I'm so sorry. I don't know why I said that. Of course I want all of us to be safe and not just him.*

I think something's wrong with her, Killian linked with me. *This is odd behavior, even for Sierra. She's never shocked herself.*

Maybe they're fated mates? I didn't want to say they definitely were, but her reaction indicated more than just attraction, and holding on to anger made it easier to deny the pull. *That* I understood. I'd been in the same situation not even a month ago.

Killian tilted his head and squinted.

While he pondered my words, I tried to ease Sierra's concern. *It's fine. We're all highly emotional. We know you don't want harm to come to us, either.*

Griffin parked the SUV in a spot at the back of the restaurant where Erin wouldn't see us. He tapped his fingers on the steering wheel. "I guess we'd better get out. It'll look suspicious if Torak doesn't pull up in the vehicle."

Soon, all six of us were standing by the store, and Sierra rushed to the driver's-side door where Torak was ready to get back in. He towered over her five-foot-eight frame by several inches and was double her size in musculature.

When she reached him, she stopped abruptly. "Don't try to kill her like you did us." She lifted her chin, but her bottom lip quivered. "But if you do, make sure she can't come back."

He smiled. "Don't worry. I'm an excellent fighter. You saw what I could do earlier tonight."

She licked her lips and tossed her hair over her shoulder. "You were all right."

Now they were flirting. Though I was all about Sierra finding someone so we didn't have to keep hearing her complain about being single, now was not the time.

Griffin cleared his throat. "Erin isn't known for her patience."

Torak took a hurried step back and opened the door. "Does anyone know what to expect? Should I know anything in particular?"

No one spoke.

Then Sterlyn rubbed her hands together. "Tom likely would have brought Erin a piece of clothing belonging to someone he held a grudge against. If asked, I would insinuate you aren't sure of the specifics but that they wronged your alpha in some way and that's all that matters to you."

"You're young enough that following orders without question is normal, and an alpha—especially one like Tom—never likes to share all the ways that someone made them look bad." Killian took my hand. "Worst case, if things go awry, we'll be there in seconds to have your back."

And I'd fallen in love with an amazing guy. Even when I'd blamed him for the disappearance of my grandparents and mom, this type of promise had made me thaw toward him almost immediately.

Torak nodded and climbed into the driver's seat.

When he moved to shut the door, Sierra damn near shouted, "Wait."

He paused and lifted a brow.

"Be careful, okay?" She fidgeted, and her gaze traveled to Sterlyn, Griffin, Killian, and me. "We kinda need you to stay in one piece so we don't blow our cover."

"Uh...thanks?" His voice rose at the end, making it sound like a question.

When he shut the door and started the engine, Sierra inched closer, her attention locked on Torak. He looked at her before backing out, and she exhaled loudly like she was in pain.

Sterlyn and Griffin glanced at each other.

"Hey," I said and patted Sierra's shoulder. "We need to move so we can keep an eye on the meeting. Are you okay?"

She spun toward me and bobbed her head. She said in a rush, "Of course. I'm *fine*."

I'm going out on a limb here and saying she's not fine. When Olive used to say that, it meant she was the opposite of fine. At the mention of his late sister, Killian smiled sadly. *And to this day, I'm not sure what the opposite of fine is. All*

I know is that it's scary, and I had a knack for making it worse.

Meaning he'd either tried to fix her problem or attempted to be understanding when he'd had no clue. Once again, he'd been a good guy, if a little misguided.

"Let's go toward the back of the parking lot." Griffin waved at us to follow him.

I gestured to the four cars blocking the back. "There's a drive-thru. We could get blocked in. It's best to go around to the front."

We were still far enough down the road and at an angle that Erin wouldn't be able to see us. Three buildings stood between us and the Shell station, so we didn't need to lurk behind the buildings, trying to remain undetected, and risk making the humans suspicious. We needed to do something to put their minds at ease...like stay in front near the road.

Torak drove past the gas station, and I froze. What was he doing? My heart pounded, and my throat constricted.

"I *knew* we couldn't trust him," Sierra spat, and her hands clenched. "We shouldn't have given him the vehicle."

He missed the exit back to the interstate, and realization slowly dawned on me. He wasn't abandoning us. "He's turning around so it'll look like he just got off the interstate when he pulls into the gas station."

Sterlyn laughed. "Thank gods he thought of that. I didn't consider that she'd know which direction Tom would be coming from. Of course she's aware this is the halfway point between where Tom was staying near the latest missing pack and Shadow City."

Sierra's tension melted away. "So he's not betraying us." The hope in her voice was thick.

You might be right, Killian linked and pursed his lips.

But I don't know if he's good enough for her. She's a pain, but she's... He trailed off, unsure what to say.

Maybe before we'd bonded, I'd have been insecure or jealous, but not anymore. I knew exactly what he meant. *Like a sister.*

He flinched. *Yeah. Sierra, Griffin, and Sterlyn were the closest thing I had to a family until you came along.*

My chest warmed. *They're still family*...our *family.*

Griffin strolled to the next building over, some sort of vape store. There was a second gas station between this store and the one at which Erin was parked, but we couldn't go there because Erin would have a clear view of us.

"We need to stay here and listen," Sterlyn said as we walked past the windows of the vape store and sat at the edge of the curb, where there weren't any parked cars.

"What?" Sierra placed a hand on her neck. "We told him we'd be there in seconds if something went wrong."

We needed to calm her before she drew unwanted attention. I bit my bottom lip. "And we *can* reach him quickly. Erin won't attempt anything too drastic with all the humans around. She might want to work with them, but she won't want them to target her."

Griffin yanked at his dark polo shirt. "Jewel's right. Think about it. Whenever there's a risk of getting caught on video, she doesn't come around, not even at the entrance to Shadow City. She doesn't want to be on television."

"She wants to stay off the humans' radar." Sterlyn lifted her hands. "Whatever the reason, I'm sure it's one that is working to her advantage and not ours."

The silence spoke to everyone's agreement. Before anyone said more, the Suburban reappeared, and Torak pulled into the gas station.

"Everyone, try to listen," Sterlyn murmured.

Obeying, I focused to filter out the traffic and other excess noise.

As soon as I keyed in on the Suburban's engine, the vehicle turned off. A door opened and closed, and steady footsteps sounded. Torak was walking toward Erin.

My lungs seized. Not being able to see what was transpiring had sweat pooling in my armpits.

Minutes passed, and nothing was said.

This can't be good, I linked with Killian. I'd figured that Erin would be in a hurry and jump right to the point. We had no clue what was going on, and the urge to check on him nearly overwhelmed me. Being able to link to him would have been amazing, but he wasn't in the same pack as any of us. We couldn't communicate with him.

"That's it," Sierra said, and marched toward the gas station.

Killian released me and snagged her by the arm, linking with both of us, *Not yet.*

Nothing is happening. Sierra jerked, trying to get free. *She must be on to him.*

"Should I know you?" Erin asked finally, and all five of us held our breaths.

Torak cleared his throat. "No."

I wanted to smack him. She was feeling out if this was the shifter she was supposed to meet, but I couldn't do anything to salvage his misstep without exposing us.

"Then I guess there is nothing further to discuss," she replied, and her high heels clacked on the cement.

My shoulders sagged. This wasn't working, and we couldn't do a thing about it because Tom was dead. This had been our one chance.

"Wait. Tom told me about you. He described you, and I

can smell who you are," Torak said urgently. "You can't leave."

"Not only did Tom not come, but *you* think you can tell me what to do," Erin replied. "Give me one good reason not to leave your ass right now."

Fear sat heavy in my stomach. If he outed us, he'd gain her trust and try to negotiate the safety of his own pack. Most alphas would do just that. Had we let our marginal trust of Sadie compromise our judgment?

CHAPTER TWO

HEART HAMMERING, I held my breath. I had to go with my gut and believe he wouldn't rat us out.

Torak murmured, almost too low for my shifter hearing, "I assume you don't want to be the one running around and *collecting* items like someone unimportant. You'd rather have someone do the dirty work for you, but if that's not the case, fine."

I inhaled, feeling dizzy. Normally, I trusted my instincts, but so much was at stake that every decision we made had a good chance of being wrong.

When she didn't immediately respond, I scooted closer to Killian, our legs brushing. Under ordinary circumstances, I'd have found it humorous that Griffin and Killian were sitting the way they were. They were both so tall and muscular that it was almost comical how uncomfortable they appeared, hunkered down on a cement block in the middle of a congested highway.

She's going to leave, Sierra linked as she plopped down beside me. *As long as she doesn't hurt him, everything will be okay.*

She won't hurt him. Killian tensed and looked around me. *We need her to believe that Tom is alive without seeing him. Levi can't pretend to be Tom for much longer.*

He was right. This was kind of a Hail Mary, and if it didn't work, we were screwed. We couldn't make Tom magically appear.

"Why didn't Tom come?" Erin asked warily.

Unfortunately, she was smart and cautious. That made things more difficult.

"Please, let him be quick on his feet," Griffin whispered from the other end of the line. Sterlyn sat between him and Sierra.

"He's buried from the battle." Torak huffed. "Didn't your contact share that information with you? Tom couldn't make it, so I came instead."

I snickered. That was a good play on words. He hadn't lied.

"Of course the contact told me that," she said indignantly. "But that doesn't mean I can't question it for myself."

Sterlyn's shoulders sagged, and my body mirrored hers. So far, Torak was pulling this off.

"I was told to give you this," Torak said.

He had to be handing her Egan's shirt.

An eighteen-wheeler rushed past us, adding more noise interference. I closed my eyes to enhance my hearing.

"This smells familiar." Erin's tone held a warning. "It smells of silver wolf."

My head dropped, and my pulse pounded. We hadn't considered that Sterlyn touching the shirt would transfer her scent to it. Though she hadn't worn it, there was enough essence for Erin to notice it.

"What do you expect?" Torak asked with intense

annoyance. "Silver wolves were part of the fight. We were all attacked and fighting, and I had to leave abruptly to get here in time."

Sterlyn chuckled. "He's good."

I had to agree. I wasn't sure I'd be so quick-thinking in his place.

"He's *all right*," Sierra interjected as her leg bounced.

She wouldn't give Torak any credit. I laid my head on Killian's shoulder and linked, *I thought when she found her fated mate, she'd be all love-struck. I didn't expect this.*

Maybe he's not her fated mate, Killian replied and wrapped an arm around me. *You could be reading into things.*

I lifted my head and glared at him.

*Tsk*ing, Erin cleared her throat. "I told Tom not to get arrogant. The last time you all were winning was by sheer luck and numbers. I'd never admit it to any of them, but the silver wolves and their friends are worthy adversaries. They somehow get involved in everything, even when it's hundreds of miles away from them."

"I can see that," he replied. "Are you going to do whatever it is you're supposed to do, or are we going to stand around all day and chat?"

"Listen here, mutt," Erin rasped. "We may be on the same side, but that doesn't mean I like or respect you. Continue talking to me that way, and I won't meet with you again."

"Fine," he gritted out. "I just want to get back to the pack."

Her heels clacked again. "And I need to get back to the city. I'll do the spell there. It's not like I can do it *here*."

She had a point. All it would take was one human

looking in her direction at just the right time to see something strange occurring.

"We need to contact Egan and Jade somehow." Griffin stood and stretched. "They could head back too soon from wherever they went and raise suspicion."

Sterlyn climbed to her feet and removed her phone from her back pocket. "I'll text Sadie. I'm sure one of them knows how to get a hold of them." She typed on her phone.

"Don't get too excited." Sierra frowned and rubbed her hands on her thighs. "He's still there with *her*. He's not out of danger yet."

Torak said, "Then how are we supposed to know where to go?"

"I'll call Tom," Erin replied slowly. "Or do you have a *problem* with that?"

She was getting suspicious. Torak needed to stop pushing her for answers.

"No, he's just eager." Torak chuckled humorlessly.

"And *that's* his problem," Erin cut in. "He's rash and doesn't think his strategy through. If he's not careful, he'll get himself killed."

This time, Torak's laugh was genuine. "You sound like you care."

"I don't care. It's a matter of convenience," Erin said smoothly. "I need him to keep the status quo for now." She moved again, and a car door opened. "I'll call Tom soon, but first, I have to get back to the city." The door shut, and a car engine started.

Killian, Sierra, and I stood, and the five of us pressed back against the brick building, even though, from this position, Erin probably wouldn't notice us.

The Suburban's engine hummed to life, indicating that Torak was in his vehicle as well.

"Let's go." Sierra waved and took a step toward the gas station. "We should get to him before he pulls out."

Killian grabbed her arm again and yanked her back to the wall with us. He murmured, "Erin hasn't left yet, and she could have backup watching. We need to go back to Dunkin' so he can pick us up."

"But—" Sierra started, but Erin's black sedan pulled to the other side of the gas station and idled near the exit.

She must be waiting for Torak to drive away.

"There's a reason we haven't caught Erin until now." Sterlyn licked her lips. "She's careful. We need to get back to Dunkin' and wait for Torak."

The Suburban pulled around to the other side of the gas station, and Griffin gritted his teeth. "If she follows him here, there's only so much hiding we can do."

Especially when we weren't inside the donut shop. I hadn't considered that she might watch him when we'd moved closer to eavesdrop.

Body coiled, I would've done almost anything to be able to link with Torak. He needed to drive away from us.

When he pulled onto the road and went in the opposite direction, my legs nearly gave out. I'd been so certain he would come here.

After a few cars had passed, Erin pulled out and followed him, and I imagined she was watching to see which direction he went. She'd expect him to get on I-75, heading back toward Knoxville.

"Let's get inside Dunkin' in case she follows him here." Sterlyn hurried past Sierra, Killian, and me, rushing back toward where we'd been dropped off.

Griffin was right on her heels, with the rest of us taking up the rear. The urgency of the situation had my wolf surging forward and wanting to use her magic. In times like these, being raised around humans came in handy. I was used to suppressing the magic inside me even when it was desperate to get out.

To soothe my turbulent emotions and magic, I used my childhood technique of meditating on music and played Debussy's "Arabesque No. 1" in my head. The beautiful tone of the clarinet had my fingers itching to learn how to play the instrument. Instead, I looped my arm through Killian's, letting his touch quash my remaining turmoil.

Are you okay? Killian asked as my emotions surged through our connection. *We're going to be fine.*

My wolf is eager to be let free. I'm fighting her a bit. That's all. I jumped down the curb as we rushed across the parking lot between the vape shop and Dunkin' Donuts.

I wouldn't have admitted that to anyone else. Though I was a silver wolf and often stronger than other wolves, depending on the phase of the moon, wolves, especially the men, tended to be antiquated, viewing women as weaker, though Dad had tried his best to change those views. Change took time. My best friend, Emmy, and I admitted our struggles to each other—but rarely. It wasn't that we didn't trust each other, but old habits were hard to get past.

Killian was different. He was my fated mate, so sharing everything with him was as natural as breathing.

If it weren't for our bond, I never would've known, he assured me. *Pull strength from me if you need to.*

As we reached Dunkin', I caught a glimpse of my reflection. My long, straight auburn hair was a little wild, and my brilliant blue eyes glowed more brightly than usual. Growing up, Chad, my friend and silver wolf packmate, sometimes thought I was linking with someone because of the shade of my eyes. But usually, I'd been deep in thought about music or a book I'd just finished.

Griffin yanked open the donut shop's side door and held it for us. "Let's get something to eat."

Though he was trying to sound normal—human—the vein between his eyes bulged.

We piled in, and the restaurant, unfortunately, was not crowded. We were the only ones inside except for the two workers behind the counter.

Killian and I took the lead, walking past the few tables on one side of the room and heading straight to the counter. Stacks of donuts gleamed from trays behind the salespeople, and I scanned the selection, knowing we needed to order something.

The woman behind the register took a step back. She tugged at the collar of her gray Dunkin' shirt. "What would...er...would you like?"

Humans generally didn't feel comfortable around supernaturals, but with the way the woman was gawking at Killian, I suspected she was reacting to his extreme attractiveness. I almost felt bad for her. He was deliciously handsome, but he was *all mine.*

My wolf growled, and I edged in front of him, blocking most of his chest and southern region. "*We'll* take the larger size of assorted donut holes." I didn't care what we bought as long as her eyes left *him.*

His chest shook, bumping the backs of my shoulders. He linked, *I love it when you get all territorial.*

Most humans would have found my behavior unhealthy, but that wasn't the case with supernaturals. When we found our fated mates, we didn't like anyone else looking at them the way we did. Our connection was a sacred bond that linked us—mind, body, and soul.

Her tawny gaze diverted to the register. "Anything else?"

"One black medium coffee and one with cream and sugar," I rattled off. Though caffeine might not be the best choice, I desperately needed it. With things calming, fatigue was setting in, and we had too much to do before I could consider taking a nap.

Sierra, Sterlyn, and Griffin joined us and gave their orders while Killian tugged me over to the table farthest from the main door to the parking lot. He pulled out a chair, and I sat, wanting to get off my feet.

Now that the meeting with Erin had concluded without issue—so far—all the other problems whirled through my mind. With our need to find the two packs that had been captured, PawPaw's pack, Mom, and Chad having trouble shifting, the world knowing about our existence, and Erin working against us, I wasn't sure if this was a war we could win. We couldn't *not try*, but we were up against so much.

Did I lose you? Killian linked and placed his hands on my shoulders. *I can tell your mind is a million miles away.*

I looked over my shoulder at him. *You'll never lose me. Now that the situation isn't as dire, everything is catching up to me.*

Yeah, your mind and body have been under so much stress that relaxing leaves you with almost too much to process. He leaned down and kissed my forehead. *I'm here for you, and my arms are always available for comfort.*

Grinning, I arched an eyebrow. *Just your arms?* For a moment, things felt normal. We were just a guy and a girl hanging out with friends.

My entire body is yours for the taking. He kissed my lips. *Whatever you need or want.*

Here? In front of everyone? I teased.

He winked. *Just say the word.*

Words aren't what I want, I linked, biting my bottom lip and catching his attention.

A faint cedar musk hit my nose as Sierra dropped into the seat beside me. She groaned and lowered her voice. "Ew. I bet even the human can smell the arousal hanging around you two." She waved a hand in front of her nose. "Please don't make me lose my appetite. It's been forever since I had a donut. Let me enjoy this."

Sterlyn placed the container of donut holes in front of me and passed a bag to Sierra. Killian sat next to me as I opened the container and popped a cinnamon-powdered hole into my mouth. The sweet taste exploded on my tongue, and I moaned.

"Where is Torak?" Watching the parking lot, Sierra didn't touch her donuts. "I figured he'd be here by now."

Standing at the edge of the table, Sterlyn kept watch, too. "Our new allies are experienced. At first, I was worried, but I think Torak realized that Erin was following him. If I were him, I would've gotten on the interstate and headed in the direction she'd expect."

"I bet you're right." Killian snatched a blueberry-glazed hole and ate it.

A phone dinged, and Sterlyn pulled out her phone and scanned the message. "It's Sadie. She contacted Egan, and he and Jade are staying where they are until Levi receives word from Erin. Also, Torak called and said he's getting off at the next exit and heading back."

At least that confirmed he hadn't abandoned us.

Griffin strolled over with a tray of four hot coffees and an iced coffee. Though he maintained a lazy stride, his jaw twitched.

Something was off.

Griffin says the humans are acting strange, Killian linked with Sierra and me.

Turning toward Griffin, Sierra placed an elbow on the table. "Really? That's normal."

"It's different," he murmured and placed the drink tray on the table, keeping his back to the humans. "They didn't ease up when you walked away. They're more than just uncomfortable."

"We're *all* tense." Sterlyn grabbed the coffee marked *cream* from the tray. "When Torak gets here, we'll leave." She swiped her phone again and typed another message.

The worker who'd taken our order said in a low voice. "Sue, does that man with dark hair next to the redhead look familiar?"

"What do you mean?" her coworker whispered back.

I flicked my gaze toward them and saw them in the farthest corner of the work area. A human wouldn't have been able to hear them, but we weren't human.

The one who'd taken our order nodded. "A certain person who's been on the news nonstop."

Sue's mouth dropped open. "Oh, my God. He does look like the man who told us about all those *creatures*."

"Exactly." The register worker glanced at us.

I averted my gaze.

"We should call the cops. What if they attack us?" Her voice quivered.

Killian's neck corded, and his nostrils flared. Guilt crashed through our bond, churning my stomach.

"I'll go in the back and call them," Sue said as she turned around and walked through a swinging door.

There was no time to spare. We had to move.

CHAPTER THREE

EYES WIDE, Sierra jumped to her feet. When the four of us didn't move, she blinked and waved a hand, sliding her container of donuts across the table toward Killian. She gritted out, "Sitting here while *Sue* makes her call seems risky."

We couldn't just run. *If we bolt, that will add to their fear and anxiety.* My gut was screaming at me to react the same way as Sierra, and the only reason I hadn't was because of my lifelong training in self-restraint.

"We have to remain calm and organized so the humans aren't aware we can hear them." Sterlyn took another sip of coffee as her attention remained glued on the parking lot. "If they realize we heard them, that will inform them that we have exceptional hearing."

Killian placed a hand on Sierra's donut bag and arched a brow. *We're going to leave. None of us want to have our faces on television and let Erin or someone in her coven see. That could hinder any credibility Torak has earned.*

Erin had made it clear she was uncomfortable meeting with someone other than Tom. If she found out we'd been a few buildings away from their meeting location, she'd piece together at least part of what had happened.

"Breathe," Griffin murmured. "Sterlyn taught me that controlled breathing helps with remaining rational. I'd think she would've taught you that by now."

Rubbing my chest over my heart, I blinked as tears stung my eyes. She must have learned that from her dad, my late uncle, since my own father had taught the same technique to our pack.

"She tried." Sierra lifted her chin and remained standing, but she didn't sprint to the door. "It doesn't work. My sense of self-preservation is stronger than oxygen."

"That means—" Killian started.

"Isn't that Torak?" I asked loudly, cutting him off. Telling Sierra that she didn't want to calm down and that was why the technique didn't work would only make her more upset.

Sierra's head snapped toward the road, and her attention homed in on a blue Tahoe turning into the parking lot.

I linked with her and Killian. *Play along. We don't need humans realizing which vehicle we're getting into.*

Head tilting back, Sterlyn nodded. "You're right. I keep forgetting that he has that new SUV." She rolled her eyes dramatically.

Though the two of us couldn't pack link anymore, she had a knack for reading situations.

Griffin's brows furrowed, but he didn't say anything. When his irises glowed faintly and his forehead smoothed, I guessed either Sterlyn or Killian had informed him of what Sterlyn and I were doing.

Everyone stood and grabbed their drinks and food. As we walked out, I forced myself to eat another donut hole to appear unconcerned. When we reached the middle door, the cash register woman hurried to the back.

I'd bet she was telling her friend we were leaving, but that worked in our favor. We walked outside just as the Tahoe pulled into the parking lot. It circled to the drive-thru as our group rushed toward the vape store.

When we reached the building, I saw Torak pass us in the Suburban. Sierra waved her hands like a madwoman while Sterlyn snatched one hand and dragged her away from the donut shop.

"What are you doing?" Sierra gestured wildly toward the Suburban. "I'm trying to get his attention!"

"I know, but you could also get the workers' attention if they come back around. We need to call Sadie and get her to let him know," Sterlyn countered.

Dropping her hands, Sierra sighed. "You're right. People can't help but notice me, so I'd better try to fade into the background. Though I doubt it'll be successful."

Griffin pinched the bridge of his nose. "I'd rather them notice you than Killian."

"Thanks, man," Killian growled. "I appreciate that." The strangling sensation from our bond returned, and I wanted to smack Griffin.

"Not helping," Sterlyn chastised, scowling at her mate. "Everyone knows Killian volunteered to inform the world about us to protect all of us from exactly what happened back there."

"Apparently, it didn't work. She lumped all of you in with me as supernatural." Killian laughed bitterly.

Sierra placed a hand on her hip and lifted the one holding the coffee cup toward him. "Remember how you always lectured Olive and me about being known by the company you keep? I guess you were right."

Now Sierra wasn't helping, and I had to remind them why the decision had been made in the first place. "They were afraid and assumed things. Believe me, I know. I was one of them at first. But now I agree that it was for the best that a friendly face informed the world instead of the demons wreaking havoc."

I love you, Killian linked. *I needed to hear just that right now.*

Sometimes, we all needed a reminder about our true intentions. In an awful situation with no good answer, we had to hold close to the logic behind our actions and remember why the risk had been worthwhile. *I'll always be here to do that very thing.* I wanted to touch him, but my hands were full of donuts and coffee. I didn't want to chance dropping either and causing a scene.

I turned around in time to see Torak making a U-turn. Instead of turning into Dunkin', he pulled into the vape store and the spot directly in front of us.

"Maybe he isn't a complete moron." Sierra straightened and hurried toward the driver's-side back seat.

I wanted to lecture her. Torak had handled the situation better than most anyone would have. The least she could do was be kind to him, but I had a feeling that if I said something, I'd be wasting my breath and energy. If they were fated mates, she was probably trying to understand those sudden and intense emotions, especially if she'd felt them while he'd been aiming a gun at us. I remembered feeling like I had a split personality the first time I met Killian.

Torak left the vehicle running and swung open his door. "Sorry it took me so long, but she was watching me like Ollie."

"Ollie?" I asked as I hurried toward the back seat. If the

Dunkin' sales girls had called the police, the authorities could be here any second.

Torak got out of the car. "Yeah—he's our falcon friend who sometimes keeps an eye out for us. We may need to call him back. He was with his nest in Florida when I learned another pack was missing this morning." He gestured to the seat he'd vacated and focused on Griffin. "I figured you'd want to drive."

"You'd be right." Griffin brushed past him and got into the car.

Since Sierra climbed in on the driver's side, I assumed she'd scoot over to the captain's seat behind Sterlyn, but when I moved to climb through the back door, Sierra was actually behind the driver's seat. I arched my brow when she didn't budge. *Can you move to the other side so we can all get in?*

You were supposed to be Torak...er... Her cheeks reddened. *I mean, sure. I'll move.* She went to the other side, and despite her being a wolf shifter, I couldn't believe her coffee didn't spill with how fast she moved.

Her unusual awkwardness made me wonder if she was trying to get Torak to slide past her so they touched. I mashed my lips together to keep the smile from my face, but she must have noticed because she sneered and glared at me.

Not wanting to add to Torak's curse, I moved to the back seat, eager to leave before the cops came.

The faint sound of sirens blared, and a lump formed in my throat. Though we weren't at Dunkin', we weren't far enough away.

Killian sat next to me and placed his coffee in his cup holder, and I followed his lead.

All the chatting stopped, and everyone buckled in.

Once the doors were shut, Griffin put the vehicle in reverse. He groaned. "Dude, the seat's warm."

"I won't apologize for that," Torak scoffed as he settled into the seat directly behind Griffin. "Otherwise, I'd be dead."

"He's scorching, so it makes sense." Sierra cleared her throat and added quickly, "His ego. That's what I meant. Not his body."

Smiling cockily, Torak glanced at Sierra and winked.

Killian wrinkled his nose. *I've never seen her act so cringey before.*

The sirens grew louder, and flickering red, white, and blue lights could be seen in the distance. The police were speeding, eager to get here.

Griffin pulled onto the road, turning toward the interstate. "At least we got out of here in time. The humans wouldn't be able to read our license plate from their location, so even if they saw us get into this vehicle, the cops won't be able to locate us."

Good point. For once, Fate might be on our side.

Sterlyn's phone rang, and she pressed some buttons on the radio so the audio came through the vehicle's speakers. "Hello?"

"How did the meeting go?" Rosemary asked. Her wings flapped, indicating she was talking to us while in the air.

"She was suspicious, but Torak handled her very well." Sterlyn looked over her shoulder and smiled at Torak. "She took the shirt and said she'd perform the spell when she was back in Shadow City. Levi should expect a call."

This was getting so complicated. We'd had no choice but to kill Tom—he wouldn't have stopped selling out packs to the humans. But I wasn't sure pretending he was still alive was the right decision, either. Erin was already suspicious about Tom not showing up, and I wasn't sure what would happen if there was a next time.

"Don't worry. Levi has Tom's phone. Zagan and Eleanor are with us, and we're rushing back to Shadow City. We'll get there before Erin so she won't be suspicious about Zagan and Eleanor being gone the entire time she was. All the dead are buried." Rosemary sounded tired. The battle we'd fought was catching up with us. "Everyone was loading into the cars when we left them a few seconds ago, so I'm sure Sadie will be calling you to coordinate the retrieval of her brother."

Sierra's shoulders sagged.

Getting on I-75 northbound toward Knoxville, Griffin asked, "Did you all find something we can use to locate the missing packs? We need time for recon so we can break them out before the humans do whatever tests they did on Hal, Mila, Chad, and the others."

I'd been eager to eat more donuts, but that reminder ruined my appetite. Mom, Chad, and my grandparents, along with their pack, had been experimented on during their captivity. We knew the men had been tortured to force them to shift, but none of us had realized why until today. When they'd shifted into their wolves to attack our enemy, they'd involuntarily changed back into their human forms. Stuck in some vulnerable mid-shift or freshly shifted into their human state, they hadn't been able to fight. So many had been killed—I didn't want to think about the numbers. I had noted at least three who'd died out of the fifteen from PawPaw's pack on our side. PawPaw had brought a total of thirty, but the other half had been with Sadie's group. There could've been more deaths on that side.

We'll figure out what's wrong with them, Killian linked and pulled me to his chest.

I dropped the donuts onto the seat to my left, needing his embrace.

"Eliza will perform a location spell on the missing pack when she and the other witches return to their coven." The wind whistled through the phone. "We can stake out the location of the captive wolves once they're found, but we have to get our vampire allies back to Shadow City and Terrace before Erin notices that a large number of them are missing, and we need more witches as reinforcements. The wolves that are struggling to shift should go back to the former silver wolf neighborhood."

Thank gods we had a coven on our side. I wasn't sure we could go up against Erin's coven alone.

Though I hated that Rosemary was right, none of us could dispute her. We needed to locate the captive wolves pronto. Once we knew how far away they were, we could plan excuses for how long we might be gone to scope out the facility. I had no telling what Erin would say when she finally called Levi back.

Kissing the top of my head, Killian sniffed before saying, "That's a good plan. For all we know, Erin might want to meet someone again."

Pulling at the hem of his shirt, Torak fidgeted in his seat. "Why don't I come back with you? I'd hate to go home and have Erin demand to meet again, and I'm three hours away. If another random person shows up, I think she'll become too suspicious and leave."

"Excellent point." Sterlyn twirled a section of her hair around her finger. "But that's asking a *lot* of you. You have your own pack to take care of."

"Yes, I'm the alpha, but only because my dad doesn't think he can be the permanent alpha anymore since he lost his eye. He'll be fine stepping back in temporarily. This is too important to just sit on our hands. The latest missing pack consists of our *friends*, and humans are targeting *our kind*. They'll move beyond wolf shifters once they get answers from us." Torak straightened his shoulders. "I mean, as long as you don't mind providing me a place to stay."

Sierra opened her mouth, but Killian spoke before she could. "You can stay with Jewel and me."

"I've heard enough insanity," Rosemary said with disgust. "Between learning that people actually want to sit on their hands and Killian believing it's wise to have Torak stay with them in Shadow Ridge with Erin nearby, I can't take anymore. I need to hang up."

I giggled. Rosemary's bluntness was admirable, though most people, like me, didn't understand the angel at first.

"What?" Torak glared at his hands. "I—"

"Please, for the love of the gods, stop." Rosemary groaned. "Whatever you all decide about Torak, make sure he doesn't stay in Shadow Ridge. We have to fly higher now, so I've got to end the call." The line went dead.

Sierra shook her head. "How many times do I have to tell her she comes off as rude?"

"She doesn't mean to." Sterlyn pursed her lips. "But she's right. Torak, if you're willing, we can let you stay with Hal's pack or with the witches. Whatever you prefer."

His attention flicked to Sierra. "Which one is closer to h"—he yanked on his earlobe—"help."

If I were a betting woman, I'd wager a whole heap of money that *help* wasn't what he was originally going to say.

"Both locations are similar distances to Shadow Ridge." Griffin moved into the right lane to get off at the next exit. "If I were you, I'd stay with the wolf shifters unless you're already comfortable around witches."

"I have nothing against witches, but I'd rather be with my kind." Torak shrugged. "I'll text Dad, Winter, and Sadie to tell them what's going on."

Now that I knew we were heading home, I was eager to get there. I wanted a shower and to lie in bed in Killian's comforting arms. We were clueless about where we'd be heading tomorrow or where we might end up staying.

Torak grabbed his phone and typed out his message while Griffin pulled off and headed southbound. When Torak's phone dinged, he read the message and put it back in his jeans pocket. "They agree it's for the best."

Twisting around, Sierra held her hand out to Killian and asked, "Can I have my donuts?"

He groaned and tossed her the bag. "There. Next time, don't throw them at me."

"I didn't *throw* them." Sierra flipped forward and landed hard against the back of her seat. "I panicked. There's a difference."

Killian wrapped his arms around me again, and I nuzzled deeper into his chest. We were heading home, and our friends and family were on their way back as well. For a moment, no one was under siege.

As my eyelids drooped, I heard the sound of the donut bag opening. Sierra sighed dramatically and murmured, "Since you did such a good job with Erin, do you want one of my donuts?"

My chest convulsed with quiet laughter. I was certain she'd bought one for him.

"I'd love one," Torak murmured.

And before I could hear any more, I fell asleep.

"SHIT," Griffin hissed, and my eyes flew open. That was the tone he used when we were in danger.

"What's wrong?" Killian asked urgently, but his voice was thick with slumber. He must have dozed off as well.

I popped my head up and noted the familiar oaks and cypresses. We were back in our pack neighborhood in Shadow Ridge. I blinked as the Craftsman-style homes came into view, and my focus landed on the hunter green house Killian and I shared, then Griffin and Sterlyn's white house with its distinct wraparound porch next door to ours. A person stood in front of it.

The scarlet red hair with black streaks was all I could focus on.

Erin.

And Torak was in the car with us.

CHAPTER FOUR

"SHOULD I TURN AROUND?" Griffin asked as he pressed the brakes.

Sterlyn shook her head, her hand grasping the armrest. "Keep moving. Doing anything else will draw more attention to us. I just linked with Cyrus and Annie. They're on their way, which is good if she wants to talk to all the shifter council members." Sterlyn's twin brother, Cyrus, was also on the Shadow City council.

Although I'd been sound asleep seconds ago, I was now fully awake, heart pounding. Just when I let my guard down, something like this happened.

Torak unbuckled his seat belt, dropped to the floor, and crawled toward the back seat.

Since I was sitting in the middle of the back row, I lifted my feet so he had room to hide behind his chair. The windows were dark, and he flattened himself against the floor.

"Dude, give me a second," Killian hissed as Torak's legs landed on top of his feet. "Let me move out of the way."

His anger rushed through our bond, tightening my

chest. He didn't normally act like that. I linked, *He's hiding from Erin. He didn't do anything wrong.* I hated to lecture Killian, but he'd been harsh.

"Sorry, man," Torak murmured, afraid Erin might hear.

Sierra glared over her shoulder at Killian.

Killian pulled his feet out from under Torak but didn't apologize. He moved so his legs curved over Torak and stretched between the middle-row chairs.

I returned my focus forward. Erin's black sedan was parked at the curb, and she stood on the edge of the lawn, near the mailbox. At least she wasn't trying to hide. Rather, I gathered that she wanted to be seen.

Sterlyn's chest expanded as she released her hold on the armrests.

Everything inside me wanted to turn around and leave, but we had to play the role of clueless allies. I'd met Erin only twice, and both times, the evilness that wafted from inside her had made my angel genes squirm. The ability to sense the essence of a person's soul was both a blessing and a curse for silver wolves, who were descended from an angel. Though it was best to know if the person you were dealing with was good or bad, it was uncomfortable to be around someone vile without letting on.

"Everyone, stay calm," Sterlyn said, and turned toward us, pointing at Sierra. "We don't need to rile her up, especially since Torak needs to stay hidden." Her attention flicked to Torak, making her message clear: we had to get Erin out of there as quickly as possible.

The one benefit of it being late December was that Torak wouldn't have to sit in a hot, humid vehicle while we tried to get the witch to leave.

Griffin drove past Erin's dark sedan and pulled into the driveway of their house.

A shiver ran down my spine, and I resented the fact she had an effect on me. I'd been born a protector and trained my entire life for battle, but her negative energy was something I didn't want to experience again.

Killing the engine, Griffin muttered, "Someone will let you know when she's gone."

After a moment, Sterlyn opened her door and got out.

Time to see what the witch wanted.

I grabbed the armrests of both chairs to climb over Torak without falling. I sat in Torak's seat as Killian followed my lead and then swung the door open.

As Killian got out behind me, I noticed that Sierra had hesitated, glancing into the back seat.

If you don't want him to get caught, you need to get out. He'll be fine, I linked with just her.

She shook her head as if I'd brought her back to the present, and she hurried out of her side of the vehicle. I turned to face Erin. She'd moved into the center of the yard, close to the driveway, and was staring at the vehicle.

Sterlyn rounded the front of the hood, with Sierra a few steps behind her. She must have waited to ensure that Sierra got out of the car as well. As strangely as our friend was acting, Sierra could have slammed the door, eager to get away from Torak, or jumped into the back seat on top of him and refused to get out. A fated mate's safety was always a priority, and remaining rational was the best way to ensure he remained undetected.

"Isn't this a surprise," Sterlyn said kindly with a forced smile as she observed Erin. "To what do we owe the pleasure?"

Lifting a brow, Erin slid her attention to Sterlyn. "I didn't see you and Griffin in the city today, only Cyrus and Annie, so I thought I'd check in."

Footsteps hurried down the road, and I turned to find Annie and Cyrus heading toward us. Annie's warm brown hair lifted behind her in the cool breeze, and her honey-brown eyes appeared duller than normal. She was short, especially by wolf standards, coming in around five and a half feet. Cyrus towered over his mate, his dark silver hair standing out against the twilit sky. His gunmetal eyes locked on Erin.

"You could've just asked them where we were." Griffin leaned against the driver's-side door and crossed his arms.

A huge smile appeared on Erin's face as the negativity swirling out from within her coated my skin. I wanted to shudder with disgust, but she'd gain pleasure from any reaction, so I forced my body to remain still.

She placed a hand on her stomach and cooed, "It wasn't a burden to come check on all of you. After all, your health is very important to me."

Oh, I'd bet it was. I swallowed a snarky comment. Like Sterlyn had said, if we engaged, the witch would stay longer.

"Aww." Sierra batted her eyes, her tone extra sugary. "You shouldn't have." Her face twisted as she wrinkled her nose. "Really."

"I must say, Erin, visiting this neighborhood twice in one week—that's a new record." Killian remained in front of the back passenger door. He placed his hands in his pockets and relaxed his shoulders.

Erin's gaze settled on the window of the vehicle's back row. "I wanted to know if you have any updates to share. We agreed to be forthcoming. Is there something I should be aware of?"

Annie and Cyrus joined us in the driveway, stopping in front of the window Erin had been staring at. Sterlyn must have told them that Torak was hiding back there, but their casual demeanor kept the fact that we were talking right outside the Suburban from seeming odd.

"You could've just asked us earlier." Annie pushed her long hair behind her shoulders. "You saw us helping rebuild the Elite Wolves' Den. We just got home a few minutes ago."

"You two, yes, but I didn't know if Sterlyn and Griffin were coming later. They do that regularly." Erin shifted her weight to one leg. "They never showed up, so I decided to drop by. Was this not okay?" She touched her chest and pouted.

Damn her and her sneakiness. If we said no, it would appear as if we were hiding something, but if we said yes, that would give her more leeway to drop by unannounced. If the circumstances had been reversed, I was fairly certain she wouldn't want us showing up on her coven doorstep.

Griffin gritted his teeth, and Killian remained silent. They didn't want to give her permission, but we didn't have a choice.

This was when my position within the pack came into play. Forcing my legs to move toward her, I brushed her arm reassuringly. "Of course you're welcome here. And you know what? I'd love to visit you and your coven soon as well. I've yet to go inside Shadow City. Maybe the seven of us could help with the rebuilding and drop by to meet some of your coven members after working for the day. I love the way you're trying to bridge the gap between us and would love to reciprocate the gesture." Dad had said to kill people with kindness, and what better way than to drop by her place as well?

Mouth open, Erin reminded me of a hungry alligator. I

was pretty sure if she could kill and devour me without consequence, she would.

Warmth exploded through my connection with Killian as Sierra linked, *I think I've been shown up and might have just fallen for you myself, Jewel. Kill, you have competition.*

Unable to continue touching Erin, I dropped my hand. An unnatural coldness clung to my skin as I breathed in her strong rosemary scent, which had me on the verge of gagging. She must have performed a spell recently to reek of herbs this much. My guess was the location spell on Egan's shirt.

Forcing myself to move slowly, I stepped back and took a deep breath. Erin's scent wasn't nearly as strong now, as if she were hiding it.

Erin stood tall. "I just dropped by because I was worried you might not have informed me of something. Not for a *visit*."

At least she'd think twice before stopping in like this again.

"Well, you'd be right." Sterlyn steepled her fingers. "We learned that another pack was taken, about three hours away from here, and we went to investigate."

Sterlyn coming right out with the information startled me, but I trusted her. We knew this wasn't news to Erin, and telling her made it appear as if we were confiding in her.

"You did?" Erin jerked her head back. "How did you obtain this information?"

She wanted to know our source. If she could figure that out and eliminate it, she could hide her involvement.

"There's been a lot of talk on the internet," Sterlyn replied without missing a beat. "We've been keeping an eye on the news for anything odd."

She was referring to the intranet I had the login information for. This was a good tactic. She wasn't lying, and Erin couldn't shut down the internet.

Erin's jaw twitched.

"Anyway, the information proved right, and Tom showed up." Sterlyn tilted her head. "I thought you were going to inform us if Tom made a move."

"I might be keeping an eye on him, but I can't watch him all the time." Erin jutted her hip. "I was busy doing other things all day, and it's clear you all made it out safely. What did you learn while you were there, and were you able to capture Tom?" Her attention moved back to the Suburban.

Why did she keep looking at it?

Cold tendrils of fear clawed into my chest. Not wanting to upset Sierra, I linked with Killian, *I think Erin recognizes the vehicle.*

Shit. I hadn't considered that, Killian replied, his alarm mixing with mine. I wasn't sure I could move if I wanted to. I could very likely be frozen in place.

"We weren't able to capture him." Sterlyn frowned.

Annie growled and clenched her hands. "So he'll just keep betraying more packs? This *has* to stop."

Clearly, Sterlyn hadn't updated the two of them yet, which was probably a good thing. Annie's reaction was genuine.

"Did we at least find out where they took the other shifters or where they might attack next?" Cyrus ran a hand down his face. "The more wolves they capture, the harder it'll be to get everyone out. When Hal, Mila, and the others left the government facility, they couldn't even shift."

At the time, we'd assumed it was because everyone was

weak and malnourished, but now I feared it was due to the experiments the humans had run on them.

Erin's brows furrowed. "Well, I'm sure it's not the last we've seen of him. You'll have another chance." She adjusted her dress and turned back to her sedan, then glanced at the Suburban again. "Did you retrieve anything I can use to help you locate the missing shifters?"

She was fishing, pretending she was being helpful. I had a feeling if we handed something over, she wouldn't give us the right location.

Standing, Griffin dropped his hands. "No, we don't have anything on us that you could help us with. I wished we had different answers." His tone lowered in sadness.

"Very well. I'd best get back to the city now that you're all safe at home." She took a few steps toward her car and paused. "But you didn't find out anything alarming or troubling?"

Killian chuckled humorlessly. "Everything we've learned can fall under that. People are kidnapping supernaturals for a *reason*, and we don't know who or why. I'm not sure what other words we could use to describe the situation."

Rolling her eyes, Sierra cocked her hip. "You keep asking us these questions, but no one's asked you the same thing yet, so I will." She narrowed her eyes. "Is there anything you aren't telling us?"

While meeting my new pack and getting into my alpha's mate role, I'd learned that many people disregarded Sierra as a mouthy attention seeker. A few even said the only reason Killian was so close to her was that she was the last reminder of his family since she'd been his sister's best friend. But there was more to Sierra. She was a master of keeping her intelligence hidden, and this was one of the times it slipped through. If she wanted to, she'd be an amazing leader.

Erin couldn't weasel out of the question.

"I've told you everything I find relevant." Erin stroked her throat. "I'll *call* if there's anything I want to share."

We stayed in place and watched Erin climb into her car and pull away. Luckily, she'd parked so her sedan was facing the exit to the neighborhood, so she wouldn't get a clear view of our license plate.

"What's going on?" Annie asked as her gaze landed on each of us.

Inhaling deeply, Sierra opened her mouth.

Don't say anything out loud, Killian linked to Sierra and me. *Erin could be listening.*

And just as quickly, Sierra closed her mouth. *I thought we got rid of the bones.*

We did, but that doesn't mean she doesn't have another trick up her sleeve, Killian countered. *Sterlyn is informing Annie and Cyrus of everything right now.*

Bones? I hadn't heard anything about that before.

Killian quickly filled me in on how witches who used evil magic could place the spelled bones of their ancestors in locations they wanted to monitor from afar.

The more I learned about Erin, the less I liked her, which was saying something. I could barely stomach being around her. Sometimes, the enemy who pretended to be your friend was the worst one of all.

They're going to head to your grandfather's pack to drop off Torak. Killian relayed the plans that Sterlyn and Griffin must have imparted.

Can we go, too? I linked. I wanted to see my family, including Chad.

Killian's eyes softened as he opened the back door for me. *Of course.*

He could read my emotions and had probably figured out why I wanted to go.

I'm going, too, Sierra announced and jumped into the Suburban before anyone could contradict her. She got in the very back—which wasn't normal—and Torak groaned faintly.

"Quit acting like a baby," Sierra muttered.

Please get in before they start arguing and Erin hears his voice, Killian linked and gestured inside.

We got back into the car, Killian and me taking the middle-row seats. No one made a noise as Griffin reversed and we headed back out of Shadow Ridge.

"Can I—" Torak started.

"Shh," Sierra said, cutting him off. "We'll tell you when it's time."

A *smack* sounded, followed by Torak's low growl.

Sierra, quit harassing him, Killian linked, scolding her as if they were siblings.

Griffin turned left, away from the quaint brick downtown shops that weren't decorated for the holiday season like usual. Killian had shown me pictures of years past. The holidays were usually a busy time for tourism in the area, but this year, with the demon war and the secret coming out, they were trying not to encourage more humans to visit. But even without the extra tourism, humans were thick on the streets with cameras, searching for paranormal activity in the city they'd seen clips of on television.

After a few more minutes, we pulled onto another road, and the Ridge disappeared behind us.

"You can get up now," Sterlyn said from the front. "We're taking you to where you'll be staying."

"Thank gods." Torak sat upright and stretched his arms over his head. "Between trying not to move and Sierra kicking me in the stomach, I wasn't sure how much longer I could be quiet."

Sierra scoffed. "Please. You can't handle that and you call yourself an alpha? More like a wimp."

"Keep it up, and I'll show you how wimpy I can be," Torak promised.

The spicy scent of arousal hit my nostrils, and I wanted to vomit. *Oh, dear gods.*

Killian jerked around and pointed a finger at them. "Cool it, you two, or I'll make Sierra sit up here with Jewel."

"Are you her brother or something?" Torak asked.

At the same time, Killian answered, "Yes," while Sierra said, "No."

My throat dried at the way Killian's head jerked back and his pain sliced through our connection. She'd hurt his feelings.

"Uh, okay." Torak cleared his throat but didn't say anything else.

I reached for Killian's hand to comfort him, and the vehicle filled with tense silence. I linked, *She didn't mean it.*

Yes, she did. He intertwined our hands, but his eyes became glassy. *Just let it go, please.*

He needed space, and that was something I understood.

Soon, the one-story houses of Sterlyn's former family pack neighborhood came into view. They weren't Craftsman-style like our Shadow Ridge homes, but rather simple and built to withstand the test of time. The surrounding oak, ash, and maple trees were bare of leaves, making the entire front section of the large, circular neighborhood visible, including the clearing in the middle.

My breath caught. Most of PawPaw's pack was in the

clearing. That wouldn't have been alarming, except it was clear they weren't training.

A large group was fighting one another while other pack members watched from the sidelines, tears streaming down their faces.

Jeremiah—the alpha of the pack that lived near the facility where my grandparents' pack had been held captive and whose pack had temporarily relocated here for safety—and his strongest fighters were out there, trying to calm several fighting men from PawPaw's pack, but they were struggling to break up the violence.

We had to get out there and help them.

CHAPTER FIVE

THE VEHICLE LURCHED FORWARD, and I pressed my hands into the back of Sterlyn's headrest to keep upright.

"What the fuck is going on?" Griffin growled.

"I'm hoping that's a rhetorical question since *none of us know*," Sierra snapped from the back seat.

Killian kept his attention locked on the fighting pack as he linked, *Let's not bite each other's heads off*.

We passed between the houses, and Griffin slammed on the brakes by the training grounds, making the tires squeal. He cut the wheel. The Suburban skidded and swerved so that the driver's side faced the clearing, coming to a stop when the tires smacked the curb.

My lungs squeezed, and my vision blurred, but we didn't have time to recover. We had to stop what looked like a mutiny.

We jumped out of the car, and Griffin and Killian made a beeline to the fight. Sean, PawPaw's beta and intended future alpha, was right in the center, with a few of his closest friends flanking him, trying to settle the fight. Sean's shaggy, buttery-blond hair was drenched with sweat, and his usually warm olive eyes held a dangerous glint. He already had a darkening black eye, and blood trickled from one nostril, telling me someone had jumped him or this had been going on for a while.

Twenty-five of PawPaw's pack were engaged in the fight. Jeremiah was in the center, pulling people away from Sean.

My stomach sank. Why was the pack attacking their beta?

Nana cried, "Jewel!" Her voice broke halfway through.

I spun around to find her in a group, watching the turmoil. She had her arms wrapped around a woman from the pack with the woman's younger child between them, facing away from the fight. Nana's long, silver-streaked chestnut hair acted like a shield, protecting the girl, and her amber eyes were filled with fear.

Rushing to my grandmother, I tried to slow my racing heart. Any sign of anxiety would only worsen an already emotional crisis. Forcing my voice to remain calm, I asked, "What's going on?"

"Fear, child." Nana closed her eyes, and when she opened them again, a tear trickled down her cheek. "Something's been off inside us since we left that facility, but everyone hoped it was due to emotional turmoil. Then, when we sensed the loss of our pack members during the battle with Tom's pack, their deaths felt odd–unnatural, as if..." She trailed off, and her eyes searched for something, but they never focused. "As if it wasn't their time. Like something had been forced on them. And then the ones who are still alive...something weird vibrated from the pack links, adding to the fear.

"Sean came to my house and waited for Hal to call to

inform us about what had happened. Our pack was in pain, not understanding what was going on, and when we got the call, Sean and I came out here to update our people. We *hoped* it would unite us so we could work together to find a solution, but all it did was escalate tensions." She waved her hand at the circle just as Killian wrapped his arms around one of PawPaw's pack members and yanked him away from the fight. "Ten minutes ago, it devolved into this. Jeremiah tried to help, but the pack was still reeling from the losses and not knowing how to fix ourselves."

I hadn't considered how their pack would react to learning that they couldn't control their wolves. What would it be like to have the part meant to protect you working against you, making you vulnerable?

If PawPaw had been here, he could have used his alpha will to stop the fight, but Sean didn't have that, and the pack was taking out their fear and frustration on him.

Sometimes, it was easier to blame the messenger.

None of the women were involved, so Nana had done her job as alpha mate and influenced those who viewed her as one of their leaders. Unfortunately, PawPaw's pack was old-fashioned, and while the men treated the women well, they didn't view the alpha mate as an authority figure.

I linked with Killian and Sierra, informing them of everything I'd learned. I placed my hand on Nana's shoulder and said, "I've got to go help them. I'll be right back."

Spinning on my heel, I hurried to the center of the action. Killian, Sterlyn, Griffin, Torak, and Sierra were working on the outside of the gigantic circle. Fifty shifters were involved, and they were all practically on top of one another.

Jeremiah stood back to back with Sean, his jade eyes

narrowed as he used his bulky frame to protect Sean's back. He was taller than Sean by an inch, but they were both muscular. His pack members fought among them, but they were pulling their punches, doing just enough to keep Sean from getting pummeled.

That was the problem when dealing with a pack that wasn't your own. Interfering with another pack's drama could irreparably strain the relationship once things finally calmed.

I glanced around, not sure what to do. We needed a distraction.

We needed to determine who was leading the brawl.

I scanned the group and homed in on Brent. He'd been one of Heather's close friends, and he was usually even-keeled. However, Heather had been the first to die at the hands of the humans who'd captured their pack. PawPaw had mentioned that between Heather's death and the torture Brent had endured, he'd been struggling. This must have been the final straw.

He was attacking the man on Sean's right, trying to reach the beta.

I took off toward the fight.

"Jewel!" Nana shouted. "Get back here!"

Under normal circumstances, I'd have obeyed, but this wasn't anything like *normal*, and it couldn't keep going on.

"I'll be fine," I called over my shoulder.

My friends continued to try to thwart the fighters from the outside, but that wasn't my goal. I'd be getting in the center first.

Keeping my attention on Brent, I bobbed into the chaos.

What are you doing? Killian linked, and his hot anger penetrated our bond, warming my blood.

Trying to end this, I answered as I ducked, missing the

elbow of someone attacking a man from Jeremiah's pack. *The same as you.*

I'm right behind you, he replied. *If you're getting in the middle of it, so am I.*

I wouldn't tell him no. Though I was confident I could handle Brent on my own, I would never complain about my fated mate backing me up.

Pushing through the mass of bodies wasn't easy. A few slammed into me, but I remained on my feet. The worst part was the stench of blood and sweat surrounding me. This had to be what testosterone smelled like.

A guy spun toward me and swung his fist. His eyes widened, but I wasn't sure if it was from realizing who I was or that I hadn't attacked him.

I threw my arm up, blocking his fist, and dropped. Kicking my leg under his, I took him down, and he fell backward into a man behind him.

Though I hadn't meant to engage in the fight, I wouldn't take a punch.

Wait for me, Killian linked, still several feet behind me.

Despite the situation, I laughed. *Because standing here is less risky than moving forward?* I wasn't trying to be a smart-ass but rather trying to get him to see reason. I was only a few people away from Brent. Standing still would just as likely get me hurt as moving forward.

His displeasure wafted through me, but some of the heat from his anger ebbed. *You've got a point. I just want to* —he cut himself off—*protect you, but obviously, you're doing fine on your own.*

He must have seen what had happened. *Remember what I told you*, I reminded him as I moved forward again, ensuring I didn't lose focus.

I know you can protect yourself. That's never been the

problem, he answered. *I just wish you didn't have to. Is that so bad?*

That logic I understood completely. If I could swaddle him in blankets and lock him in our room, I wouldn't hesitate. But then he wouldn't be the man I'd fallen in love with. *No, but you need to understand that it's never going to happen.*

A man's shoulder slammed into my neck, and I stumbled backward into Brent. Pain shot down my spine from the impact, but at least I'd reached Brent faster.

Killian growled. *Oh, I do. And it's taking everything I have not to rip that asshole's head from his body.*

They aren't thinking. They've never acted like this before. But that was the thing with fear—the emotion could make people act out of character.

Brent remained focused on the man he was fighting. He kicked him in the stomach, causing him to crumple and giving Brent access to Sean. Brent growled, "Don't tell us to calm down."

I had to act.

As Brent reared his arm back to throw a punch, I leaped onto his back and wrapped my arms around his neck.

What are you doing? Killian linked. *You weren't engaging until now!*

He's the most aggressive, so I'm shutting him down, I answered. At least, I hoped I was going to take him down.

"What the—" Brent started and turned his head toward me.

I couldn't give him a chance to react, so I tightened my hands around his neck, cutting off his oxygen supply.

His hands gripped mine, slackening the hold.

With the almost new moon, my angel magic wasn't

much help, so he was stronger than me. This wouldn't work —I needed a different strategy.

A snarl emanated from him, and I expected him to shift, but the sound of breaking bones never came.

My chest constricted. This was worse than I'd expected. Brent was likely trying to shift but couldn't, fueling his terror.

He pulled my right hand away from his neck and backed up so we rammed into some people behind me. Since my back was to them, I couldn't tell how many.

A man growled, and then something slammed into my kidney. Pain erupted in my stomach, and I nearly fell off Brent's back. Brent pried my left hand from his neck, and the agony in my kidney allowed him to drop me.

"That's my *mate*," Killian rasped from behind me, and the sound of crunching bones followed.

Thank gods he'd followed me.

Brent moved toward Sean again. I didn't have any time to lose.

Gritting my teeth, I lunged at him and slid both hands under his armpits. Then I clasped them behind his head, locking my fingers together. My shoulders were soaked from his armpit sweat. I was all in.

He tried to grab my hands, but he couldn't with the way I was holding him. After a second, he tried using his shoulders to dislodge me, but I pressed down firmly, countering his move. I gritted out loudly, "Calm down, or I'll break your neck."

That wasn't an idle threat. I'd put on more pressure to offset his resistance, and it would eventually injure him.

His sudden lack of resistance was my answer.

Killian, Sterlyn, and Griffin appeared beside me and immediately mirrored my hold on the three closest men around Sean and me. I glanced around for Sierra and Torak and found the two of them shielding a group of women as some of the fighting men got too close for comfort. They herded the men away, trying to keep the bystanders safe.

With our three instigators restrained, the fighting stopped. Everyone froze in place, their attention locked on the four of us as their chests heaved from the exertion.

For a moment, the entire area was silent.

You'd better say something, Killian linked.

Bile churned in my stomach. *Uh, no. Sean needs to.*

He did, and this is what happened. Killian nodded to the men in front of us. *Someone else—someone with a connection to Hal—needs to step up.*

I had no desire to be anybody's leader. Being the alpha's mate was a bigger role than I'd ever desired, and I'd accepted the role only because I couldn't live without *him.*

Sean took a step forward, but as soon as he did, a man on the edge raised his fist.

The words *don't kill the messenger* sank into my mind, chilling my bones. This was why Killian had chosen to protect his friends by becoming the person who outed the supernaturals: to be the target of all the anger. But Killian's message hadn't generated the fear of losing our magic.

"This isn't Sean's fault." I winced. That probably hadn't been the best way to allay panic, but this was not my area of expertise. "It's purely the fault of the people who kidnapped you."

Brent laughed darkly. "You mean it's the fault of *your mate,* who informed the humans of our existence, creating this entire mess."

I should've kept my mouth shut, but the damage was done. "Killian did that because demons were trying to induce worldwide panic. The past few months have been one horrible situation after another with no good solutions. We're all trying to make the best decisions we can."

I'd give anything to have Dad here. He had a way of knowing what to say to offer hope.

Hope.

That was what these people needed.

"Fighting one another won't solve your problem." I inhaled, trying to calm down and keep a level head. The right words weren't coming to me. I'd have to go with my heart. "Working together is the only way we'll find answers. This anger, *believe me,* will only make the problem worse because you're giving the issue life. Think of *Heather*. She, along with *Killian,* the silver wolves, the Shadow City alpha, and so many others sacrificed so much to get you out of that hell. Don't make Heather's sacrifice mean nothing."

Brent's body sagged, and he dropped to his knees. I had to shuffle my feet so I didn't fall on top of him. His shoulders shook, and he sniffled.

He was crying.

I released him. I'd only put him in that hold to get him to calm down. If he felt remorse, then he'd moved beyond anger.

"Jewel's right," Sterlyn said as she released the man she'd restrained. "No one *here* has done anything to hurt any of you. Fear has a way of bringing out the worst in us, and by letting it, we allow the enemy to win."

Sterlyn should've spoken, I linked with Killian. She had a way of stating things that made the truth so easy to see.

Warmth wafted through our bond, and Killian replied, *You don't give yourself enough credit.*

You're right. I almost made the mob turn on you. I couldn't believe that the first words out of my mouth had made people immediately point their fingers at Killian. The hell I'd put him through when we'd met would be one of the biggest regrets of my life, and having him reminded of what others thought of him had made that worse.

Killian and Griffin released the men they were holding, and Brent and the other three men slowly stood. Their faces were red, likely from embarrassment. Not only had they been the most riled up, but they'd also gotten their asses handed to them in front of everyone.

"Y'all are right." Brent kicked at the ground. "I'm sorry, Sean. It's just...when you said that our pack can't shift correctly and that we should calm down after losing five more of us, I snapped."

"*Sorry* doesn't cut it." Sean's jaw twitched. "Every one of you who attacked will be punished. Striking out against your own kind is inexcusable."

Several spots in my chest warmed as pack members who had fought Tom with us earlier today came within range. The rest of our group was arriving home.

I glanced at Nana, who was rubbing her chest. She must have felt PawPaw and the others from their pack returning, too.

Now that the situation had calmed, I hurried back to Nana and linked with Sierra and Killian, *I'm going to discuss Torak staying with them.*

I'll stay back while Sean finishes talking, Killian replied.

Good idea. Emotions were still high, and though I doubted they'd rally to fight again, it was safer for Killian, Griffin, and Sterlyn to be on standby.

When I reached Nana, she smiled at me. The little girl and mother were now standing beside her. "I'm proud of you," Nana said as she hugged me. "You remind me so much of your father."

My cheeks warmed. I'd always striven to make Dad

proud, but I wished he'd been here to handle the situation. He could have deescalated it without getting physical. "Thanks, but I came here to ask for a favor."

She pulled back. "Anything. What do you need?"

I gestured at Torak. "Do you mind if he stays with your pack? We need to keep him hidden."

"Not at all. He can stay with your grandfather and me. We have an extra bedroom." She patted my arm. "After all, your friends are letting us stay here. I'd be honored to help them out in any capacity. They've already done so much for us, especially you and your mate."

"I love you," I murmured. I never used to say the words, but after Dad's death, I wanted to let the people I cared about know that I loved them as often as I could.

"I know, and we love you, too," she said as she dropped her hand.

Hurried footsteps raced toward me, and I turned to see Killian with strain on his face. I glanced at Sterlyn and Griffin and found their expressions in a similar state.

My stomach dropped.

CHAPTER SIX

TAKING A DEEP BREATH, I forced my brain to stop swirling over potentially horrible scenarios. I linked with Killian, *What's wrong?*

Nothing. He winced. *Well, there isn't an immediate threat. Though things have calmed for the moment with the pack, fear is powerful. They could easily explode again at any moment.*

My body sagged. *When PawPaw returns, that should make things better.* Though I was certain PawPaw was just as scared, he was an amazing alpha and would know how to handle his pack members due to his special connection with each of them.

Killian reached my side and took my hand. *That's true. He'll ease some of the turmoil, but it may not be enough if we don't get answers.*

Yet another thing added to our ever-growing list of shit to deal with. No matter how badly I wanted to, it wasn't as if we would find the answers now. *Then why do you, Sterlyn, and Griffin look like something worse has happened?*

The concern etched into each line on his face had to be from something more than the current fight.

Chad and Mila linked with Sterlyn. They arrived back at the neighborhood where the coven is staying, and Eliza just performed the location spell. The missing packs are outside Rockwood, Tennessee, so about an hour and a half from here, he linked and squeezed my hand.

My lungs froze. I'd hoped it would be the same place they'd kept my mom, Chad, and my grandparents' pack. We already knew that setup and would have only needed to get a feel for the current security measures. This would be a whole new building with new *everything*, and it would take longer to determine the best way to get everyone out. *So we're starting over.* Though that wasn't necessarily true since we now had Levi pretending to be Tom, and Tom's pack was no longer an immediate threat. We still had to determine what Erin was up to while our group split apart to monitor this new building.

He nodded. *We're planning logistics since Erin will be watching us. We also need to calm the turmoil inside your grandfather's pack and pick the scout team.* He squeezed my hand again reassuringly. *We need to head back to Shadow Ridge, and your grandfather hasn't returned.*

"Jewel, are you okay?" Nana asked, pulling me back to the present. She lifted a shaky hand before clasping it to her chest.

I knew her well enough to realize she was hiding her nerves from her pack, wanting to be viewed as strong. Not too long ago, I would have agreed that showing vulnerability was a weakness. Though I wasn't ready to share my concerns with everyone, I was beginning to learn that fear wasn't something to be afraid of, and holding on to it only allowed it to control you.

"Yes. We were trying to coordinate something, but it's nothing you need to worry about," I assured her. She and PawPaw had enough to deal with, and right now, we didn't want to ask for their help. Their pack needed to remain together and safe while we searched for a solution.

Vehicles approached the entrance of the neighborhood. PawPaw and the others were finally home.

"Thank gods Hal's here," Nana murmured, confirming my suspicions. "If you six hadn't shown up, I'm not sure what he would've come back to." Her brow creased, and she placed both hands on Killian's shoulders. She smiled and said, "At first, I was worried about whether you were truly worthy of my granddaughter, but every time I'm around you, I see exactly why Fate put you two together. And I'm proud to call you family."

Warmth exploded through our bond, and Killian's bottom lip trembled for a second. He released his hold on my hand and hugged Nana, whispering, "You don't know how much that means to me. And I'm glad we're family, too."

A lump formed in my throat. Killian had lost his family, and even though Sterlyn, Sierra, Griffin, and the others were like blood to him, I understood the impact that being accepted by my family was having on him. In a way, his family had grown, and now, everyone who meant so much to each person was merging into one unit.

Ten Suburbans pulled into the neighborhood, and everyone on the grassy knoll went quiet as if impending doom had arrived. In a way, I guessed it had, since fewer pack members were coming back.

Sterlyn, Griffin, Sierra, and Torak stood behind us as the first vehicle pulled in. PawPaw climbed out of the driver's seat and hurried over to us. His nostrils flared, and his dark brown eyes studied the men in the center. The gray in his hair and beard seemed more prominent than it had earlier today, standing out against his normal dark shade. Even though he was a tad paler, his olive complexion was still darker than mine.

The other vehicles parked, and everyone climbed out, with Jeremiah's grown children—the twins, Ruby and Birch—getting out of the sixth vehicle.

We need to leave, Killian linked. *And they need to tend to pack business.*

He was right. Though I'd stayed with PawPaw's pack for the past several months, I wasn't one of them...not truly. And now that I was mated, I'd begun my own family.

PawPaw stopped in front of us and kissed Nana's lips before pecking my forehead. "Sean and Nana informed me of everything. I owe the six of you and Jeremiah a lot for getting the pack back in line."

I shook my head and said forcefully, "You don't need to thank us. What's family for?" He should have known that I'd...that *we'd* do everything in our power to help them out.

He chuckled, catching me off guard, and smiled proudly. "You remind me so much of both of your parents. Your dad's words but your mother's tone."

My heart ached with sad happiness. To be compared to both parents was oddly satisfying.

The faint scent of cedar musk wafted around us as Jeremiah appeared beside me. "I'm sorry we interfered. We were trying to make sure things didn't escalate."

"I appreciate your involvement," PawPaw said as he patted Jeremiah's arm. "We're friends, and because of you, my granddaughter, and the others, the situation didn't worsen."

Jeremiah exhaled. "I figured you'd say that, but it's still good to hear."

"If there's nothing else you need, we should get back to Shadow Ridge." Killian glanced at the rising almost new moon. "We came to drop Torak off, but we can find him another place to stay."

Torak scratched the back of his neck. "I can stay with the witches. It's no problem."

"Absolutely not." Nana clutched her waist. "We already invited you here. You can come with me, and we'll get you set up."

In other words, she'd get him settled while PawPaw talked to the people who'd been fighting.

Griffin pulled the keys from the back pocket of his khakis and spun the keyring around his finger. "You have our number if anything changes."

My chest expanded with pride. To be part of a group so willing to help others was something I'd never imagined.

Not wanting to leave without hugging them once more, I wrapped my arms around my grandparents. "I love you."

They returned the hug and murmured their love before I untangled myself.

As Killian and I followed Sterlyn and Griffin, I noticed Sierra and Torak several feet away, staring at each other as if they were the only two people in the world—a sensation I was all too familiar with.

Sierra, we've gotta go, Killian linked, his hand tightening around mine.

Though we did, I hated that he hadn't given them a moment longer together. *They're saying goodbye. They just need a minute.* The first time I'd been separated from Killian after meeting him had been so hard.

Sierra's head tilted back, and she jutted out a hip. "Try

not to shoot anyone while you're here, especially since you don't *know* them."

And I remembered thinking that arguing with him would make leaving easier. She'd soon learn that the only way to gain clarity was by succumbing to the bond.

Torak growled. "I'm not in a threatening situation, unlike—"

"Aw, I do have a way of making men feel threatened." Sierra beamed and ran her fingers through her hair. "I'm sorry that I intimidated you, but it's hard not to with looks like these."

"Who the hell have you intimidated with your looks?" Torak squinted, and his hands clenched into fists. "I'd *love* to know."

This wouldn't end well. Despite just getting on to Killian for interfering, I rushed over to Sierra and looped an arm through hers. "We need to get going. Erin's already suspicious." That wasn't a lie and would result in Torak wanting her to go for her own safety.

"Fine." Sierra rolled her eyes but relented. "I need to drop in on my parents, anyway."

"Bye, Torak," I called over my shoulder, keeping a firm grip on Sierra. "We'll check on you tomorrow."

Nana took Sierra's place, waving at Torak to follow her, and the two of them trekked off toward the back section of the neighborhood. Both Sierra and Torak kept pausing to take yet another glance at each other.

Soon, the five of us got into the vehicle, and Griffin hurried us back to the Ridge with Sierra complaining about Torak the entire time.

When Griffin pulled into his driveway, the sky was dark.

Sierra jumped out of the car, muttering her goodbyes. She wasn't acting like her chipper self, but she had a lot of emotions to sort through. She was likely overwhelmed and needed time alone. I'd needed that when I'd gone through the same thing.

As my feet hit the driveway, the urge to rush home next door was damn near overwhelming. Knowing we'd be leaving again in the morning made me want to get home and spend the little bit of time we had alone with Killian.

"Do you need me to go with you to return the car?" Killian asked out loud for me, since I was the only one here who couldn't pack link with Griffin and Sterlyn.

"No, man." Griffin shut the driver's door. "Sterlyn and I will head to the city in a few minutes, and we'll drop it off when we check in with Ronnie and Alex."

My body tensed. Here I was, thinking about heading home when Sterlyn and Griffin weren't even done for the day. "Do you want us to go with you?" I'd never been inside the city, and truthfully, I had no desire to go there. We faced enough risks *outside* its walls. I would never purposely go within them unless it was necessary.

Sterlyn strolled past the hood of the vehicle toward us and smiled. "No, you two need rest. We'll head inside and figure things out."

She was being careful about how she worded things in case Erin was somehow listening.

Killian linked, *She's afraid that if she and Griffin go with us to check out the new facility, Erin will notice and cause more problems. They're going to stay in the city.*

I hadn't considered that. Sterlyn and Griffin had been with us from the beginning, and the thought of them staying behind made me feel vulnerable, but they were doing it to protect us.

The three of them talked via the bond, and I tried hard not to feel left out.

"Well, we'd better get home," Killian said as he led me toward our hunter green house. "Talk to you later."

We said our goodbyes, and as we walked onto the lawn that joined our yards, Killian connected, *Sorry about that, but we can't chance Erin hearing anything. Sterlyn and Griffin will be seen in Shadow City, and she's talking with Cyrus about Darrell, Martha, Emmy, Rudie, and Theo going with us tomorrow to scope things out.*

Since I'd been born into the silver wolf pack, I trusted each person he'd named with my life. *That's a strong group.* Even though Martha and Rudie were mates and not silver wolves themselves, they were strong in their own right. *And who are we taking from ours? Lowe?*

I was thinking Lowe, Sierra, and April.

We passed the area between the houses, where we could see the empty pool with its large slide in our backyard. We walked up the few steps to the small front porch and entered our home.

That sounds good, but if we take Sierra, we should take Torak, too. They couldn't be apart easily, especially now.

After he'd shut the door and locked it, Killian spun me toward the entryway to the living room. The comforting blue-gray walls felt incredibly welcoming. His fingertips brushed my cheeks, and he murmured, "I know we have a lot to discuss, but that can wait until morning. I'd like to focus on you while we're alone."

My body heated, and I moved closer to him, nodding. My hands snaked around his neck, and I tilted his head down so his forehead brushed mine. "That sounds like an excellent plan."

Eyes closing, he touched his mouth to mine. His tongue swept inside, filling mine with the faint citrus taste that I would never get enough of. His fingers snagged in my hair, and he pulled hard enough to tilt my head back so he could deepen the kiss.

I moaned in pleasure, never imagining that I would like even the faintest hint of discomfort.

Let's move to the bed, he linked.

Though that was exactly what I wanted, we'd been in battle earlier. *Let me jump into the shower first.*

He pulled away, his mocha irises lightening. *How about I join you?*

Now that *sounds perfect.*

He bent and tossed me over his shoulder, then rushed toward the bedroom. The living room and hall blurred past me, but I didn't mind since my eyes were locked on his firm, tantalizing butt.

Wrapping an arm around his waist, I brushed his groin as he walked through the master bathroom door.

He missed a step, almost falling. "You're naughty."

"Then I guess you'll need to punish me," I teased as he gently set me down on the light gray tile floor. A large bathtub sat to the right and his-and-hers sinks with granite tile in front of us. To the left was a large walk-in shower with two showerheads, one on either side. The toilet sat between the shower and the sink.

He stepped into the shower and turned on both faucets as I grabbed two towels from the center oak drawer and placed them on the edge of the sink.

I took in the warm yellow walls and stepped back so we both had room to undress. When I removed my shirt and dropped it to the floor, I found Killian staring at me, the air heavy with the scent of his arousal.

"You are so damn gorgeous," he murmured. "Inside and out."

That wasn't a word I would use to describe myself, but I was damn glad he did. *And you're sexy and amazing.*

He gave me a cocky grin as he removed his shirt. His abs constricted, priming my body for him.

I traced his muscles with my fingers, and he shivered, empowering me.

His hands reached around me, and he had my bra unfastened in a second. He removed it from my arms and tossed it.

Steam filled the bathroom, adding to the heat he already had me feeling.

We unfastened each other's jeans, and soon, both of us were naked. His mouth fused to mine once more as he led me into the shower.

Water cascaded down our bodies as his head lowered and he captured one of my nipples in his mouth. His tongue caressed my skin, and his fingers slid between my legs and began to circle, the friction already building inside me.

Leaning my head against the cool tile, I tried to catch my breath as he worshipped my body, causing every cell inside to spark. I reached for him and stroked, refusing to be the only one getting pleasure.

His hips rotated, increasing the speed as his mouth sucked desperately and his fingers increased their rhythm. An orgasm exploded within me, and my body shivered as he continued.

Time stood still as we devoured each other. I'd never get enough of him. His taste, scent, and touch were the only things I ever wanted.

A second wave of pleasure coursed through me, but his fingers weren't enough. I rasped, "I need you. Please."

He moved to the corner of the shower with a small tile seat, and I climbed his body. As he sat, I slid him inside me, and ecstasy swirled through me again. My head grew dizzy as I rode him, increasing our pace to the speed I desperately needed. We opened our bond to each other, and his love washed into me, making me whole. This was the connection that only sex could bring between two fated mates, the connection where the two halves of a soul were one, even if just for those few moments.

His pleasure built with mine, and we surrendered to each other. He moaned, somehow turning me on even more, which I hadn't thought possible. He linked, *I love you.*

I love you, too, I replied, though those words didn't feel like enough.

His body convulsed, and we sagged against each other.

"Now that was perfection," he whispered as he peppered my face with kisses.

He again made me feel completely loved, and we had time alone for the rest of the night.

ARMS TENSED AROUND ME, and my eyes opened. I'd been in a solid sleep, but the tension pulsing through our bond and the stiffness of Killian's body had woken me. I blinked and lifted my head from his chest to find his eyes glowing.

I wanted to ask what was going on, but that would be futile since whoever had linked to him had just started talking.

Seeing me awake, he sat up and said, "Demons are attacking humans."

CHAPTER SEVEN

MY HEAD SPUN, and I scooted against the oak headboard of our king-size sleigh bed. Out of every possible situation, that wasn't one I'd expected to hear. I'd expected the humans to have gotten in touch with Levi or *something*. Not this.

Dizziness set in. My emotions were getting the best of me.

I played Rachmaninoff's Symphony No. 2 in my head. The soothing memory calmed me, and the world stilled so that the blue-gray walls weren't caving in and mixing with the mustard-yellow plaster ceiling.

Killian snatched the remote from his end table and turned on the TV mounted on the wall dividing the bedroom and bathroom.

"Don't we need to leave?" I asked. If demons were attacking, we needed to fight them.

"Under normal circumstances, yes, but it won't do any good," he replied as the screen filled with familiar brick buildings.

I couldn't swallow. That was Shadow Ridge's downtown.

Humans were running in every direction, slamming into each other as they shrieked and batted their hands in the air as if they were being attacked.

The chaos with PawPaw's pack was *nothing* compared to this.

Unable to continue watching the trauma, I ran my hands over the fluffy navy comforter and stared at the huge fan directly above our bed. "Why aren't we helping?" Doing nothing when chaos was only moments away didn't make sense.

"The demons have taken a hostage." Killian hung his head. "What you're seeing is the aftermath, and showing up will only make *us* a target."

He was skirting the truth, but I knew him so well that he didn't have to say it. Because of me, he regretted outing our world to humans. Not only had he found his fated mate days after appearing on TV, but my family had been the first to feel the consequences. His decision had caused so many problems between us, but he'd done it to protect those he loved. I knew that now, and it was one of the reasons I'd fallen for him despite how much I'd blamed him in the beginning.

Since finding me, he'd stayed away from cameras. Part of the reason was that there hadn't been time—we'd been dealing with one threat after another—but I feared the main reason was me.

I inhaled and racked my brain for the best way to say what I needed him to hear. "The damage is done. We got chased out of a Dunkin' Donuts because humans recognized you."

He closed his eyes and gritted his teeth. "You don't have to remind me. I was there."

Clearly, I wasn't handling this correctly. His sensitivity toward the whole ordeal didn't make it any easier.

A woman's voice played over the footage. "A man was just dragged across the road toward the woods behind me. We don't know where he's gone, but several wolves ran after him."

The camera zoomed in on a woman with tears streaming down her face. Her eyes were red and swollen, and she wiped her nose with the back of her hand and spoke with a broken voice, "My fiancé. I told him we shouldn't come here, but he insisted. He thought this was some sort of ploy, and now..." A sob shook her body. "He's...gone."

My stomach revolted. This was worse than the video of supernaturals fighting each other. This was a live feed of a supernatural attacking a human. "Who's going after her fiancé?"

"Billy and a few others who were on the night shift." He opened his eyes again, and they were haunted.

Night shift.

I glanced at the digital clock on my end table. The blue letters glowed back at me. It was six in the morning. Not extremely early, but at the end of December, the sun wouldn't even peek above the horizon for another two hours.

Throwing off the covers, I placed my feet on the dark gray shag carpet. I scurried to the oak dresser under the TV and opened up the top right drawer, where my underwear and bras were kept. Once I'd grabbed one of each, I rushed to the large walk-in closet and chose a pair of jeans and an olive shirt.

Babe, we need to stay here, Killian linked, *and out of the way of the cameras. They've already broadcast that wolves are tracking him—we don't need to remind the supernatural world that there are silver wolves here, too. We need to keep you safe.*

I tossed my outfit onto the bed and changed. *I didn't plan on going as a wolf.* Now I wanted to on principle, but I couldn't let my pettiness cause me to deviate from the plan. I'd be letting my anger control me like Mom tended to do. "I'm going to go look for the woman's fiancé and talk to the humans."

The covers fell from his bare chest as he turned off the TV and jumped to his feet.

For a moment, all I could do was stare at him. His muscular body was like a siren calling me home, and he was *all mine*. My *mate*.

"You *are not* going out there with them," he bellowed, and clenched his hands. "We're staying home and packing."

His words shocked me. Anger coiled inside me, ready to explode. "I wasn't asking for permission." He hadn't even given me a chance to explain. Instead, he'd jumped in, telling me no.

"I'm your—" he started.

"You'd better stop there," I cut in, suspecting what he'd been about to say. "Because if the next words out of your mouth are that you're my alpha, they're going to cause a whole new set of problems between us."

He exhaled and ran his fingers through his hair. "I'm not trying to be an asshole. I'm trying to protect you."

"Protect me?" I laughed. "From what? My grandparents' pack being taken? My mom's insane ex-boyfriend who was hell-bent on revenge? Or the death of my father? What will you protect me from?" I hated talking to him that way, but I couldn't allow him to run all over me. He *was* my mate and my alpha, but that didn't mean I didn't deserve respect —something he'd always given me. "Please tell me. What exactly are you shielding me from? How many times will we have the *same* conversation? Because frankly, I'm tired of it."

Heart aching, I lifted my chin to prove something to myself. Now I was the one acting like a douchebag, but he had to see how ridiculous his behavior was.

"You're right. I get it." He sat on the edge of the bed. "But that one time I was on TV is *still* on replay. I don't think it would be smart to be seen on camera again. The news feeds would have another fresh message to play nonstop."

I bit the inside of my cheek, using the pain to ground me. "I know you wish you could undo being on television, but that's not possible, nor should you want it to be. At first, I resented you for it despite the tug of our fated mate bond." *Resented* was putting it nicely, but I could never use the word *hate* when referring to him. Not anymore. "But after being around you, seeing the person you are, and learning why you did it, I *chose* to fall in love with you. I stopped fighting our bond because I saw you for the man you are. Someone who will do *anything* to protect the people he cares about. And that's what you're trying to do now."

I moved to him and brushed my fingers across his cheek. His mocha scruff was rough against my skin, stirring desire inside me, but I shook my head. I had to remain focused. "But if you stop controlling the message, it'll spiral, or worse, someone else will step in to do it. Right now, people could use a friendly face promising to protect them."

He turned his head, pressed his lips against my fingers, and wrapped his strong hands around my wrists. He linked,

I don't like it, but you're right. All they'll do is play my message on top of the clip unless I give them something new.

"If anyone should be the spokesperson for supernaturals, there's no one better than *you*." I pushed my sincerity toward him, wanting him to hear *and* feel it behind my words. Killian was an amazing man, maybe even better than Dad, and if I was going to be the mate he deserved, I had to stand my ground when I was convinced what the right course of action was.

I love you, he linked and stood, pulling me into his chest.

We didn't have time for this, but we also couldn't risk not fixing things between us. Our bond made us stronger when we worked together. "I love you, too. But if you ever try to pull that alpha card on me again, you won't like my reaction."

"I know. I was wrong. Hell, you could easily take over as the pack alpha. Everyone knows you're stronger than me," he replied, leaning his forehead against mine. "But after what happened to you and your family, I worry about what will happen if I go public again. I can't put you through more pain."

"If you don't reassure them that there are good supernaturals out there, I'm afraid something will happen regardless." I kissed his lips softly and continued via our bond, *We can do this together. Me and you.*

No, just me. He pulled back, but his eyes were warm. *I don't want a bullseye on your head. Sterlyn and Griffin are on their way to help with the hunt for the man the demons took. They want Sierra, Emmy, Chad, and us to leave during the chaos so we'll be harder for Erin to track. Let me say a few words, and then we'll go to the witches.*

Chad? I hated to question him coming with us. He was

like a brother to me, but he was still struggling to shift. I worried he could be a liability.

"He begged to come along, and he knows what it was like inside the last facility. As long as we don't engage in battle, he should be fine." Killian headed to the door.

I snarled and clutched his arm, forcing him to turn back to me. *You're forgetting your clothes.* Though it was urgent that we leave, he had time to put on a shirt and jeans.

He grinned. "I was just seeing if you'd notice." He booped me on the nose and rushed into the closet.

I wasn't sure if I found that funny or if it made me just plain angry. At the moment, my feelings didn't matter. There was too much at risk to waste any more energy.

While he dressed, I quickly packed clothes and bathroom supplies for several nights. I wasn't sure how long we'd be staying to scout the area, but I didn't want to pack too much. Wherever we rested would likely have a washer and dryer so we could do laundry.

Killian strolled out of the closet and snatched the black duffel bag off the floor.

We walked down the hallway past his sister's old room and turned left toward the living room and the gigantic kitchen. I couldn't remember the last time Killian had cooked me breakfast in there. Memories of him leaning over the stove and pulling utensils from the dark oak cabinets tugged at my heart. What I wouldn't give to have time to sit down and share a meal with my mate.

I hated that we'd woken up earlier than we'd planned, but even stopping downtown to help with the demon situation, we should be able to reach Rockwood by sunrise.

As we passed the living room, part of me wanted to lie down on the sizable brown leather couch. The few nights Killian and I had enjoyed watching a movie on the TV mounted across the room above the tiled chimney were some of the most relaxing times we'd spent together so far. Not knowing when we'd be back, I let my gaze drift out of the five windows overlooking our backyard.

Killian paused, his attention darting to the portrait of his family that hung over the couch. He always glanced at it whenever we returned home or left, as if he were telling them what was going on.

Where the hell are you two? Sierra linked. *You woke my ass up at the butt crack of dawn, only to make me wait out here?*

Why don't you go grab Emmy and take one of the Suburbans the vampires left us to get Torak? Jewel and I have something we need to do first, and we'll meet you in the neighborhood, Killian replied. *Sterlyn said Sadie and a few of our new allies are meeting us at Rockwood to add to our numbers since we can't take many from here, and Torak wants to go.*

That eased some of my panic. I'd been worried about only the four of us going. *What if he needs to meet with Erin?*

We can't risk them meeting again. Not after she potentially recognized the Suburban, Killian replied as he led me through the kitchen and out the garage door.

All right, we're heading out, Sierra linked, not even asking what Killian and I were up to. That wasn't normal, proving how much she wanted to see Torak again.

Killian opened the garage door, and we watched as Sierra damn near ran over our mailbox while backing the huge SUV out. Emmy's gray eyes widened as she swung her head toward the back, causing her dark brown hair to fly to the side. Her rosy complexion was pinker than usual, likely due to the surprise.

"Are you sure she should be driving?" I asked as I walked around Killian's black Chevrolet Silverado.

He opened the driver's door. *No, but I don't want Erin to watch the news and see another Suburban.*

That was why he wanted to take his truck—for things to appear ordinary again.

We rode downtown in silence. I tried to enjoy the comfort of the cool leather seat against my hot skin, but even that couldn't ebb the anxiety swirling within. When we pulled onto the two-lane road to the center of town, I noticed more news cameras around than last time.

Pulse pounding, I reached across the console and took Killian's hand.

He pulled up in front of a restaurant a few blocks from the woods where the demons had dragged the human away and turned off the vehicle. "Why don't you stay here?"

"If you think I want to be on television with you, I don't." If he hadn't already appeared across every news station, I wouldn't have wanted him filmed, either. But that was a done deal. "I'll be a few steps behind you, but I want to be close." Another demon might attack, and Killian couldn't see them in shadow form. I could. "Either way, I swear I won't do anything to attract attention."

His expression softened. "Okay. I won't be long. I just want to tell the humans we're working on finding that man." He kissed my lips, tossed me the keys, then got out of the car.

I watched him stroll to the group of humans. There had to be fifty people and at least fifteen cameras focused on the woods, as if they expected the demons or the man to reappear.

Once Killian had crossed the block, I climbed out of the

truck and followed him. I scanned the tops of the buildings and the dark sky for any sign of the demons.

I spotted nothing.

When Killian was about ten feet away from the first human, a middle-aged man with his hands clasped behind his back glanced Killian's way before refocusing on the woods. Then he did a double take. "Oh, my God," the man gasped. "That's *him*."

I stopped in my tracks as the rest of the humans turned their attention and cameras on my mate.

The man removed his hands from behind his back, and I saw that one held a microphone. "You're the man who confirmed that supernaturals are real. What do you have to say about this disappearance?" He thrust the mic into Killian's face.

The humans who didn't have cameras gathered close. A few frowned as if they weren't happy that they weren't the ones asking the questions.

Killian stood tall and lifted his chin. "I can't stay long, but I wanted to reassure you that *most* supernaturals aren't bad. There are a few, just like humans, who enjoy instilling fear in those they view as weaker. My friends and I are doing everything in our power to find that man and bring the demon who kidnapped him to justice."

A woman in her mid-twenties stepped forward, shoving the first man aside, and asked, "What does 'justice' mean to supernaturals? Does that mean killing?"

Of course she'd assume violence.

"It means he will be captured, and if he resists, we'll do what is necessary to protect everyone." Killian placed a hand on his chest. "I want everyone to be aware that we're working to contain the threats. They aren't being ignored."

"When you say 'everyone,' who does that include?" an older woman reporter yelled from the back.

Killian's brows furrowed. "I don't understand the question."

"'Everyone' as in all supernaturals, right? Humans aren't worthy," she asked more clearly.

She wanted to depict us as heartless and point out the divide between supernaturals and humans. I wanted to punch her in the face, but I was certain that wouldn't go over well.

"Everyone who has a heart—which, for the record, includes both *humans* and supernaturals," Killian spoke slowly. "Each one of us needs a heart and blood to survive. The only difference between supernaturals and humans is that magic flows through our veins. If you take it away, we're the same as you."

I loved his answer because it was the truth. I was part human, but I also had wolf and angel magic. I needed to eat, breathe, and love the same as humans.

"But that's the key. Magic," the woman pushed.

"I need to check in with the searchers, but know we're working tirelessly to ensure everyone is treated fairly." Killian turned on his heel and headed toward me.

"Wait," a man in his early thirties called out. "I didn't get to ask anything."

The horde of reporters chased after Killian. There was no stopping them.

As I rushed back to the truck to prepare his getaway vehicle, two dark shadows dropped in front of me, blocking my path.

CHAPTER EIGHT

I CROUCHED, ready to fight the two demons in shadow form in front of me. I scanned the surrounding area to see if anyone was close. I noticed a couple across the street, holding hands, but they were human and unaware of the threat.

The reporters couldn't see the demons, either, since they weren't of angel descent, which was one reason the humans were reacting so extremely to the man's disappearance. It was as if the air had dragged him away.

Two demons are with me, I linked with Killian. I wasn't sure what to do. Launching an attack could cause more chaos.

Do whatever you have to do to stay safe, Killian replied, and his footsteps moved toward me.

My attention flicked back to the demons, whose red eyes glowed brightly. They must know I could see them. One pulled out a knife, lifting it inches from my face.

They were taunting me.

I gritted my teeth, readying myself for the inevitable, but I would force them to make the first move. I didn't want to be blamed for fighting in front of humans, so any action on my part would be in self-defense.

Still, I murmured, "If you're going to do something, do it." I didn't want them to mistake my hesitation for fear.

The eyes of the one on the right narrowed as if he were smiling.

I hated the conclusion I'd come to. They were in control. I wondered what had taken them so long to pull this in the first place.

Their negative energy swirled around me, making me feel dirty even though I'd showered not twelve hours ago.

One of the reporters behind Killian gasped. "Do you see the floating knife?"

Now that the demon had the human's attention, he raised the knife slowly, desperate to add more fear.

I'd hoped the reporters would be so preoccupied with Killian that they wouldn't notice. Wishful thinking.

Try to distract them, I linked and lifted my hands, prepared to block his attack.

The attention of the demon on the left tilted skyward. "Jabe, we've got to go."

"Not until I get one swipe in." Jabe slammed his arm down.

He was trying to trick me.

I caught his wrist just as the other demon hissed, "We've got to go. *Now*."

Jabe's gaze flicked toward the sky, and he growled. He jerked his wrist from my hold, catching me off guard.

"Fine, but this isn't *over*," he vowed, and both shadow figures hurried away.

My ears rang as I spun around, searching for what had caused them to run. Jabe had been determined to cause a scene and hurt me.

Four demons in shadow form soared toward us from Shadow City. I noted their eyes—not red, but a variety of human-like colors—and no vileness floated off the figures. They were on our side.

Killian strode up to me, worry etched on his face. Though I'd told him to distract the others, he clearly hadn't complied. He searched the area behind me. *Where are they?*

He didn't realize the demons had vanished. I connected, *They just scurried away. Four demons from our side are coming our way.* I took his hand in mine. *They're almost here.*

I'd expected the anxiety flowing through our bond to lessen, but instead, his turmoil increased. He snagged my hand and dragged me toward the truck. *We need to get you out of here.*

I dug my feet into the concrete, standing firm as the middle-aged male reporter yelled, "It looked as if you could see something the rest of us couldn't. Can you tell me how that's possible?"

Shit. I hadn't considered they might catch me on camera. I hoped they hadn't filmed my brief interaction with the demon.

I quickly followed Killian. I hadn't meant for my face to be plastered all over the news with his, but I couldn't do a damn thing about it. Maybe that was why the demons had shown up—to create more supernatural havoc. I shuddered. I didn't want to give them credit for being intelligent, but I knew better. Dad had taught me to never underestimate my enemy, and here I was, purposely trying to do it.

My face burned. He'd be ashamed.

I tossed the keys to Killian, and we hurried into the truck. The reporters rushed after us, reminding me of paparazzi chasing after celebrities. I'd always thought that was exaggerated...until now. Clearly, people were desperate to get whatever story they were after.

Killian stomped on the gas and peeled out of our spot. Since it was still early morning, there weren't many vehicles downtown, so we didn't have to dodge anyone.

I was thankful our demon allies had been heading our way. I feared what trouble the malicious demons would've caused had they not arrived. Though I was confident I could have handled the demons, that would've given the humans more of a show and instilled more terror in them.

We drove out of downtown, and I leaned back against the headrest. Killian had been right—we shouldn't have come. "I'm sorry. That was a disaster. I thought if you went on the news to reassure—"

"No, you were right. I needed to do that. The demons showing up was the problem. It was as if they were targeting you." The farther we got from downtown, the more Killian relaxed, but his anger didn't subside.

My scalp prickled. I couldn't disagree with him. The demons *had* targeted me, the only person there who could see them. It could have been coincidence, but I was beginning to believe less and less in that sentiment.

At first, the abduction of my grandparents' pack had seemed random until we'd learned that Tom, Mom's revenge-seeking ex-lover, had chosen them. All the packs that had been taken since then were regional, with Tom having provided items to locate them. The connection was Tom. Now we knew Erin had been working with him, but we didn't know why. We still had a huge picture to put together, and we were missing large pieces of the puzzle.

"I don't know." That was the only thing I could say for certain. "They might have. But why?"

"Maybe they knew it would reveal that you're different.

That you can see things I can't." He banged the steering wheel with his palm. "But how would they know that?"

Good question. I would say it was because they could sense my goodness, but Killian was good, too. Goodness wasn't reserved only for those of angel descent. I couldn't sense that they were demons, but I could sense the vileness floating off them, the same as for any evil person. I knew they were demons only because they'd been in shadow form. Someone would've had to tell them who and what I was. "I...I don't know."

Killian reached over the center console and took my hand. *It doesn't matter. Nothing will happen to you. I'll make sure of it.*

I wanted to argue with him—he was making a promise he had no way of keeping—but if saying that made him feel better, I wouldn't contradict him.

We passed the *Welcome to Shadow Ridge* sign and headed for the two-lane highway that would lead us away from here.

Dark shadow forms appeared on either side of the car. A scream lodged in my throat, but then I noticed the familiar hickory-brown eyes of the demon on my side.

Bune. Levi's father.

I glanced at the demon on Killian's side. Brilliant black eyes with diamond-like sparkles stared back at me—Zagan.

Two demons I *knew* were allies.

Their shadow forms dispersed and became more like smoke. I'd seen them do that a handful of times and only when they were slipping through cracks.

They must be planning to come inside the car.

"Jewel, what's wrong?" Killian asked. He looked from side to side to see what I kept staring at. "Are you seeing demons?"

I hadn't considered what he'd feel through our bond. Of course he would sense my reaction. "Yes, but it's Bune and Zagan." As I said the words, their smoky presences seeped into the truck, even though the windows were rolled up. They'd found cracks large enough to get through. "And now they're in the truck with us."

"What?" he gasped, his panic surging through the bond. His hands jerked on the steering wheel, and we swerved off the smooth road onto the side, hitting grass and kicking up dirt as Killian slammed on the brakes.

Bune and Zagan materialized into their human form in the back seat.

"What the hell, Killian?" Zagan smirked, his eyes twinkling. He wore a black shirt and slacks as if that would make him hard to see in physical form. He flipped his shoulder-length raven hair out of his eyes, the black strands contrasting with his clay-colored complexion. "I thought you were used to demons popping up unannounced."

Killian spun around and glared. He gritted out, "I am, but this is the first time demons have sneaked into my *moving vehicle*."

"Sorry about that." Bune lifted one coffee-colored eyebrow and directed a look of warning at Zagan. He scratched his short golden brown beard. "We wanted to check on you two, and Levi and Rosemary asked us to go with you to Rockwood to stake out the area. Since you were already heading out and those humans are trying to catch up with you in their news van, we thought it would be ideal to join you this way."

Growling, Killian pressed the gas and headed back onto the road. Our bodies lurched as we transitioned from uneven ground to asphalt.

I leaned toward the center console and noted two vans gaining on us. "That must be them."

Rolling his eyes, Killian increased our speed. "We'll be fine. It won't be hard to lose them, but damn, they're persistent."

He was right. Though humans could drive fast, since it was dark, they'd have to drive slower or risk causing an accident. The four of us could see just as well in the dark as we could if the sun were shining brightly.

Sierra, are you and Emmy okay? Killian linked.

She answered immediately. *No, I'm not. Why did you have me come get him? He couldn't just stay with Hal?*

I grinned, knowing exactly what to say to get her to react. *You know what, babe? Why don't we leave him there and ask Ruby to keep an eye on him?*

He cut his eyes toward me, a look of warning. He murmured, "Do not encourage her. I'd rather he stay behind."

I thought Torak had proven himself trustworthy. Apparently, Killian still had doubts.

No, it's fine, Sierra backtracked immediately. *He's annoying and loves waving his gun around, but I can handle him. After all, Sadie wants him with us, right?*

Exhaling, Killian replied, *She does. Look, can you all meet us at Rockwood? Bune and Zagan have joined us, and I like the idea of bringing the truck in case we need to split up.*

In other words: so we didn't roll back into the neighborhood in another Suburban in case Erin showed up again.

Yeah, I'm down, Sierra answered. *Being behind the wheel for once is kinda nice. If someone doesn't like my music, tough. If they've gotta pee, they have to wait until I say they can. If they annoy me, I can kick their ass out. I have the power, and now, I'll never want to give it up.*

Turning onto the road to the interstate, Killian shook his head. *Then maybe you should learn how to drive better, because Jewel and I aren't riding with you while you're behind the wheel.*

Hey, Jewel's her own person and can make her own decisions, Sierra shot back. *If she wants to ride with me, she's more than welcome. In fact, Jewel, I can pick you up at the McDonald's a few miles away, if you want. Then Torak can ride with Killian, and you can be in the amazing girl SUV.*

Under normal circumstances, I'd be up for it. Spending time with Emmy would be fun, but listening to Sierra's musical mashups would give me a headache, and after seeing her almost run over an unsuspecting mailbox not even an hour ago, I'd rather stay with my mate. *I hate to say it, but after the past day, I could use some soothing music.*

Girl, I love The Little Mermaid. *Sebastian's voice inspired me on so many levels when I was a little girl. I'm not sure which one was Bach, but if he has the same rhythm as the crab, he can do no wrong.*

My mouth dropped open, and I could form no words.

Jewel was talking about classical music. Killian grinned and squeezed my arm.

Oh. Sierra paused. *Ew. Yeah, Torak stays with us. She rides with you. We'll meet you there. We're getting in the Suburban now.*

I laughed at the dismissal. Our tastes in music didn't mesh.

"Is everything okay up there?" Zagan leaned forward, staring out the window.

We were all on edge, even though we weren't in Shadow Ridge anymore.

Killian kissed my hand and answered, "It's just Sierra."

"Say no more." He settled back in his seat and looked out the window.

Everyone knew Sierra. She had no shame and never hid who she was. It was one of the things I liked most about her, though at times, it could be overwhelming. I asked, "Do you guys mind if I put on some classical music?"

Bune sighed. "No, I'd love it. Marissa used to play the piano, so it reminds me of home."

My heart ached. The thought of having to live without my fated mate hurt so badly, it took my breath away. To live through it...I didn't even want to imagine. Not wanting to push, I flipped the radio on and settled in for an hour's ride, trying to stay calm.

THIRTY MINUTES FROM ROCKWOOD, Killian's cell phone rang. His phone was connected to the car's Bluetooth, so when he answered, all four of us could hear Sterlyn.

"Hey, it's me, and I'm with Griffin, Cyrus, Annie, Alex, and Ronnie. The human just called Levi, and there's a problem," Sterlyn said. "They want us to capture the pack tomorrow."

My stomach sank. How were we supposed to do that when there wasn't even a pack to take?

CHAPTER NINE

EVERYTHING SEEMED to be working against us, and I wasn't sure how we were going to win. Each step forward resulted in us taking two giant steps back. Though I'd expected the humans to want more shifters, I hadn't known they would demand a turnaround time of twenty-four hours, especially since they'd obtained a new pack just days ago.

The corners of Killian's eyes tightened. "Well, that's not happening."

"I know," Sterlyn replied, sounding flustered. "I thought we'd have more time before we revealed our hand."

There had to be a solution. We'd never planned on handing over a pack, but this changed things. I glanced at the sun, which was now rising, soft swirls of pink giving way to a gorgeous winter sunrise. Its magical beauty struck a chord inside me. "Wait. I know we hoped that we'd have the two packs out when we concocted this plan, but what if we use this opportunity to make Erin look bad?"

Bune chuckled. "That's actually brilliant, but if you do

that, you'll basically confirm to Erin that you know she's involved."

"But she pretty much knows that anyway, so that's not a huge change." Killian tapped his fingers on the black leather steering wheel. "How can we make her look bad?"

All the paranormal stories I'd read when I was younger were finally coming in handy. I loved a good anti-hero who could warp my mind just a little. "We have Levi tell the humans that when we got there, *no one* was there. There wasn't even a hint that anyone lived there." The best way to insult a witch was to say her magic was impotent.

"Now that's downright evil." Zagan leaned forward between Killian's seat and mine, his face lit with mirth. "If I didn't know better, I'd swear you were raised in Hell."

For some sick reason, I puffed out my chest as if I were proud.

"I don't know if I should be impressed or concerned," Griffin deadpanned over the line. "But it works."

"She would never expect it from us," Ronnie agreed. "But we'll need to be careful."

"And we'll need to make sure Egan and Jade are okay staying put until it's settled." Sterlyn sighed. "Once we call out her magic, she'll try to locate them again."

I glanced out my window, running through every plausible scenario. We needed to think like the witch to figure out how she'd react.

We drove down US 27, a four-lane highway. There were more cars on the road than I'd expected, but they were going in the opposite direction, likely for work in the town we'd passed ten minutes ago. Trees lined both sides of the road, indicating we were more in the country than near a big city.

The last government facility had been remote, but this location was even further off the grid.

"We should ask them first, but I assume they'll say yes," Annie answered. "They kind of have to. Wherever they go, Erin can locate them."

I closed my eyes and cringed. We should've thought of that before running off. She could find them as long as she had Egan's shirt.

"Which means we'll need to get the material away from her so they can go home," Cyrus growled.

"That will be hard." Alex's regal, almost British accent held a hiss. "I'm sure she took it to her coven, and no one ever visits their territory. At least no one has for as long as I've been alive."

"Maybe Rosemary will know something. When we meet up with her, we can see if she has any ideas," Sterlyn said. "Either way, we'll have to determine a solution for Egan and Jade."

"Witches are powerful." Bune cleared his throat. "Worst case, Eliza and Circe's coven should be able to block Erin from locating them."

Killian blew air from his cheeks. "But for how long? Whether we like it or not, Erin is smart, and it won't take her long to figure out whose magic is blocking her."

I took a deep breath. "There's one solution with the best outcome, but it's the more difficult one." Out of every option, if we could execute the plan, it would be safer for all of us.

Turning his head toward me, Killian nodded. "Getting the cloth away from Erin."

"I wonder if that's why she waited overnight before making the call." Sterlyn's voice hardened. "She was hoping we'd try to steal it."

My heart skipped a beat. That could be the case. Luckily, none of us had made any such attempt, and I was certain no one would've tried to pull it off without informing the others. That wasn't how this group operated, and the openness of our bonds was one thing I treasured most about us.

"Doesn't matter since we didn't try," Annie interjected. "That just proves she might try to bait us. Whatever we decide, we've gotta handle it the right way."

In any situation, there wasn't a "right" way but rather a "best," and even that was up for interpretation.

"Why don't you all see what you can glean from inside the city?" Killian's hands gripped the steering wheel once more.

"Sounds good." Sterlyn's voice grew louder as if she were closer to the phone. "Griffin's mom just arrived, so we need to go, but I'll step outside and call Sadie to give them a heads up."

"Just let us know." Killian pressed the hang-up button on his steering wheel.

Zagan settled back in his seat. "I thought when we left Hell, things would get stagnant and boring, but I was wrong. In fact, I think Earth is more chaotic than Hell ever was."

Sometimes it was weird thinking about the existence of an alternate dimension, but I'd heard enough to believe it, even though I hadn't been around to help during the demon war.

"That's because, in Hell, there were only bad choices, so none of it mattered. Here, there's hope, and that's more powerful than fear," Bune replied wisely.

Looking at Bune, you would think he was in his forties rather than older than a millennium. That was how long

Shadow City had been around, and he'd left for Hell before the gates had been shut and the city had been established.

A handful of buildings appeared in front of us, the first cluster since the last town we'd gone by. According to the GPS, we were getting close to Rockwood.

Killian linked with Sierra and me, *Where are you?*

The sign overhead at the traffic light says West Rathburn Street. There's an El Patron and Little Caesars ahead. We've just entered Rockwood, she answered.

You're ahead of us, but we shouldn't be far behind. We're passing a Peggy Ann Truck Shop, which is an all-blue building, I connected.

She answered, *We're probably five minutes ahead of you. Torak just got a text from Sadie to meet them at a Walgreens up ahead. I'm asking Aurora to send us a picture of where the government building is on the map so we can find a place nearby to stay.*

Killian's brows rose. *Uh...sounds good. We'll be there with you soon.*

His surprise floated through me, causing me to rub my arms. I linked, *What's wrong?*

Nothing. His forehead smoothed. *It's just, she's thinking things through. I'm not used to her doing that.*

Maybe Torak is influencing her, I suggested. Fated mates were supposed to bring out the best in each other, and Torak had a level head on his shoulders.

He frowned. *Stop with that. They probably aren't even fated mates. You know how Sierra would be if she found hers. Do you think she'd be fighting it?*

Was he being serious? Surely not. *From what I've heard, every single fated mate in this group fought their bond at first. Why would she be any different?* I understood he was protective of her, but there had to be something more going on...I just wasn't sure what. *Don't you want her to meet her fated mate? She's made it clear she wants to.*

Of course I do. He placed his arm on the door rest. *I want the best for her. I just don't think that's Torak.*

He's proved himself to us and seems like a good guy. Why wouldn't you want it to be him? I now fully trusted that Fate knew what she was doing. Every fated couple I'd met showed she'd done one hell of a job.

Killian bit his bottom lip. *Just stop wishing for it to be that bond. You could influence her, and she could get hurt.* His annoyance swirled between us. *We need to focus on the missing packs and not play matchmaker.*

Head tilting back, I blinked a few times. I had to replay the words he'd just spoken to ensure I'd heard him correctly. This wasn't the time for us to have a disagreement, so I tried to process them without being emotional. *I'll stop pushing if you stop being so closed-minded. Of course I don't want her to get hurt, and I haven't even hinted to her that I think they could be mates. But you need to prepare yourself. Even if it's not Torak, Sierra could find her mate—or choose one—at any time.*

The Mexican restaurant she'd mentioned appeared on the right. It was a brick building with a dark green roof, and the signature orange and white building of Little Caesars was just past it. We were close.

You think I don't know that? Killian's jaw twitched. *I want her to be happy, but she doesn't need to rush into anything.*

I wanted to snap at him. Of the two of us, he'd been ready to cement our bond almost immediately. And now he had the audacity to act like Sierra shouldn't have that same chance?

"Shouldn't someone reach out to Sierra?" Bune asked

from behind me. "Since Torak is with her and we have no clue where they're located."

We'd been arguing instead of filling in our demon friends. Grimacing, I remained quiet and allowed Killian to inform them of the plan.

"There's the Walgreens." Zagan pointed between the seats to the left.

The standard red cursive letters of the logo sat on top of the brown siding on the side of the roof. Large windows made up a portion of the wall, and the rest was brick, but the place was smaller than any pharmacy I'd ever visited.

We found the Suburban idling next to a large white van. "I bet the van is Sadie and the others," I said. We hadn't seen their vehicle before, but that made sense.

Killian pulled up into the spot beside the van just as Torak rolled down the window of the back passenger seat. Emmy rolled down her window, as did Roxy, who was in the van.

I reached for the door handle, then realized the video of Killian and me from earlier this morning was probably playing on repeat, and we didn't need anyone recognizing us.

As if reading my mind, Killian stayed put. I could see that Lillith was in the driver's seat of the van, with Sadie next to her. Roxy sat behind Lillith, with Axel across from her. Donovan leaned forward from the very back.

Roxy tossed her bright red locks over her shoulder. Her color was that vibrant even in wolf form. Amazing. She smirked and waggled her brows as her hazel eyes glowed. "So, we saw Jewel making headlines next to her man."

My face burned, but I refused to look away. Not only would that encourage her, but I hadn't done anything wrong. "That unfortunate occurrence wasn't meant to happen."

Axel scratched his head. "What my mate meant to say is, what happened back at your place? What the hell was going on with those demons?"

"Causing chaos." Killian scowled and dropped his hands into his lap. "Demons were why we informed the world about our existence in the first place. They arranged for the humans to be there to see everything that went down."

A breeze lifted Sadie's rose gold bob, and her light ocean-blue eyes narrowed. "They enjoy the attention. It reminds me of a man I used to know."

"Don't get me started," Donovan growled. His navy eyes were so dark they could have passed as black, and his shaggy jet-black hair fell into his eyes. Despite it being winter, he wore a short-sleeved shirt, his tribal tattoo peeking out from under the sleeves.

Whoever they were talking about, no love was lost between them.

What the hell happened? Sierra linked as her attention landed on Killian and me.

He connected, *Demons attacked a human downtown, and we were trying to reassure people. We'll have to deal with the repercussions later. Right now, we need to get the packs out before everything falls apart.*

"With those two's faces plastered on television"—Lillith tilted her head in our direction, making her dark bob bounce—"I'd rather find a place to get settled." A faint red rimmed her dark eyes, and I wondered if her vampire side was bleeding through.

She did have a fair point.

"Did we find the location?" Sadie lifted her pink

phone. "Because that would help with finding a place to stay."

Emmy laid her arm on the outside of the Suburban. "Aurora just texted us back. There's a hidden government building in the southeast section of Mount Roosevelt. It's off the map, but from what the witches have gathered on some special witch intranet, a coven stumbled upon it several decades ago. Nothing happened, but they sensed the stench of death around it."

Death. Lovely. That was exactly what I'd wanted to hear. I tried to push away the thought since that could have easily been my mother and family.

"They rented a cabin for us a few miles out. We check in at four today, so we should leave our cars in the parking lot and stake out the area." Emmy tapped on her phone. "I've just plugged in an area where we can leave our vehicles, if you want to follow us."

"What are we waiting for?" Torak rubbed his hands together. "Let's go. I want to save Cujo and his pack."

Cujo. Like the dog? I wanted to say something, but I figured it'd be best if I didn't.

Everyone nodded, eager to do something other than sit in a vehicle. Killian rolled his window up, and we followed Sierra and Lillith through back roads to a large, windy path up the mountain.

My ears popped as the air pressure changed. We were getting close, and soon, we'd find out what the humans had done to those packs, or if we'd find a solution to the suffering my grandfather's pack was going through.

As we neared the top, Sierra swerved onto another road.

"She really shouldn't be driving," Zagan muttered.

I hated to agree, but she'd nearly driven off the road several times.

A small parking lot opened up ahead. The trees were thick around us, indicating we were well into the woods.

Home.

My wolf surged forward, wanting to come out, but now wasn't the time. We needed to be able to communicate with each other.

We got out of our cars, and Donovan paused as he stepped from the van and stared at our demon companions.

"Hi, I'm Zagan." The demon tipped his head and gestured with his thumb. "And this is Bune. We're here to help."

"And what, exactly, are you?" Donovan sniffed. "You sure aren't shifters or vampires."

"Demons." Zagan winked and smiled proudly.

Sierra pressed the lock on the Suburban's key fob and shook her head. "What would Eleanor think about you flirting with someone else?"

His face fell. "I wasn't flirting. I was being friendly."

I tried not to laugh.

"Tell him, Emmy." Sierra swirled her finger in the air.

"Eh." Emmy grimaced. "It could go either way. Who's teaching you how to interact like that?"

"I don't know." Roxy crossed her arms and squinted. "He had a constipated look like he was desperate but also searching for a bathroom. Are all demons like this?"

Zagan lifted both hands. "Rosemary said that when humans are being nice, they wink, smile, and lean toward someone."

"See, that was your first mistake." Sierra lifted a finger. "You're listening to an angel who just got her emotions back and takes everything literally. There's an art to interacting that can only be learned by watching others. Like—"

"Now's not the time," Killian said and rubbed his forehead. "Let's go find this building so we can see how many scouts are needed around the clock."

"We'll have time to teach Zagan how to be friendly later," Sadie said as she patted Zagan's shoulder. "But hey, you're trying. That matters."

Donovan's expression twisted. "I'm not so sure."

Torak huffed and walked off toward the woods, heading southeast. Cujo must be a better friend than any of us realized.

"Come on. Let's go before Zagan tries to flirt with one of us," Lillith said loudly enough that everyone could hear.

Exhaling, Zagan scrunched his nose as if he smelled something putrid.

"Don't worry, son." Bune's shoulders were shaking. "I'm sure everything will be okay."

Sierra rushed after Torak, with Sadie, Donovan, Axel, Roxy, and Lillith right behind her. Bune, Zagan, Killian, Emmy, and I took up the rear. I stood between Emmy and Killian, and our group merged into the oaks, red cedars, and yellow birches that surrounded us. Animals scurried through the underbrush, which was comforting. Nothing too horrible was going on close by. Elk leaped past us, and red hawks swooped overhead as we continued our trek into the woods. From what the GPS had said on our way out, there were about eleven thousand acres of state forest.

After being cooped up in the car for so long, the walk would calm our animals.

Killian intertwined our hands, and we moved so closely that our arms brushed.

Two miles in, gunshots rang in the air.

CHAPTER TEN

KILLIAN BLOCKED me as I spun toward the sound. Air sawed through my lungs as I stepped to the side to search for the threat. I didn't want anything to happen to him or the others, either.

A few northern cardinals scattered from some red cedars, flying away from the area. The only sounds were of their beating wings and our group's heavy breathing. No other shots were fired.

"We'll check things out," Bune said, and he and Zagan flickered into their shadow forms and soared in the direction from which the noise had come. At least they could find the threat undetected.

Sierra, are you okay? Killian linked.

When she didn't immediately respond, fear dug its sharp nails into my chest. I stepped around Emmy and found Sierra wrapped in Torak's arms as he shielded her from the potential attack.

"Damn it, Dewayne," a deep voice shouted from about half a mile away. "You missed the damn deer."

My shoulders relaxed. We weren't under attack, but rather, people were hunting.

Torak loosened his arms and took a step back. Sierra shook her head and finally responded, *I'm fine.*

Donovan frowned. "I thought this was a hiking area."

"Me, too." Sadie removed her phone again and swiped the screen. After a few seconds, she closed her eyes. "Apparently, only a section is reserved for hikers. The area of Mount Roosevelt we're heading through is open for hunting."

Well, *we* weren't being shot at.

Rolling her eyes, Lillith groaned. "Of course it is. Why should things get easier for any of us?"

"Maybe you can do your teleporting thing and take us all there." Roxy forced an exaggerated smile, and I swore every tooth in her mouth could be seen.

"Whoa." Sierra lifted a hand. "You can *teleport*? How are we just learning about this?" She narrowed her eyes and glared at Torak.

I was kind of in agreement. Teleporting would be epic right about now.

"What the *hell*, Roxy?" Donovan rasped, his irises glowing as his wolf surged forward.

Sadie placed a hand on his arm and said, "It's okay. She wasn't thinking."

"Clearly. Should we just sit here and share secrets in the middle of a fucking hunting area?" Donovan clenched his hands at his sides.

"Calm down, man." Axel stepped in front of his mate. "She didn't mean—"

Things were escalating, and for once, it wasn't Sierra's fault. I was used to being a peacemaker with Mom, so I drew closer. "Hey, look, it's fine. We won't say a word. We'll forget it was even said."

Speak for yourself, hussy, Sierra linked, her attention locked on Torak. *That would've been helpful to know when your grandfather's pack was being slaughtered.*

Emmy karate-chopped the air. "Look, I can forget about it easily. But if you can teleport, right now would be an excellent time."

"I have to know what the place looks like to get us there, and it takes a lot of my energy." Sadie licked her lips. "It's draining for me to take myself, and to take this many people would be impossible."

"Forget the group. How can you do it, period?" Emmy asked as she leaned toward Sadie.

Sadie lifted her chin. "I'm half fae."

Heat flushed through my body, and I poked my tongue into my cheek. That wasn't possible. Fae rarely visited Earth, and their magic was tied to their realm, or so legend said.

Killian touched the base of his neck. "Impossible."

She smiled like he'd told a funny joke and said, "I assure you, it is. My father is fae, and he went to school for a short while on Earth and met my mother. My fae magic is tied to Earth, but it's slower to recharge."

Pacing, Donovan scowled and grumbled, "We don't have to tell them *everything*."

He wasn't happy that she'd shared that with us, and I couldn't blame him. As cautious as we were with them, it only made sense they'd be the same way with us. Trust was earned.

Since she just trusted us, I'm going to share what I am with them, too, I linked with Killian. *Trust has to begin somewhere.*

He nodded, but his face was stoic. *Just don't tell her everything.*

That was fair. Sadie had told us only a little bit about her abilities. "I'm a silver wolf." I wouldn't share that Emmy was as well, though it wouldn't be hard for them to figure out.

"All of you with the same color of fur are, right?" Lillith cupped her elbow with a hand and took a step toward me. "But what's interesting is that we've researched what you could be but never found any information on it."

"We're part angel and part wolf." Like Sadie, I'd tell just enough. Truthfully, my heritage would eventually become common knowledge, especially since our kind was on TV. "We were created when Shadow City was built."

Two shadow figures floated toward us as the demons returned. They landed behind Killian and me and shifted back into their human forms.

Startled, Roxy stumbled back a few feet. "That's still so damn disconcerting. Hell, demons and angels aren't even supposed to be real, and now we've learned there are half-angel wolves."

Smirking, Zagan put his hands into his jeans pockets and leaned back on his heels. "I assure you, we're all real."

"Sorry to surprise you, but it's best to investigate in a form in which most people can't see you." Bune nodded and rubbed his hands together. "There are a ton of hunters out here, so we'll need to be careful."

"No other threats?" Emmy arched her brow.

He shook his head. "They were all human."

"And each one was wearing brown and green clothing with a horrible orange vest over it." Zagan waved a hand in front of his chest. "Maybe it's for that college football team everyone likes?"

I laughed. "You mean the Volunteers?"

He glanced at me like I had two legs. "No, not volunteers. I didn't realize people who wanted to help had to wear that same color. I meant the football team."

Roxy snorted. "That's the name of the football team."

"They're wearing that color so other hunters can see them." Donovan pinched the bridge of his nose. "That's it. It would've been a good thing to know so we could've done likewise."

We were over-complicating things. "If there's a hiking trail, let's just go back and take it until it ends. That should save us some trouble," I said. Though we wanted to remain undetected when we arrived at the building, we could take a safer course. This early in the day, not many people should be out here, and those who were probably hadn't seen the news clip of Killian and me that was likely going viral.

Scratching his chin, Torak smiled. "That's very simple and a great idea."

My cheeks burned, but something like pride wafted through Killian's and my connection.

"That's because she sees the bigger picture," Killian murmured, and took my hand. "Since she's been around, I've noticed that sometimes, we make things harder than they should be."

Killian sounded just like Dad.

"What are we waiting for?" Sierra clapped her hands, being unnecessarily loud. "Let's get out of here before we do get shot at. I've already had someone *aim* a gun at me far too recently."

Torak scoffed. "I didn't know you were allies. How many times do I have to tell you that?"

"As many times as it takes for you to apologize to me." Sierra smacked her chest.

His nostrils flared. "You're so damn infuriating. Can't you let it go and embrace my boyish charm?"

"Please. Killian has more charm than you," she growled and marched past Torak toward me.

Stopping in his tracks, Killian turned to her. He pursed his lips and linked, *That was not a compliment. You do realize that.*

I know. It really sucks for him. Sierra scrunched her face. *Hopefully, he'll find a way to improve.*

I mashed my lips together. I wasn't sure if she was trying to insult Killian, but her timing was perfect.

Exhaling, Killian turned around and tugged my hand again. He linked, *See, not fated mates. You've gotta let that go.*

With each step, Sierra's feet pounded harder. Even without my sensitive shifter ears, I would have heard her for miles. If she wasn't careful, the hunters might think a herd of elk was nearby.

Emmy caught up to Sierra and murmured, "Let's not get the hunters' attention. I'd rather not get shot at again."

"Fine," Sierra grumbled, and quieted down.

I glanced over my shoulder to find Torak and Lillith right behind Sierra and Emmy. Torak's eyes were homed in on the back of Sierra's head, and his bottom lip stuck out a little. He was pouting. He must not like Sierra being mad at him but didn't want to apologize. The latter had to be his wolf's influence since he was an alpha in his own right. Apologies were hard for them when they didn't believe they were in the wrong.

Sadie and Donovan followed behind, with Axel and Roxy trailing them. Bune and Zagan took up the rear.

At this point, I did trust Sadie and the others. They'd proven themselves. But it still comforted me to have two of our own at the very end.

Soon, we reached the cars again.

Lifting her phone, Sadie pointed a little farther down the road. "A hiking trail starts there. It goes around the edge of the hunting area, stays close to the road, and ends at the edge of Mount Roosevelt, right where we need to go."

I know I suggested this, but are we sure this is a good idea? I usually didn't second-guess myself, but we had to be careful that no one recognized us.

Trust me, Killian linked and released my hold. He jogged over to his truck and opened the driver's door.

"Wait. We're leaving?" Sierra asked, her mouth dropping.

Emmy placed a hand on my shoulder. "She wouldn't be standing here if that were the case."

Reaching inside the vehicle, Killian removed two baseball caps. He tossed an Atlanta Braves one to me and placed a Tennessee Volunteers one on his head. The hat enhanced his sharp cheekbones and was something I'd definitely want to see him in again.

I'd never been one for hats, but at least they would obscure our faces a little, so I pulled the ends of my hair through the back as we followed Sadie's directions into the woods.

The trail was fifteen feet wide, so people could walk side by side or pass one another easily. The ground was covered with autumn leaves, and the sun now shone down on us.

Sweat sprouted underneath the bill of my hat from the heat of the sun. Wolf shifters ran hotter than humans.

A trio of rabbits hopped away from us, and a blue jay sat

perched on the branch of an oak a few feet away. If we hadn't been on the hunt for kidnapped packs, this would have been a peaceful walk in nature.

Feet pounded on the mulch about a mile away, coming closer. The rhythm sounded like someone out for a morning run. These trails were well used, so that wasn't surprising.

Emmy appeared at my side, a knowing grin on her face.

I would've loved to be able to pack link with her. I tilted my head, trying to figure out what was going on, and she discreetly gestured behind us.

Glancing back, I noticed Torak and Sierra walking side by side. And Killian said they weren't fated mates, but I wouldn't point it out to him. He would come to terms with it in his own time.

The runner appeared, his chest drenched with sweat. My stomach hardened, worried he would notice us, but as he passed by, he didn't even glance our way.

The rest of the way was uneventful, and the trail came to a sudden end.

We hadn't passed another human. Though no one was behind us, I glanced around to double-check.

"What's wrong?" Axel asked, following my gaze. "Is someone back there?"

I shook my head. "Just checking the area. My dad taught us to always remain cautious because a threat could be imminent."

"Wise advice," Sadie said kindly.

Emmy gave me a side-arm hug and said, "He was a wise man and an amazing alpha."

My heart ached. That he had been.

Do you need a minute? Killian asked, his hand squeezing mine.

Of course he could feel my emotions. *No. We need to*

get there and stake out the area. Having something to do is the most helpful.

That I understand.

Our group stepped into the thicker woods. Though we were no longer in the hunting area, we were still more at risk off the main path.

We spread out, moving in a line. Now that we weren't as worried about humans, we picked up the pace. The terrain was uneven and similar to the areas we chose to run through.

Killian led the group, which I was more than happy with. We moved at a steady pace for twenty minutes. The presence of deer and elk was more evident here than back where the hunters had been. Animals had a knack for sensing danger, especially after hearing gunfire.

An all-brick building appeared through the bare tree limbs.

We were getting close.

With every step, the structure seemed more massive. The construction appeared new, and I detected a faint stench of death and decay that reminded me of decomposing bodies. Maybe this was the facility Aurora had learned about on the intranet—perhaps the government had redesigned a building for experimenting on supernaturals.

I decided I didn't want to know.

The trees thinned, giving us a clear view of the building we'd need to break into. Five guards were posted on either side.

Killian stopped. We needed to stay within the tree line for cover. I breathed in the smell of humans, sensing nothing that would identify them as a supernatural race. The human guards were searching the area.

This particular building consisted of two rectangles that

joined at one corner, making a ninety-degree angle. A road led to the building, but the parking lot was underneath it, with metal garage doors keeping it secure. Worse, the building had no visible entry on this side.

We needed to see the other side, but we had a huge problem: there was no tree cover.

Is it me, or is there no way inside? Sierra linked.

I cringed. I didn't have an answer.

Killian sighed. *This is when Bune and Zagan come in handy.*

"Am I the only one seeing a problem?" Lillith murmured. "Or am I the only one who can't link to discuss that?"

"Don't worry, I can't link, either." Emmy smiled sadly as her gaze flicked to me. "So you aren't alone."

"Bune—" Killian started.

"We're on it," Bune replied as he and Zagan shifted into their shadow forms.

Reaching out, Roxy placed her hands on Zagan's invisible form. When her hand stopped, she hissed, "Holy shit. That's insane. I feel him, but I can't see him."

"And I would truly appreciate it if you stopped feeling him *now*," Axel gritted, his teeth clenching. "You're *my* mate."

Zagan's eyes narrowed, and he inched toward the building.

When he left, Roxy nearly toppled over, her eyes wide. She stumbled a few steps toward a tree...and a net wrapped around her body, lifting her up so she was hanging from a high branch of a red cedar.

CHAPTER ELEVEN

OUT OF EVERY scenario I'd thought through, this had not been on my radar. Yet here we were, staring at her ass through a net. Of course, that would be the main thing we could see from down here.

"Don't just stand there," Roxy hissed through clenched teeth. "Get me down."

A guard jerked his head in our direction and asked, "Did you hear that?"

She had to be quiet. Freeing her without making more noise might be impossible, but we didn't need her talking and having them come check their traps even sooner.

I spun around, hoping to ask either Sadie or Axel to communicate with her, but Sadie's eyes were already glowing.

Roxy growled faintly, confirming my assumption.

A female guard standing in the middle of the group glanced our way. She narrowed her eyes as she tried to see. "I can't tell if a trap was launched. Why don't you go check it out?"

Throat closing, I struggled to swallow. Having an angel here to fly Roxy down would have been helpful right now.

"Me?" the guy asked, his tone rising. "Alone?"

"Yes, *alone*," the woman huffed. "It's just some animal like all the other times."

His hesitation would buy us more time. I scanned our surroundings for an answer to our problem, but we had no way to get her down without dropping her and making a lot of noise.

"Does anyone have an idea?" Axel rubbed his temples as he breathed shallowly. "They'll come over here soon."

A breeze swung Roxy from the top branch. A few branches cracked as if Fate were giving us the middle finger.

Killian tensed, his panic swirling into me. Any second now, he'd try to talk me into leaving, but I would remain right beside him.

"Something's over there," the man on the opposite end of the line said gruffly. "Go take a look. It's probably nothing."

This wasn't out of the norm for them. That could be why they weren't rushing over.

"There's no way to get her down quietly." Killian's jaw twitched. "We'll just have to do it and hope for the best. We have to get out of here before the guard discovers us."

"What does that mean?" Torak stepped toward us, nostrils flaring. "We can't leave my friends in there."

This wasn't good, and one person could diffuse him the quickest. I linked with only Sierra, *Calm him down.*

Sierra tilted her head. *Me?*

She truly had no clue what they were to each other, so maybe Killian was right, but we'd soon know. *If you're fated mates, your touch will help reason filter in. He's worried about a pack he cares about, and he's getting confrontational.*

I remembered exactly how it had felt when my grandfather's pack was taken.

Her eyes bulged. *You think we're fated mates?*

Was anyone thinking clearly? I replied, *Just try, please. We're running out of time.*

Obliging me, Sierra clutched Torak's hand, and he stopped moving.

"Fine," the original guard grunted. "I'll go see, but if something happens—"

"For the love of God, just go," the woman groaned. "We all have walkie-talkies, but if you scream, we'll hear you."

Donovan walked past me toward the guards and whispered, "I'll take care of this."

That was the worst thing he could do.

I grabbed his arm, and he froze while Sadie tensed and Killian's gaze locked on my hand.

Calm down. I'm preventing him from leaving and making a huge mistake. I tried not to roll my eyes. Now wasn't the time for possessiveness. I dropped my hand and spoke out loud, "There aren't any good options, but that's the worst one. We need another way out of this."

The guard's footsteps drew closer. I surveyed the area again, hoping something would pop into my mind. My attention landed on Lillith.

Vampire.

We could use that.

Sadie rubbed her hands together. "I'll beam them and not let them get too close."

That would immediately inform them that supernaturals were here. "I have a better idea."

Exhaling, Emmy muttered, "Lillith."

I wasn't surprised she'd figured out my plan. She and I had been inseparable growing up, and she knew how I thought. I nodded and said to the vampire, "You can mess with his mind when he gets here."

Lillith winced. "Okay, but what do you want me to say? If I tell him he didn't hear anything, his cohorts won't believe him."

She was missing the point. "Act like you got lost in the woods and wound up here. Then make him believe he saw a deer and let it go. That will account for the noise."

Pride swarmed through our fated-mate bond, and I straightened my back. Killian linked, *You are damn smart.*

"But what if it doesn't hold?" Lillith nibbled on her bottom lip. "I'm a horrible actress."

Torak snorted. "That's true."

"You just have to get close to him so you can use your mind juju. You can do this. I believe in you." Sadie hurried past Torak and placed her hands on the vampire's shoulders, staring her straight in the eyes. "Talk to him someplace where the other guards can't see you. Then distract him long enough for us to get Roxy down. When you hear the noise, tell him to wait a few seconds before checking the trap and implant the memory of him finding a deer."

Closing her eyes, Lillith inhaled shakily.

"Girl, you've got this." Sierra patted her on the back a little too roughly. "You're confident and a badass. Now go show that asshole who's boss."

"Yeah." Lillith stuck out her chest. "He's an asshole who's okay with locking supernaturals up. I can do this."

The guard was in the tree line and would be on us in seconds.

"Go." Axel gestured toward the building.

Lillith disappeared from view, using her vampire speed to head the human off. We had to move.

Emmy strolled to the red cedar. "I'll climb the tree."

"You don't have to do that." Sadie backed up a few steps, her gaze trained on the top of the tree. "My beams can cut the rope."

Stepping next to me, Killian placed his hand on the center of my back. The buzz of our connection sprang to life. At least we had each other in less-than-ideal circumstances.

"I hate to be the pessimist here, but..." Sierra flicked her wrist. "What if you miss and take down the tree?"

Roxy whimpered, and I wanted to strangle Sierra. If Emmy climbed the tree and tried to release Roxy, it would make her swing around even more, and the other guards might come to this one's aid. It was too bad Zagan and Bune weren't here; they could have easily gotten her down in their shadow form, but hopefully, they were inside the building, and we had no way of signaling them for help.

This time, Torak placed his hand on Sierra's shoulder. Her body relaxed, the connection of the fated mate bond soothing her.

"This is one of the skills I'm most comfortable with." Sadie smiled, but concern was etched on her face.

Noticing how she'd worded that statement, I wondered how comfortable she truly was. If she struggled with teleporting, maybe all her fae abilities were unpredictable.

"Oh, sorry!" Lillith gasped from several yards away.

We all went still.

The silence stretched for several seconds, and then the guard asked, "Who are you?"

"Lost." Lillith's voice trembled. "I...where am I?" She was playing her part well, which meant she was a better actress than she'd let on.

I turned my attention back to Sadie, who lifted her

hands so her palms faced the top of the tree where the rope was.

My lungs froze, and I fought the urge to close my eyes. Any sign of distress would add tension to the situation.

Donovan stood next to his mate, their arms brushing. If that wasn't a sign of a supportive mate, I wasn't sure what was.

"I was hiking in the woods and got separated from my group, and I—" Lillith continued her ruse and stopped as her breathing grew rapid.

Hands clenched, Axel stared up at his trapped mate. The breeze picked up, causing her body to rock harder and the trees to creak louder.

"Listen, I've got to check on something. Let me radio my coworkers so they can help you." The guard's voice sounded strained. "It might not be safe out here."

Eyes tightening, Sadie shot pink beams from her hands. One hit a branch right next to Roxy, and the other one hit the rope. Both snapped, and she fell toward the ground with the branch beside her.

Standing right underneath, Axel stretched out his arms to catch his mate, and the impact slammed them both into the ground, with Roxy landing on top and his arms tangled in the net.

If we hadn't been in a highly volatile predicament, I'd have been laughing.

"What the hell was that?" the guard asked, and his footsteps hurried toward us.

Sadie and Donovan rushed to untangle their friends as Lillith commanded, "Wait." There was the sound of a struggle as Emmy ran to Roxy and removed her knife from her back pocket. She cut through the net while Donovan and Sadie worked to free Roxy from the never-ending mess that surrounded her.

"Some of us should head into the woods," Killian murmured. "We need to get back to the cars as soon as Bune and Zagan arrive, and the less noise, the better."

Hurt wafted through me, but when I turned to him, he wasn't looking at me. His attention was on Sierra. He was telling her to go ahead and retreat before everyone else.

That was different, but I wasn't complaining.

Lillith repeated what we'd told her to say earlier. She was messing with the guard's mind.

We needed to move. Though she could make him forget about us, the more memories she had to change, the likelier his mind was to fracture over time. I didn't expect there to be a problem before we freed the two packs, but I didn't want to take any chances.

Sierra crossed her arms, not wanting to be left out. There was something she could do, and Torak would want her out of harm's way. More supernaturals could be working with the humans anyway. I said, "Torak, you two should go make sure no one is following the path we took here to sneak up behind us—"

You bish, Sierra linked, just as Torak nodded. *I hate to leave—you all need me.*

The problem was, the more of us who stayed close to the facility, the greater the risk of discovery. I wasn't leaving because I was a trained fighter and might be of help here.

"Come on, Sierra." Torak took her hand and tugged her to the woods. "Let's get out of the way and not cause any more problems."

Displeasure swirled from Killian, but I lifted my chin, refusing to feel ashamed.

Go with him, please, Killian told Sierra. *We'll be a few minutes behind you. We just need to make sure no supernaturals are tailing us while we're preoccupied, and once we know the plan worked, we'll be right behind you.*

Fine, she replied, and she and Torak retraced our steps here.

When Roxy was finally freed from the netting, tears burned my eyes. I'd almost believed we wouldn't get out of this situation.

Axel got to his feet as well, and the five of them followed Sierra and Torak's path, moving deeper into the woods with us right behind them.

Lillith's and the guard's footsteps picked up speed, heading in our direction, indicating that Lillith had heard us scamper away.

As we stepped deeper into the thick trees, my pulse pounded in my ears. That had been way too close of a call, but now we knew they'd laid traps in the woods. We'd have to find them all, which would be hard.

That was a problem for later.

Lillith appeared in front of us. Her face was paler, and her brown irises held a hint more red. "It's done. He's fixing the net now."

The female guard's voice sounded on his walkie-talkie. "Bruce, is everything okay? You've been gone a while."

A second later, he responded, "Yeah. You were right. A huge deer got caught in it. I cut it down, and it ran into the woods, but the net's ruined."

"Roger that," the woman replied. "One of us will grab a new one."

Killian leaned into me and wrapped an arm around my waist, relief evident in his body language and through our connection. We'd all been worried that something else would go wrong.

"Will Zagan and Bune know where to meet us?" Torak asked as he leaned against a tree next to Sierra.

"They'll head in the direction we came from," Killian answered as he pulled me in front of him. He wrapped his other arm around me, holding me from behind.

Unable to resist, I sagged against him, enjoying a quiet moment after the chaos.

"I sound like an old man, but damn, my back hurts." Axel rubbed his lower back, which had taken the brunt of the fall. "It felt like a ton of bricks landed on top of me."

Roxy spun toward him and arched her brow. "*What* did you just say?"

"What?" Axel's brows furrowed. "You were ten feet in the air. It was gravity."

She placed a hand on her hip as she regarded him. "That's a little better. I haven't gained an ounce of weight since we've been together."

"How is that—" Axel started.

"Man." Donovan did a cutting motion with his hand. "Stop. Trust me."

Sadie nodded slightly.

"You two—" Roxy pointed her finger at Sadie and Donovan.

Two shadows in the air caught my attention, and the rest of my tension vanished. They'd made it back. Now we could find out what was set up inside the building. "I hate to interrupt, but Zagan and Bune are here."

Roxy snapped to attention. Her eyes scanned the sky right above her, searching for the two figures. "Aha!" she exclaimed and gestured above her head. "They're there. Aren't they?"

Emmy chuckled, then mashed her lips together and

tried to cover it up by clearing her throat. "No, but close." She winced. "Kinda."

If by *close* she meant *within a mile*, she was right.

The two demons landed in front of us and changed back to their human forms, their faces strained. Bune squinted at the group. "Did something happen?"

"That's a question with a long answer." Axel shifted his weight and grimaced. "One I would appreciate sharing on the way back to the vehicles."

Sadie and Donovan hurried to the front, leading the way. My wolf surged forward, not liking it, but I tugged her back. They were alphas, too, and they'd been following our lead. It made sense for them to have their turn.

Taking my hand, Killian squeezed. *It's hard. I know.*

For a second, I was confused, until I remembered he could feel my emotions. I wasn't trying to hide anything from him, so of course he knew. *You don't seem to be struggling with following their lead.*

For the same reason you held your wolf back before I needed to say something. He walked in sync beside me and continued, *And I have a lot more practice, thanks to my friendship with Sterlyn and Griffin.*

That was odd, because I didn't have a problem following their lead, the same as I wasn't bothered by Cyrus or Annie. *But following them doesn't bother me.*

Because when you met them, you thought of them as your alphas. I didn't, but interacting with other alphas was something my dad prepared me for. As an alpha, you have to be aware and respectful of power dynamics, or you turn out like Tom. It's something you'll become used to now that you're an alpha's mate and interacting with others outside your pack.

I hadn't considered how the change in my role would

affect me. I'd always been a strong wolf, but I had more of a leadership position now than I had ever wanted. *Thank you for explaining.* I didn't have my dad here to do that anymore.

Always. He leaned over and kissed my cheek. I smiled and went quiet, content to listen to Sierra, Roxy, and Lillith babble on, telling the demons about everything that had happened.

FINALLY, we arrived at the log cabin we had rented for the next week. Granted, *cabin* was an understatement. It was huge. When Sterlyn and Griffin said they'd rented a place close by, I hadn't expected one this size. It would easily accommodate the twelve of us.

We parked in the driveway, located on the cabin's uphill side by the top floor. The place had three floors and was surrounded by woods, with no other cabins close by. The top floor had a huge wraparound deck with a rectangular table and a red umbrella outside. A set of stairs led down to the second-floor deck and the hot tub. A large staircase near the tub led from the second floor to the ground level by the woods.

Before going inside, we walked down the stairs to the woods to get a good sense of our surroundings. We'd be coming and going and needed to familiarize ourselves with the normal noises we should expect.

Killian and I climbed back up behind Zagan, who was behind Roxy. Axel was in front of her, moving slowly, I assumed, because of their fall, but he refused to be left behind.

"Any day now would be great," Sierra yelled from behind us.

Leave it to her to hound the wounded.

A whoosh had me glancing toward the sky. A low snarl escaped Axel, and he quickened his pace. Between one blink and the next, his foot gave out, and he stumbled. Roxy caught him, keeping him upright, but she staggered from the additional weight and fell into Zagan's chest.

Wrapping his arms around her, Zagan stabilized Roxy, and a loud hiss came from above us.

I looked up again to see Eleanor flying overhead, her golden hair making her appear every inch the angel she was, until I saw her sneer. Her attention was locked on Zagan and Roxy, and then she flipped her feathers to a side that looked sharp and darted toward them.

CHAPTER TWELVE

THE WAY ELEANOR'S focus homed in on Zagan and Roxy could mean only one thing: she was upset he was touching her.

She soared toward them as quickly as a bullet. Zagan pivoted so Roxy was standing behind him and growled, "Stop it, *now*."

Eleanor's wings swept backward as she stopped her forward progression, her body coming back into clear view as she hovered. Her golden hair flew into her face before settling around her shoulders. When her face was revealed once more, her nostrils flared, and she gritted out, "Maybe it was a bad idea for me to come. None of you are taking the threat seriously."

Even though her expression was twisted with anger, hurt rang in her voice, and her eyes darkened with grief.

Uh...am I the only one missing something here? Sierra linked. *If I didn't know that Eleanor feels nothing but hate and resentment, I would swear she has feelings for Zagan.*

Could they be mates? From the limited information I

knew, angels hadn't had preordained mates for centuries, until Rosemary and Levi had met.

"She was about to fall, Eleanor." Zagan lifted his hands, palms facing her. "I merely caught her. She has her own fated mate." His tone was even and steady.

Her nose wrinkled. "Then why didn't her *mate* catch her?"

Axel exhaled loudly. "Because I was the one who caused her to lose her balance." He rubbed a hand down his face. "I'm not thrilled about him having his arms around Roxy, either, but it was better than her falling down the stairs and knocking everyone else over, too."

Arching a brow, Eleanor sniffed. "A wolf shifter who can't walk up some stairs?"

"What is it with angels?" Roxy glanced around Zagan's shoulder and pointed a finger at Eleanor. "The other one isn't nearly as bad as you, but still, it's the overall demeanor."

Flipping her wings back to the sharp side, Eleanor huffed.

"You need to *stop*." Zagan's tone changed to one of warning. "Axel got injured earlier, but he wanted to familiarize himself with our surroundings, same as everyone else. If something sounds off, we all need to be aware."

She rolled her eyes, but her breathing calmed marginally.

Killian cleared his throat and placed a hand on my shoulder. "Not that I'm not glad you're here, but why *are* you here? Is something wrong?"

Eleanor crossed her arms. "Why do you always think something's wrong? Since the council members and Levi are busy with Shadow City and demon attacks, I was one of the few who could sneak away relatively unnoticed. I thought I could be of assistance. That's all."

I suspected her presence had more to do with a certain demon here.

"We can use the help, especially since you can fly." Sadie exhaled from the front of the line midway up the stairs. "The humans have traps set everywhere."

"Really?" Roxy frowned. "You want her help after she tried to *kill* me?"

"At least she didn't hold a gun to your head," Sierra called from the back of the line.

Torak huffed. "You'll have to let that go some time. I didn't know you were inside the vehicle."

"Honestly, none of this would've happened if Axel would've just taken a sip of my blood." From her spot behind Sadie, Lillith grinned and batted her eyes.

Hanging his head, Axel sighed. "Knowing that I'll be fine in the morning, I didn't want to risk weakening you, especially with the limited amount of blood we have on hand for your food supply, but maybe that would've been better than the bloodbath we might have on our hands now."

Our group was disintegrating, and now someone was insinuating we might have an actual brawl. We had to remind everyone about our common goal. "Guys, we need to get inside so Zagan and Bune can tell us about the facility," I said.

"Breaching this facility will be more difficult than the last place," Bune said from behind Torak.

Lovely. A shiver ran through me, and it wasn't the kind that Killian gave me, which was very unfortunate.

"Then let's get moving." Donovan turned forward again to march up the stairs.

When Eleanor jerked her head to the side, I didn't doubt she was up to something. Before I could ask anything, she'd swooped down and scooped Axel into her arms.

"What the—" Axel started, his eyes bulging as Eleanor leaned forward.

But Roxy cut him off. "That bi—" Her voice dropped until it turned into a complete growl.

Eleanor didn't hesitate. She flew him up the stairs and landed at the top, releasing Axel onto the porch in front of the hot tub.

Everyone rushed up, ready for the situation to unfold.

As I stepped onto the porch, I found Axel and Roxy standing next to the hot tub with Sadie and Donovan between their friends and Eleanor and Zagan. Lillith was on the other side of the hot tub, leaning against the door with a twinkle in her eyes as she watched the craziness. I'd expected Roxy to go off on the angel, but Zagan's body shook with anger.

"What the *fuck* was *that*?" Zagan rasped and clenched his hands at his sides.

Eleanor shrugged. "What?" she asked a little too innocently, especially for her.

Now Emmy, Sierra, Torak, and Bune were behind Killian and me.

"You *carried* him." Zagan's face turned pink.

Pulling her wings into her back, Eleanor kept her expression indifferent. "You said he was injured and nearly fell. I thought that would be safer for everyone involved."

She had him there, but I mashed my lips together. I wasn't stupid. She'd done that to make him feel jealous.

Bune hurried around Killian and touched Zagan's arm. The older demon said, "Everyone needs to calm down. You two fighting is only adding more tension and stress to an already difficult situation. Eleanor, if having you here is going to create more problems, maybe you should go back to Shadow City."

Zagan winced, and Eleanor frowned. Despite their mutual anger, they wanted to stay close to each other.

Ah...the struggles of the mate bond.

"Seriously, I thought if he was injured, I could help. I didn't ask for permission because these wolf shifters are stubborn and don't like to accept help, especially when they aren't in immediate danger." She nibbled on her bottom lip. "I'm..."—she straightened her shoulders before continuing —"sorry for doing what was best since I made decisions for others."

The sulfuric stench of a lie was missing, but that didn't mean she'd told the entire truth.

Now those *two are mates*, Killian linked with me. *They remind me of Griffin and Sterlyn when she was pretending to date me.*

My body tensed. Even though I'd heard the story, thinking of Killian with anyone other than me made my blood boil. He was *mine* and no one else's. *They act similarly to Sierra and Torak. The main difference is that Torak has a calmer demeanor.* Sierra was also a loyal and thoughtful person. That hadn't been an option for Eleanor for most of her life, and she was learning to deal with all the new emotions angels were suddenly experiencing, just like Rosemary but without the friends to keep her grounded or a completed preordained mate bond.

No one said anything until Roxy blew out a loud breath. "Though her decision was less than ideal, it did prevent Axel from hurting himself more so...I've gotta appreciate that, even if *begrudgingly*."

"Hey." Axel's brows furrowed. "Shouldn't I have a say in this?"

"Nope." Lillith popped the *p* and waggled her eyebrows. "You've been with Roxy for years now. You should know better."

He bobbed his head from side to side as if Lillith had a point.

"If it's going to be a problem—" Killian said, backing Bune.

"No, it's fine." Zagan relaxed his hands. "She was trying to help like I did with Roxy." He rolled his shoulders as if trying to unwind.

"Aw, look at everyone getting along." Sierra sniffed and pretended to wipe a tear from her eye. "Maybe Torak can learn something here."

Torak grunted and rubbed his temples.

He was struggling, and I could only imagine I'd put Killian through something similar when I'd been ornery. I linked with my mate, *I'm so sorry I put you through hell before we completed our bond.*

Where did that come from? He took my hand in his and squeezed.

Watching this. Though each couple had to come to terms with their relationship in their own time, they'd soon learn that the resistance was futile. *All that time, I thought my anger was about letting my pack and family down and being distracted by you. It took seeing this to understand that most of my anger came from trying to deny our bond.* What had been so hazy and confusing a month ago was now crystal clear. The anger had needed to take over for me to finally see how irrational I had become. Hopefully, these two couples would get there soon, and Killian would accept that his found sister belonged with the man she loved.

"She's right," Killian said, and winked at me. "We need to strategize and split up the group so we can figure out who's on which shift, especially since we can't see how many vehicles are in the facility parking lot."

He was right. We had no clue what was going on inside. If it hadn't been for Bune and Zagan, we'd be going in blind.

Lillith turned to the door that led inside. She glanced at the keypad. "Anyone know the code?"

"3445258," Emmy replied. "Dad sent it to me when he booked the cabin."

After typing in the number, Lillith opened the dark gray door and stepped inside.

The rest of us followed her in, and I couldn't believe that the owners even called this a cabin. It was much fancier than my grandparents' house. We entered a ginormous kitchen on the right with a large, light oak rectangular table to the left. The cabinets were a light oak that matched the hardwood floors, and the countertop was white granite. The stove and refrigerator matched the counters, and nothing even slightly clashed. A sizable peninsular countertop divided the kitchen from the dining area, and a section of the counter was raised, with four bar stools underneath to give more eating space.

I was relieved that they'd rented such a large space. With so many people here, including members of two packs that were still getting to know one another, we needed to spread out.

"Now this is what I'm talking about." Emmy chuckled as she walked into the sizable living room adjacent to this area. A light gray L-shaped couch for six sat directly across from a gray brick chimney. Strangely, there was no TV.

Sadie walked to the far side of the kitchen table, her back to one of the four windows that overlooked the huge staircase we'd climbed and the stream at the bottom of the hill. "Before we begin exploring, maybe we should sit down and discuss a plan."

Nodding, Emmy took a seat at one end, so I hurried over and sat next to my best friend. Everyone else filled in, Killian next to me with Sierra on his other side, Torak next to her, and Bune taking the end directly across from Emmy. Donovan sat next to his mate with Axel beside him, and Roxy took the last spot between Bune and Axel.

"Thanks," Lillith grumbled. The feet of one of the bar chairs squeaked against the hardwood as she pulled it out. "I guess I'm stuck back here with the demon and angel."

Glancing over her shoulder, Sierra beamed. "In a way, you fit better back there than with us. Demons did create your kind."

Lillith bared her teeth. "I'm suddenly feeling mighty hungry, and wolf blood doesn't sound half bad."

"Oh!" Roxy's eyes widened, and she clapped her hands. "I see the resemblance to demons now."

"Right!" Sierra placed her elbow on the table and flicked her wrists.

The entire exchange was odd, but Bune's expression made it damn near comical. His face was scrunched like he was constipated, though I was sure it was his look of confusion.

I linked with Killian, *You need to get Sierra to focus.*

He cut his eyes to me and replied, *Really? No one can.*

She respects you. I held back my snicker. *She'll listen, even if reluctantly.*

Emmy kicked me under the table and tilted her head at Sierra. She was trying to have the same conversation with me that I'd had with Killian. Sometimes, the two of us were way too similar.

"I'm assuming the inside is heavily secured and very well organized," Killian said as he placed a hand on my thigh.

My body warmed, and I fidgeted. Now wasn't the time to get aroused, especially when we were discussing strategy around a ton of other people who could smell it.

My wolf refused to listen.

Bitch.

No one seemed to notice. At least, that was what I chose to believe until I noted Emmy giving me a strange stare.

"Yes. Zagan and I did a quick sweep." Bune steepled his fingers. "I went to the building on the east side. This place has more guards inside. The bottom of the building is a parking garage, and the top floor has various rooms into which they've divided the packs."

"Like men, women, and children?" Donovan asked, his jaw twitching.

Bune shook his head. "That's what was disturbing on my side. It was a mixture of ages and genders in each room, as if they're split up into different test groups and kept in a *controlled* environment."

My stomach churned, and the desire wafting through me dampened.

"How many rooms were there?" I asked. Last time, they'd had three.

"There were five rooms holding shifters, a lab, and one room with surgical equipment." Bune leaned back in his chair as he tapped his fingers on the table. "The wolves appeared to be in worse condition than Hal's pack was in when we freed them."

Eleanor leaned against the door as if eager to leave. "Of course they are. Fate wouldn't allow this to be easy for us."

"Don't be so heartless." Zagan narrowed his eyes. "You're not the one being experimented on...for now."

She inhaled sharply. "Is that a threat?"

"No, I'm just saying that if we don't find a way to stop this from happening, it's only a matter of time before one of us gets taken...again."

He was right. Chad and Mom had been captured and experimented on along with PawPaw's pack. My racing pulse dizzied my head. I had to focus on what I could control. I looked at Zagan. "What did you see?"

Zagan pulled out one of the bar stools two seats down from Lillith, close to where Eleanor stood. "Same setup as Bune's. The only difference was that three of the rooms were in use, not all five. And they were in use divided up into men, women, and children. They're locked in those cages again, with the IVs. It looked as if the humans are doing blood tests on them."

"That must be the pack that was more recently taken." Emmy rubbed her hands. "Bune, were the shifters you saw sedated?"

"No." He scratched the back of his neck. "They weren't. Most of them were just leaning against the wall in a daze."

"They could've been drugged." Torak stood abruptly and placed his hands on the table. "We've got to do something before it gets worse."

He was worried about his friends, and I couldn't blame him. I knew what my grandfather's pack had gone through, how they were still suffering, and Torak knew as well. His friends would meet the same future if we didn't get them out of there in time.

"We can't overreact, Torak," Sadie said softly. "We'll get them out, but Roxy almost got caught. We have to scope out the area."

He slammed a hand on the table. "Then why are we just sitting here? We should be *out* there doing the work so we can rescue them sooner."

"Listen—" Donovan said.

Sierra pointed a finger. "He's right. We need to get out there and look. We need to split up and figure this out...now."

If Killian still couldn't recognize they were mates, then he was purposely not seeing it. Sierra didn't want Torak upset and hurting.

"Look, I'll go with Torak." Zagan climbed to his feet. "That way, I can scope out both buildings while Bune gets some rest. He can relieve me early in the morning."

"Which means I should go as well. I can watch the shift change and fly lower while the sky is dark." Eleanor placed her hand on the doorknob, ready to leave.

"I'll go, too!" Sierra jumped to her feet. "I'll help Torak look for traps."

"Absolutely not." Killian shook his head. "You will stay here until someone I trust can go with you."

She pivoted on her heel and snarled, "Torak can be trusted. He's helped us several times."

My chest constricted. *Maybe you should—*

Ignoring me, he grabbed Sierra's arm. "You're *not* going."

I sucked in a breath. I couldn't believe how he was treating Sierra and me. That wasn't the Killian we knew.

"I'm going. End of story." Sierra lifted her chin and jerked her arm from his grasp.

Torak stepped between Sierra and Killian and said tensely, "Don't touch her that way." He glanced over his shoulder at Sierra. "But I agree with him. You should stay here where it's s—"

"If you say *safe*, I'll kick you in the nuts," Sierra snarled. "I can make my own decisions, and I'm going with you. That is, unless Killian decides to alpha-will me and take away my *choice*."

Hurt wafted through our bond as Killian inhaled deeply. "I wouldn't take away your freedom of choice unless there were absolutely no other way to prevent your death."

"Then that settles it. I'm going." Sierra turned on her heel and marched to the door without a glance back.

I touched his shoulder, wanting to comfort him. He was hurting, and I had no clue why.

"Keep an eye on her," Killian rasped.

Torak chuckled darkly. "I will. You don't even have to ask. Then again, you don't trust me." He turned his back on my mate and walked out of the kitchen toward Sierra.

Normally, my touch would have soothed Killian, but his body was shaking under my hand.

"I'll keep watch on her, too," Zagan vowed as he and Eleanor rushed after the others.

Killian growled and banged his fist on the table while the rest of the group showed varying expressions of anger and concern. He had just insulted one of their own after they'd proved themselves as allies.

Emmy's eyes flicked to Killian and the door. She wanted me to talk to him, and though I wasn't sure what the conversation would result in, I had to do something before everything exploded and we lost the alliance we'd made.

"I hope you don't mind excusing us. We'll be right back." I grabbed my mate's arm and pulled him outside to the back deck.

This was going to get resolved.

CHAPTER THIRTEEN

OUTSIDE, Sierra and Torak were at the bottom of the staircase, sprinting to the tree line with Zagan and Eleanor hovering over them. Killian stalked to the top of the stairs, watching the two of them as they disappeared from view. I shut the door behind us.

He hadn't fought me about going outside, which mildly surprised me. Maybe he'd wanted to try to stop Sierra again. They'd hurried to get away, which *wasn't* surprising. Sierra knew Killian, and though he was kind and understanding, he was also a strong alpha—her alpha—who she hadn't even pretended to listen to.

The sun had set behind the trees, bringing on twilight. The stream trickled below, and a gentle, cool late December breeze wafted past me. Any other time, this would have been a peaceful moment far away from civilization and immersed in nature—the perfect combination for any wolf shifter.

But too much turmoil hung over us for me to relax.

I'd hoped that Killian would start talking, but his frown deepened as he took a seat on the stairs. He was brooding.

Hurt and anger continued to swirl through our bond, and I didn't understand it.

I pushed past the sting from when he'd been short with me and took an empty spot beside him. I kept my attention on the sky, though I wanted to stare at his face.

I took a deep, calming breath, then exhaled, pushing out all my negativity to keep a clear mind. However, the lump in my throat remained lodged. "What's going on with you? You insulted Torak right in front of his stepsister and friends." Normally, Killian wasn't so careless.

He rubbed his temples, and some of the weight fell from my shoulders. This was more the Killian I knew...the man I loved.

"Yeah, that wasn't my best moment." He took my hand. "I'm sorry for being short with you in there. You were just trying to help, but I don't like Sierra going with *him* to scope out the area."

And there it was again. "What do you have against him? Yeah, he aimed a gun at the Suburban when we pulled up to help them, but we would've done the same thing if we'd been in their shoes and didn't know who was arriving. He didn't even know what we looked like, and as soon as Sadie said stand down, he did without a second thought." I understood why Sierra kept harping on him about it. Still coming to grips with what he was to her, she was using anger to ground herself. It was what I'd done when I'd met Killian, so I couldn't judge her for it, but Killian was a different story.

"That's not the problem." Killian leaned his head back, looking at the sky.

Now I was more confused than ever. That was the only thing Torak had done to give us any pause; unless he'd done something I wasn't aware of, but I was confident that Killian would've told me prior to now. "Then why don't you like him?"

His cheeks filled with air, and he blew it out. "I actually *do* like him."

My breath caught. I was so confused. I'd hoped that his answer would provide clarity, but it was the complete opposite. The more I pried, the less sense any of this made. "*What* is the problem? Because you kind of showed your ass back there to everyone, and I'm trying to understand why. You're giving me nothing here."

He snorted, and his chocolaty irises locked on me. A sad grin spread across his face. "You almost sounded like Sierra."

"Now you're deflecting," I said as I placed my hand on his arm and scooted closer. "What is going on with you?"

"I wish I knew." He turned to me. "But the idea of them spending so much time together irks me."

Chest clenching, I tried to keep my breathing steady. If I hadn't been secure in our relationship, I would've felt threatened. Hell, even feeling secure, it was hard not to wonder what that meant. "But you have me," I said a little too forcefully, and grimaced. I was trying to get him to talk to me, not make him defensive.

His smile turned genuine. "Oh, I know. There's no one else in the world I want. You should know that."

All my anxiety melted away. "I do, but still, hearing something like that gives a mate pause." I winked to reinforce I wasn't upset. "But you'll have to get over that because they're—"

His lips turned downward, and his body tensed. "If you say fated mates *again*, I may lose it."

And the irrational Killian had returned. "Why?"

He stood and paced in front of the hot tub.

Wanting to watch his every expression, I climbed to my feet and leaned against the railing.

His face twisted in anguish as the oddest combination of emotions wafted through our bond—hope, happiness, fear, guilt, and longing. As soon as I landed on one, another sensation replaced it, as if it were a moving puzzle that changed so quickly I couldn't piece it all together.

I straightened my shoulders and asked again, "Why, Kill?"

"Because I can't lose her," he spat. As soon as the words were out, his eyes bulged. He stopped in his tracks and breathed raggedly.

Unfortunately, the wide range of emotions made sense now. I didn't know why I hadn't put it together. "How would you lose her?" I already knew the answer, but I needed him to realize it.

"Because when she completes the bond with Torak, she'll be part of his pack instead of mine, and I'll lose what feels like the last bit of family I have left," he murmured, his head hanging. He ran his hands through his hair and muttered, "I'm a moron."

My heart ached, and I took a small step toward him. "You have me."

"I *know* that." He lifted his head, his now dark chocolate eyes focusing on me. "You are my world, and there is no one else I would ever want by my side. Jewel, I can't wait until we have a child together—to create a small person that's half of you and me. But Sierra, she's my..." His brows furrowed as if he were searching for the right word.

"The last link to your sister and parents?" I offered. Tears burned my eyes, but this wasn't about me. I'd come to grips with my dad's death and Mom's horrible way of dealing with it. Not that it got easier, but I was finding my peace with it. Unlike Killian and the death of his family, I didn't feel like my decisions had resulted in Dad's death.

"Yeah." He strolled to the edge of the porch and ran his hand along the wooden rail. "She was always at our house, and she and Olive would get on my nerves. It was crazy. They'd barge into my room, talking about something that had happened at school or asking questions about my friends as if they were interested, just to drive me up the wall." He licked his bottom lip. "And now I'd give anything for them to do it just one more time. Instead, I let Olive and my parents go check out a threat without me, and they died."

A tear trickled down my cheek as the sorrow flowing through our bond intensified. He had to stop blaming himself, and he had to understand he wasn't losing Sierra. "You do realize that if you'd gone with your parents, you'd likely be dead, too?"

"Maybe." He shrugged and stared at the woods. "Or maybe I could've made the difference."

I knew that feeling all too well. "You know, that's exactly what haunted me about Dad's death. If the pack had just stayed together, would he have died? If I hadn't run off to my grandparents' pack...if I'd just sucked it up and stayed around, could I have saved other silver wolves...my extended family?"

"You couldn't have known what would happen." Killian pivoted toward me, his eyes glowing from his wolf surging forward. "And that would've only put you in danger."

"It's the same *for you.*" He needed to see that he couldn't reassure me with those words when he didn't believe them himself. "I knew Dad was in danger, and I should've left to go fight with him, but I didn't. Neither you nor your parents took the threat seriously because they didn't take backup. You had no way of knowing what would happen, so stop beating yourself up."

He closed his eyes. "I *know* you're right. I actually see your point, but forgiveness..."

"Takes time." I put one foot in front of the other, slowly approaching him. My heart fractured with the pain he'd gone through, mixing with the regret I was immersed in myself. "I'm still working on it, but if you're actually realizing what I'm saying is right, the rest will work itself out slowly." I placed my hands on his chest and stared at his face.

His hands covered mine, and, returning my gaze, he whispered, "But that doesn't help with Sierra." His guilt and sorrow were now the main emotions swirling through our bond.

I kissed his lips. "You will never lose her. She loves you just as much as you love her. Yes, she may not be part of the pack any longer, but that sisterly bond and friendship will never stop. She needs you just as much as you need her."

"I don't know." He grimaced. "I've kinda been an ass."

My cheeks hurt from smiling so widely. "I'm not denying that, but you were acting that way because you love her so much. I have a feeling the two of you will get through this." Even though Killian was an amazing person, he had his faults and sometimes made bad choices. That didn't take away from his character. Admitting he was wrong only made him stronger.

He kissed me, his tongue slipping between my lips. His faint citrus taste washed over me and made me feel as if I'd come home.

How did I survive so long without you? he linked as he deepened our kiss.

My chest shook with quiet laughter, but I didn't dare

pull away from this bliss. *I'm not sure, but I'm here now, and that's all that matters.*

A low growl emanated from his chest as his arms wrapped around my waist and pulled me against him. *That* is *all that matters.*

I closed my eyes, concentrating on the buzz of our connection. His firm lips were on mine, and his hands slipped under my shirt, sparking an inferno inside me. Between my desire, the heat of his body, and the fated-mate bond, nothing was more important to me than *him* in that moment.

Whimpering, my wolf surged forward. Both she and I wanted to soothe our mate in the best way possible—by uniting our two souls.

Feeling the same way, he grabbed my butt and hoisted my legs around his waist. As my legs tightened around him, he walked past the hot tub to the second staircase, which led to the top deck.

Let me get down, I linked, not wanting him to fall.

Nope. He moved his head back so he could see each stair as he climbed, keeping his hands firmly around my butt.

I laughed, unable to hold it in. The world felt right, and the two of us were carefree. He reached the top and walked to the driveway. He jogged past our cars and jumped the small red cement wall. Then he walked into the oaks and red cedars that grew thick behind the house.

Where are we going? I asked as I kept my hold on him. I loved how his body rubbed against mine and the inferno inside intensified. My body and soul wanted him, needed to feel like one, even if for just a little while.

Deeper in the woods so I can take you without fearing

anyone will hear us. His mouth landed on mine. *Seems fitting since our first time was in the woods.*

The memory stirred something deep within. When we could no longer hear the trickling of the water, Killian slowed and placed me on my feet. The trees were thick around us, and the darkness engulfed us.

His hot mouth was on mine again without restraint or hesitation. We were alone, each desperate for the other.

Clutching the hem of his shirt, I removed it from his body. He countered my movements by slipping his hands under my shirt and unfastening my bra. When he pulled back, he removed both the shirt and bra at the same time, leaving both of us topless.

He paused, his eyes examining me. He smirked sexily as he cupped my breast with his palm. His fingers caressed my nipple as his free hand slid down to my jeans and unfastened them. I stumbled back a step, my back hitting an oak tree trunk as pleasure rolled through my body.

Not wanting to waste a moment, I undid his pants. Then he released his hold and slid my jeans and panties off.

As he rose, his hand slipped between my thighs, and he sucked on my nipple. He circled his fingers in my folds as his tongue flicked over my nipple, building tension inside my body.

I leaned my head back as I stroked him in rhythm with his gentle caress. His hips quickened our pace, and an orgasm ripped through me. I moaned as my hips rotated against his fingertips.

You're so damn sexy, he linked and pushed his desire and love to me, heating my body even more.

When I came down from the temporary high, my wolf howled. That hadn't satiated her. I needed more of him. I pushed him off, turned to the tree, and then bent over a little.

An animalistic snarl came from him, and my breathing quickened.

He positioned himself and circled an arm around my waist. He slipped inside me, filling me, and my vision went black. As he pumped inside me, the friction grew. His fingers found my folds again and fluttered around my core as my hands held on to the trunk for dear life and the bark pressed into my skin, adding to the sensations. This felt different than anything we'd ever experienced before, hungry and eager, like we were finding salvation in each other.

As we opened ourselves, our souls merged. *This* was what we were so desperate to achieve—this place where we could be ourselves, where our feelings were clear about how we felt for each other. We were more than in love, more than each other's oxygen—we made up each other's essences.

His ecstasy blasted through our connection, and I shuddered. We climaxed together and rode through the bliss.

When it was over, he peppered kisses down my back. *I love you so damn much.*

My heart felt so full, it could burst. *I love you, too,* I replied and turned toward him to kiss him. *And I can't wait to start a family with you, but we just need to make sure things are more settled.*

His eyes glowed as he brushed my cheek. *Then we'd better hurry and settle them.*

I'm all for practicing so we can get it right when the time comes, I teased and slipped my tongue inside his mouth. *They say practice makes perfect.*

Oh, I think what we do is beyond perfection...whatever

that word might be, he replied as his fingers dug into my skin.

Now that was something I couldn't disagree with.

"Jewel!" Emmy called from back at the cabin. "Where are you?" Her voice was full of concern.

We'd sneaked off without thinking that someone might come looking for us. *We've got to get back.*

Killian stepped away, giving us room to put on our clothes as I called out, "We're coming!"

My heart hammered as I reached down and snatched my clothes from the ground. Both of us quickly dressed and rushed back toward the cabin.

When we hurried back to the deck where Emmy stood, waiting in front of the door, she tilted her head. She glanced at me and then at Killian before her attention settled back on me.

My cheeks heated. She had to know what we'd been up to. Part of me wanted to turn invisible, but I lifted my chin instead. "Yes?"

"Lillith and Roxy are getting more upset over the things Killian said, and when I came out here, the two of you had vanished." Emmy crossed her arms and tapped a foot. "Did you two really sneak off to have—"

"Roxy and Lillith are upset?" Killian interjected and clapped his hands. "I should probably go in there and apologize."

You jerk! I linked. *You're going to leave me out here alone with her to have this conversation, aren't you?*

She is your best friend, and I don't want to talk about sex with her. Killian beamed at me. *With you, anytime. I'm even willing to show you whatever you need assistance with. But her? Not so much.*

My frustration melted away. How could I be upset over that?

"Wait. You're going to apologize?" Emmy blinked and cupped her ear as if she had misunderstood.

"Jewel showed me the error of my ways and helped me gain some clarity," he said and pecked my lips.

"And how, exactly, did she *show* you?" Emmy smiled sweetly. "I'd love to know."

Killian chuckled. "By talking and making me realize why I didn't like the idea of Sierra and Torak together." He nodded to the door. "Let me go in before they attack me."

When she moved out of the way, Killian opened the door and walked in.

He wouldn't be facing them alone. I looked at Emmy. "I'll come back out after the meeting so the two of us can talk, but I need to be with him for this."

I moved to enter the cabin, but Emmy blocked me. I growled in warning, but she reached into my hair and pulled out some bark.

"Okay, but after you're done, I want to hear all about this *talk*." She waved the piece of bark in her hand. "And I'll come with you in case you two need backup."

If I thought I'd been mortified before, I was speechless now. I had no retort. Obviously, Killian and I had had sex, but that didn't mean I wanted to talk about it with anyone. What happened between the two of us was private, but the longer I put Emmy off, the harder it would be—no pun intended.

So I threw back my shoulders and entered the cabin, determined to be a supportive mate. Then I heard Roxy say, "Oh, maybe we should leave since he doesn't trust any of us."

CHAPTER FOURTEEN

I WASN'T SURPRISED that Roxy was being confrontational. In a way, it made things easier for Killian to get the apology out. It wasn't as if they harbored any resentment.

No one was in the kitchen, so I continued into the living room, where Roxy, Axel, Sadie, Donovan, and Lillith were sitting on the couch. Bune stood in front of the fireplace, arms crossed, appearing very uncomfortable.

My gut hardened. Maybe we shouldn't have slipped off to have sex, but Killian and I had needed that connection. He needed to know I was there for him in all ways.

As I took my place next to Killian, he took my hand and said, "I'll apologize to Torak and Sierra when they get back. Jewel helped me understand why I was upset, and I said things I didn't mean. I do trust Torak, and I appreciate every one of you, especially for staying."

Roxy pouted and huffed, and my throat closed. She wouldn't let this go that easily.

But Sadie smiled, her beautiful eyes twinkling. "We understand, but thank you for addressing it. To be fair, we're all on edge. There's no telling who might disappear next, and that's alarming."

"If he wanted things to continue to go smoothly with us, he didn't really have much of a choice with Roxy around." Donovan lifted a hand in surrender.

"Now I wish I hadn't said anything." Roxy blew a strand of red hair out of her face. "He came in here and was *nice*. If I keep ragging on him, I'll be the asshole and not *him* anymore."

"To be fair, Sierra is still riding Torak about the gun," Lillith said as she leaned forward to see past Sadie and Donovan to Roxy.

Axel snorted. "Oh, I *bet* she is—"

I cleared my throat loudly, wanting him to be quiet. Killian was just now accepting that Torak was likely Sierra's mate, but what Axel insinuated might push him back over the edge since he thought of her as a sister.

"So...has anyone determined the room situation?" Emmy asked as she leaned against the threshold that divided the kitchen from the living room.

Once again, I owed her. She knew me well enough to sense I needed help. We'd had this routine locked down since we were young and Mom would suspect the two of us were up to something. We'd been pretty good at diverting her attention, though she'd normally come back to the question whenever Emmy left the house.

"From my quick walkthrough, there appear to be four bedrooms." Bune gestured toward a staircase that started in the corner of the room and led up a floor. "One has a queen bed with a connecting bathroom that opens to the top porch. Another overlooks the driveway and has three full beds. The upstairs corner room has a queen bed and a couch, and the room down here behind the fireplace has another three full-size beds."

Every couple would want one of the rooms with a queen bed, so this would be fun to figure out. I tried not to groan, but it was tempting.

"Donovan and I can take the queen bed with the couch, and Torak can room with us," Sadie offered as she laid her head on her mate's arm. "Killian and Jewel should have the other queen bed since their pack did cover the house."

The corners of Killian's mouth curved upward, and I rolled my eyes. He was thrilled that her arrangement would prevent Sierra and Torak from completing the mate bond. I should have scolded him, but I would miss linking with Sierra, too. I still struggled over not being able to talk with Emmy like we used to. Though I loved her, our connection wasn't the same, and we had to work harder on our friendship.

Emmy rubbed her lips together, one of her quirks when she was uncomfortable. What must be bothering her hit me: she didn't really know everyone here. "And maybe we can run out and get an air mattress or something so Emmy can stay in our room," I suggested.

Wait. What? Killian linked with me.

Yeah, I probably should have run that by him first, but Emmy was my best friend. I couldn't put her in an uncomfortable situation. *Sorry, but she doesn't know Bune, Zagan, Sierra, or you like she knows me. She won't be comfortable sleeping in the common area where people will be tromping by. Besides, we'll be working in shifts, so we probably won't be sleeping on the same schedule, anyway.* I had no doubt Killian and I would be on watch together.

"I can sleep on the floor." Emmy nodded ecstatically.

"We used to do it all the time when I stayed over at your house."

That was true. We'd never slept in my bed. Rather, we'd built a fort on the ground and slept in that.

"Well, if Axel and I have to share a room with two other people, I do *not* want to bunk with that insane angel and Zagan. After what happened earlier, I'd rather stay with Lillith and Sierra." Roxy crossed her arms.

Oh goodness, there was no telling what kind of trouble the three of them would get into, but I wouldn't argue. I didn't want to get in the middle of those two again either.

That meant Bune was stuck with them instead, but I suspected he could more than handle it.

With all that squared away, my stomach growled. I couldn't remember the last time we'd eaten, and I was famished.

Killian chuckled. "I'm going to order some pizzas. My mate is hungry."

"You'd better hurry." Emmy wrinkled her nose. "Because that sound means you have less than thirty minutes before Jewel becomes Jaws."

I stuck out my tongue at her. At that moment, our friendship had completely dissolved. She, Chad, and Theo used to call me that nickname when we were little, mainly because they knew how to prevent the beast within from emerging.

Food.

Most people didn't realize that when I got hangry, my inner diva came out in style, and unfortunately, we were reaching that point. I could own it, but that didn't mean I couldn't pretend to be offended.

"Jaws!" Lillith leaned forward, placing her elbows on her knees. "Now this is a story I need to hear."

Humor wafted from Killian as he pulled out his phone. "I'd better get on it." He winked at me as he walked away, and in that second, I somehow fell more in love with him *again*.

THE NIGHT HAD FLOWN by quickly, and Killian and I were on the back deck, waiting for Sierra and Torak to arrive. At nearly two in the morning, Emmy, Bune, Donovan, and Sadie had woken and left to relieve them.

Tom was supposed to attack the unsuspecting made-up pack in the morning.

Are you sure you don't want to get some rest? I linked and placed my head on Killian's shoulder. We were sitting on the edge of the hot tub, watching the stream trickle by below with the moonlight shimmering off the ripples. The air was chillier tonight, meaning it had to be near freezing. Though I wasn't truly cold, a shiver ran down my back.

I was an ass, and I hate that Sierra's upset with me. Killian pursed his lips. *I need to talk to her, because who knows what tomorrow will bring?*

I couldn't argue with that point. Even if making Erin appear incompetent didn't work, we had a whole day of scoping out the facility ahead. Either way, we would all be busy, tired, and on edge. *Just don't push too hard. She might need space.* Sierra could either be open and willing to listen or angry and reactive. Her attitude would have a lot to do with how she and Torak had interacted.

He propped his chin on top of my head and linked, *I know. I can feel her, and she doesn't seem quite as upset. I think it'll be okay.*

The sound of flapping drew my attention skyward, and

I could make out Eleanor's golden hair and light-colored wings. She was high in the sky but low enough for us to see her clearly. Zagan's demon form hovered closer to the tree-tops, likely right above Torak and Sierra.

The two of them soon stepped from the tree line, hand in hand.

Unease filtered through Killian as he lifted his head.

I looped my arm through his to ground him and pushed my love and pride through our bond. This was a big step for him, and it was more about beginning the process of him forgiving himself than him not wanting Sierra to be happy with her fated mate.

Torak paused and dropped her hand, and Sierra flinched as if she was hurt. She followed Torak's gaze and scowled.

She must have figured out he was taking a step back because Killian was watching them.

Straightening her shoulders, she marched toward the staircase and took the stairs two at a time. Torak grimaced but quickly followed her, and I suspected he didn't want her to confront Killian alone.

Eleanor and Zagan floated to the porch and landed next to the back door. She entered the code and threw open the door to march in, but he stayed in place. "What are you doing?" she huffed. "We've been out all night, and I don't want to hear them prattle on about something asinine."

"I want to make sure they don't want me for something." Zagan flickered back into his human form. He was homed in on me and Killian.

I forced a smile. "No, it's fine. Everything's okay." I trusted my mate to do the right thing, especially now that he was aware of the real issue. Killian wouldn't let his cowardice and fear control him. His actions had proven that time and time again.

Zagan examined Killian. He must have found whatever he was searching for because he nodded and followed Eleanor inside, closing the door.

Sierra reached the top of the stairs with Torak on her heels. She wielded her finger as if it were a weapon. "Are you *seriously* out here to continue our fight from earlier?" Her head bobbed. "Because let me tell you something. Just because you're my *alpha*—"

"I'm sorry," Killian said softly.

Her body froze with her mouth wide open. She blinked a few times. "Did I just hear what I *think* I did?"

Of course she wouldn't be Sierra if she didn't goad him.

Killian grinned. "You heard me, but I'll say it again because I was an asshole." He paused, and his discomfort surged through our bond. He smoothed his face, masking his anxiety with confidence. "I'm sorry for not listening and for being bullheaded." He glanced over her shoulder at Torak. "And I'm sorry for treating you like I don't trust you. I just fear what you represent."

Warmth spread through my chest, not only for Killian overcoming the past that haunted him but for his honesty. He was owning up to his actions.

Scratching his head, Torak swallowed. "Thanks?" Then he winced. "Sorry? I'm not sure what the right answer is here."

Sierra turned around and smacked the back of his head. "What he means is, why in the *world* would you fear him?"

Torak waved his finger back and forth. "No, that wasn't what I meant at all."

I mashed my lips together and swallowed my snicker. That interaction was more mate-like than anything I'd seen between them. I stepped closer to Killian so our arms brushed and linked, *You're doing amazing.*

Doesn't feel that way. He licked his lips and then answered Sierra's question. "You're the closest thing I have to a sister now, and when you two complete your bond, I'm afraid I'll lose you."

Heart swelling, I opened our connection. He'd admitted he knew they were mates even after fighting me for even referencing it. He was so damn amazing.

The anger on Sierra's face melted into adoration. She placed a hand over her heart, and her gray eyes glistened. "Is that what this was all about?" She broke into a fit of laughter, and her chest heaved as she tried to take a breath.

My shoulders slumped as I debated what was going on with her.

This isn't very comforting, Killian linked, wearing a scowl on his face. *She's laughing at me.*

I could do only one thing to try to fix this. I linked with her, *Sierra, what's wrong with you? You're hurting his feelings.*

Her laughter stopped abruptly, and Torak stared at her with furrowed brows. He looked as confused as the rest of us.

She wiped the tears from her face and sniffled. "Sorry, it's just hilarious that you think you could actually get rid of me."

My body grew light again. I had a feeling she was going to say exactly what I hoped she would.

Killian waved his free hand toward me and explained, "When Jewel and I completed the bond, she joined my pack. When you and Torak—"

"First off." She lifted a finger in front of her face. "I'm still not certain I've forgiven him enough to complete said bond between us, but *if* I ever do, my changing packs won't change *our* relationship." She moved her hands as if they were scales. "Other than you being my alpha. But let's be real, you let me get away with almost anything I want. So..."

The tension wafting from Killian diminished as he took a deep breath, though I could feel him hanging on to some concern. He pushed, "But you'll move away, and—"

"And come visit every month." Sierra took his hands in hers. "My entire family lives in Shadow Ridge, and that doesn't include just my parents and brothers. That includes you, Jewel, Sterlyn, Griffin, Ronnie, Alex, Rosemary, and Levi. There is nothing in this world that would ever change that, and *if* Torak and I cement our bond, all that means is my family gets a little bigger. It doesn't take *anything* away from you."

Thank gods we were having this conversation now, because it was clear she and Torak had realized who they were to each other. It was only a matter of time before the pull grew too strong for them to deny it. Had this conversation come after their bond had been completed, I was certain it wouldn't have gone as well as it was going.

I stepped away as the two of them hugged. Normally, I wouldn't like any woman touching my mate like that, but this was something *he* needed, and it was between family. I wouldn't get in the way of that.

Poor Torak, though, shook his head. "Why do you keep saying *if*? We're *fated mates*. Why are you so difficult? I want you, even though you're the most frustrating woman on this planet."

Sierra pulled away from Killian and winked at me. She glanced over her shoulder at him and shrugged. "Then I guess you'd better figure out a damn good gesture to win me over, since your first impression was less than subpar." She spun on her heel and sashayed through the door, leaving the three of us gaping in her wake.

Killian cleared his throat. He punched Torak in the arm as he said, "I hope there are no hard feelings."

"None at all, man." Torak spread his hands out in front of him. "I knew something weird was going on, and I always thought Roxy and Lillith were something, but she's...indescribable, and I can see that if you felt like you were going to lose her, it'd be like losing something larger than life. But just know, *when* we complete the bond, you'll become my family. And I'm a big believer in remaining close-knit."

Happiness swirled through our connection, and my heart felt full. This conversation had gone better than I'd ever dreamed possible.

I yawned, unable to fight off fatigue any longer.

Killian wrapped his arms around my waist, and I leaned my head against his hard chest. He snickered. "I need to take my mate upstairs to our bedroom to get some sleep. You two probably want to eat and get some rest as well."

"If I wasn't famished, I'd forgo the leftover pizza." Torak rubbed his stomach. "But I gots to keep my strength up."

"There're drinks in the fridge," I added as another huge yawn overtook me.

Killian nudged me forward, and when I opened the door to step inside, he hollered over his shoulder, "And good luck with her."

"Thanks," Torak muttered. "I'll need it."

Without another word, we passed by Eleanor, Zagan, and Sierra, who'd already started eating, and headed straight to bed.

THE SUN SHONE through the thin curtain that covered the double sliding glass door to the balcony of the bedroom Killian and I were staying in. The maroon paisley comforter hung off the bed, and the thin white sheet covered us from the waist down. My head lay on Killian's bare chest as his arms anchored me to him. I groaned as my eyelids fluttered open. I could've sworn wolfsbane had laced my Coke last night.

Killian's phone buzzed on the only nightstand, which was on his side of the bed. He growled, "Who has the nerve to wake me at this hour?" His joke fell flat because we both knew who was calling and what it was about.

I untangled myself from him reluctantly, my body still buzzing from his touch, and linked, *You'd better answer it.*

He grabbed the phone and frowned at Sterlyn's name flashing across the screen.

It wasn't quite eight, and the front door downstairs opened. From their voices, I knew Sadie, Donovan, Emmy, and Bune had come back.

Killian swiped the screen and put Sterlyn on speaker. "Hey."

"Hey," Sterlyn replied, and at least another five other people were breathing in the background. She must have us on speaker, too.

"Emmy called her dad this morning and told him that Roxy got caught in a trap last night and Axel got hurt trying to get her down," Griffin said. "Is everyone all right?"

"Yeah. Luckily, he wasn't injured badly, so he should be fine this morning." Killian yawned and placed an arm behind his head. The muscles in his chest flexed, distracting me. "But there are traps out there. The recon team just returned."

"If you need me to come help out, let me know," Ronnie offered.

Alex growled. "You know we can't do that. Erin is watching us like a hawk shifter."

"Well, we can send some other demons out there to help if we need to," Levi interjected. "If you all need more hands on deck."

"There's no boat there, so how would having more hands help?" Rosemary scoffed. "Either way, though these demons are undecided, they're still getting acclimated to Earth and helping defend the city from the ever-growing demon attack problem. We have to be careful who we send."

Demon problem. Yet another issue to contend with.

"Love—" Levi started, then stopped. "You know what, never mind."

He was likely trying to inform Rosemary of what that saying meant. I smiled. Now that I wasn't threatened by her, I found her literal nature very endearing.

"We were calling to let you know the humans called, and the story worked. Their leader is *very* annoyed with Erin." Sterlyn sighed with relief. "He hung up a few minutes ago to call Erin immediately."

"So we did hurt her reputation?" I asked carefully. I didn't want to assume since I hadn't been on the other line.

"Yes, he was very annoyed." Griffin chuckled. "I'd almost feel bad for Erin, but the bitch deserves it."

"They're supposed to call back any second to tell us our next move. They don't trust Erin anymore," Ronnie said excitedly.

Someone's cell phone rang on the other end.

"It's him," Levi informed us, and he changed his voice to sound like Tom. "Hello?"

My heart pounded, and I could faintly hear the words of the man on the other end.

"Erin is supposed to be locating that pack again," the human said in frustration. "This is unacceptable."

"I agree." Levi represented Tom's pompous ass perfectly. "If she fails us again, we'll have to find more wolves another way."

"Even if she does, I'm done with her." The man scoffed. "You'll need to find us another witch who we can..." He trailed off.

"Are you there?" Levi asked brashly.

"I'm here." The man cleared his throat. "What I was saying was...uh..."

Something strange was going on, and the heaviness of sleep vanished as my blood began pumping.

"You were saying?" Levi snapped.

After a second, the man's voice turned colder. "Who the *hell* is this? And how did you get my phone number?"

CHAPTER FIFTEEN

NONE OF THAT MADE SENSE. If I hadn't been on the line when Levi had received the call, I wouldn't have believed what I was hearing. The man sounded confused. A hint of fear had replaced the usual disgust in his voice.

"Is this a game?" Levi demanded, sounding even more like Tom. "You called me about supernaturals—"

Killian pressed mute on the phone as he fidgeted on the bed and the mattress creaked.

A strange laugh came from the other end. "Please, there are no such things as supernaturals. It's a figment of your imagination."

"I've captured—" Levi sounded strained.

Something odd had happened. He'd gone from telling us we needed to find a replacement for Erin to pretending he didn't even *know* us. *Kill*, I linked and sat up in bed.

I'm as clueless as you, he replied, his muscles tensing.

My chest squeezed so hard my heart might shatter. Though I wasn't sure what was going on, one thing was crystal clear: this wasn't good.

"Look, we've got things handled, so don't worry." The

guy on the other end was growing frustrated. "For the love of cheese, do *not* try to capture any supposed supernaturals. Just call and report it to the hotline. And don't call me *ever* again. I'll be changing my number."

A loud click sounded as the line disconnected, followed by silence.

After a second, Alex hissed, "*What* just happened?"

"I'm not sure," Ronnie exhaled. "But did he really say 'for the love of cheese'?"

"Cheese is quite delicious," Rosemary answered. "But I did find that odd since it was so irrelevant. Erin had to be behind that."

Sterlyn growled, "That's my thought, too. But how? She wasn't anywhere near him."

"In Hell, the witches created a way to perform amnesia spells without having to be near their target." Levi sounded like himself again, which was comforting. "All they needed was an item, a picture, or a location they could visualize—something to anchor the spell to wherever the person was located. However, if they target a general area, then anyone there will forget."

I was fairly certain that didn't matter. It would have been nice to know where this *man* was located, if I could even call him that.

"An amnesia spell makes sense." Griffin's words were almost inaudible.

No one was looking at the bigger picture. I linked to Killian, *If Erin made him forget supernaturals, that means she knows we're the new Tom, and she might suspect we know where the packs are.*

He went still before unmuting the phone. His jaw twitched. "Jewel just pointed out something *very* disturbing." He repeated what I'd said.

I placed a hand on his arm as my throat constricted. Not many men would give credit to someone else since I'd willingly brought it to his attention, but Killian was everything a man should strive to be.

"Fuck," Griffin rasped. "She's right. She'll want to screw us over like we did her. If we wait too long, there's a huge chance she'll stop us from getting them out."

His anxiety fueled mine, and my pulse pounded in my ears. "That means we need to get them out *tonight*." Even that could be too late if Erin was making a move, but striking in daylight without any cover would be foolhardy. Remaining unseen would be better than having humans call reinforcements as soon as we stepped onsite.

Killian scratched the back of his neck. "Okay, we need to inform everyone downstairs about what happened, and Jewel and I need to get out there to keep watch. If we manage to get these packs out, we'll need a way to transport them."

"We'll take care of that," Sterlyn assured him. "Just focus on what you need to do."

"And someone has to keep an eye on Erin," I said. At this point, we needed to know if she even farted weirdly.

"We'll put Cyrus and Annie on it." Sterlyn grunted. "They've been connecting with the Shadow City citizens, which has been amazing for Cyrus getting support as a council member, and I hate to risk my nephew and niece becoming orphans. The two of them have sacrificed enough, and having them here will help conceal us from Erin."

"Oh, please." Ronnie snickered. "My niece and nephew are the ones winning those people over—them and Midnight." Midnight was Annie's biological mother. "She's been right there beside them, watching the kids while they help rebuild the city."

"Can you send more fighters here?" Killian grimaced. "I hate to ask, but we could really use the help."

"I'll send a few vampires, but we can't send as many as before," Alex answered. "Though Erin is focused on us, she's keeping an eye on the Terrace as well. I can send ten. I'll make sure Joshua is among them."

"Does it matter, though, since we know that Erin knows about us?" Levi groaned. "Wow. That was confusing, but you know what I mean."

"Yes, it matters," Rosemary scoffed. "If we stop pretending, Erin will become more blatant. We have to be strategic. After all, these asinine political games are the only thing Erin has ever known. Me, too, for that matter, though I find them rather cumbersome."

Good point. Some of the tension left my body. Erin likely wouldn't deviate from her political games, which would make it harder for her to come here and make it magically difficult for us to get the shifters out tonight, especially if Annie and Cyrus kept a close eye on her.

"We'll ask Sadie if more of her pack can come and help fight." Killian threw the covers off his legs. "Even ten vampires would be amazing, and if there's any way you can direct some of my pack to come here undetected, even better."

"We'll work on it and call you back shortly." Sterlyn paused. "Just put your phone on silent, and you all be careful. Though we want to save the packs, we don't want to lose any of you in the process."

My lungs worked easier. Sterlyn truly cared about everyone. Knowing she was my cousin filled me with pride. She had similar qualities to my dad, and I could only assume they'd been passed down in our family.

"We will," Killian assured her as he stood. "You all do

the same. Talk soon." He hung up the phone and hurried across the wood floor to snatch his shirt from the top of the chest of drawers.

Not wanting to be left behind, I jumped out of bed and picked up my jeans, which had fallen on the floor. I wiggled them on and glanced up to find Killian watching me. His chocolate irises were filled with love.

My cheeks burned. "I never said I was graceful."

He walked around the bed and kissed me, then linked, *You're adorable, and I'm so damn lucky to have you.*

I smiled, and my body warmed. This might be our last moment alone for who knew how long, and though I tried to focus on the present, I could feel it was fleeting. *You mean everything to me.* Though he knew I loved him, I didn't want to forget to say the words as well. I wanted to make him feel treasured in every way possible.

And I'll kill anyone who tries to take you from me, he linked as his determination slammed through our bond.

Even though Killian wasn't that sort of man, he meant every single word. He'd lost his family, and Sierra would eventually leave the pack. This was his way of telling me we were in this together...forever.

I kissed him as the vow settled over me. The words excited me in a way I'd never known, and I realized I felt the same way about him. We wouldn't set the world on fire, but we'd take out anyone who tried to interfere with our bond.

His tongue swept inside my mouth, and his unique taste filled me.

A loud knock on the door interrupted us, and Emmy called out, "I know we're sharing a room, so in theory, I should be able to walk in without knocking, but the door is locked, and I can smell the arousal from outside."

I giggled, the sensation feeling odd, and pulled back. Our moment was officially over, but at least we'd had this time together. "We're heading out right now."

Killian's face smoothed into a mask of indifference, the very expression I'd learned meant there was a serious matter at hand that usually included risking our lives. He placed his cell phone into his back pocket and intertwined our hands as we headed to the door.

When he opened it, I found Emmy leaning against the wall. Her hair was half out of her ponytail, and she had dark circles under her eyes.

She hadn't gotten enough rest yesterday.

Hell, none of us had, not even Killian and me, and we'd stayed behind.

"We came back so we could be here for the call." She yawned, not bothering to cover her mouth. "So here we are."

"They called just as you all got here," I replied, hugging her. I hated that we were depleted. It was never good to be exhausted before battle, but in war, there usually wasn't a choice.

Emmy was like a sister to me, and I wanted to send her away so she wouldn't get hurt. But that would be futile. Right now, every supernatural was at risk of being captured, and I respected her too much to consider asking her to stay behind. The two of us had grown up training together, and I knew how capable she was.

Realization punched me in the gut, damn near kicking the breath out of me. This must be exactly how Killian felt about me—knowing I was capable of holding my own but wishing I didn't have to. And here I was, giving him hell because he cared about me so much that he wanted me safe. He wasn't right, but I could've been understanding. His protectiveness came from a place of love, not from devaluing the worth he found inside me.

Are you okay? he asked, and my stomach clenched at his concern.

I'm fine. Just wishing I hadn't given you such a hard time when you wanted to keep me safe. I repeated what I'd just realized to him.

He smiled as he continued toward the stairs. *Which wasn't right, and I'm sorry. But you're correct. That's exactly why I did that.*

Working through his guilt over his family's deaths and his fear of losing Sierra had strengthened our relationship overnight. Maybe the two of us were finally healing together.

Refocusing on Emmy, I cupped her cheeks with my hands and said, "Why don't you go get some sleep?" I worried about her. She was always taking care of me and neglecting herself.

"And miss that conversation?" Emmy shook her head. "Not happening. You should know better, especially with that serious look on Killian's face and yours." She paused and tipped her hand. "After you all get done doing the *deed*, I expect to hear what it's like."

Flames licked my face, and I averted my gaze. "Em—"

"Oh, no." She lowered her head, making sure she stayed in my view. "You are not getting out of this. Unlike Sierra, I've respected your boundaries, but J, *come on*. Help a sister out."

"First off, no. You will not think of my *mate* that way. And two, it's private and magical, but I might be able to tell you some things I've learned." Maybe the bare basics that didn't involve discussing anything about *my man*. "But first, we go downstairs and listen to the conversation you were determined to learn about two seconds ago."

She opened her mouth to argue, but I clutched her arm and yanked her toward the stairs.

As we walked down the steps, the living room came into view. Sadie, Donovan, Bune, Lillith, Zagan, and Roxy sat on the couch, with Axel behind Roxy, his hands on her shoulders, standing tall as if he'd never been injured.

I exhaled.

Eleanor stood in front of the fireplace, her wings lying limply at her sides. Torak and Sierra stood hand in hand behind Sadie and Donovan on the couch.

My attention flicked to Killian standing in the middle of the room. I hurried to him and took my place at his side. Emmy stayed at the bottom of the stairs and leaned against the railing.

No one spoke, ready to hear what we had to say.

Killian informed everyone of the entire phone call, and I watched their expressions. Emmy, Bune, Sadie, and Donovan were exhausted. The four of them would need to rest while Killian, Lillith, Roxy, Axel, and I watched the area.

By the end of the update, everybody's face was tense. Torak released Sierra's hand and pulled out his phone. "I'll get thirty of my men here to help with the rescue. They aren't more than an hour or so away."

Donovan nodded. "And I'll reach out to our pack back in Nashville. We should be able to get twenty here. I'm sorry it's not more, but that's all the people we can spare, especially with someone out there hunting shifters."

"What about Egan and Jade?" I asked. Having some dragons on our side would be hugely beneficial. They could easily take on double the amount of fighters as the rest of us and carry injured shifters away to safety—if they were willing. With the goodness that wafted from them, I had no doubt they would offer without us having to ask.

"They were staying away because—" Sadie stopped herself. "Which they don't need to do anymore, since Erin is on to us."

Eleanor fluffed her feathers. "I'd have them wait until closer to nightfall to arrive, so if Erin does perform the location spell again, they'll still be wherever they're hiding."

My head tilted back. *Has she ever offered strategic advice before?*

Sierra's eyebrows lifted, but her lips tipped upward. *Only to argue against Rosemary.*

And the snarky Sierra I knew and loved returned.

Keeping a schooled expression, Killian nodded. "True. But if they're willing to send some of their subjects, we would greatly appreciate that."

"Their *subjects*?" Roxy asked, and leaned back in her seat. "I have no idea what you're referring to."

The sulfuric stench of a lie was undeniable.

"Seriously, Roxy." Lillith waved a hand in front of her nose. "With *that* smell, you might as well admit it."

Roxy straightened and squared her shoulders. "Hey, I tried."

"With the deference that tall guy showed Egan and Jade, it wasn't hard to figure out that they're the king and queen." Eleanor rolled her eyes.

"It doesn't matter anymore. It's clear both sides can be trusted." Sadie stretched out her hands. "We'll call them, and I'm sure they'll send some dragons."

Scratching his scruff, Bune said, "Are there any other people we can ask for assistance? I can talk to Levi and discuss having more demons come help."

"I wish I could ask Dad for help, but the fae realm is very peculiar. It was hard to get them to accept me, and that was after they tried to kill me multiple times." Sadie bounced one foot. "Asking for guards and people to come here could cause another civil war."

"We definitely don't want to create problems for any other realm." Killian rocked on his heels. "So don't feel bad."

"We do need to get people back out there watching." Emmy pushed off the rail. "We saw the first shift come in, but anything they do might give us clues about traps and their general movements."

She was right. We needed as many eyes as possible on the facility until we launched our attack. "We can strategize with each other and through pack links, and readjust when we know our numbers," I said. That was the nice thing about how the group was set up: we had, at minimum, one person in each group who could always communicate with the others.

"I'm going with the morning group." Zagan stood. "That way, I can focus on locating more traps outside and keep an eye on things inside."

He was right. He was weightless and invisible.

"Me, too." Bune inhaled as if he were gathering the energy to stand once more.

"You need to call Levi and make plans with him, then get some rest. We need one of you alert on each shift," Killian said gently.

My chest puffed with pride. He was great at handling delicate situations diplomatically.

"Everyone who hasn't just been on watch should go," I added and stepped closer to Killian.

Lillith stood and rubbed her hands together. "What are we waiting for?"

Without another word, our group dispersed. Killian, Lillith, Roxy, Axel, Zagan, and I grabbed some leftover pizza and headed out.

THE NEXT FEW hours were painfully dull. No one came to the facility or left, and five guards were posted at each corner like before.

Every hour, one guard from each side walked a certain area of the perimeter and checked the traps, which helped us identify where they all were. The humans must not have sensed our presence. Roxy and I stood watch at one end of the building, while Lillith and Axel stayed in the center to focus on the middle set of guards, and Killian took the opposite end. We stayed back in the trees since our supernatural eyesight allowed us to see well enough. I hated to be separated from Killian, but this way, we could easily communicate across the different pack links and with Lillith.

Zagan went inside the buildings to find out what was going on during the day.

Even with the cold air of late December, the sun beat down on us, making me uncomfortably warm. I had to keep reminding myself that at least it wasn't August.

The woods and surrounding area were quiet, except for the occasional deer that traveled by—until the sound of rumbling engines drew closer.

Roxy's gaze met mine, and I knew I wasn't the only one hearing it.

Vehicles were coming, and by the sound of it, large ones.

We have incoming, I linked with Killian.

I couldn't see him, but I could feel the moment my comment registered. Dread soared through our bond.

Ten Suburbans rumbled by and pulled up in front of the building. Six people climbed out of each vehicle.

We were severely outnumbered.

CHAPTER SIXTEEN

MY LEGS TURNED WATERY. Sixty more guards had arrived on the scene, wearing bulletproof vests and carrying tranq guns. I couldn't believe this was a mere coincidence. The human in charge had called in reinforcements. Erin had to suspect we were here.

From what I could tell, no supernaturals had shown up. I doubted the guards would be comfortable fighting alongside us. All the other times, we'd fought either humans or wolf shifters, and it was either/or despite their alliance, so I doubted they'd reached the comfort required to fight side by side in just a few short days.

"This is *lovely*," Roxy muttered, and I fought the urge to shush her.

If there were any supernaturals among the guards, we'd know soon enough since she'd spoken out loud. I understood we had to communicate verbally since we didn't have a pack link, but we weren't in danger yet, and saying that had been unnecessary.

I held my breath as I waited to see if anyone had noticed.

When the guards didn't pause, my breathing steadied again.

What happened? Killian linked.

He could feel my trepidation. *Roxy said something out loud, and I was worried that a guard might have heard her. It doesn't appear they did. Sorry, I didn't mean to alarm you.*

It's our job to worry about each other. His concern eased through the bond.

I grinned as some of the worry rolled from me. *That's very true.* And I noticed he'd said *we* worried about each other. I'd have bet money that one week ago, he'd have said it was his job to worry about me. We'd both grown so much in a short amount of time.

The guards hurried to meet with the sixty new arrivals. As they talked, the body language of the fifteen original guards became stiff and unwelcoming. *Something is going on, but I can't hear what they're saying over the engines.*

Dammit, I can't hear them, either, Killian grumbled.

Glancing at Axel and Lillith, I noted they were leaning forward as well.

One of us needed to hear the conversation. I closed my eyes, a trick Dad had taught our pack. If you needed to improve one of your senses, you had to eliminate another.

I locked onto their voices and relayed what I was hearing to Killian. *The new arrivals are telling the guards to go inside and keep watch in there. The original guards aren't happy and insist they should stay outside since they know where all the traps are located.*

They were having a dominance standoff. That was one thing about humans, especially the ones who sought power and control: they acted similarly to the alphas of the supernatural world, and I was certain that if humans had thought pissing on something would lay claim to it for real, they'd do so without hesitation. We had a lot more in common than either side would freely admit.

Surprise flickered through our bond. *You can hear them?*

I'd missed what the woman had said because Killian had distracted me. I answered, *Yes, but I need to concentrate. Give me a second.*

"Don't be an idiot," a deep male voice said. He was one of the new arrivals. "You know the inside of the building better than we do and the vulnerable point of entry. Six of you need to stay out here to familiarize us with the area outside and the traps. We'll split into six groups."

Six groups. They planned on increasing their watch on both sides of the building. My shoulders tightened.

The female leader of the original guards scowled but nodded. "Fine. How big will the groups be?"

"A total of five," the deep-voiced man answered. "The five includes one from your team. The rest will help guard the inside as well, specifically around the cages."

Some of the tension left the woman's body. "That sounds good."

She seemed better with that plan, as if they were on even ground. But I suspected the newcomers would take over inside as well. They were likely a specialized division and wouldn't sit back and take orders from the current guards.

We had numbers, but I worried about the total on their side. We'd be attacking shortly after twilight, not wanting to wait too long and have more backup arrive. We couldn't risk waiting much longer.

"Gary," the woman in charge said as she turned to a man on the edge of their group. "Go open the garage so they can pull their vehicles in. We want to make sure that if anyone shows up, they won't have any idea about our numbers here."

The man with the deep voice glanced over his shoulder, his green eyes icy. "How do you know they aren't already out there?"

I fisted my hands. These new arrivals were smart. Dad had said to never underestimate your opponent. That was the best way to end up dead. Now I understood his warning, but I didn't like having it used against us.

"Because fifteen of us are out here at all times, and we check the traps every hour," the woman grumbled. "And all we've ever caught are rabbits and other small critters. Well, except for a deer the other day."

As I gritted my teeth, my hearing became impaired. I forced my jaw to relax, refusing to allow stress to take over my body. If I didn't get myself under control, I wouldn't be able to hear what else they said.

"Ugh," Roxy grunted. "None of us can hear a damn word they're saying."

"Shh," I breathed. "I can barely hear them."

"Wait," she gasped. "You can—"

"Not when you're talking."

"Gotcha. Quiet." She squatted and practically leaned over me.

At this moment, she reminded me of Sierra, and I forced myself not to push her away. She'd only complain, and I wanted to keep listening in.

"—to head inside." The deep-voiced man pointed to multiple groups of four and waved the rest toward the Suburbans.

I'd missed the last part of the conversation due to Roxy, but at least I'd heard something. I opened my eyes as the deep-voiced man and twenty-three guards moved off the road that ran in front of the building and stepped into the grass. The remaining thirty-six split up into the ten Suburbans, and the nine original guards headed to the building on the left.

As the cement garage door opened, I leaned forward. Luckily, the noise didn't interfere with our vision. Fifteen vehicles were already inside, all parked on the right, with the left half of the garage vacant. That had to mean the stairs or elevator were on the side where the day workers parked.

They're forming six groups of five outside, I linked with both Killian and Sierra back at the cabin so she could inform everyone there. *Three groups will be covering the front of the building and three covering the back. Each group will consist of one original guard and four of whatever special team just showed up.*

Faint surprise pulsed from my pack link with Sierra. *How do you know this? Roxy and Axel just told Sadie they couldn't make out anything since they kept the engines running.*

This was one benefit of the packs splitting up and keeping everyone informed—we all had a way to communicate with one another.

Just a trick Dad taught us. Any updates from anyone else? The past couple of hours had been relatively quiet as people napped and rested, getting ready for the grand finale tonight.

Draco, Katherine, and a few other dragons should be here at any minute, Sierra answered. Some pride wafted through our link. *And as Donovan promised, twenty of his pack members will be here around five, along with Egan and Jade. Donovan's pack had to settle things before heading this way, but Torak's thirty pack members should be here within half an hour.*

I suspected Sierra's pride came from being in a position to impart information. That would be her new role once she and Torak established their bond because she'd be an alpha mate, the same as me.

I pulled my cell phone out of my back pocket and looked at the time. It was almost three. We'd been out here longer than I'd realized. My stomach growled, confirming it had been far too long since the cold-pizza breakfast.

Good, Killian responded. *Griffin texted me earlier—Levi found twelve demons to send our way, and they're en route, following two Suburbans full of vampires and three full of wolf shifters that Billy has heading this direction. Eliza, Herne, Aurora, and Lux are on their way from the coven to help us wake the shifters.*

Despite the good news, the hairs on the back of my neck stood. Our numbers would almost match theirs, but there was no telling what we would run into on the inside. The last time we'd breached a facility, we almost hadn't made it out before Tom's pack had ambushed us in the woods. If they'd been a little faster, they could've captured us all inside. Dread sat heavily on my stomach, but I didn't want Killian to feel the sensation. He was under enough stress, and burdening him with mine would make it less bearable. I searched deep inside me where our connection was rooted and tugged on the strand on my end to clamp down on my negative emotions.

We had to save these packs. The more time Erin had to plan an attack, the more our chances of getting the packs out dwindled.

Torak and I can head over there and relieve you two,

Sierra replied. *You guys should have some downtime before the fight.*

No, you two need to be there when Torak's pack arrives, Killian linked.

My knees weakened, and intense love overflowed inside me. I'd never imagined I could love someone this much, but every day, I fell for him a little more. This time yesterday, Killian hadn't even wanted to consider that Sierra could be mates with Torak, and now he was telling her she needed to stay with Torak and meet her future pack.

Her surprise sent a shockwave through our link, and I smiled.

How about Eleanor? I asked. From what Killian had told me, angels didn't require as much sleep as the rest of us. *Could she come here and keep watch for a little while?* I hated to exclude anyone from the planning process, but someone had to keep watch to ensure nothing changed at the facility.

Fifteen previously cooled pack links warmed in my chest. Our arriving pack members were in range. I rubbed my chest, enjoying the warmth. Packs were meant to stay together, and when we got out of range from one another, the bond cooled and felt empty.

Is everyone okay? Lowe linked.

I wasn't surprised that Billy's son was part of the group heading our way. Billy had been Killian's dad's best friend and was now Killian's beta. He'd even handled the alpha responsibilities for a couple of years while Killian had tried to find his way after losing his family. Billy had stayed behind to run things and address any issues at home so no one would be wise to our absence.

Killian's side of our connection eased as he replied, *Yes. Have you all run into any issues?*

Nope. But I'll tell you, I'm sick and tired of Suburbans, Lowe answered. *It's like, whenever I go anywhere, it's in one of the big-ass vehicles.*

Guys and their rides. Chad and Theo were the same way about things that didn't matter to me. *It's actually smart. They blend in with what the enemy uses,* I replied. I hated the word *enemy* because we shouldn't be that. We should be allies. We all needed oxygen to breathe, water to hydrate, and food for energy.

Every single one of us.

We weren't that different.

April linked, *That's what I told him, but he ignored me.*

They must have been within thirty miles of us to link. That was a very good thing. I linked, *Sierra, when the pack arrives, have Eleanor show them the way here. Maybe bring us something to eat. They can get an idea of the land before we start the rescue.*

I thought you were coming back to rest, Sierra replied.

I winced and connected with just Killian, *I'm sorry. I didn't mean to take charge.* He was the alpha, and I was bossing our pack around.

You have nothing to apologize for. His warmth exploded through me. *I actually found it hot, and you're right. As much as I wanted to head back, if people are arriving, we should stay here and make sure nothing changes.*

We were the ones who'd been here for the past seven hours and knew who had come and gone.

Killian repeated that to the pack, supporting what I'd said.

We'll be there soon, Lowe replied.

The thirty guards had split up and taken their positions. Now there were three groups spread out evenly in front and at the back of the buildings. The garage door was shut, and the woods were relatively silent.

"Our pack members will be joining us shortly." Scanning the area, I thought of another issue, and my stomach dropped to the ground. "We need to figure out a way to document all the traps." Our group knew where each one was, but none of the others did.

"Please, Axel and Lillith have that covered." Roxy waved her hand and smiled. "Lillith was an art major and brought her sketch pad everywhere. She has a pocket-size pad she carries around in case she gets bored. She's been drawing things the entire time we've been here, including the location of each trap."

Thank gods these people were our allies. I hadn't considered doing that until it was damn near too late.

I settled back under the brush and waited.

THE NEXT TWO hours flew by way too quickly. The good news was that nothing had changed on the outside, not even a guard shift, but that was also the bad news. That meant they were expecting an attack, and they were smart enough not to say it out loud.

Everyone had joined us in the woods, including Jade and Egan and more dragons, my mother, and members of our various packs. We had a total of one hundred and eighteen people, but Zagan had informed us that inside, there were sixty guards with bulletproof vests and forty lab technicians. With the thirty guards outside as well, we were still outnumbered. Plus, we had two hundred and fifty captive wolf shifters to free and get to safety.

No problem at all.

The worst part was, we had two security measures to get through. First, in the lobby of each building was a voice authenticator. We'd need to get a guard to help us in. The second one was a scanner, and Zagan and Bune hadn't figured out what it read. Worse, each day, the guards rotated who was authorized to unlock the rooms using this feature. But luckily, today we knew which person to nab.

This time, we knew what we were up against.

Our plan was simple. Everyone would head inside except Katherine, Chad, Mom, and April. That way, each person would be able to link with someone inside, and Katherine would survey the area to ensure a pack didn't attack us from behind again. We would try to stay in our human forms, and our packs and vampire allies had brought guns, knives, and daggers for everyone.

Killian stood next to me as we stared at the buildings. Twilight was upon us, and we were waiting for the darkness to spread. We hoped they'd expect us to attack late like last time.

Bumping my arm, Emmy looked at me sternly. I turned, and Martha, Darrell, Chad, Mom, and the four witches stood right behind her. All nine of them had their eyes locked on me.

"No self-sacrificing this time." Emmy arched her brow. "We've all seen that side of you too often. Fight, be strategic, but don't try to save everyone by risking your own life."

My face burned. In the past, I'd tried to prove to everyone I could hold my own. Now I was ashamed that I'd acted so foolishly. The only person I'd needed to prove something to was myself. "I promise."

Killian exhaled and glanced at the sky. "Thank gods."

It was then I realized how much I'd worried everyone.

"I should go with you all in there." Chad chewed on his

bottom lip and narrowed his smoky topaz eyes as a trickle of light reflected the gold from his wheat-colored hair. "I mean, to stay out here and—"

But we all knew why he couldn't go inside. It was the same reason PawPaw's pack wasn't here to help, and Ruby and Birch, who'd helped us fight last time, had stayed behind with them in case Erin tried something in the Shadow City area. Under pressure, their shifting was uncontrollable, so they needed wolf shifters who weren't struggling to shift to remain with them. Ruby and Birch had stayed behind to protect the people I loved.

Darrell, Sterlyn and Cyrus's backup in the silver wolf pack, shook his head, causing his long midnight-brown bangs to fall into his blood orange eyes. "You know why we need you out here. Keep an eye on everything, and keep in touch with Sterlyn and Griffin about when the buses will arrive at the park's entrance."

Alex's sister, Gwen, had found Savannah, a human who'd been involved in kidnapping PawPaw's pack but had switched to our side, and made her remember us. She'd convinced her brother to let us borrow three of his school buses again.

Aqua eyes shining, Darrell's mate, Martha, ran a hand through her short, dark auburn hair. "We need to listen to Darrell instead of arguing with him."

"Just...please be careful, baby," Mom said in a broken voice. Her cognac eyes darkened as she hugged me. "I can't lose you, too." Her cinnamon-brown hair covered my face.

Tears burned my eyes, and the grief of losing Dad slammed back into me. It was never far from my mind and heart, but now wasn't the time to fall apart. Killian touched my arm, anchoring me like always.

The sky darkened, and I surveyed the wider group.

Torak's father, Titan, stood behind him. His short brown hair and matching goatee, along with his black eye patch, gave him a pirate-like appearance. Winter, Titan's mate and Sadie's mother, placed her hands on her daughter's shoulders. Winter's shoulder-length blonde hair was slightly longer than Sadie's, but their eyes matched perfectly.

Leading the new vampires, Joshua kept inching closer to Lillith. His mocha eyes flicked in her direction every few seconds, his medium-brown skin glistening in the night despite the moon almost being blacked out.

It was nearly a new moon, and the angel magic that usually buzzed in my skin was almost gone. A full moon, or what we silver wolves called a Silver Moon, would've been ideal so I could have been stronger and twice the size of a normal wolf when I shifted.

Eleanor edged over to Zagan. She was going inside in case we needed help to break the locks on the cages. Everyone was waiting for the signal, and Killian had just lifted his hand when the guards' walkie-talkies went off.

An urgent voice shouted clearly despite the static, "Supernaturals are right on us, and they're about to attack."

Well, there went our surprise.

CHAPTER SEVENTEEN

I NEARLY CHOKED on my gasp. This had to be a sick joke, but the way the guards were spreading out solidified that they did, in fact, know we were here.

"How in the world could they know?" Lowe asked as he moved to Killian's other side. His pecan-brown hair was pulled into a low ponytail, reminding me of Torak's hairstyle, and he rubbed his fingers over his copper-brown chin scruff.

That was the million-dollar question, and I could come up with only one clear answer.

"It has to be Erin," Eliza answered. The witch's sea-green eyes narrowed to slits as she retied her light caramel hair into a bun on top of her head. She normally appeared younger than her sixty years, but the crow's feet around her eyes were pronounced from stress. "I just felt a spike of magic around the dragons."

Killian exhaled and winced. "She still has Egan's shirt. We need to move before more backup arrives."

"Backup has already come," Sierra stated as our group edged toward the building.

We were all anxious to act, but we didn't want to be reactionary.

"This is the government. They probably have more people nearby, just in case," Darrell said. "They wouldn't want us to know their complete numbers."

Hurrying toward us, Sadie had her mouth pressed into a hard line. She whispered, "Are you ready to go? We were almost ready to attack."

I focused on the one good thing that had resulted from this situation—getting to know Sadie and her friends. She and Donovan could've tried to prove they were the most dominant and launched an attack, but instead, she was here to make sure we coordinated our actions. They were true friends and allies and not out to make a name for themselves, which was a relief since Sierra would more than likely end up part of them. If I'd thought they were a horrible pack, I would've been struggling with Torak being her fated mate.

Instead of answering, Killian glanced at Darrell. Since Cyrus and Sterlyn weren't here, Darrell was in charge.

He nodded.

All the wolf shifters were ready.

"Egan and Jade informed us they're ready to move as well." Sadie rubbed her hands together. "How do we want to split up? I'm assuming in a way where everyone can communicate."

We hadn't paired off yet, which was problematic. The guards were evenly spread out with their rifles at the ready. My heart pounded in my ears, and I took charge. "Every group breaks in half. You can split however you like, but we need to move. Mates are best kept in pairs so they won't worry about the other person, and they're stronger together."

Warmth spread through Killian's and my connection, granting me more confidence. With a mate like him, I had a feeling that in a few years, I wouldn't have any insecurities because he made me feel whole.

Without pause, our group began to divide. Seven of Killian's and my pack headed to our side, including Sierra, while Lowe led the remaining eight to the spot behind Sadie. Axel and Roxy, along with ten of their other pack members, moved to our side with Zagan and Eleanor, along with five demons. Emmy, Martha, Darrell, Circe, Aurora, Torak, and fifteen others from his pack headed to our side, along with Jade, Egan, two other dragon shifters, and Joshua, who brought five of the vampires with him, Lillith falling in behind.

Everyone else went to Sadie.

Eleanor squeezed through to the front of the groups and turned around. "Let me and the demons attack first. That way, the guards will be distracted, and hopefully, none of you will get shot when you break into view."

That startled me. Though Eleanor helped us routinely, she'd never seemed to be the most caring person. This was the kindest offer I'd heard her make.

"I was about to suggest that," Zagan added, his forehead wrinkling.

Clearly, I wasn't the only person thinking that. Maybe being around us was changing her.

"That would be ideal, especially since the humans can't see you in demon form." Killian's shoulders relaxed. "If the vamps can use their guns and get closer, using the trees for cover, that would help, too."

Chad snickered. "Remember the chaos the demons caused last time? It terrified the humans."

"They aren't the only ones terrified," Lillith grumbled

with a frown. "I thought Sadie's teleporting abilities made me uncomfortable. Oh, how wrong I was."

"You aren't kidding." Joshua exaggerated a shiver. "And now Shadow Terrace is overrun with demons. I'm still not used to them popping up randomly. I never know when someone might be listening."

A demon with long, wavy, light brown hair snickered. Her olive green eyes twinkled despite the impending fight. "Believe me, Joshua. No one is sneaking up on you or hovering nearby. All you ever do is complain about your breakup. We're staying clear."

Lillith groaned faintly, as if she were in pain.

He frowned. "It's been months, and I'm doing better."

This was the first time I'd met Joshua, but kindness radiated from his soul. Between that and Ronnie and Alex trusting him, I had no question in my mind he was good people, and I hated to hear that he'd been going through something difficult.

"Golda," Bune warned from his spot beside Donovan. "Stop your sass, and leave Joshua alone."

So the olive green–eyed demon's name was Golda.

Footsteps shuffled near the facility, and a human guard asked, "Do you see anything?"

Tension thickened throughout our group.

Emmy and Killian edged closer to me as if they expected me to run out. Though I wouldn't have done that even a few weeks ago, some of my choices had clearly made them uneasy.

April, get Katherine and scope out the area. We need you to watch the perimeter and ensure no other packs show up unexpectedly. Stay a safe distance away, and start the watch, Killian commanded.

He was right. If the humans were working with another pack like Tom's, it could show up at any time.

Mom and Chad were having a hard time with not joining the fight, but we didn't have much of an option. I spun around to hug Mom and murmured, "Killian told April to run the perimeter. Can you two keep her safe?" I made sure I said the words quietly enough that April wouldn't hear from the back of the group. She was the weakest of the four going, but I wanted Chad and Mom to know they were protecting someone, too. That we thought they were worthy.

Mom returned the hug and glanced at Darrell, her cognac eyes glowing.

I didn't have to be part of the pack link to know what she'd said. I'd bet she asked him to watch after me.

When my usual anger and frustration didn't come, I paused. I didn't need to replay one of my favorite songs in my mind to calm my nerves, either. Instead, I understood she was worried. All this time, I'd thought the concern had been about my abilities, but it was nothing like that.

"Shadow now," Bune commanded as his body flickered into shadow form.

My throat dried. The battle was here.

Zagan and the other ten demons followed suit, and our new friends hissed a few gasps behind me. They hadn't been around demons before.

"They disappeared like magic," a tall, older male wolf shifter whispered from the back of our group.

Eleanor bolted toward the sky, and when she reached the treetops, a female guard yelled, "Look!"

Five vampires rushed past Donovan and me and hunkered down behind several trees. They spread out, each one settling behind an oak so they wouldn't have any leaves to shoot through.

Flipping her wings to the sharp side, Eleanor flew straight again, and within seconds, shots were fired at her. She wrapped her wings around her body and spun. The bullets deflected off her wings, and she barreled toward the guards in the center, right where we'd need to run and figure out how to open the garage.

"Watch out!" the tall guard yelled as he lowered his rifle and stepped backward, realizing Eleanor would land close to their position.

Chaos was descending, and my breathing increased.

Out of the corner of my eye, the other five vampires got into position fifty yards away, using oak trees to hide them as well. They'd spaced themselves so that both vampire groups were firing at the guards on each edge. The only problem was that we weren't getting the guards on the other side, and they were staying in position, despite their colleagues being attacked. I could only assume they were afraid we would eventually attack the other side or use our current attack as a distraction.

The twelve demons soared into view, but instead of fighting the guards directly in front of us, I watched as they flew over the building toward the back.

My wolf surged forward, ready to help in battle, but I forced myself to remain still. With gunfire on both sides, it would be easy for one of us to be harmed.

Egan and Jade hurried to the front of their group, and two dragon shifters who were part of our group followed right behind. The man appeared to be the same age as Egan but at least six inches shorter. His ginger hair made his sapphire eyes look bright. The female shifter beside Jade was only a few inches taller than the dragon queen. Her violet opal eyes were narrowed as she pulled her dark brown hair into a ponytail.

When the four of them joined us, Egan's pupils turned to slits. "Should we shift to help fight outside, or would it be better if we stayed in human form for inside?"

Having dragons out here would add to the chaos, but we might need their strength inside.

"I would normally say shifting would be great, but when the shifters wake, seeing dragons might petrify them. They'll be in an already vulnerable state." Killian pinched the bridge of his nose. "If things become dire, then obviously yes, shift."

"We won't be able to fit into the building well in our dragon forms," Ginger Dragon said as he straightened his shoulders, then grimaced. "But I'll listen to whatever my king decides."

Jade chuckled as her face softened. "You know Egan appreciates you speaking your mind."

A scream forced my attention back to the battlefield as a guard who'd been stationed on the other side of the facility tumbled into view. A tree trunk stopped his forward motion.

Eleanor had barreled into the center of three guards, who were now unconscious on the ground. She was fighting two more. The female guard would shoot, and Eleanor would flick her wings to deflect the bullet as she punched the male repeatedly in the face.

The vampires continued with their gunfire. The guards wore bulletproof vests and helmets to protect their hearts, lungs, and faces. But that wasn't what our strategy was. We wanted to incapacitate them, so the vampires stayed focused on their real target: the guards' arms and legs.

Everyone was preoccupied.

"Are we good to move?" Sadie shouted, not worried about the humans hearing us.

Killian glanced at me, then at Eliza, Darrell, Torak, and Egan. We all nodded, not needing words to communicate.

"Let's move, but remember: do not kill unless it's absolutely necessary. We don't want to prove to them that we are the monsters they fear," Killian replied, then linked to our pack, *Stay in your groups and be careful. We protect ourselves and fight, but also don't take unnecessary risks. Your lives are just as important. Got it?*

I was again reminded of how good of an alpha he was. He'd reminded his pack that their lives mattered to him. Not many alphas would have made a point of saying that.

Determination and pride filtered into me through the pack links, the sensations stronger than before I'd become an alpha's mate. I knew Killian could feel them even more.

Though we weren't one pack, our group moved as one. The vampires remained in position, not needing instructions on what to do. They continued to shoot at the humans, who were now retreating.

Screams and panic ensued on the other side...or that was what it sounded like. Another human guard was launched into view on our right, the same side our group was heading toward.

A shadow form soared at it, ready to finish the job.

My stomach sickened. I hoped to the gods they weren't killing the guards unless they had no other option. I understood that killing was par for the course, but that didn't mean we should do it blindly.

Get down, Killian linked, and his body crashed into mine. We stumbled a step.

Something hit the ground an inch past my foot. Grass and dirt exploded onto my navy sneakers. My attention turned to the guard who'd been firing at Eleanor. Eleanor spun around and grabbed the woman's head, jerking it. A loud crack rang in my ears, and the woman's body tumbled lifelessly to the ground.

Bile inched up my throat. I'd been distracted, and the guard had noticed. I would have been injured if Killian hadn't been there.

I had to keep my head in the game and not worry about death. The humans had started this war.

Are you okay? Killian asked as he grabbed my hand and tugged me toward the nearest garage door.

I wanted to snap at him, but that wouldn't be right. I was angry at myself, not him. *Yes, I was worried about the demons killing the guards, but that's foolish. Of course we'll have to kill some of them.*

If I know Bune and Zagan, they won't tolerate killing for pleasure. Remember, these demons have chosen not to succumb to their dark urges, Killian assured. *That's your "protector" nature coming out.*

That was a double-edged sword for silver wolves—we were born protectors of the world, not just supernaturals.

The guards the vampires were firing at were wounded and falling apart. Though the shots hadn't been fatal, most were losing blood and growing weak.

"Jewel! Killian!" Emmy shouted from the garage several feet ahead. "Come on."

The first few steps forward were hard, but each one grew easier than the last. Soon, Killian and I were racing to catch up with the others. When we reached the large cement door, I surveyed the area for an opener, but found nothing. Not even a scanner.

Bune and Zagan hadn't told us how to get in.

"Is it just me, or is there no way inside?" Sierra stood

where the ends of the buildings intersected, glaring at the other garage door. The other group was there, searching for their own way in.

"Maybe we can cast a spell." Aurora lifted her hands.

Eliza pushed them down. "We need to conserve our energy. We have to wake up all those shifters, and last time, Rosemary had to recharge us."

And she wasn't here to do that.

"I've got an idea." Egan removed his shirt.

"Though I do enjoy your shirtless form, now isn't the time." Lillith waved her hands around at the chaos.

Jade snarled but didn't say anything as scales began to cover Egan's body.

That reminded me of the other day when he'd sprouted wings while keeping the rest of his body in human form. I'd never seen a wolf shifter half-shift before, but apparently, dragons could.

When his face was mostly scaled over and his mouth had elongated, smoke trickled from his nose. He then shot flames from his mouth, hitting the concrete door.

"What is he *doing*?" Sierra asked as she moved to the other side of Roxy and Axel.

"Weakening the cement," Axel replied simply.

Thank gods we had the dragons because I wasn't sure what our next move would've been. "Can one of you do that on the other garage door as well?"

Draco answered from behind me. "No. He's the only one who can half-shift."

That was interesting. Probably only the strongest of the strong could manage that.

I turned around and saw Draco scowling at Egan. I wasn't sure what their relationship was, but Draco seemed to feel responsible for his king and queen.

"Let me try my beams." Sadie stood in front of the other garage, gesturing for the others to move away, and lifted her palms.

Donovan, Titan, and Winter moved behind her. When the area was clear, pink beams shot from her palms and slammed into the concrete.

Glancing behind us, I saw the vampires run from their hiding spots and attack the guards lying on the ground. Screams still sounded from the other side of the building, but much less frequently.

Heat from Egan's flames licked my arms, and when the air cooled, I refocused in time to see Egan's face smoothing back into skin.

"Let me try getting us in," Eleanor called from overhead. "Move out of the way."

Killian took my hand, the buzz of our connection sparking to life as we slid to the right. Emmy, Darrell, Martha, Sierra, and Torak followed our lead, and as soon as the last of us were out of the way, Eleanor dropped from the top of the building, spinning with her wings wrapped around her body for protection. She hit the cement right where Egan had concentrated his flames, and her body ricocheted off the wall. She thudded onto the concrete ground.

A low hiss came from behind as Zagan yelled in a panic, "Eleanor!"

Yeah, they were mates, all right.

The cement fractured and crumbled, large chunks landing on top of Eleanor. She'd protected her body with her wings, but the impact could have knocked her out.

Eleanor's wings loosened, and she groaned and sat up, dust covering her face and hair.

"She did it," Donovan said with relief, and I spun around to find Sadie pale, with sweat beaded on her forehead. Her beam had created a large hole to get the second group inside that garage. She'd obviously stretched herself thin, but now both buildings had a way in. We just had to find a route upstairs.

I glanced around. The vampires were knocking out more guards, and the other demons were racing toward us.

The terror in Bune's dark hickory irises made my blood run cold.

"Get inside," he shouted just as a creaking sound caught my attention.

I glanced up at the building's windows and saw five gun barrels lined up and pointed at our group below.

The guards weren't waiting for us to come in. They were going to pick us off out here.

CHAPTER EIGHTEEN

CLOTHES RIPPED, and I spun around to find Draco shifting into his dragon form. Navy scales covered his skin as his body grew.

I'd never seen a dragon shift before, but I forced my attention back to the guards and noticed that their guns were tilted in various ways as if they weren't aiming.

Draco must have distracted them as well. *Kill, we have to move,* I linked.

Skin tingling, I knew Killian was looking at me, so I nodded upward. His terror slammed into me and mixed with my own.

"You heard Bune. Go," Killian murmured loudly enough for all the supernaturals to hear without alarming the humans. "They're going to shoot us from the windows."

Draco flapped his wings, lifting from the ground as the demons soared to help him. Though the humans couldn't see the demons, they would unfortunately see Draco.

Bune flickered back into human form. Roxy gasped next to Sierra and stumbled backward.

I clenched my hands and bit my tongue, resisting

scolding her about being afraid of a demon on our side when humans had guns trained on us.

Egan bent down to lift Eleanor, but Zagan shook his head. The demon scooped her up and cradled her in his arms, then he stepped through the jagged opening she and Egan had made. That was enough to get the rest of us moving.

"They're going inside," a male guard gritted out.

"Move, now!" I commanded and waved my hand. Though I didn't want to get injured, I couldn't run into the garage until our pack and allies had made it in. This was one of the scariest parts about being a leader, which I'd realized while watching my dad sacrifice his needs and safety for the rest of us.

At this moment, the decision felt *right.*

Glancing over my shoulder, I watched as the other group hurried through the hole Sadie had made. Just like Killian and me, Sadie and Donovan stood and watched as their people ran inside.

A loud roar vibrated the ground as Draco huffed fire from his nose and mouth. The ten demons slipped into the windows just as the guard who'd alerted the others fired at the dragon.

Between the roar and gunshots, my ears rang as I stood helplessly below, unable to assist. I watched, eyes widening, as the bullet barreling toward Draco slowed until it hovered in the air.

I blinked twice, thinking this had to be a figment of my imagination, but then the bullet slowly descended to the ground.

That shouldn't have been possible, yet I'd witnessed it with my own two eyes. I glanced up and noted a large sweat mark on Sadie's pale pink shirt. She'd obviously exerted more energy.

The world tilted as I tried to process what I'd seen.

Screams of terror rang out through the windows, confirming the demons had begun their assault. With the demons and Draco, we should be able to make it inside. Now I was worried about what we might find.

Roxy, Axel, Sierra, and Torak were the last four Killian and I were waiting on. Once they were in, Killian clutched my hand and dragged me into the garage as if it were actually safer.

I almost lost my footing. With the new moon upon us, he was faster than me. *I have shorter legs than you*, I reminded him. *I'm moving slower than you're used to right now.*

As we walked through the hole, I paused, looking behind us to see Sadie and Donovan rush inside their opening to the other building's garage. Everyone but the vampires, Chad, Mom, Katherine, April, and Draco was now inside.

Usually, I'm the one struggling to keep up with you, he replied as some of his guilt wafted through our connection, tightening my chest.

I hated to remind him that I wasn't at my strongest, but I didn't want my arm yanked off.

He slowed, now underestimating my speed, so I removed my arm from his grasp and sped up. I walked around the group, sliding between two sedans parked between load-bearing columns. A column was placed every two spots throughout the garage, and all the vehicles were parked on the side with the closest access to the elevator and staircase.

"Hey!" Sierra called after me. "We waited for you, and

now you're leaving our asses behind. That's not very friendly."

Torak groaned. "Keep up with her instead of complaining."

I didn't need to turn to see her face. I could already picture the affront.

And I like him even more now, Killian replied as he caught up and kept pace behind me. *He's probably the only person who can get away with talking to her like that.*

Maybe, but they haven't completed the mate bond, so he'd better tread carefully. I didn't want to waste time worrying about Sierra.

When we finally made our way through the maze of SUVs, Zagan was standing in front of the steel doors of an elevator, holding Eleanor. Killian and I rushed to the demon and angel to check on her. The fact that she might be unconscious for a while could be disastrous. Last time, Rosemary had used her wings to unlock the captive shifters' cages, and Eleanor was the only angel here.

Aurora, Eliza, Emmy, Martha, Darrell, and Lillith fussed over Eleanor beside Zagan. Lillith held out her wrist, making it clear about what she wanted to do—give Eleanor some of her blood.

Zagan shook his head. "We can't. She's pure angel. Your blood won't work on her."

My stomach dropped. I hadn't considered that. Demons had been angels before the fall, and they'd created vampires. It made sense that vampire blood wouldn't do anything to them.

"Then what do we do?" Roxy asked from behind us.

"I could use magic on her." Eliza rubbed her hands together. "But it might deplete me."

"No." Eyes narrowed, Martha straightened. "Save your

energy. I'll stay down here with her." She surveyed the area. "We'll go to the far end and hide behind that column"—she pointed—"so if humans come down here to get away, they won't see us immediately."

Ideally, the humans wouldn't make it down here, and we were wasting time standing around.

"What? No." Darrell scowled, his blood orange irises darkening. "I want you upstairs with me."

Martha smiled. "I'll be fine. Besides, you and Emmy are the better fighters."

That was true. They had been training since they were young. Martha had been an alpha's daughter prior to meeting Darrell, and her father hadn't wanted her trained to fight. That had changed since she'd become part of the silver wolf pack, but silver wolves were inherently better fighters.

Lillith pressed her lips into a hard line. "I will, too. If people come down here, I can use my vampire speed to disorient them."

"And I can link with you if we hear anything suspicious," Martha assured Darrell as she cupped her mate's cheek.

He groaned and nodded. "Fine. Just stay safe."

"I should stay—" Zagan started.

I wouldn't even let him finish that statement. "No, we need you upstairs. You know the layout and which guards and techs can disarm the biometric security." I understood that they were mates, but we needed him more right now.

"Jewel's right." Killian punched the demon in the shoulder. "And Eleanor will be adequately protected. If we need Eleanor for the cages, Zagan, you come get her."

"Fine." Zagan made sure Eleanor's head remained

cradled against his chest as he marched to the place Martha had designated.

Emmy hugged her mom while Darrell kissed Martha's cheek. After that, Martha and Lillith followed Zagan to their hiding spot.

As Lillith walked past Roxy, Roxy gave her a side hug and said, "Be careful, and don't die on me."

Lillith rolled her eyes but grinned. "You, too."

"Let's not talk about death." Axel wrinkled his nose. "It's bad luck."

I had to agree with him there. I focused on the elevator. A scanner had been installed on the right, and none of us had a badge. We had to find another way up.

I studied the area around it and noticed a small scanner in the middle of the wall fifteen feet down from us. I could make out the doorway.

Lovely.

What's wrong? Killian linked as his hand brushed my arm.

Jolts of our connection buzzed to life, comforting me. This was part of the plan none of us had thought about. We'd been focused on getting into the lab and the doors and hadn't considered how to get up there.

"We need a badge." I gestured to the scanner on the wall. "Both the elevator and stairs require one."

"Oh, yeah. I forgot about that," Zagan said sheepishly, but then he didn't hand us anything. "Hold on."

If he didn't have a badge, there had to be another way in, and we didn't need to give them more of a heads-up about our arrival than we already would.

A low growl came from Troy in my pack. His fern-green eyes narrowed, and he shook his dark red-brown hair. "I could really use that spell that allowed us to see the demons again."

There's a spell for that? I had so much to learn.

"We don't have Rosemary's and Levi's blood, so it can't be cast." Aurora slipped a hand into her jeans pocket. "And it isn't something any of us should have regular access to. Blood magic is powerful."

I understood what she meant. Magic like that should be used only as a last resort.

Zagan flickered as he transitioned back to human form. When he was visible to everyone again, he had a keycard in his hand. "Bune and I stole one earlier. Sorry, when Eleanor—"

Marching toward him, Sierra plucked the card from his hand and said, "Explain later."

I hadn't seen this side of Sierra before, and for a second, I was certain I was seeing a different person.

She headed to the scanner, but panic squeezed my throat. "Wait."

"We've waited long enough." Sierra exhaled and spun back around to face everyone. There was a gleam in her eye that hadn't been there before, one I recognized so very well: determination. I suspected after Torak got on to her, she was going to prove to him she could handle herself.

"Sierra—" Killian's Adam's apple bobbed.

He didn't need to fight my battle for me. Besides, scolding her in front of Torak would only increase her desire to prove us wrong.

I refocused her attention on me by saying, "Every human up there who isn't fighting a demon is waiting for us. That means if we all crowd into an elevator, we'll be easy targets."

Emmy snapped her fingers. "You're right. We should

split up, but then whoever's in the elevator will still be at the biggest risk."

Pushing up his sleeves, Killian smirked. "Unless we let them think someone is coming up in the elevator and they aren't."

That was an amazing plan. If we hadn't been in a life-or-death situation, I'd have kissed him.

"I can go up in demon form." Zagan held out the badge. "That's what Bune and I planned to do, anyway."

So that's why we hadn't heard anything from the others. They were probably already on their way.

"No, they'll account for demons now and shoot the entire space." Darrell leaned back. "One of us should stay down here and press the up button when we're all in position."

"It'll have to be someone from one of the packs so they can link." Egan crossed his arms, and his muscles bulged everywhere.

Roxy huffed and placed her hands on her hips. "I'll do it, but Egan and Jade, you keep an eye on Axel."

"Me?" Axel tensed. "What about you?"

"I'll hang back with Martha, Eleanor, and Lillith. That way, we can alert two different packs if something goes wrong."

We didn't have time to argue. Right when I was about to say something, Roxy snatched the badge from Zagan and scanned it on the stairwell access panel.

The door slid open.

She shrugged and headed back to the elevator.

Killian took my hand, and we headed to the stairs. Everyone followed right behind us.

The white walls of the stairwell were damn near blinding, especially with the fluorescent lighting. The stairs were the same gray cement as the garage. Even though we were shifters and light-footed, my steps and Killian's echoed inside. Halfway up the stairwell was a landing where the stairs turned in the opposite direction.

People could be up there waiting for us, I linked with Killian. Though I wasn't trying to keep my thoughts secret, I didn't want to alarm anyone else. I sniffed but only detected a faint smell of humans.

He nodded and lifted a finger, telling me to wait. He went up the stairs, and I wanted to go after him. He'd scolded me about taking unnecessary risks, but here he was, doing the exact same thing.

At the landing, he stopped just as Zagan's shadow form floated over his head.

"It's clear," Zagan said.

Killian stiffened since he hadn't known the demon was there.

Everyone rushed forward. I climbed the last set of stairs and stopped next to Killian as Zagan's shadow turned smoky and slipped through the crack of the door.

A walkie-talkie sputtered to life. "We've got a read on a large group in the stairwell."

I hadn't expected that they'd know this. I glanced in the corners of the room but couldn't find any cameras. So I glanced down at the corners of the floor... and my heart stopped. There were infrared scanners.

Something dinged outside, and then we heard shuffling. A guard said, "Why is the elevator here? I thought he said they're in the stairwell."

Someone must have told Roxy to send up the elevator. I grabbed the door handle as Egan, Torak, and Axel stood right behind Killian and me, ready to launch into action.

I bent down and removed the dagger from my ankle, then nodded and opened the door.

Ten guards stood in the center of a gigantic stark-white room with beige laminate floors, five facing us and the other five facing the elevator. They were dressed like the guards outside, in all black with bulletproof vests and helmets. But that was fine. We could still kick their asses.

Our group dropped and rolled into the room as gunfire erupted from the five guards who'd expected us to be standing there. I focused on the guard closest to me as the rest of our group swarmed inside. I had to trust that the others would choose one and fight; otherwise, we wouldn't make it out of this alive.

As he aimed at my chest, I stabbed him in his right shoulder, messing up the arm he'd been counting on to pull the trigger. His arm dropped, but he gritted his teeth, trying to raise the gun.

More of our fighters poured in, and someone hit my back. I collided with my opponent. The barrel of the rifle dug into my chest, and a stabbing pain stole my breath. Tears burned my eyes, but I didn't have time to give in to the agony, or I'd get shot.

Jewel! Killian linked.

I'm fine. I promise, I assured him. *I fell. That's all.*

Gunshots sounded all around me, but I couldn't take my eyes off my enemy.

I grabbed the end of my dagger and yanked hard, and the man groaned underneath me. He kicked me in the stomach, throwing me off him. I crashed onto my side. My hip smarted, but my lungs filled with air once more. My head cleared, and I jumped to my feet as the guard leaned on his left shoulder, trying to get up, his back to me.

That should've gone against everything he'd been trained to do.

Using his mistake to my advantage, I kicked him in the back, and he fell onto his stomach, whimpering. I dug my heel into his back as I reached down and yanked his helmet off his head. Not wanting to kill him, I fisted his caramel hair and banged his head against the floor hard. His breathing smoothed out as unconsciousness claimed him.

Grabbing his uninjured shoulder, I turned him over and untangled him from the rifle. Though I despised weapons, we might need them. One of the captive shifters could use it.

I scanned the area, and bile inched up my throat.

Five of our people already had gunshot wounds, but with our numbers, there were two of us fighting each guard.

Demons drifted down the hall from where they'd attacked the guards at the windows and joined the fight. I looked for the person who needed the most help.

Killian and Axel fought well together side by side, and everyone else had their fight under control.

When my gaze landed on Torak, near the middle of the room, I knew that was where I needed to be. Sierra and Torak had positioned themselves in front of the witches, likely so they wouldn't need to use their magic, but when a guard lifted his gun at Torak, Sierra jumped in front of him.

She was going to get them both killed.

I pushed myself toward them, dodging Killian, Axel, Egan, Jade, Darrell, and Emmy. The guard aimed at Sierra's head, and I lifted my arm.

Just as his finger twitched to pull the trigger, I jumped on the guard's back, pushing his firearm down. The gun fired a split-second before I had his arm at his side, and a shriek echoed in my ears.

The guard spun around, and I kicked him in the chest. He stumbled back.

"Motherfucker," Sierra snarled, and pain trickled into our bond. "He *shot* me."

Hot anger boiled inside me. I was tired of people I loved getting hurt, and it ended here.

Lifting my pilfered gun, I let the rage fuel me and mimicked his actions. I fired a shot into his knee. He crumpled to the ground, and I charged him and kicked his rifle from his hand. It skidded across the room, and I raised my dagger, ready to even the playing field.

I sliced into his vest, cutting the protection away from his body. All these humans hid behind their weapons and gear. At least this time, they'd have to fight fair.

"No!" the guard pleaded. Even though I couldn't see his face, his tone conveyed his fear.

If he thought I would kill him, he was so wrong. He didn't deserve death. Instead, I'd allow him to suffer. I wouldn't reinforce their misguided view that we were all killers, and maliciously, I'd let them know we'd outsmarted them. I'd raised the dagger, ready to injure him so he couldn't come after us again, when Zagan screamed, "Stop!"

CHAPTER NINETEEN

MY HAND that held the dagger dropped, and my wolf surged forward, wanting me to incapacitate this guard. I managed to maintain control and keep my hand at my side. My neck stiffened as I gritted, "If I don't knock him out, he'll come after us."

"He's the one we *need*," Zagan emphasized, his icy black-diamond eyes narrowing.

Of *course* he'd be the guard we needed to let us in. I wanted to roll my eyes, but instead, I reached down and yanked off his helmet.

He was young, maybe in his mid-twenties. His curly dark hair was matted with sweat, and his large eyes were an almost disconcerting blue. That was when it clicked—he had no negativity wafting from his soul. The usual hate that most of our enemies directed our way was missing.

This reinforced what I'd learned. Some of these humans were targeting us because they were just scared or following orders. The female guard we'd taken hostage last time, Savannah, had wound up helping us then and now. Who's to say these people wouldn't change sides if they'd take the time to get to know us?

Sierra stomped her foot and glared. "He *shot* me."

Blue Eyes lifted a hand and panted, "In fairness, it's just a graze, and I didn't intend to shoot you."

She growled, "That doesn't help. Shooting at *him*"—she gestured to Torak—"is worse than trying to shoot me." Her bottom lip trembled, revealing she was trying to be tough for Torak.

Now I realized how I looked when I was determined to save everyone and not accept anyone's help. No wonder Killian had been beside himself all those times.

Pain surged into my throat, and I linked to Sierra, *I'm so sorry you got hurt.*

It's not your fault, she replied, her nose wrinkling. *If it weren't for you, I'd be dead.*

That might be true, but I couldn't help but feel responsible.

To calm myself, I began playing Chopin's Nocturne No. 2 in my mind. Between the peaceful music and my realization that only two guards remained standing, some of my worry fell away. The demons continued to fight them as Killian and Axel came over to us.

The rest of our group fidgeted as they waited for our next move.

Icy tendrils of fear emanated through my connection with Killian and squeezed my heart. Something had to be wrong, but when I glanced at him, his gaze was locked on my hand that clutched the dagger.

Are you hurt? he linked, his jaw twitching. *You made it sound like you weren't earlier.*

I followed his eyes and noted that blood had dried on the blade. He must have thought it was mine.

No, that's from the guard. The barrel of his gun hit my chest. That's what caused the pain. As soon as I'd said it, I wished I could take it back. That sounded worse than what had happened.

His eyes bulged.

A shifter fell into me. The guard didn't mean to... I trailed off. I couldn't salvage this. Anything I said would only paint a worse image in his head, and he wasn't trying to shield me from the fighting. *Just...I'm not hurt. I'll probably have a bruise for a day.*

The lines etched on his face relaxed marginally.

Something thudded on the floor, but Blue Eyes was focused on me, so I couldn't take my attention off him.

I kicked his foot. "Get up."

"What?" He stared warily at the dagger I held. "Why?"

He must have thought I was going to attack him. "If I were going to hurt you, I would've done it a few minutes ago, despite Zagan telling me to stop."

Egan and Jade marched up beside me. Jade's emerald eyes were fierce as she said, "You're going to get us inside."

She was a little rough around the edges, which was one reason she and Rosemary had butted heads when they'd met, but she was strong...a survivor. I could tell by the way she held herself, and I respected her for it.

The guard cleared his throat. I glanced over as the last guard ran away from the demons, straight into Darrell and Emmy. Emmy kicked the guard into her father's chest, while Darrell wrapped his arm around the guard and squeezed, cutting off his air supply. The man soon slumped to the ground.

I stared around the lobby. It contained no furniture, just white walls and laminate flooring throughout. Even the door in the far corner was white. A screen about shoulder height was set into the wall next to it.

Blue Eyes shook his head. "I...I can't. I'll lose my job."

"You'll lose more than that if you don't help us," Egan whispered, the softness adding more of a threat to his vow.

Ready for this entire situation to be over, I lifted the dagger and pointed it at the screen. "And we don't have all day."

"But—" Blue Eyes started.

Killian grabbed his arm and yanked him up.

Axel followed his lead, gripping the guard's other arm, and the two of them dragged him through Torak's, Donovan's, and our packs to the door.

I hurried to where Blue Eyes' rifle had skidded and swiped it up. As I stood, I noted that Troy's shirt was wet with blood.

How many of you are injured? I asked Troy and the other eight pack members here with us. Since I couldn't fully feel their pain, just discomfort that could've been bruising from fighting, I had to ask.

Troy closed his eyes and didn't respond.

I understood that look. He didn't want anyone to know.

Everyone assured me they were fine...all except Troy. He knew we'd be able to smell his lie. I didn't want to embarrass him, so I didn't call him out on it.

Three other wolf shifters were injured, too. Somehow, the dragons had come out unscathed, along with Lillith, Aurora, and Eliza.

Killian growled, "Get us in there."

"A third round of backup is on the way. You can't get all the prisoners out before they arrive. You should leave while you can," Blue Eyes stuttered.

Unfortunately, no sulfuric stench of a lie swirled around us.

"Is that true, Eliza?" Sierra groaned in pain as she leaned against Torak, and his face twisted with worry.

Something blurred past me, and Lillith stopped a few feet away from the door and tilted her head. "Why would you ask that? It's obviously true, or we'd all know."

"What? Really?" Blue Eyes gasped.

"There's no magic surrounding him to hide his lies." Eliza pursed her lips. "So there's no time to dawdle."

Floating over Blue Eyes' head, Zagan turned smoky again. "The other demons and I will go inside and eliminate any threats while you deal with *him*."

Head snapping upward, Blue Eyes frantically searched the air above him. His breathing quickened, and he visibly shivered. "That's what's attacking us? Demons?"

Sometimes, I forgot how little humans knew, even though they were aware of our existence.

Seeping through the crack, the five other demons followed Zagan inside. At least we had one advantage over the humans.

"Get us in there, *now*," Axel commanded as he shoved Blue Eyes in the back.

Blue Eyes shook his head.

Intimidation wasn't working. Dad had said that sometimes, sincerity was the only thing that worked.

Inhaling deeply, I kept playing Chopin in my head. I needed something soothing to hold on to in order to better connect with him.

I linked to Killian, *Can I try something?*

He tilted his head and nodded. *You never have to ask.*

Placing my hand on Killian's arm, I guided it down. His brows furrowed, but he didn't stop me.

I slid next to Blue Eyes, and he flinched, thinking I was going to hurt him again. First impressions were a bitch...or that was what Mom had said time and time again. "Look, I know humans are uncomfortable around us. But—and pay attention—we didn't kill any of your friends. They're only knocked out." I could hear just as many heartbeats as when we'd arrived. "We just want to save our friends and families. How would you like it if someone kidnapped your family and experimented on them?"

He swallowed hard and glanced down at the vest I'd cut open. "Fine, but only because what they're doing doesn't sit right with me. I doubt getting you in will help, though."

My legs nearly gave out. I hadn't expected him to give in so easily. Now I was glad I hadn't hurt him.

"But shooting *me* did?" Sierra snapped from behind.

I clenched my hands. Now wasn't the time for her snark.

His eyes narrowed as he turned his body halfway to see her. "You all came in here and attacked us. I thought you would kill us."

"Well—" Sierra started, but then raw power surged through the pack links.

I'd never experienced it before, but I immediately knew what it was.

Alpha will.

Sierra, for the love of gods, be quiet. Don't say another word about your injury until we're out of here, or unless you get hurt worse, Killian bellowed, the power vibrating through every word. *Jewel already got through to him.*

Her anger was palpable, but I was glad Killian had done that. I knew it had to be difficult for him, especially knowing she was on the verge of leaving our pack.

Rushing across the room, Emmy reached my side and

plastered a soft smile on her face. I knew it was one of the fake ones she reserved for winning over her parents, but no one else had ever caught on. "It means a lot to us that you're willing to help us save all those women and children," Emmy murmured, and touched Blue Eyes' shoulder.

All the tension left his body. He reached up and pressed a button on the scanner. "This is Bleu."

The screen showed jagged lines as it processed his voice. I held my breath and waited for whatever happened next.

When the door clicked open, I pressed a hand to my chest. I hadn't been sure it would work.

Killian yanked open the door, and we stared into a long, sterile white hallway. There weren't any guards here, but straight ahead was a door to a gigantic lab. Technicians scurried around behind the door's glass window.

That was when it hit me. They were behind some kind of security they didn't expect us to break through.

"How many of us do you need here?" Darrell asked. "Some of us should go outside and head off the cavalry."

"Good suggestion." Killian nodded. "Everyone who's injured should go. We need about ten here."

A weird noise came from behind me that sounded like Sierra, but her words were muffled.

Cold realization settled hard in my chest. She had to be trying to complain about being shot.

"What's wrong?" Torak asked with concern.

We didn't have time for this.

"Torak, help Sierra out of here," Killian commanded. "Why don't Axel, Lillith, Jewel, Eliza, Aurora, and the demons stay?"

Jade scoffed. "What about us?"

"He wants us outside in dragon form." Egan's pupils turned to slits again. "Don't you?"

"If you don't mind. The demons can get into locked spaces, and you guys are strong. We need our strongest fighters out there since we've eliminated most of the threat in here." Killian bounced on his feet, and his eagerness pulsed through our bond.

My chest swelled. I was so proud he was mine. He'd just acknowledged that the dragons were stronger than we were while complimenting everyone he'd asked to head outside. He was an amazing leader.

"That's what I was thinking," Egan agreed, and touched his mate's arm. His golden eyes flickered similarly to a wolf shifter's, indicating he was talking to his mate.

Jade exhaled and shook her hands at her sides. "It makes sense. We just need to let the others know."

"I'll tell Sadie." Axel nodded and entered the hallway.

We were all eager to get moving.

"Everyone, be careful, and alert us if you see anyone approach," Killian said as he clutched Bleu's arm and led him inside with us.

"Hey!" Bleu exclaimed as he tried to dig his feet into the tile. "You said I just needed to get you inside." His valiant attempts to stop didn't do him any good. Killian was much stronger than him.

We're in the lab, Killian linked with the entire pack. *How are things next door? We've learned backup is coming, so most of our group is heading outside to hold them off if they arrive before we get out of here.*

Bune is getting the guard to let us in, Lowe replied. *Several in Donovan and Sadie's pack are injured. I'll tell them what you're doing and follow suit.*

I hated that more people were hurt, but I held on to the fact no one had died.

As our smaller group entered the hallway, my nose burned from the smell of disinfectant. As Bune had said, there were five rooms—three on the left and two larger ones on the right. Straight ahead was the lab with a full window and a steel door.

When I reached the first door on the left, vomit churned in my stomach and up my throat. This was worse than the last facility. Instead of individual cages, three huge cages were each crammed with ten people.

One child was placed in each cage along with a mixture of older and younger men and women. Each person wore a gown, and the cage on the left included a small shifter in animal form. The wolf lay on its belly, whimpering with a faraway look in its hazel eyes.

"Oh, dear goddess." Aurora's voice cracked, and she clung to my arm to stay standing.

I shared the same sentiment. In the first room on the right, it was the same situation but with five cages. The same mixture, but half of the captives had lost their hair.

Screams filled the lab, and I jerked toward the noise. The demons were harrying the technicians into chaos. The door to the right opened, and the lab techs ran out. Then they locked eyes on us and froze.

Five more ran out, and a pale, lanky man slammed straight through the women in front. He was so focused on what was behind him that he ran into Axel's chest.

"Oh, *fuck*, no," Axel growled. "Just, no. You don't just *run* into someone. This guy doesn't have any survival skills. I have to teach him a lesson."

The guy's eyes widened as he stumbled back, but it was too late.

Axel hissed, "This is for your own good." He then punched the tech in the face.

A female lab tech in front screamed, her face turning red.

Red Face continued to screech, and I fought the urge to cover my ears. *I think she's screaming on purpose.* They must have determined through testing that our hearing was super sensitive.

Lifting a hand, Eliza chanted, "*Fac eam ut sileas*!"

The woman's screams vanished, though her mouth was wide open. Good enough for me.

But we had no clue what other information they'd learned about us. "We need to knock them all out."

"What?" the dark-haired woman beside Red Face asked. Her bottom lip trembled, confirming her fear.

Another fifteen technicians ran from the lab, giving us twenty to handle while we got the captives out.

"That's all of them," Zagan yelled as the five demons followed him into the hall. He shut the door hard so that no one could run back inside...not that it would matter.

I sprang into action. Wanting to shut Red Face up permanently, I took the butt of my dagger and smacked it into her head. She dropped, and I spun around, looking for my next target.

"Make sure he doesn't escape," Killian told Eliza and Aurora, nodding at Blue Eyes as he and Axel ran into the group of technicians.

I spun into the sea of white jackets and knocked another woman out. Out of the corner of my eye, I saw a petite woman come at me with a syringe.

I hadn't expected that since they'd run from the lab in terror. She aimed at my arm, but I pivoted out of the way, colliding with a male tech. I grabbed him, using him as a shield, and the woman stuck the needle into his chest.

Her eyes widened, and I grasped her wrist before she could yank the needle from her coworker's chest.

"Get it out!" the guy screamed and tried to jerk from my grasp, but I wrapped my free arm tightly around him. Though moon magic wasn't buzzing under my skin, I was still stronger than any human.

Her face strained as she tried to remove it from his chest. Shield Man bucked against me, so I depressed the plunger. His eyes rolled back, and I released him as he crashed to the floor.

Syringe Woman's mouth opened and closed like a fish.

"I hope that wasn't lethal." I shrugged, but worry sat on my chest like a weighted blanket. When her attention flicked back to me, I punched her in the jaw, and her neck snapped back.

I might have hit her harder than necessary, but the bitch deserved it.

I looked for another technician to take out of commission. Only one wasn't detained. I raced toward her, but she lifted her hands in surrender. It was enough to make me pause. Then a loud, shrill ringing distracted me.

I turned to find Zagan in human form with Syringe Lady in his arms. He was holding her hand up to a black biometric scanner, and a gigantic 30 was flashing red across the screen.

The numbers began counting down. 29...28...

CHAPTER TWENTY

ANOTHER FUCKING COUNTDOWN.

I shouldn't have been surprised. We'd run into this issue at the last facility when we didn't know who the key was to open the doors, but this time, Zagan had watched to *see*. None of this made sense.

"I thought you knew who the right person was." Eliza grimaced as she rubbed her hands together.

Axel snarled, "Obviously, he didn't, and we're running out of time."

The timer now said twenty-five seconds, and none of us had moved.

"I know who the right person is," the lab tech said, voice quivering. "I'll tell you as long as you swear not to hurt Bleu or me."

"We can't trust her." Zagan tossed the unconscious tech aside. "We'll just keep trying."

Killian lifted the older female tech closest to him and hurried to the scanner.

Something about the woman's plea stopped me. She was only a few years older than me, and as a sweet essence wafted from her, I couldn't believe she would willingly deceive someone without good reason. If she lied, we'd know by her scent alone.

The tech's icy hazel eyes locked on the guard and filled with concern as she twirled a piece of her light ash-brown hair around her finger. She was petite, and her white lab coat was several sizes too large.

As Killian lifted the older woman's hand, the young tech's bottom lip trembled. "If you scan her hand, you won't be able to get the captives out. They've got backup measures for a bomb to detonate inside each room."

Killian dropped the tech's hand. There was no sign of a lie, and if it was true, then everything we'd risked to save everyone would be in vain.

12 flashed on the screen.

Killian linked with our other pack members, informing them of what we'd learned before they ran into the same issue.

"Who is it?" I asked. This entire situation was insane. If she pointed us at someone, we might have a chance.

"Him!" She pointed at the male guard who had slammed into Axel, the first one knocked out.

That could've been why he'd been so desperate to get away.

"Of course," Axel growled as he bent down and threw the guy over his shoulder. He ran to the scanner and turned his back so the lanky guy's hands could reach it easier.

Zagan snatched his right hand and placed it on the scanner as *5* flashed like a strobe on the screen.

My heart pounded in my ears as we all waited with bated breath for what happened next. Explosions could detonate at any second.

The flashing stopped. Five loud clicks confirmed that

the woman hadn't led us astray, and I wondered *why*. There had to be a reason beyond their safety since we weren't killing anyone.

We still needed to help our pack members and friends in the other building. "Do you know who can let the others out next door?" I suspected she wouldn't, but I had to try.

"I'm not sure, but tell them that a young tech named Stephanie will help them the same as I did." She clasped her hands as if she were begging me to believe her.

So far, she'd been forthcoming. I just hoped it didn't burn our asses, but again, there was no hint of a lie.

Killian linked and repeated the information to our pack members. Since his focus was there, I hurried to the first room on the right with the hairless shifters. "Aurora and Circe, take the first room on the left. Zagan, handle the middle one, and Axel, the last one on the left. Killian will take the last room on the right. Will the other demons keep watch on these two and ensure no one gets in our way?"

"Wait!" the tech exclaimed. "You need a key. Each tech person has a set, and the cages are marked."

"Britney." Bleu rubbed his forehead. "You won't get away with helping them. You know what Central Med will do to you."

"I don't care. *This* is wrong," she hissed through clenched teeth. "If we stand by and let these helpless people suffer, then we're no better than the people who were excited to capture them and run tests on them."

Not wanting to listen to their bickering, I snatched the set of keys from her hand and rushed to the hairless shifters who needed our help. Out of the corner of my eye, I watched as the others went through the pockets of the closest tech to them and took off to where I'd told them to go.

As I hurried into my room, my heart nearly broke in two. The smell of feces was damn near overpowering. These shifters had been broken, humiliated, and experimented on, and my stomach roiled with disgust.

What's wrong? Killian linked. *Did you run into an issue?*

Calling *this* an issue would be a true understatement. *I didn't expect the smell of urine and poop.* The familiar anger I kept at bay curled inside, sitting heavy like lead.

I breathed through my mouth to keep the horror at bay, but it didn't help. I ran to the first cage, where a man who was larger than the others stood protectively in front. He bared his teeth, and his light amber eyes narrowed with suspicion. "What do you want now? Haven't you done enough?"

A lump formed in my throat. Why would he think I was here to hurt him? He should have recognized me as a fellow wolf shifter.

Lifting my hands in surrender, I jiggled the keys. "I'm here to get you out."

Someone gasped behind him, sounding full of hope, and murmurs came from the other two cages on my right. I kept my attention on Amber Eyes. He was either their alpha or a wolf strong enough to protect his pack members. Either way, he deserved respect.

They all did.

His forehead wrinkled, and if he'd had eyebrows, they would've furrowed. "Is this a trick?" He sniffed, and his face twisted in even more agony.

He couldn't smell me. A deep pain stabbed my chest, and I wasn't one of the affected. I could only imagine what they were going through, living like this. It ended now.

"It's not a joke." Not wanting to waste any more time, I

kept my hands raised and hurried to the lock of the cage. "On the paranormal den's intranet, a Knoxville moving company shifter owner posted about two of his younger helpers not coming in to work. He dropped your pack's address, and several of us went to your place to determine what happened to you because we'd just rescued another wolf pack that had been held captive." I wanted to ease their fear by explaining how we'd gotten here.

Amber Eyes' face smoothed, and some of his distrust vanished. "But how did you find us?"

I slid key after key into the lock, searching for the one that fit. "Friends of ours performed a location spell." I didn't want to say too much in case the rooms were being monitored beyond the people who were here.

A key clicked into place, and I opened the cage door. The group inched forward. I could only assume that the hope of freedom was overpowering whatever little mistrust of me was left.

Killian linked with our entire pack here, *Sterlyn, Griffin, Cyrus, Levi, and Rosemary are here. They're going to pick up the freed shifters at the parking lot by the trail we walked the other day. Tell everyone, and get someone to help them there. There are four buses.*

Moving out of the way and hurrying to the next cage, I said, "Go down the hallway and out the door. The guards are knocked out. Take the elevator or the stairs to the first floor. Someone will lead you to the pickup location. Follow their steps exactly, because there are traps out there."

Amber Eyes nodded and stepped from the cage, waving his people on. "You heard her. Go! I'll be there shortly."

Either they realized they could trust me or that it didn't matter. If they detected a slight chance of freedom, they'd take it.

"Wait!" I shouted as I slid the key into the next cage's lock. "There are dragons, an angel, and demons out there. Demons you might not be able to see, but they are on our side. All of them are allies. You can trust them." Most supernaturals, including me before I'd met Sterlyn and the others, hadn't been around other types of supernaturals.

"Dragons? Angels? *Demons*?" the younger shifter from that cage parroted. She was half my height, but I couldn't gauge her age with the condition she was in. Judging by her voice, she was seven or eight. "I thought they weren't real."

Any other time, I would have bent down and comforted her, but getting her out of *here* was the priority. "I'll tell you all about it later, but I need you to trust me." I tried to make my voice soft and reassuring while remaining firm.

She bobbed her head as I opened the cage to the second set of shifters. The woman with kind sage-colored eyes rushed toward the smaller girl. She wrapped her arms around her, pulling her into her chest. "You heard the nice lady. Let's get going."

Their musky cinnamon scents were so similar that they had to be family. As the girl burrowed her head into Sage Eyes' chest, she murmured, "Mama," confirming my thoughts.

"Go!" I hated to ruin the moment, but our time was running out.

Footsteps pounded the hallways as the shifters were let out. I hurried to the third cage and glanced over my shoulder, only to see actual wolves running past the door. *They can shift?* Hope surged through me, warming the cold tendrils of fear that had constricted my heart.

No, they were wolves when I got in here. I don't think they can shift back, Killian replied, his fear growing and cooling the hope that had momentarily lifted my soul.

So one room had people who had lost their hair and senses while the other room had shifters stuck in their animal form. Even if I hadn't believed in coincidences, this was something that couldn't be ignored.

With each cage I opened, the shifters scurried out without hesitation.

"I'm clear in here!" Axel shouted.

"Same!" Eliza and Aurora responded in unison.

How is everything over there? Killian linked with our pack members in the other building. *Was Stephanie able to help you?*

Lowe replied, *Yes, she did. We're getting everyone out. We have a slight problem, though.*

Of course, with things going relatively easily, there had to be a problem.

Stephanie wants to go with us. She's a shifter and has been working here to figure out what they're doing so she can reverse it, Lowe continued.

That was a *good* problem to have as long as we could trust her. *Do you think she's sincere?*

I do, Lowe replied, sounding strange. *Uh...I feel a strange connection to her, and I don't want to leave her.*

Through our fated-mate connection, Killian's distrust felt like a noose around my neck.

I understood not wanting to take her, but Lowe had never acted like this while I'd been around. And I wondered if this lab tech could be his fated mate. If she was, he'd refuse to leave her behind. I linked solely to Killian, *We should let her come with us.*

What? His surprise slammed into me.

Spinning on my heels, I turned to find Amber Eyes walking through the door. When he saw Britney, he stopped in his tracks.

I hurried toward him, wanting to end whatever confrontation might go down. *Because these shifters need medical help, and my family and friends back at Sterlyn's childhood pack home need help. We'll have people watching her at all times, but Killian, if she's willing to help us, she'll know what they've done and how to reverse it.*

His surprise changed into acceptance. *You're right.* He admitted Lowe back into our conversation. *Bring her, but keep an eye on her. Do you understand?*

Of course. We'll be heading out soon, Lowe answered.

"You," Amber Eyes murmured.

As I stepped into the hallway, I found everyone outside their respective rooms, with Zagan standing between Bleu and Britney.

"I'm so sorry—" she started, but her own quiet sob cut her off.

"No, don't apologize. You're the only reason Suzy got better last night," Amber Eyes replied, his voice thick with emotion.

Clearly, this woman had been trying to help before we'd come. I hated to ruin the moment, but we had no choice. "Backup will be arriving, and we need to go."

Killian nodded. "Aurora and Eliza, can you handle these two so we don't have to knock them out, but also make it look like they didn't help us?"

"We can put them to sleep." Eliza lifted her hands. "If you don't want to fall, lie down on the floor."

The two of them obeyed and were smart enough to make their bodies lie haphazardly. The two witches lifted their hands, their palms facing Bleu and Britney, and said, "*Dormiant.*"

Within seconds, the guard was snoring, and Britney's breathing steadied.

Of course, that was when Bleu's walkie-talkie went off, and a deep male voice said, "We're five minutes out."

A lump formed in my throat. This was exactly what had happened last time. I could only pray this backup didn't include other supernaturals, but at least they wouldn't expect dragons.

"You all go on," Zagan gestured to the hallway door. "We'll stay here in shadow form and destroy the lab."

Though we'd destroyed the last lab and they'd still been able to pick up where they'd left off, it would be harder for them to start testing again immediately. "Just be careful."

Zagan winked. "Always." He sobered. "Make sure Eleanor gets out of here."

"Of course, man," Axel said as he clapped Zagan on the back. Then Zagan flickered back into shadow form, and Axel stumbled back.

"Where did he go?" Amber Eyes rasped.

"He's in demon shadow form. Remember, I warned you," I replied and gestured for Eliza and Aurora to go.

Axel and Amber Eyes hurried after them, with Killian and me taking up the back. Killian linked with our pack, informing them about what was going on, but they'd also heard from a nearby walkie-talkie.

Luckily, Herne and Lux had been able to wake the shifters on the other side, and everyone was evacuating the other building as well, but they were moving slowly. We'd have to hold off the new arrivals heading toward us.

We ran down the hallway and into the lobby. The last few shifters were heading down the stairs. They were limping and not in the best physical health. There was no telling what they'd gone through, but I didn't blame them for opting for the stairs instead of the elevator. I wouldn't want to risk getting trapped inside another cage.

We caught up to the last few people, and I fought the urge to tell them to hurry. Panic would only create more fear and possibly cause them to fall.

I hadn't needed to employ my calming mechanism as often since meeting Killian, but this evacuation had my anxiety levels peaking, so I played Massenet's "Meditation" from *Thaïs* in my head, focusing on the violin section, which spoke to me in a way very little operatic music did.

When Aurora and Eliza stepped through the door and we could see the garage, my heart lightened. Maybe we could get out of here before the backup arrived.

As Amber Eyes and Axel hurried through the garage, Eleanor wobbled out from behind the column with Martha, Roxy, and Lillith. Nodding, they hurried toward the opening to the outside. If we could reach the tree line before the vehicles got here, we should be free.

But then all eight dragons roared, followed by April linking with our pack, *We have incoming! They're here.*

CHAPTER TWENTY-ONE

I COULDN'T HEAR any vehicles. My heart pounded, and combined with the trampling footsteps ahead and my almost nonexistent angel magic, it hindered my senses.

Then I heard the thrumming of helicopters, and I stumbled over my feet.

That had to be them.

How many helicopters? I asked April. She was the only eyes my pack had outside.

After a pause, she answered, *Two, but I hear other vehicles coming, too.*

They were attacking by land and air. The dragons should be able to help, but I feared we'd suffer casualties on our side.

We'd never trained for an attack from above.

Get the shifters into the woods as quickly as possible, Killian commanded as he picked up his pace. *The trees are our best protection.*

But it was also winter, and half the trees were leafless. We'd still be decent targets running through the area. It would be best if we could shift, but the captives would struggle with that.

Roxy's face paled as she exhaled shakily and ran to Axel.

"What's going on?" Eleanor asked as she limped toward us. "It's pure chaos. And where's Zagan?"

"He's inside, destroying the lab, but he's fine." We could've used the demons with the helicopters, but they should be back with us soon. "People are arriving via car and helicopter to attack us."

"I'll help with the helicopters." Eleanor spread her wings and flapped them, but she didn't take flight. She kept trying, but her timing seemed off.

I'd opened my mouth to tell her to stop when Killian linked, *Babe, I don't like her flying injured, either, but one thing I've learned through Rosemary: if an angel is determined to help and you tell them not to, they'll only snap at you.*

I swallowed hard. He was right. I did the same thing when I was hurt but determined to help. You couldn't change anyone's mind once it was set.

Eleanor lifted off the ground and slowly flew out of the garage.

"Come on," Killian said as he grabbed my arm. "We've gotta get out of here and see what's happening."

The scene was like an apocalyptic movie where a fantasy world and the modern world collided. Two black helicopters flew in low with four soldiers stationed on each side, two behind automatic weapons and two with rifles. From the helicopters alone, we had sixteen fighters with guns, and the majority of us couldn't fight them.

Four dragons attacked one helicopter and three the

other. Flames poured from their mouths, but the dragons couldn't get too close with the guns shooting at them.

The vampires had taken cover in the brush and were shooting at the helicopters, but they couldn't fire frequently due to the dragons.

April linked with us, *There are ten Suburbans heading this way.*

If they held the same numbers as earlier, that meant we were facing sixty additional fighters. There was no telling if more were behind them or if they had supernatural allies in the woods.

"There are ten Suburbans," I murmured, ensuring Lillith, Roxy, Eliza, Aurora, and Axel were aware of the incoming threat. Though they had Katherine out there on their side, they couldn't link with her.

Something blurred from the tree line, racing toward the sky. It flew fast, and I couldn't tell what sort of creature it was. I swallowed hard, hoping it wouldn't attack our dragon allies. When the creature stopped and hovered, I saw that it was a small dragon. It breathed fire on one of the automatic riflemen, and he screamed.

Whatever type of dragon it was, it appeared to be on our side.

Tearing my attention away, I focused on what was in front of me. Most of the captives were following a trail of rocks that someone had left while we were inside, showing the way toward the tree line without getting caught in a trap.

Whoever had done that deserved a freaking medal.

Our problem, though, was that captives were still evacuating the other building. They were moving slowly and seemed groggy, confirming they'd had to be awakened by

Herne and Lux like my grandparents' pack. They stumbled every few steps. We had to hold the Suburbans off.

Some of us need to shift, I linked with Killian, wanting him to make the official call with the pack. We had backup clothing at the house, and if I knew Sterlyn, she'd sent enough clothes for anyone who ripped through theirs to find something to wear until we made it home. *It's the best way to stop the vehicles since we can sprint faster in that form.*

Dread pooled through our bond as the weight of the situation hit us hard.

Fine, I'll tell them to shift, but I need you to lead them while I tell the vampires to help us fight the vehicles. We need Eleanor, the demons, and the dragons to attack the helicopters while we focus on the enemy on the ground.

My chest expanded, and butterflies took flight in my stomach. He was asking me to lead our pack and trusting my instincts instead of asking me to run and hide. This was all I'd ever wanted, but the weight of the responsibility settled hard on my shoulders.

He needed me, and I couldn't shy away from it. *Okay. Just be safe.* I hated to think of him running into the trees where the helicopter men were firing, but they were focused on the dragons instead of us.

As promised, Killian linked with the pack, *Everyone who isn't helping the captives flee, shift and be ready to fight the Suburbans under Jewel's lead. We have to hold them off long enough for the captives to break free.*

Five of us are helping the captives, Troy replied. *I'm one of them.*

That meant thirteen from our pack could help fight.

Torak sent twenty of his pack members to intercept the vehicles. We'll be there shortly, Sierra linked. *The rest of Torak's pack is helping the captives to the buses.*

Killian darted across the driveway toward the brush the vampires were using as cover, and part of me wanted to chase after him. Gunshots rang out everywhere, especially in that area as the guards attempted to hit the dragons. But he needed me to lead the pack, and I had to let him do what he needed.

"What the hell is he doing?" Roxy rasped.

"Getting the vampires. Come on, we need to head off the vehicles. I'm going to shift so I can run faster and coordinate with my pack members. Eliza and Aurora, please get there as quickly as you can. We could use your magic if things go south." I refocused. *The shifters with me will take cover in the woods on the left while the rest of you stay to the right and head down the road. The farther away we can cut them off, the better for getting the captives to safety.*

Tugging at my wolf, I propelled her forward in my mind. My body changed as my spine transitioned to all fours. My clothes ripped from my body as I transformed into a wolf.

"Sadie and Donovan are heading over, and we're going to come with you," Axel bellowed, his voice almost a growl.

I turned my head to find him half-shifted and quickly conforming to four paws, with Roxy just a few seconds behind him.

Though shifting would make it harder to communicate, it was the best bet we had.

Sadie ran toward us, her eyes wide and her rose-gold bob flying everywhere. Her mate was already in wolf form at her feet as she ran toward the witches. She stopped and opened her arms. "When we were scouting, I made sure to follow the road so if I needed to teleport anywhere, I could visualize it in my mind. Let me take you both a mile up. It sounds like they're still a few miles out, and that will help us get there at the same time as Jewel and the others."

Before, Sadie had seemed hesitant, but now a lot more was at stake. Though she looked tired, it wasn't a long distance, but it wasn't my call to make.

"Let's do it." Aurora nodded and lifted her chin.

Eliza smoothed down her flowy brown shirt, looking less certain. "I'm—" She blew out a breath. "Fine. Let's just do it."

That was enough for me. I didn't want my pack or the witches to get there long before I did.

Unable to communicate verbally with the others anymore, I ran toward the left tree line.

I'm right behind you, Lowe linked to me, and I heard Donovan, Roxy, Axel, and a few other paws giving chase.

Using the marginal amount of angel magic running through my veins, I tried to pick up my pace. It didn't help much, and a few of the normal wolves kept up with me, though not all.

Emmy and Darrell came racing from the trees on the right, and for a second, I wished I could tell them to stay put, but I suspected it wouldn't change their decision.

I ran between a red cedar and an oak, enjoying the feel of the woodsy ground. Wolves weren't made to run on cement, and being in nature eased some of the worry in my soul.

I glanced back. No one else had joined us, so we only had seven on this side. The other eleven from Killian's and my pack would be on the right side.

No animals were stirring, the helicopters and dragons having likely scared them into hiding. The almost new moon rose, barely giving off any light, which helped our side since humans struggled to see at night.

The thrumming of the engines grew louder. They'd be upon us in minutes. I focused on the pack bonds. Nothing of concern was wafting through Killian's and my connection. He hadn't been hurt...yet.

I'm heading your way, Killian linked. *The vampires should catch up with you momentarily.*

His tug on our connection was like a life vest saving me from drowning. Though I hadn't felt pain from him, communicating with him meant he was definitely still alive.

Okay. Let our group head out in front and hold them off. Everyone on the right side, get ready to attack, I commanded. *You'll know when it's time.*

The first Suburban came into view, the others close behind. Now we stopped them.

I threw my head back and howled, wanting them to hear how close we were, and then I ran through the red cedars onto the road in front of them. Emmy and Darrell were right behind me, realizing what I was planning to do—create a distraction so the other wolf shifters could attack.

Though I'd intended to do this alone, everyone knew wolves traveled in packs, and our silver fur matched perfectly, making us appear more pack-like.

As expected, the first Suburban slowed when Lowe, Roxy, Donovan, and Axel hurried from the tree line as well. My chest seized as I feared that Lillith would follow suit, but my lungs began to work again when she stayed put.

In wolf form, we must not have seemed as threatening to them, especially since they undoubtedly had guns.

The Suburban stopped, and I kept my attention locked on the ten vehicles I could now see. The passenger door of the first one opened, and a woman in the familiar all-black guard suit appeared.

I had to blink to make sure it wasn't an illusion. *Savannah* was standing in front of me.

My knees buckled, so it was a great thing I was in wolf form. At least the humans wouldn't be able to see that. *Savannah is part of this group. Did anyone know that?*

No, Killian replied. *I'll talk to Sterlyn.*

Savannah flicked her eyes around the trees as she said, "Look what we have here, boys. I'm finally ready to get my revenge after being held captive. They should've killed me before I got away."

I crouched and bared my teeth, making it clear we wouldn't be moving. If we ran, they'd continue to the building and see the captives escaping. Savannah must have thought we were trying to get away, and I had no way to tell her otherwise besides standing my ground.

The back doors opened, and two guards climbed out, guns raised. The thicker guard rasped, "If that's a shifter, their human side must be dormant to be standing in front of guns like this."

Little did they know my heart was pounding.

Jewel, what's the plan? Lowe linked, his terror seeping through the pack link.

I couldn't scold him for his discomfort; my own skin was crawling. More guards got out of the vehicles, and none of them had tranquilizer guns. *When they attack us, everyone in the woods jump out.*

I almost winced, waiting for Killian to scold me. When he linked with me, his fear was high. *They didn't know she'd be here.*

Shit, then they likely had guards looking for the buses.

"What are you doing?" Savannah murmured low enough that only wolf shifters could hear. "You need to go."

I shook my head slightly so she would understand—no.

"What are we waiting for?" The guard behind her stepped forward, his weapon aimed at my head. "Let's go."

Now! I linked, spinning on my heels and crashing into Lowe. If I hadn't done that, the bullet would've hit him since he was standing directly behind me. It nicked my leg, the sharp sting burning through me, but it wasn't fatal, thank gods.

Lillith blurred over and yanked the gun from the thicker guard's hands, then smacked him on the head. He fell as the wolves on the right side of the road joined us. They charged the other guards, attacking them with vigor.

I leaned onto my back paws, the sting uncomfortable but nothing I couldn't handle. Gods knew I'd experienced way worse.

Something materialized beside me.

Sadie, Aurora, and Eliza.

Maybe things would be all right.

But Fate had to be laughing, because as soon as I thought that, Aurora and Eliza dropped to their knees and vomited.

Lovely, but we'd be okay.

More guards climbed out of the SUVs, and I pushed myself hard to reach them. *Anyone who's free, attack the people in the back.*

Emmy and Darrell caught up and flanked me. The three of us were in sync despite not being able to link. We'd all had the same training, and hell, Darrell had been one of my main trainers growing up. We'd better think similarly.

"Get them," a lanky guard from the last SUV yelled as he aimed his weapon at us.

As if by mutual agreement, the three of us ran in the zigzag pattern Dad had drilled into us. The point was to make our movements look random.

But when all ten of them trained their guns on us, I knew it was only a matter of time before we got injured or worse. Lanky Guard and the man beside him aimed at me while others focused on Darrell and Emmy.

Right when I slowed to change direction, hoping to disorient them, Lanky Guard anticipated the move, and his finger twitched.

A gunshot rang out, and I closed my eyes, preparing to meet the end. I linked with Killian, *I love you*, and waited.

CHAPTER TWENTY-TWO

A LOUD GROAN SOUNDED, and I opened my eyes to see Lanky Guard with a bullet hole between his eyes. His body dropped against the Suburban, and the guard beside him jerked his head around and lowered his gun.

We're here, Killian linked, his terror mingling with mine and nearly strangling me.

I didn't have time to pause, so I rushed to the second guard.

Just in time, he continued as I lunged, aiming for the man's throat.

His eyes bulged, and he tried to lift his arm, but my teeth sank into his neck and pierced his artery. Blood spluttered in my mouth, and my stomach roiled at the metallic taste. I hated the taste of blood and, more than that, killing.

But death was part of war.

Not wanting to dwell on it, I released my jaws and dropped back to all fours. The guard's body hit the cement hard, and I spun around, looking for my next target.

Thankfully, the vampires were here and shooting at the guards, causing them to retreat into the cars. Since we were attacking in wolf form, we were shorter than the humans, and the vampires could shoot at their targets more easily.

The guards on the passenger side of my Suburban hurried back into the vehicle, and the driver shifted into reverse.

I pounced into the open back door and landed in the middle-row captain seat. Luckily, only five people were in this vehicle, and two of them were dead. *I need backup when someone can get here. I'm inside the last vehicle.*

"Shit!" the guard next to me yelled as he swung his gun toward me, but I didn't pause.

Claws tearing into the leather, I slashed his cheeks, digging in deep. Crying out, he dropped his gun and kicked at me, then grabbed his face.

The driver punched the gas, while the guard in the front passenger seat twisted around and aimed his weapon at me. I used the backseat guard's chest to push off and pounce on him. I bit his shoulder and swatted at the hand that held the gun. Then something hard gripped the back of my neck. The hand yanked on the skin, pulling me off the guard.

It was the driver.

Before he could pull me too far away, I dug my claws into the guard in the front passenger seat for leverage and threw my entire body into the driver. My head hit his nose, and bones cracked.

His grip on my neck slipped, and the Suburban swerved.

Get out of the car, Killian linked, his panic slamming through me.

I glanced out the front windshield in time to see we were rushing into a tree.

"Whoa!" the guard in the passenger seat yelled as he

reached across the center console and my body. He was more worried about grabbing the steering wheel than fighting me.

The hairs on my neck rose as I instinctively turned toward the back seat just in time to see Backseat Guard aim his gun at my head again.

I'd taken my attention off him for too long.

Tensing, I dove to the back floorboard just as the vehicle crashed. My body jolted hard into the back driver's-side door, causing pain to explode through me, and then the impact had me tumbling toward my enemy. I whimpered, unable to hold back the sound.

Heart pounding, I forced myself to focus on my surroundings. The guard who'd aimed at me was unconscious, blood trickling down his face.

Jewel, Killian linked, cold thrumming through our bond from her fear.

I shook my head, trying to get my thoughts together so I could respond, but before I could, the door next to me opened.

Everything in my mind yelled at me to move, but my body didn't respond.

Strong, familiar arms wrapped around me and pulled me into a muscular chest that smelled like home.

Killian.

The guards, I replied weakly, not wanting to leave his arms. The buzz of our connection sprang to life, diminishing some of the pain twisting inside me. I could see over his shoulder where the Suburban had hit a large oak tree. No wonder the impact had been so jerky.

The other vehicle doors opened just as Killian replied, *I brought backup*.

I laid my head against his shoulder, not caring that if a

human looked at us right now, they'd see a man hugging a wolf.

Humans.

I wriggled down and dropped to all fours, wincing from the agony in my side. Though I hadn't broken any bones, I was most definitely bruised. *We need to help the others.*

No. Eliza and Aurora have recovered. The vampires have shot out the tires. Sadie is using her beams, and the wolves handled the majority of the guards while you were enjoying your car ride, he replied.

When I looked at his face, I expected to see anger or annoyance, but instead, I only found relief. His irises were his normal brown color, and though his eyes were tense in the corners, it was his usual expression when facing dangerous situations. Most important, he wasn't glaring daggers at me. *You're not mad?* As soon as I asked, I wished I hadn't. If he hadn't realized he should be mad, I'd just given him permission to be unhappy.

He arched his brow. *About you jumping into the vehicle alone?*

I wanted to hang my head. Not because I'd done something wrong or wasn't strong but because I wouldn't have been happy if he'd made the same call. *Yeah.*

I'm not happy, but I understand why you did it. If they'd gotten away, more vehicles could have left and regrouped to come back with a better strategy. He shrugged. *So I'm not mad. Just wish that it had been me instead.*

That I could understand.

"Come on." Killian nodded toward the facility. "We need to check on everyone and see if the dragons, Eleanor, and the demons need our help with the helicopters."

The sounds of the engines echoed his words.

We needed to get the hell out of here before someone else showed up. I wasn't up for another battle.

Joshua stepped around the hood of the vehicle and lifted the keys. "They were knocked out in the wreck, so we're good to move. We're grabbing the keys and hiding their guns in the woods."

I trotted beside Killian as we hurried back on the narrow cement road. The other vehicles had their doors open, and there were numerous guards passed out on the road.

Savannah stood in front of the first vehicle with her arms crossed. Her forehead was wrinkled. She opened her mouth just as her walkie-talkie went off and a frantic male voice yelled, "We're going down. Mayday! Mayday!"

Sierra stood in wolf form a few feet away next to Torak. She linked, *I thought they only said that in movies. They say that in real life?*

A deafening explosion rattled the ground, almost as if someone were trying to prove to Sierra that this was real life and not a movie.

My heart stopped. Had someone on our side been hurt in the crash? I had to go check.

"Someone knock me out," Savannah shouted. "I need to look the same as the others, or they'll know something's up."

"It might be best if we erase your memory," Joshua started.

"No. I've been racking my brain, trying to remember what happened while I was *missing*. I don't want that again. Besides, you might need my help on the inside so no more people die on *either* side."

"Just knock her out." Killian sprinted toward the facility. "We've got to *go*."

Not wanting to be left behind, I took off, staying next to Killian.

"Fine," Joshua grunted, and I heard a loud *whack*. When a body hit the ground, I didn't have to guess who that might be.

Everyone in our group raced back toward the facility. The vampires sped past us, using their supernatural speed, while the rest of the wolf shifters ran together.

Since Killian was in human form, he was running more slowly with Eliza, Aurora, and Sadie. I didn't want to leave them or my mate behind, so I slowed to the back of the wolves.

Darrell and Emmy peeled away from the group, no doubt using the slight extra jolt of angel magic to increase their pace.

My paws hit the pavement, feeling unnatural. I yearned for the soft mulch of the woodland floor, but this straight shot would get us to the facility sooner. I kept my hearing attuned to our surroundings, listening for any sounds of an incoming threat from air or ground.

Smoke trickled up from the helicopter crash site, dark and thick even in the night sky. The smell burned the back of my throat.

Memories of my grandparents' burning pack neighborhood surfaced in my mind—the choking sensation of soot in our lungs and how we'd lost Heather. All the losses hung heavy on my heart and mind, threatening to pull me under.

As the facility came into view, so did the dragons, wolves, and Eleanor. But one thing didn't make any sense. I linked, *Where are the demons?*

Chasing after the second helicopter to make sure it doesn't circle back, Lowe answered. Someone else must have asked the same question. *We're heading to the buses. The demons are going to meet us back in Shadow Ridge.*

"Are all the freed shifters secured?" Killian asked, slightly out of breath from the fast jog.

Eleanor nodded. "I watched the last of them get out of here unharmed."

"What about Mom and Chad?" I needed to make sure they were okay. I couldn't lose the last two members of my family who were tied to Dad.

"They led the shifters to Sterlyn's group at the buses," Killian answered, and pushed the warmth of his reassurance to me. *Sterlyn informed me, but I got distracted while you were in danger. I'm sorry.*

That didn't matter. They were safe. *It's fine. Thank you for checking.*

"Then we have no reason to stay," Sadie said as she hurried to the rock trail that led out of the woods. "And I don't have much magic left to teleport or use my beams."

Our group took off, eager to get away from the facility. The helicopter fire continued to grow.

The dragons and Eleanor flew high into the sky so if a human noticed them, they would resemble large birds, but they stayed close enough to keep an eye on things.

Eliza was breathing hard, so Killian, Darrell, Emmy, and I slowed to stay with the older lady. She still moved more quickly than a human due to the magic that blessed her blood.

When the trees thickened around us, some of the tension eased from my body, but not enough to fully relax. Every time I thought things were getting better, Fate proved me wrong, so I stayed wary.

Sterlyn informed me that the buses are moving out. All the captives are loaded, and a police car was spotted driving past them, Killian linked with the rest of the pack. *All our vehicles are at the cabin, but we need to get back to Shadow Ridge. Let's pack up and head out.*

The police car must have arrived in response to the helicopter crash and fire. Good thing we were gone. And I was ready to go home, even though the cabin was so nice.

Killian repeated the information out loud for the witches and the wolves who weren't part of our pack. That picked up everyone's pace.

Even when the huge staircase to the cabin came into view, my heartbeat didn't truly steady. It wasn't until we'd all shifted back, changed, and loaded into our vehicles that my breathing leveled out.

Now we had another issue to resolve: getting enough resources for the captives since they couldn't return home. The witches were occupying the finished houses from the second silver wolf backup location, and my grandparents' pack and Ruby's pack had taken all the houses in Sterlyn's childhood pack neighborhood. These wolf shifters would have to live in the unfinished homes and in the woods in the backup location. Sadie and her friends would stay with the captives there, especially since Torak knew one pack well.

Emmy, Torak, and Sierra were riding in the truck with us back to Shadow City. Sierra was stuck in the middle, but she had her head on Torak's shoulder while their hands were intertwined.

For once, Sierra wasn't the agitator.

"Seriously, Sierra. Jewel refuses to tell me *anything*," Emmy said loudly. "I keep asking questions, but she's tight-lipped because Killian is her *mate*."

I rolled my eyes at my best friend's antics. I loved her tremendously, but there were certain things I'd never expected to not want to discuss. When we'd agreed to divulge everything once one of us had gained experience, I hadn't understood I wouldn't want to because it was something sacred between mates. Maybe I'd have felt differently if I'd slept with someone before him, but talking about Killian *like that* disrespected our relationship.

"What?" Sierra gasped. "What do you wanna know, girl? I got you."

Now Emmy was the one who sputtered. She hadn't expected Sierra to be so accommodating. "Uh..."

Killian cut his eyes to me and pursed his lips. Confusion swirled through our bond.

Great. He didn't realize what Emmy was asking about, so I'd make it clear for everyone. It might teach Emmy a lesson. "She wants to know what sex is like."

"*Oh.*" Sierra coughed. "Uh..."

My mouth dropped open. I'd expected Sierra to know. She was so confident and so big on sexual innuendos and obsessed with chick flicks. I'd just assumed she was experienced.

"Wait," Torak's voice cracked. "Are you a virgin?"

"Hey!" Sierra shouted, and I turned around to watch her wield her finger. She poked Torak's chest and straightened her shoulders. "I may not have *actual* experience, but I'm amazing with my hand and a glass of wine!"

Torak's head tilted back as Killian groaned.

"For the love of gods, Sierra. I don't want to hear that shit." Killian folded into himself as if he had a bad image in his mind. "You're like my sister, for fuck's sake."

Emmy's cheeks were bright red. She hadn't counted on Sierra taking the conversation further than she'd imagined it could go.

Tapping a finger to her lips, Sierra averted her gaze to

the ceiling of the truck. "I've always wondered. Is it for fuck's sake singular, or fucks' sake plural?"

I grinned, unable to prevent myself from jumping in. "It depends whether it's one fuck or multiple fucks."

Sierra's eyes bulged as if I'd solved the biggest riddle in the world. "So Killian only has one. I hope for you his one move makes it worthwhile." She winked.

And I wanted to die. Somehow, she'd turned that around on me, and I'd gotten burned. Karma was a bitch. I'd set Emmy up, and I'd wound up falling alongside her.

"What just happened?" Torak blinked. "I learned she's a virgin, and in the next breath, she's talking about another guy's moves."

"First off. Move. Singular. He has one fuck. And see." Sierra pounded her chest. "I don't need experience to know what to do. You'll see."

Killian pinched the bridge of his nose while Torak beamed.

And I smiled, enjoying a peaceful moment.

All too soon, we pulled into Shadow Ridge. The odd sensation that I wasn't thrilled to be here shocked me. I'd been desperate to get back, but an uneasiness had settled over us as we'd coasted closer to our home.

Downtown seemed the same. We'd missed Christmas while we'd been freeing the captives, and though supernaturals didn't celebrate human holidays, the stores were brimming with humans and cell phone videographers all around. Demon attacks were growing more frequent, and humans were attracted to either the fear or the thrill of being close to death.

Now that we were home, we'd need to gather blankets, pillows, and other supplies we could spare and take them to the backup silver wolf neighborhood for the freed wolves. Sterlyn had informed Killian that the lab tech who'd left with us was making a list of items we needed to determine how to resolve the shifters' issues. Apparently, the girl had contacted her pack and told them to find temporary shelter elsewhere, knowing the government would come searching for her. She didn't want her family caught in the crosshairs.

We coasted into our pack neighborhood, and my attention landed on Killian's and my home. A woman stood in front of Sterlyn and Griffin's white house, which was next door. She appeared to be in her twenties, but she had an ageless quality about her.

Her waist-length, deep-forest-brown hair framed her face and brought out the twinkle in her coffee-brown eyes, making her seem mischievous. She wore all black, similar to Sterlyn but more formal, including a black dress, black tights, and black heels, with her lips painted the same shade as if to blend in with the night.

"Who is that?" Emmy asked as she leaned forward. "I haven't seen her around before."

"I haven't, either," Killian said as he pulled into our driveway. "But we're going to find out."

As soon as the truck turned off, the five of us got out. I was on the side closest to the stranger, so I marched toward her while Killian jogged around the hood, catching up.

Goodness radiated from this woman's essence, and then her herbal-jasmine scent made everything click into place.

She was a witch, and not from Eliza's coven.

Unlike me, Killian smiled and asked, "Can we help you with something?"

"I'm looking for Griffin and Sterlyn." The woman

licked her lips. "Do you, by chance, know where I can find them? My aunt sent me here."

"Your aunt?" I had a feeling the answer would tell me everything.

The woman shifted her feet. "Yes, I'm Breena. My aunt is Erin."

Then it clicked. She was a Shadow City witch. "They aren't here right now, so you'll have to come back later."

Breena shook her head. "I...I can't. For your sake and mine. My aunt...she'll ask questions, and I can't lie, or she'll know."

Sierra laughed and marched up beside me. She placed a hand on her hip. "Do you think we were born yesterday? There's no way you're trying to help us, so quit the act and leave."

"I—" Breena stopped and exhaled.

Killian stepped forward, his jaw twitching. "Now hold on, and listen to me."

CHAPTER TWENTY-THREE

WHEN KILLIAN TURNED to the side so he could address Sierra and Breena, I was confused. I'd expected him to tell Breena where she could go.

But I couldn't get over the pureness she radiated. It was drastically different from what I'd sensed from Erin, and if I hadn't heard her admit she was the niece of that evil tyrant, I wouldn't have believed it.

"Sterlyn asked that you stay here. She and Griffin will arrive shortly." Killian wrinkled his nose and linked to me, *This doesn't make sense.*

Did you ask Sterlyn why? The last thing any of us wanted was a witch from Shadow City near us for longer than necessary.

She said she's on her way and to ask Emmy and Darrell to gather the supplies and take them over. Killian's hands clenched. "Emmy, can you handle that thing?"

"Yeah, sure," Emmy replied, but I recognized her tone. She'd do what she'd been asked, but she didn't want to leave our side.

I couldn't blame her. I'd feel the same way, but we both

knew they wanted only a handful of people to know about the silver wolf backup location, and Emmy was one of the few who already knew. It made sense to send her.

She brushed past me, and our eyes connected. She tilted her head, conveying everything in that one move—that I better not hesitate to call her if I needed her.

I gave her a slight nod, and she exhaled then hurried toward her house.

Other vehicles carrying our pack members went by, each one heading home. I could feel the stares of each shifter driving past.

Killian gave the pack a brief update, though he didn't specify which coven Breena was from. No one asked, which was a blessing. I doubted they'd handle the news any better than Sierra was.

"I promise I'm not here to cause problems." Breena rubbed her chest and bit her bottom lip. "It's just...Erin thinks you guys are up to something, and she asked me to check things out. I don't want to head back and tell her you weren't here. That would only make her more certain, and... I don't want that to happen. Things are already bad enough."

"Oh, please." Sierra lifted a hand. "Don't act like you're on our side." She turned to Torak. "She's part of the witch coven inside Shadow City who think only of themselves."

"Sierra," Killian warned. "You need to calm down. Sterlyn asked her to wait. Why don't you go home or take a walk to cool off?"

She huffed and gritted her teeth, ready to argue again.

Though I loved Sierra, she sometimes let her emotions get the best of her common sense.

Torak took her hand and nodded toward the neighborhood. "I thought you wanted me to meet your family. Let's go do that now."

Her cheeks turned pink, and she inhaled deeply. *He's trying to get me to leave so I don't keep talking, isn't he?* she linked with just me.

Times like these proved Sierra noticed more than she let on. Most people thought she was a hothead, which she was, but it wasn't because she was irrational. It was because she cared so much. I suspected being Torak's mate would make her more level-headed. *Yes, but it's a damn good excuse, and you shouldn't snap at him.*

But... Sierra forced a tight smile at him as she continued, *I don't want you all to forget who she is. You have bleeding hearts.*

I snickered, and both Breena and Killian stared at me. I hadn't meant to let that escape, but the fact that Sierra saw forgiveness as a weakness amused me. Forgiveness was harder than holding on to anger and a grudge. I linked with her, *I promise that none of us will forget who her aunt is. Just go spend time with your mate and your family. I have a feeling that your life's about to change very quickly. Just trust us...if not me, then Killian. Has he ever steered you wrong?*

Her chin trembled, and I hoped it was from the impact of my words.

Are you okay? Killian linked, his forehead lining with concern.

I deserved that question. *Sorry, it was Sierra. She was linking with me and said something that caught me off guard.*

"Sierra," Torak prodded again and intertwined their fingers, tugging on her. "Why don't we go?" He exuded confidence, except for tapping the fingertips of his free hand on his thigh.

Poor guy. He must not be certain how she would react to his intervention, but he was trying to help. If I hadn't known Sierra would comply, I'd almost feel bad for the guy.

"Fine," she growled, but she paused and pointed a finger at Breena. "But if anything happens because of you—"

"Look, I'm here because Erin pushed it, but she's going too far." Breena rubbed her hands along her arms. "I've been looking for a reason to leave the city and talk to you all, and Erin handed it to me today. She knows that out of all the Shadow City witches, I'm the likeliest to get you to trust me. Why would I admit that if I wasn't sincere?"

Sierra scoffed. "To get us to trust you, of course."

Please, Sierra, Killian linked. His frustration rang through our bond, and I knew she was pushing him too far.

I thought— I started.

Sierra lifted a hand, cutting me off. "Let's go, Torak. You're right. You should meet my family. They want to interrogate my future mate."

Fingers relaxing, Torak smirked. Then a gleam darkened his green eyes. "I'm already your *mate.* We just need to formalize it."

Maybe I'd rather she threaten Breena than listen to Torak's suggestion. Killian scowled, his sadness weighing down our bond.

Though he'd finally come to terms with them being fated mates, he wasn't looking forward to Sierra leaving our pack. I didn't blame him, but it was something she had to do, no matter how much we'd miss her.

As the two of them strolled away, I kept my attention trained on Breena. I didn't want to lose focus and have her trick us. For all we knew, she could be masking the stench of her lies, which meant we had to listen to her heartbeat and breathing for any signs of abnormality.

I touched Killian's arm to ease some of his momentary grief. *How much longer until Sterlyn is here?*

A few minutes, Killian replied. *They're turning onto the road that leads into Shadow Ridge.*

That meant when they'd heard Breena was here, they'd immediately taken off from the backup location.

"You're saying she went too far, but what does that mean? If she's your priestess and aunt, I would think you'd want to stay firmly on her side." I shrugged and leaned my head on Killian's shoulder. "But I'm new here. What do I know?"

Killian's shoulders shook enough for my head to bob slightly.

"Ask Sterlyn, Griffin, and Rosemary. I've never fully supported my aunt, but I used to believe she thought she was doing the best thing for the coven." Breena glanced at the sky. "And she's some of the only family I have left...her and my sister, Diana. They've always gotten along so much better than I have with either one of them since Mom passed." Her voice broke on the last word, and her eyes glistened with unshed tears. "I tried to believe in the story Erin told our coven, but something always felt off. I couldn't truly pinpoint what...until the past week or so."

Throughout her entire speech, I not only listened to her words and inflection but to her breathing and heartbeat. Nothing seemed out of the norm. Dad had taught us that very few people had harnessed the ability to lie by believing that whatever they said was the truth undoubtedly. It was hard to do, and most who trained to achieve it usually fell short.

She homed in on me, and our gazes locked, the two of us

searching for something within the other. If she was telling the truth, I was looking for some undeniable sign, whereas she was wondering if I believed her. My gut said to trust her. Nothing seemed amiss, but Erin was working against us, and we couldn't trust her without a solid reason. I linked to Killian, *Do you believe her?*

I don't know, he responded as he wrapped an arm around my waist. *But Sterlyn, Griffin, and Rosemary will have a better gauge than we do. I haven't been around Breena much, but I will say, when those three complain about the witches, they usually name Erin and occasionally Diana. I've never heard them talk about Breena, and if they did, it wasn't negative.*

Some hope warmed my chest. If we could find an ally among the Shadow City witches, maybe we could figure out a way to stop humans from hunting supernaturals.

Headlights flickered between the bare branches, and I looked over as Griffin's Navigator drove in our direction.

A chilly breeze picked up, and an owl hooted a mile or so away, close to the river. The reassuring sounds of animals reinforced that they didn't sense a threat.

"That's them," Killian said as the Navigator disappeared around the bend.

Silence descended until the Navigator pulled into their driveway. As soon as the engine turned off, Griffin, Sterlyn, Ronnie, Alex, Cyrus, Annie, and Eliza scurried out. Two people were missing.

I asked, "Where are Rosemary and Levi?"

My answer came with the sound of flapping wings. I looked up to see Rosemary descending beside me with Levi's shadow form floating right next to her.

Annie waved a hand at the vehicle. "There wasn't

enough room, but even if there were, it wouldn't matter. Rosemary prefers to fly."

"Being trapped in metal isn't natural...not for me." Rosemary landed gracefully and pulled her wings tightly to her body. "The sky is where an angel is meant to be."

"In fairness, that's plastic." Griffin patted the hood of the Navigator. "I wish they were still made of metal, but that changed years ago."

Oh, dear gods. She's going to get him to whine about how he wishes cars were still built like they were in the eighties, Killian complained before clearing his throat and saying out loud, "I'm thinking Breena came here for a reason."

Sterlyn took a step toward the front door. "Maybe we should go inside."

"No." Breena flinched. "I've already stayed too long, and if Erin tries to check on me, I'll feel the magic more easily out here before she can hear anything I say."

I wished I could link with Sterlyn and Griffin to get their take on Breena. Though we'd talk after she left, I'd much rather hear it now to know how to proceed when we heard what she had to say.

Eliza's lips mashed into a line. "What she said is true. It's easier to feel magic when you're outside in the elements." The older woman lifted a brow as she flicked her wrist, likely casting a spell.

At least we had another witch here to confirm whether what Breena said was true.

Shivering, Breena flinched and glared at Eliza's open palm, but she didn't say anything. Instead, she inhaled deeply as if trying to calm down or come to grips with the situation.

"Okay, then. What's going on?" Sterlyn asked as she stood between Killian and Griffin.

We formed a half circle around Breena, who stood in the center of the driveway. Alex stood closest to the Navigator with Ronnie between him and Eliza, then Annie and Cyrus with Levi on Cyrus's other side. Rosemary stood firmly next to her mate. Sterlyn, Griffin, Killian, and I stayed on Breena's other side.

Squaring her shoulders, Breena dropped her gaze to the fescue grass of the yard in front of my feet and Rosemary's. That was a submissive act for a wolf shifter, but I'd learned it wasn't viewed the same by humans. I was rather certain her action stemmed more from the guilt she was carrying for betraying her aunt and sister—if that was in truth what she was doing.

Alex scowled. "Breena, are you wasting our time? Because we're busy handling delicate matters, which is why we left the city in the first place."

I was surprised at his admittance, though he'd carefully worded his statement so it could mean almost anything, as if he were testing her.

"Oh, I *know*." Breena creased her brows. "That's why I'm here. I'm supposed to ask you where you've been...to play these games the council always does...but I'm tired of it all. I'm tired of Erin trying to force me to be more like her and mold me into this heartless bitch. So I know where you were. You were freeing the captives that Erin helped catch."

My head jerked, and I nearly stumbled back. If I hadn't been leaning on Killian for support, I might have fallen on my butt, which was saying something for a wolf shifter. I'd expected her to tell a partial truth to make us think we were on the same side, but she'd demolished any pretense among us.

I still wasn't sold that she could be trusted. Maybe that

had been the point—to shock us so we came forward with more information. *Kill...*

Don't worry. Sterlyn and Griffin don't fully trust her, either, Killian assured me, and pressed his fingers into my side, just enough for comfort.

Alex crossed his arms. "I was not on any sort of rescue mission, so you're misguided."

Batting her eyes, Ronnie shoulder-bumped Annie as she said, "And neither were we. I'm sorry if you were expecting something else."

Thankfully, three of us could say that without lying. Between setting things up for the captives and needing a few alibis, we couldn't all be at the facility. Also, Annie had stayed behind with her twins.

"I swear, everyone must think I'm an idiot." Breena stood straight with her chest out. The hint of the guilt-ridden woman from moments ago had been replaced with one who appeared far stronger than I would've expected. She lifted her chin. "I've been pushed around by my aunt for the last five years, but I'm tired of people discounting me. Yes, maybe you *three* were here, but I highly doubt anyone who didn't just speak up was here."

None of us could disagree without confirming her statement, so we were forced to remain silent, which was just as telling.

"Fine." She rubbed her palms on the front of her dress. "I'll tell you why the demon attacks are increasing."

Levi snorted. "Because the demons who chose evil love chaos. That's why. It's rather simple, but it's endearing that you think we might believe you have insider knowledge."

"It's not just that." Breena wrapped her arms around herself. "It's what finally made me realize that my aunt has gone too far—well, that and helping capture other supernaturals."

Cyrus stepped forward, tilting his head. He examined her like he was trying to piece together a puzzle. He waved a hand. "Please tell me."

She rubbed her hands together and closed her eyes like she was regaining her balance. When she opened them back up, she murmured, "She's controlling them. She started in small stages, trying to cause chaos, and gradually increased, but that's about to change now that she doesn't have Tom to help her catch more wolf shifters. She'll need a helping hand—evil demons."

Is that possible? I didn't know much about demons, but that sounded improbable. How could a witch control a demon? Something powerful would have to bind them together.

"That's highly unlikely." Eliza laughed bitterly. "You aren't spelled to hide your lies, but there has to be something strange going on. To control a demon would require a huge sacrifice. Something a mortal witch wouldn't have access to."

I frowned. If Eliza didn't believe Breena, I couldn't think of much any of us could counter with. We didn't know how magic worked the way a coven did, and I knew for a fact that everyone trusted Eliza without question.

"But she does have access to something like that." Breena gestured to Rosemary and Levi. "How else were all the residents of Shadow City able to see the demons during the war?"

A loud gasp came from Rosemary, and she clutched her chest. "No." Rosemary shook her head, her purple-mahogany hair swinging behind her. "She wouldn't *dare*."

Levi pulled her into his side to comfort her while he pleaded with Eliza, "Please tell me that's not possible."

"I..." Eliza paled. "It's actually plausible. I'd have to do some research, but you two are preordained mates, and the demons were originally created by the spell that fractured their own mating bonds. With both of you descended from archangels, your blood would definitely be powerful enough."

"Unfortunately, that makes sense." Levi's nostrils flared. "Dad, Zagan, and I have been trying to figure out why the fallen demons vanished without a trace. A few of the righteous demons who stayed behind said they didn't want to risk death and haven't done anything to help us locate them. All of a sudden, it's like they've decided not to, but we thought they just got bored and comfortable."

That also made sense, but some of them might have gotten bored and decided to act out. The timing of Breena's explanation and the attacks could be a coincidence.

"Either explanation is plausible." Sterlyn arched her brow. "We can look into that, but is there anything you can tell us to help us know whether we can trust you more immediately?"

Alex nodded. "She's right. It's not like we can storm your coven neighborhood and attack so we can destroy the blood. That could be exactly what Erin wants so she can prove we're unfit to be on the council. It might be yet another ploy to gain more leverage in Shadow City ."

"One thing we'd like to know is how you got a human to forget they knew Tom." Eliza pressed a hand to her stomach. "If you can answer that, we might be willing to trust you more."

That means a lot, coming from her, Killian linked. *Their two covens don't get along.*

I'd gathered that from the little time I'd been around them.

"I don't..." Breena lifted her head skyward as if she were searching for answers.

Eliza snorted. "I figured."

"Wait..." She trailed off as her eyes widened.

Either she'd realized something or she was afraid. I hoped like hell it was the first one.

"Wait?" Annie murmured and leaned toward Breena. "Is something wrong?" The sincerity of her concern dripped from her words and again reminded me of how good of a person she was.

"Several days ago, Erin came back from town in a hurry with a vial of blood that smelled sweet like syrup." She bounced on her heels. "We've never used vampire blood in our spells, but she hurried inside, saying she had to try a new spell. A few minutes later, she said that it worked and that she'd figured out a spell to make the human forget about you."

"Sweet-smelling blood." Ronnie turned her head toward Alex. "That would be a vampire."

"We can alter memories." Alex tugged at the collar of his button-down shirt. "So, could that work?"

"It could, and that would be easy to test. Even if it's just a small memory...like what someone had for breakfast." Eliza smirked. "And we might be able to figure out a way to use it to our advantage."

Anything that might help us get ahead of our enemies, I was all for trying.

Breena tensed and scanned the area.

I spun around, ready to confront whatever had alarmed the witch.

CHAPTER TWENTY-FOUR

I TURNED TOWARD THE STREET, expecting to see Erin. Killian's anxiety swirled through our bond, feeding off mine. My throat was so thick I couldn't swallow.

Every single one of us pivoted in that direction...except Eliza.

"Turn back around," Eliza hissed through clenched teeth. "We can't let our *guard* down."

Great, maybe this was what Breena had been working on. Eliza had admitted that she'd wanted to make the human remember us, confirming to Breena that we had been talking to him.

Rosemary frowned, but she followed Eliza's instructions. Levi kept his hand on the small of her back. When Annie, Cyrus, Alex, and Ronnie also obeyed, I did, too, but I kept an eye out in my peripheral vision.

Why are we not watching the area? I linked with Killian, hoping to get some sort of answer.

"So...you're saying you didn't leave the surrounding areas?" Breena asked in a colder voice. She wrinkled her nose as if she were disgusted by our answers. "You all scurried out of the city for no reason?"

I think Erin is checking in, Killian replied. *We can't feel their magic, so we wouldn't know.*

That didn't make me feel any better. Though Breena had suggested this could happen, I'd expected it to be more evident. Instead, being watched and not being able to tell caused a shiver to run down my spine. I tried to hold still, but I was certain my reaction would've been visible to anyone watching.

I almost felt like prey. Now I felt worse for the humans whom the demons were attacking. This must be what they'd experienced.

"The reason is none of your concern, but we didn't leave the area." Ronnie rolled her eyes and crossed her arms. "How many times are you going to ask the same question? The answer won't change."

"Fine. But why is *she* here?" Breena asked and pointed at Eliza. "This is our coven's territory, not *theirs*."

Killian stiffened and snarled, "This is not *your* territory. This is *my* pack's home. Your coven has stayed behind the walls of Shadow City for centuries while my ancestors protected *these* lands. And I say that Eliza is welcome here any time she desires. If you have a problem with it, stay inside the city."

Though it was a very inappropriate time, my body warmed. Hearing him being all alpha and commanding was *very* sexy.

Breena stepped back, her jaw dropping as if she hadn't expected such an intense scolding.

At least no one had noticed my arousal.

"Ah, love." Levi chuckled. "It smells as if Jewel likes a dominant male, just like you do."

Okay, obviously they had. My face burned, and I fought the urge to hide it. I wasn't ashamed of my desire for Killian, just that everyone knew I was turned on.

Don't let them faze you. Killian growled, and his eyes glowed. *I enjoy your reaction to me.*

Breena coughed, and her face turned slightly pink. "Um..." she stuttered before composing herself. "We were worried when all of you took off at once...like you'd learned something you might want to share with us. I just wanted to drop by and make sure nothing is wrong. But you're all here, and nothing seems out of sorts...other than the *witch* being here."

"There's one easy way to solve that problem," Ronnie offered as she stepped toward Eliza. "*You* can leave. Killian made it clear which witch is welcome."

Yanking on the sleeves of her dress, Breena stood tall. "I'm a council member the same as you, and it would be nice to have a show of mutual respect."

At that moment, I could see she wasn't the same as Erin. I couldn't make an informed comparison with Diana since I'd never met her, but I was beginning to suspect that what Breena had told us before her aunt tuned in was true. Breena desired to give and receive respect, whereas Erin thrived on fear and control.

Sterlyn lifted a hand and cleared her throat. "If you want respect, you have to be worthy of it. I, too, would like to work harmoniously with your coven, but that means each side has to be transparent. Now, if you'll excuse us, we have matters to attend to. Thank you for stopping by to check on us, but as you can see, we're all here and well."

My heart twinged. That was how Dad would've handled the situation. He would've ended the confrontation, even if it was just a show for Erin. If we went too far, the priestess would know. Unfortunately, she was a worthy adversary. All the books I'd read growing up portrayed the villains as smart, but sometimes, the news and TV equated bad with ignorant, which was not the case. I guessed worthy adversaries were hard to capture, and we thus didn't hear much about them.

"Fine," Breena said tightly, but her body relaxed. She didn't like the animosity hovering between us, even if it was pretend. "But this town is technically the property of Shadow City, and I have as much right to be here as anyone."

My hands fisted at my sides. If Erin was watching, Breena couldn't be nice, but she was handling being abrasive really well. Maybe it wasn't an act.

"I expect you to remember that when we visit your coven," Griffin said as he beamed and lazily placed his arm around Sterlyn's shoulders. "No one outside the witches has ever visited there, not since my dad or I have been alive."

Breena's head jerked back, and she frowned.

I didn't know all the history of Shadow City, only the parts that affected the silver wolves and now Killian's pack, whose history had been impacted by the silver wolves vanishing to survive. Killian's pack had stepped up to watch over the city from Shadow Ridge, while the vampires had demanded they run Shadow Terrace to manage their own blood supply.

"If you visit us uninvited, it could ruin the spells we need to keep in place." Breena bit her lip. "Which would cause horrible side effects. You should know this."

Rosemary fluffed her wings. "That's what you witches keep saying, but I think there might be more to it."

"Give them credit for sticking to the same story, love," Levi replied, stepping closer to his mate. "Didn't the angels believe a skewed version of the truth for almost the same amount of time? Lies have a way of coming out."

Breena lowered her head. "I have to head back before my coven worries. Just remember, if you learn anything that the council or Erin should know, it's your duty to inform us. Otherwise, it could be seen as a betrayal of the city."

Now *that* sounded like something Erin would say. I wasn't sure if Breena's true colors were finally coming out or if that was something Erin had forced her to rehearse.

"The same goes for all of you as well," Alex replied, his strange accent slightly stronger than before. "Haven't we learned what can happen to our city when we're divided?"

I linked with Killian, *What does he mean?*

He's referring to the events of the past several years. Our city has grown more fractured over time, and the demon world nearly destroyed it. Yet here we are, with Erin pulling the same shenanigans, Killian answered, his attention locked on Breena.

Instead of responding, Breena hurried away. She didn't have a vehicle, and I wondered how she'd arrived.

Hey, Lowe linked with Killian, April, Billy, Sierra, and me. *The four of us are heading out with Torak, Darrell, Emmy, and Martha to deliver some camping gear. We're taking four of the large trucks and have them loaded up.*

I wasn't surprised, especially if Lowe had a connection with Stephanie, who was out there with them.

We should go with you, I suggested. I hated not being there to check on Mom, Chad, and my grandparents. There was also a lot that needed to be done to set up the camping grounds for the displaced packs.

Killian intertwined our fingers and replied, *Erin could be watching us. None of us should leave. Them going is risky enough.*

We'll pretend to head downtown and make sure we aren't followed, Billy replied. *If the two of you go with us, that could raise more questions after that witch showed up.*

Unfortunately, they were right, but that didn't make accepting it any easier.

"We can talk freely now." Eliza shook out her arms. "Breena is out of range, so Erin can't listen to us anymore."

"Can't they listen anyway? They did before." Cyrus scanned the area as if he expected to find someone lurking in the bushes.

Tucking a stray strand of hair behind her ear, Eliza pursed her lips. "No. She must have had a charm or something around Breena to listen and monitor her. Before, they had witch bones, which are significantly more powerful. Since we destroyed them, they can't listen in as easily, especially in this large of an area. I felt a slight change in energy at the same second Breena reacted. It was faint, so if I hadn't been searching for a sign the entire time, I might have missed it."

Once again, it seemed like Breena might be trustworthy. My head swam, and my thoughts blended together.

Killian hugged me to his side. "I have pack members heading out to the houses if you'd like them to come pick you up."

"That's probably for the best." Annie pouted. "I wanted you to spend time with the twins, but I'm not sure we could get you home."

"I can hide the trucks to ensure no one can follow us," Eliza agreed and hugged Annie and Ronnie.

The trucks came into view around the bend, and Killian lifted a hand and linked, *Can one of you stop and take Eliza?*

Within the next few minutes, Eliza had gotten into the truck with Billy and headed out.

"As much as I hate to leave, I need to get back to the city." Rosemary spread her wings, ready to take flight. "The longer we stay away, the more questions Erin and the others will ask."

Sterlyn yawned. "I think we should all settle in for the night. If Erin snoops again, we should give the illusion that everything is normal."

Though I wished we were helping the freed captives, I knew we couldn't, and I was eager for some time alone with my mate.

Our group said goodbye, and within seconds, Killian and I were at our front door.

As we entered the house, some tension vanished from my body. I'd been running on fumes. Walking into the living room, I inhaled deeply. I loved Killian's sandalwood scent. It wafted throughout the entire house and made this place feel like home.

Hey, he linked as he turned me toward him. We stood behind the loveseat positioned across from the windows that overlooked the backyard. It had to be approaching midnight. My body was heavy with fatigue, but my mind was racing.

He cupped my cheek, and the buzz of our bond sprang to life. My breath caught as butterflies took flight in my stomach. I'd never tire of him.

What are you thinking about? He kissed the tip of my nose.

The sweet gesture warmed my body again, but at least this time, we were alone. *Just processing everything Breena said and wondering whether we can trust her.*

Wrapping his arms around me, he pulled me against his chest. He lowered his head to my forehead and replied, *Time will reveal that, and I have a feeling, if even some of what Breena said was true, we'll learn sooner rather than later.*

Good point. If Erin was controlling the demons and the humans didn't have supernaturals to help them capture more shifters, she'd have to up her game. *So we wait and figure out who the humans will target next?* That would drive me insane. Though I didn't have a better option, I hated sitting around and waiting for someone else's move. I wanted to thwart their attempts and gain the upper hand.

Dad used to remind our pack that acting rashly usually resulted in bad outcomes. He'd preached patience, whereas I had Mom's temperament when it came to these types of situations.

"You left me again." He chuckled and booped me on the nose. "I guess that means I'll have to do better."

I'd opened my mouth to ask him what he meant when he kissed me. My mind short-circuited, and I responded in earnest, not even remembering what I'd been planning to ask.

His faint citrus taste made me dizzy, and I wrapped my arms around his neck, pulling myself closer to him.

He pulled away, and I groaned.

"Go take a shower." He released his hold and stepped back. "I'll warm up the oven to cook a few frozen pizzas. We both need to eat after the crazy day we had." His stomach grumbled, reinforcing what he'd said.

If not for that, I would've told him to screw food. I wanted the one thing only his body could provide, but he was clearly hungry, and I needed to take care of my mate.

Twenty minutes later, I strolled out of our bedroom to the kitchen. I'd needed a shower more than I'd realized. Maybe Killian had known that when he'd pushed me to take care of myself.

I stood at the round kitchen table, breathing in the heavenly scent of pizza, and the view was even better. Killian was bent over, biceps bulging, as he pulled two pizzas from the oven. He wore the fish-print pajama bottoms I'd bought him after learning he enjoyed fishing, though he hadn't been able to do that lately with all the threats around town. His white cotton shirt hugged his body, and I licked my lips with hunger—for him and the food.

He quickly cut the pizza and set a plate down in front of the chair I stood behind and the one beside me. Without saying a word, we scarfed down the food I again hadn't realized I needed.

He watched me take the last bite of pizza, and as soon as I swallowed, he got up and cradled me to his chest.

My body blazed, knowing exactly what he wanted. We had been so worried about each other, and we needed the connection from our bond that we could only achieve through sex. He'd held me off, wanting to take care of me, but now that we were cleaned and fed, it was time to pleasure each other.

He didn't break his stride as he carried me to our bed. Once he'd laid me down, he gripped my red flannel pajama bottoms and yanked them from my body. Breathing raggedly, he watched me with glowing eyes. "You aren't wearing any underwear."

There had been no doubt about what my dessert would be, and I'd wanted to eliminate any time wasters that would prevent him from getting inside me. I winked. "And I'm not wearing a bra, either."

He groaned. "That I already figured, but hearing you say it..." He trailed off with a deep, sexy growl. Leaning over me, he grabbed the buttons of my matching flannel top and ripped the shirt open. The buttons flew across the bed. His desperate desire for me had me damn near purring, and I was most definitely not a cat.

He hooked his thumbs into the waistband of his bottoms and pushed them down his legs. All of him was on display for me, and between the hardness and the scent of his arousal mixed with mine, I had no doubt he was just as ready.

When he climbed on top of me, I shook my head, and he paused. I gestured at his white cotton shirt and commanded, "Off." I wanted to feel his skin against mine. Nothing less was acceptable.

A wicked grin peeked through as he pressed his hardness against me. I grabbed the hem of his shirt and whipped it over his head. He chuckled and helped me untangle his arms from the shirt, but as soon as he broke free, his mouth went straight to my nipples.

No more distractions, he linked as his tongue flicked my tender skin.

Pleasure washed over me, and I didn't bother tossing his shirt to the floor. Instead, I clutched the navy comforter with both hands as he focused all his attention on my body. His free hand caressed the neglected breast, and his hips rolled, building friction between my legs.

I spread them wider, wanting him to slip inside me.

Not yet, he replied. He rolled to his side, taking my other breast in his mouth and sliding his free hand between my legs.

Though that wasn't what I'd wanted, an orgasm ripped through my body, taking me by surprise. He knew exactly how to touch me.

His lips captured mine, swallowing my moan as our tongues danced together. His fingers continued their steady pace on my sensitive area, but that wouldn't cut it anymore.

I pushed him onto his back, and he gasped as his surprise filtered through me. I hadn't meant to dominate him, but the thrill of his reaction empowered me. It was my turn to pleasure him.

Straddling him, I threw my head back as he filled me. His hands cupped my breasts while I rode him, slow and steady.

His eyes locked with mine, the glow brightening as our connection opened more to each other. I tore my gaze from his and quickened the pace, watching his muscular chest and abs convulse with each thrust. He was the sexiest and kindest man in the entire world, and he was all *mine.* Possessiveness swirled through me, and I further opened myself to him.

Times like these were my favorite, when we were so connected we felt like one person, our emotions and pleasure blending together.

We kept our rhythm slower than normal. I dug my fingernails into his chest, loving how his muscles moved underneath my hands. I didn't know if our bond was getting stronger or if we'd made so much progress during our fight and in our relationship that our connection had also evolved, but he'd trusted me and hadn't asked me to hold back, and this felt like our sweetest lovemaking yet. Maybe we were letting some of our demons go together.

His pleasure built, and the friction in my body swelled in sync. His hands gripped my waist, urging me to move slower.

I'd expected the speed to be boring, but it was more intense in an emotional way. He filled me so completely, and my stomach clenched.

My body quivered as ecstasy swirled between us. His fingers dug deeper, and I could feel his hands shake. We climaxed together, and I braced myself on his chest for support from the overwhelming sensation. The world rocked around me, and it was exhilarating.

He rolled me off him and cuddled me against his chest. We didn't even bother to get under the covers. Spooning, we fell promptly asleep.

THE NEXT DAY passed without issue. Sterlyn, Griffin, Cyrus, Annie, Alex, and Ronnie headed back to Shadow City to keep up appearances while Killian and I stayed in the pack neighborhood as if nothing were out of the ordinary. Fortunately, the others had gotten the new packs settled, and Chad, Theo, Rudie, and Mom had returned here with Billy, Sierra, Torak, April, Stephanie, and Lowe.

Mom, Chad, and Emmy were at our house, and Killian was grilling hamburgers on the back porch for dinner. The early January air was chilly, even to my wolf shifter skin, and the four of us stayed inside since Killian insisted he needed to work alone.

The truth was, he was giving me alone time with my family and friends.

Since Mom was here, Emmy wouldn't harp on about sex again. She would wait until I was alone, especially after her last attempt had backfired.

Mom sat on the edge of the couch, her eyes bright with hope. "Stephanie thinks she can create a cure for *all* of us within a week, especially since she has the whole lab at Shadow Ridge University to herself while the campus is between semesters. She'd already been working on a cure at night in her lab after each work day with her friend Brittany."

"That's amazing," I said as I sat between her and Emmy. "At least we found someone who has the knowledge to help us."

Chad ran a hand down his face. "I want to be able to fight again."

I understood that sentiment all too well.

"Also, Aurora and Circe have been on the intranet, talking with covens around the world." Mom leaned her head back against the couch. "They think there's merit to the vampire amnesia spell."

This was the most at peace I'd seen Mom since Dad's death. It was almost as if she'd found something worth living for again.

Emmy snatched the remote from the end table. "Well, we need to take advantage of Sierra's absence and actually catch up on what's going on in the world and not watch some rom-com." She flipped on the TV and changed it to the news.

Shadow Ridge appeared on TV. Downtown was in utter chaos.

CHAPTER TWENTY-FIVE

TIME STOOD STILL. I couldn't believe what I was watching. All the other attacks downtown had involved only a handful of demons, but this was different. Twenty demons in shadow form were darting down to harass unsuspecting humans and shifters.

Was Erin behind this? Or only the demons?

Killian, downtown is under attack, I linked as Emmy, Chad, and Mom jumped to their feet and headed to the front door.

The lid to the grill slammed shut, and Killian ran inside just as they reached our door. Mom shouted over her shoulder, "The silver wolf pack is coming to help fight the demons downtown."

Though I wasn't part of the pack anymore, I was still a silver wolf and could see the demons, and I'd be damned if I stayed behind. "I'm going with you."

"Fine, meet us there." Emmy's voice had turned into a growly rasp, as she had already begun shifting into her wolf.

I hurried to the door and saw silver fur sprouting on her arms. "Emmy, don't!" I exclaimed, my stomach churning. I wasn't her alpha, but she wasn't making the right decision. "A wolf running into the attack will only freak out the humans further."

Her feet stopped as she tried to steady herself, fighting against the shift she'd called.

"She's right," Mom said sadly. "Chad and I shouldn't go. We'll wind up scaring the humans more if we lose control and shift. If he tries not to shift, he will, and if he tries to shift, he won't be able to. Either way, it'll be a cluster."

My heart ached for them, but we didn't have the luxury of remaining still.

I'm coming, too. You aren't going alone, Killian linked.

He couldn't even see what he was attacking, but I had to tread carefully. *You can calm the humans. You are the face of the supernaturals, and we need someone who cares to help them.* I knew he wouldn't agree to be left behind, and I understood that asking him to do so wasn't right. We were a team, and we worked better together.

Instead of getting aggravated with me, he rushed to the kitchen and grabbed the keys from the counter. *You're right. I can try to calm the humans... if it's possible.* "Let's take the truck. Emmy can ride with us."

"Okay." My heart pounded from either exultation that our relationship kept growing stronger or the anticipation of a fight. Maybe it was a combination of the two.

Emmy frowned deeply as she raced back into the house. She was upset. "I told the other silver wolves not to shift, either. I can't believe I didn't consider that."

Some of the weight fell off my shoulders. She wasn't upset with me.

The three of us ran through the kitchen to the garage. I paused in the mud room and snatched two knives from the block we kept near the garage door. I linked with

Killian, *If Erin is behind this, she'll be close by to see her handiwork.*

His trepidation slammed into me as he opened the garage door. *I'm linking with them now, and I'm telling April to stay behind to watch the neighborhood,* he replied.

We climbed into his truck, Emmy getting into the back seat behind me. Killian slid into the driver's seat, then shut his door and pressed the gas. Tires squealing, we sped down the driveway into the street. He slammed on the brakes, cut the wheel, and thrust the shifter into drive.

Not missing a beat, we sped from the neighborhood toward downtown.

Killian gripped the steering wheel. "Sterlyn is calling Breena to see what the witch has to say."

"Like she'll admit to anything," Emmy snarled from the back. "But whatever. Just get us there so we can kill these assholes. I don't know why they have to congregate here. Every damn supernatural attack messes with our town."

I gripped the handlebar and tried to control my breathing. I began to play Mozart's Eine kleine Nachtmusik" in my head to hang on to my calm and stay rational. "If *Erin* is the one in charge, she'll want to make them attack within a certain range to test her control."

My throat constricted. If she was growing desperate, as Breena had insinuated, *this* was escalating matters, but we couldn't assume anything until we found proof that someone beyond the demons was behind this.

No one responded. We were all processing the information as best we could. Killian pushed our speed, and the trees flew past my window. My head spun, and my stomach grew more upset.

Killian linked with Billy and me, *We were just informed about the demon attack on the city. Emmy and Sterlyn are coordinating with the silver wolves, so I need you to help on our side. Though we can't see the demons, it would be helpful if some of the pack came to help me split up the humans so we aren't gathering them in one area for the demons to pick off.*

That was great thinking. If we moved the humans to one location, the demons would follow. Splitting them up would divide the demons as well and make our counterattack more effective.

I bent down, securing the knives around my ankles. I didn't want to go running past humans with weapons until I needed them.

On it. We'll be there shortly, Billy replied.

Though I hated to interfere, Killian failed to say one thing. *Our first instinct is to shift, and though I understand that, we need everyone to stay in human form when they arrive so we don't further terrify the humans.*

I'll make sure to communicate that as well, Billy replied.

The brick buildings of downtown came into view, and the mayhem was worse than what we'd seen on TV. More demons were in shadow form, and a thick line of them hovered over the city streets, swooping down to terrorize people.

Even with all the silver wolves on our side, it would be hard to come out on top. People were running away, panic clear on their faces. A slender man clutched a heavyset man's hand, attempting to drag him down the street, but the heavyset man was turned toward a woman under attack, watching her blood spill. He seemed frozen in terror or afraid to turn his back on the sight, as if watching would prevent him from being next.

Every demon had someone as prey. The demons didn't discriminate, and a mixture of people of all ages and genders were clutched in various evil hands. Red eyes flamed in each shadow as if terror were fueling them.

"Shit!" Killian exclaimed as a woman carrying a younger child ran in front of the truck. He turned the wheel and hit the curb ten feet away from the first brick building into the city. The truck lurched to a halt, jerking our bodies forward. I braced my hands on the dashboard. The vehicle stopped mere inches from a thick oak tree where the woods gave way to downtown.

A blood-curdling scream rang in my ears.

"Is everyone okay?" Killian asked as I reached for the door handle.

"Better than they are!" Emmy quipped as she swung her door open and jumped from the truck.

I climbed from the truck and linked, *I'm fine. But I need to help Emmy. Can you calm the humans and guide them somewhere safe, out of the downtown area?*

Yes, but be careful, he replied. *And let me know if you need me. That's the only way this will work.*

The same goes for you. Just because you're helping humans doesn't mean you won't become a target. That was the risk of him being there, but I couldn't sideline him, especially since I didn't want him to do that to me.

I ran behind the bed of the truck and faltered. Bile burned my throat. The twenty-five demons had humans in their clutches, and several bodies littered the ground.

The sound of engines grew louder, and Billy linked, *We're almost there. We're following the silver wolves.*

Some of my worry eased. They were close, and they were all driving. That would be hard to do in wolf form, so Emmy must have communicated the need to remain human to the silver wolf pack as well.

A group of teenagers passed me, eyes wide as they ran

haphazardly. Fear had taken control, which meant I had to keep my focus steady.

I pivoted, narrowly missing the smallest teen in the back. Human and demon scents mixed together, making it hard to get a sense of how many of each were nearby, but the worst part was the negativity that felt like sludge on my skin.

Emmy was only a few feet ahead of me. She bent down and grabbed the dagger she typically wore around her ankle with jeans. That was the place we silver wolves carried our weapons when mixing with humans, easy to reach but out of sight.

A few reporters were on the street, filming the brutality. Yet another way the humans' fear would grow. I wasn't sure how supernaturals would survive having all of humankind turned against us, or why Erin was behind it.

As we reached the first two demons, Emmy lunged at the one attacking an older man. The man cried, begging for his life, which only fueled the demon.

I squatted as a man in his twenties ran at me. Blood smeared his face, and he couldn't see well. Spinning to the left, I barely got out of the way as he rushed by. I took the opportunity to dislodge my knives, then planted my legs underneath me and stood.

A demon had her hands around a young woman's neck, choking her. Her shoulder-length violet hair swung as she flailed desperately, trying to grab whatever was attacking her. Each time she hit the demon, her body trembled harder, as if feeling something she couldn't see fed her fear.

The demons were relishing the torture and prolonging the suffering.

I lifted my knife, and the young woman's brown eyes locked on me over the demon's shoulder. They widened as I raced toward her and the demon. She likely thought I was coming for her. Her mouth opened, but though her lips moved, no air came out to form words.

The demon chuckled. I could only assume it was because she thought the woman's fear had grown. Little did she know she would be taking her last breath.

I stabbed the demon in the back where I suspected her heart to be. Blue blood splattered my face, the smell as putrid as the essence inside her.

Releasing her hold on the young woman, the demon sagged and spun toward me. Her red eyes dimmed, and she snarled. My knife was still inside her, cutting deeper with each movement.

As the demon crumpled, the woman gasped for air.

Doors slammed shut behind me, and Billy linked, *We're here and heading your way, Killian.*

A strangled groan escaped the demon as she dropped and her heart stopped beating. Now that my adversary was dead, I removed the knife and scanned the area to find twenty-some-odd pairs of demon eyes locked on me.

Lovely.

"Head out to the main road. You'll find someone there who can lead you to safety," I commanded the human.

Without nodding, she raced off in that direction, eager to get away.

Good.

Out of the corner of my eye, I watched Emmy take her demon down. The older man bawled as he attempted to run away but tripped over his own feet.

Under normal circumstances, I'd have found it amusing, but the urge to scream at him to get himself together nearly overtook me.

Darrell, Cyrus, Annie, Theo, and the rest of my former

silver wolf pack ran past us. With Sterlyn still in the city, a total of seventeen of us were here, but I'd still take our odds over the remaining demons.

All the demons let go of the humans they were terrorizing. They were smart enough to realize they should focus on the threat instead of indulging themselves. We had to get to them before they scattered.

Again, I wished our enemies were dumb. It would have made things a whole lot easier.

The reporters were still recording, faces pale with fear, but not enough to make them run. I rasped, "Get the *hell* out of here, or I'll make you."

That was enough to get them to retreat, but they left their cameras recording. It wasn't like it would make a difference.

The wolves split apart, each of us focusing on a demon. At least six wolves would be targeted by two demons, and I remained alert as I pulled my knife from the dead demon's back. It came out with a sick sucking noise that had vomit surging into my mouth. Not wanting to show weakness at this pivotal moment, I swallowed it, the horrible taste burning my throat.

Blood dripped from the edge of the blade, staining the cement underneath me. We'd have to clean all this up later.

The freed humans ran into the road. A few screamed in terror, while others cried, and some were silent, emphasizing how everyone reacted differently to being frightened close to death.

Killian, Billy, and a few other of my pack members were directing the humans to safety.

The two demons closest to me locked their crimson eyes on me. Not wanting to wait for them to coordinate their attack, I lunged toward them.

"Jewel!" Darrell growled, unhappy with me taking the lead.

But since I couldn't link with him, I had to do what I thought was best.

The two demons soared toward me, countering my move. Both lifted a dagger, the blades glinting in the streetlight.

The slightly longer demon aimed for my right arm. I leaped back, and the blade sliced my skin. The sharp pain seared, and warm blood trickled down my arm. The wound wouldn't impact my ability to fight.

Shorter Demon went straight for my throat. I ducked, and the dagger whooshed over my head.

From my crouched position, I thrust up and stabbed Longer Demon in the chest, aiming for his heart. The quick intake of air and shaky exhale made me think I'd hit my mark.

That gave Shorter Demon time to correct himself. He raised his dagger over his head and swung it down, aiming for my heart in turn. I lifted my left hand and used my other blade to block his attack. The impact of the blades sent vibrations down my arm. The demon's blade was bigger, and I gritted my teeth as I pressed through the discomfort to hold it back.

I kicked Shorter Demon in what was either his crotch or his stomach—I couldn't tell in his shadow form—and smiled as he flew back a few feet from the impact. I switched the knife into my other hand so I could fight with my dominant arm.

As the demon glided toward me again, another shadow cut him off, lifting a weapon that was also somehow a shadow.

I'd never seen anything like it.

"You should've known not to come back here and cause trouble," a familiar voice said.

Levi.

My legs weakened. I hadn't expected him to come.

A sinister sensation quivered up my spine, and I spun around, expecting to find Longer Demon there, but he was still lying where he'd fallen, dead.

Something was stalking me.

Following the sinister essence, I jogged toward the truck and saw Killian and Billy helping separate the human victims, passing them to different pack members, who guided them away from the demons. Fortunately, the negative sensation disturbing me seemed to emanate from a spot in the woods near the truck and not across the road, where they were ushering the humans and spreading them apart.

If a demon was hiding and watching the attack, I needed to slip behind them and catch them off guard. I hurried across the street as if I were following Killian and the humans. The pack was taking the humans to different hotels beyond the main street.

Instead of heading to the hotels, I bore left and used the trees along the road for cover. They weren't as thick as the woods across the street, but they, along with the darkness, should be enough to hide me.

I jogged half a mile down, and then I ran across the empty road and into the woods to circle back.

No animals were out. The negativity was so thick, it was suffocating, and sounds of terror still rang in the night.

The new moon didn't provide any light, but my wolf eyes didn't need it. I jogged back toward town as quickly as I could while remaining as silent as possible.

The negativity swirled around me so much that I struggled to breathe.

Blinking, I stepped past a cypress, unable to believe what I saw.

Erin stood near the edge of the tree line with a black scarf wrapped around her scarlet hair. She was trying to blend in with the night. She stood deep enough in the trees not to be easily seen, but she could still see enough to get a sense of what was going on. Her hands were lifted and covered with blood while her lips moved in a chant.

Erin's here, I linked with Killian. *She's doing a spell on the demons.* Breena might have been telling us more truth than any of us had expected.

How do you know? Killian asked. *I didn't see her.*

I'm in the woods. I felt something negative and thought a demon was trying to sneak up behind us. Little had I known that Erin's essence was just as evil as that of the demons we were fighting. I'd sensed her vileness before, but she must have been masking it. *It wasn't enough to be more than one, so I came alone. I didn't expect it to be her.*

Jewel, wait for me before you attack her, Killian replied. *I'm on my way.*

No, don't. She might sense you. She has no clue I'm here. I didn't want to give away the one chance I might have to kill her. *I have to try.*

His displeasure and worry washed over me, but he didn't say anything. Maybe he knew it was futile, but at least he wasn't telling me not to do it like he would've before.

I'm still heading that way. You need someone there in case it goes wrong, he replied, determination wafting through the bond.

That's fine. You won't be far behind me. If I got into trouble, he'd be here in minutes.

I tiptoed toward Erin. She was so focused that she didn't notice me.

My heart pounded. I didn't enjoy killing, but with this particular woman, it was the best choice. She wouldn't stop hurting us.

I crept up behind her and raised the knife. Just as I was ready to stab her in the back, her head turned, and her gaze landed on me.

With every ounce of strength I had, I swung the knife, but she chanted, "*Deturbare arma*!"

The knife dislodged from my hand and flew several feet back. *Damn it.* I should've retrieved the other one from the second demon I'd killed, but I'd been worried about a surprise attack.

I lifted my hands, refusing to give up. I'd take this bitch down one way or another. I punched her in the jaw, and she stumbled back.

She scowled as she said, "*Tenebrae me abscondunt.*"

And then she disappeared from sight.

CHAPTER TWENTY-SIX

MY BREATHING TURNED RAGGED. Every sign of her was gone. The negativity, her scent, everything. She'd literally disappeared in front of my eyes, and I had no way of finding her.

Erin vanished, I linked with Killian.

I surveyed my surroundings, searching for any hint that she was near as I squatted and retrieved my knife. My breathing quickened as I waited for her to attack, but nothing happened.

Strange.

Damn it, Jewel, Killian replied, his anxiety causing my pulse to pound harder. *I'm almost there.*

Footsteps rushed toward me. I could hear his desperation to reach me in the noise he made.

The sounds of the battle ceased, but I couldn't afford to divert my attention in case she attacked. I backed up slowly, inching toward Killian. The last thing I wanted to do was remain here and be the target of an invisible witch.

For the first time, I understood how non-angel descendants felt when fighting demons.

Killian's scent swirled around me, and a moment later, his hand touched my arm as he stopped beside me. His jaw twitched as his attention darted around. *Has she attacked again?*

No. This whole situation was bizarre, and I wanted to get away. *Let's get out of here before she tries something.* I turned around, though my head screamed at me not to. I'd trained my entire life to never turn my back on my enemy, but for all I knew, she was already standing behind me.

I took Killian's hand, the buzz jolting between us. My pulse slowed a little just from his touch. This was why mates were stronger together.

He didn't argue as we hurried back toward downtown.

The streets were eerily quiet. Erin had stopped chanting and disappeared, which seemed too timely to be a coincidence. *I think Breena told us the truth.*

I was thinking the same thing. Killian glanced over his shoulder. *Sterlyn, Griffin, and Rosemary are watching the Shadow Ridge gate for her. Alex and Ronnie are on the Shadow Terrace side. Whichever way she tries to get in, the gate will have to open, so they'll stay there to catch her.*

That sounded logical, but I didn't believe that would accomplish anything. Erin was proving to be more resourceful than I'd expected. I highly doubted she would just reappear and demand the gates be opened.

Hand in hand, we moved in sync, darting around trees and branches. We passed Killian's truck and rejoined the group on the main street.

Despite the small downtown area, the attack had occurred at the end farther from Shadow City, which added up. Erin would want it to seem like no one from the city was involved.

Instinct had me frantically checking on my former pack

members. They were grouped together near the center of the corpses, and Cyrus and Annie were talking with Levi. Theo had a cut on his cheek, and other pack members had similar injuries.

But they were all standing.

Blue and crimson blood splattered the cement and puddled under the bodies of the five dead demons and multiple humans scattered down the road. I couldn't see the demons' eyes. It was like the light had been turned off, and they were dark gray blobs.

My chest constricted, and I stopped in my tracks. "Did only evil demons die?" Levi had been here, so other good demons might have come to help.

Killian paused as Levi turned toward us.

His face twisted in agony as he answered, "Yes, though it's still heartbreaking. These were people I grew up with, who only recently turned after the princes of Hell were defeated. But they forced our hand, so there wasn't much we could do."

I understood the guilt of not being able to help your people. That was still something I was working to overcome.

"We need to take care of the demon bodies and bring the humans to the morgue before the humans leave the hotels." Killian ran his free hand through his hair and scoffed. "Those reporters will be back to get their cameras. I would say let's trash their videos, but it would be pointless. They've either been broadcast live or stored digitally."

I hated the ruthlessness of the humans determined to catch the next big story. It was hard to believe they would risk their lives to capture footage like this.

Cyrus rolled his eyes. "They are relentless."

"Fear motivates, dear." Annie rubbed blue blood from

her cheek and wiped it on her already blood-speckled white shirt. "And people handle it the best way they can."

Her words were so close to my earlier thoughts. I hadn't considered that the same thing could be driving the reporters.

"Someone check on the humans. Lowe, Randall, and I will stay back and handle the bodies." Darrell bent down and grabbed the midsection of the demon closest to him. "Distract them so they don't see us carrying invisible beings away."

"And the rest of our pack can clean the blood from the cement." Emmy rubbed her hands together, which caused flakes of blood to float to the ground.

Annie nodded. "Yeah, there should be chemicals at the university we can use to clean this up."

"And the police station and Shifty's Bar. We've had our fair share of blood cleanup," Killian said as he tugged me toward the hotels.

Part of me felt bad about leaving the silver wolves. I was used to helping my childhood pack, but my place was beside Killian.

"I need to head back to Rosemary." Levi flickered into his demon form. "If Erin or her coven attacks, I need to be there with my sword." He floated off.

"But Erin..." Cyrus called out. "She could access the gate if you go back now."

Levi laughed humorlessly. "Something happened inside the city, too. A shifter and vampire were attacked, so Sterlyn, Ronnie, Alex, and Griffin had to manage that situation. Rosemary is worried that it was a coordinated effort by the witches, so she went with them."

That could have been a distraction to get them away from the gate so Erin could get in.

Without waiting for our response, Levi soared toward the city and his preordained.

Killian and I hurried back to the hotels. At least the demons weren't attacking anymore.

Would she really try to get back into the city? I didn't understand the point. I'd *seen* her in the woods. There was no question.

Killian's hold on my hand tightened as he replied, *She wants to say she was there the entire time. She probably wants one of our friends to accuse her, and the guards wouldn't have it documented that she left, which would only strengthen her stance against us.*

In other words, she'd call me a liar. It would be her word against mine. Though my friends would believe me, the majority of the city wouldn't...at least, not her allies.

The two of us were almost to the door of the first hotel when April linked with Killian and me, *You have a visitor who says she needs the two of you urgently.*

I growled. April had stayed back to keep an eye on the neighborhood while we were gone. Of course we'd have a visitor now.

Killian's brow furrowed. *Who is it?*

I don't know. She's about our age and smells like herbs... so a witch. April had measured her response as if she were attempting not to sound alarmed, like she was regulating her emotions.

Killian and I tensed, our concern crashing into the bond intensifying. It could be Breena. Unless Erin or someone else had altered their appearance. Our pack could be in danger.

Sweat pooled in my armpits, and I hoped to the gods I hadn't forgotten to apply deodorant after my shower.

We've got to get back to the neighborhood. A witch is

there, Killian linked with Billy. *Can you manage the humans, or do you need us to stay?*

Even before Billy responded, Killian and I had turned toward his truck.

We can handle them, Billy assured him. *Go check on things back there. I haven't heard anything alarming, other than what you just told me.*

The pack didn't feel threatened. That could change in a minute.

We ran back around a brick store and onto the main road. Emmy had disappeared, and Annie had pulled out a hose from a nearby restaurant.

She glanced up from the pool of blood she was rinsing away. "What's wrong?" The corner of her eyes tightened as she lowered the hose.

I caught her up as Killian continued to the truck and climbed in. The engine started, and he backed out beside me so I could climb into the passenger side.

Her face paled. "I'm coming with you. If something else happens, I need to be with the twins." She dropped the hose and sprinted toward me, her honey-brown eyes glowing as she linked to Cyrus.

As soon as Annie and I were in the truck, Killian punched the gas. Once again, we were rushing toward a threat without knowing what we were facing.

Is everyone okay? Killian asked April.

Yes, she's just standing in front of your house. She keeps watching the side of the house and bouncing on her heels. I think she's in trouble, April replied.

When we reached the split in the road, Killian stayed left, heading toward the neighborhood and away from downtown Shadow Ridge. The trees closed in around us.

Now that we were close to the pack neighborhood, woods filled in the area between the road and the river.

I had the random thought that one day, I hoped things calmed down enough that Killian could take me fishing. I wanted to enjoy some of his hobbies with him when we could catch our breath and stop worrying about another attack.

"Midnight's with the kids a few houses down, and nothing seems out of sorts." Annie exhaled, some of the tension leaving her voice. "Hopefully, it's one of Eliza's coven members whom the other wolves aren't familiar with."

While we'd worked with a handful of members from the coven, most of the witches kept to themselves. If someone who didn't usually interact with us was here, I wasn't sure that meant things were less dire. But I kept my mouth shut, not wanting to upset Annie when she seemed less anxious.

I kept my attention locked on the woods and our surroundings, searching for any dark shadows—anywhere a demon could be trying to camouflage itself.

When the entrance to the neighborhood came into view, Killian's breathing became more ragged. *Whoever it is could be waiting until we get here to attack.*

My face burned. I hadn't considered that, and it bothered me.

As we rounded the last bend, I locked onto the front of Killian's and my house. I blew out a breath. Breena was in our driveway, with April, Martha, and Rudie standing several feet away, close to our mailbox.

The tension in their bodies told me everything. Breena had her arms wrapped around her waist as if to protect herself. She kept fidgeting, avoiding looking at the three women.

The three wolf shifters had their arms crossed, glaring at the witch. Lines of distrust were etched on each of their faces.

Good. They needed to be wary.

Killian pulled over to the curb in front of our house a few feet away from the mailbox and turned off the engine. The three of us were out of our vehicle in seconds and strolling toward the driveway. We passed the three women keeping an eye on the witch and placed ourselves in front of Breena.

Dropping her arms, Breena faced us and tapped her fingers on her black leather pants. "It's about time you got here."

A laugh built within me, and I swallowed it. This wasn't funny, but I couldn't believe her audacity. She reminded me of her aunt.

"Do you expect us to apologize when we were fighting demons that were attacking humans in our downtown? Maybe you're not so different after all, Breena." Killian arched a brow.

She closed her eyes and winced. "No. I'm sorry. It's just...I came here at a huge risk."

"Then why *are* you here?" My patience was wearing thin. I was tired of the bullshit and games. "There are humans who could use our help back there and blood to clean off the streets."

The corners of Annie's mouth tilted upward as she nodded at me and said, "She has a point."

"I told you why." Breena bit her bottom lip and huffed. "Erin has gone too far, and *we* have to do something about it."

We?

"Are you saying you're joining us against your aunt?" Martha lifted her chin and regarded her.

Breena paused as if to gather her thoughts. "That's why I'm here."

And here we went with the games again. I opened my mouth, but Annie spoke before me.

"I understand that Erin is your aunt, and if you're willing to help us, you feel like you're betraying your family." Annie placed a hand over her heart. "But if you don't tell us what you know and things go further, can you live with those consequences?"

A lump formed in my throat. I'd been about to bite this poor girl's head off without thinking about what she must be struggling with by being here. If she was a good person, she would have a hard time betraying her family. Now I understood why Mom respected Annie so much. She empathized with the person standing before her, unlike me. I just grew frustrated with the situation.

"You're right." Breena shook out her hands. "I have to keep reminding myself of that."

Lifting both hands, Killian said softly, "Breena, why are you here?"

The patience in his voice was heartwarming. I was so damn proud to be his mate and hoped one day I'd be worthy of the gift Fate had bestowed upon me.

"Can I talk alone with the three of you?" Breena asked and gestured to Killian, Annie, and me. "It'll be hard enough, but I know Annie is mated to Cyrus, and the two of you are best friends with Sterlyn and Griffin. I..."

She felt uncomfortable with three shifters she didn't know. Now *that* I understood.

April? Killian linked.

The young woman was already backing up. She didn't want to be here. *Yup. Just let me know if you need me.*

Eyes glowing, Annie had to be linking with Martha and Rudie. After a few seconds, the two other wolf shifters nodded and followed April.

I had a feeling the three of them wouldn't go far.

Flipping her wrist, Breena sighed. "Thank you. I've just spelled us so no one beyond the four of us can hear me. I can't risk Erin tapping into my connection with the coven."

A nifty trick that we might need to learn more about later.

She continued, "This morning, Erin told Diana and me to watch your friends and make sure they stayed in the city. I knew something was up."

"And you didn't warn us?" Annie rocked on the back of her heels.

"Would you have trusted me if I had?" Breena straightened. "You still aren't convinced I'm telling the truth. So by not contacting you, I accomplished several things."

I hated to admit it, but Breena was right. I linked with Killian, *We would've at least considered that she might be leading us into a trap.*

Who's to say this isn't one? he replied.

We couldn't be blinded by distrust, either. *We have to consider she could be trustworthy, too.*

True, he replied, then said out loud, "What were those things?"

"I realized she had to be testing her control over demons. The humans she's been working with called, demanding she find another group of supernaturals for them. She hopes the demons are her answer. I knew she'd be leaving the city and I'd have my only shot to bring you this." Breena used the hand that wasn't holding the silent spell and opened her palm. Two sizable black cauldrons appeared at the corner of our garage door, and the stench of blood hit my nose.

Not prepared for the thick, coppery scent, I swallowed hard to keep my stomach from churning. "Is that blood?"

Breena winced. "Yes. The last bit the coven had from Rosemary and Levi."

The world spun, and I grasped Killian's arm to keep myself steady. If this was true, she'd solved one of our huge problems. "Why would you do this?"

"After what happened, it should be a day or two before Erin realizes those are gone. She won't want to risk performing another spell like that too soon and with how closely you guys are watching her." Breena exhaled. "And because she'll behave in the meantime, she won't be able to help capture any other supernaturals so humans can do goddess knows what to them."

Her sincerity washed over me and shattered the walls I'd built around my heart. I believed her.

"So what are you going to do with the blood?" Killian stepped forward, then stopped himself.

"Give it to you. I cloaked myself and left the city when Levi came to help you. It was the only chance I had to come here without raising questions." Breena waved her hand at the bowls. "Dispose of it however you see fit. Just make sure it's done. I want you to verify it's their blood so you'll finally realize I'm *your* ally."

"Okay." Annie nodded and shrugged. "That's fair, and we truly appreciate it."

Breena exhaled. "I didn't do it just for all of you."

"Thank you nonetheless." Killian smiled sadly. "I know Erin's been like a mother to you. I know what it's like to lose your parents, and I know the guilt and burden you carry. I can only imagine how difficult it was for you to help us." His voice grew thicker with grief, and his sadness surged through the bond. "I'd give anything to know what happened to my parents, and I've sworn to never let anyone down again. Not like I did them."

Something unreadable crossed her face. "You didn't let them down, Killian."

"If you knew the story—" he started, but Breena lifted her hand.

"That's the thing. I do." Breena lowered her hand and stared at him. "None of you were supposed to survive, including you."

CHAPTER TWENTY-SEVEN

I COULDN'T BREATHE. The pain coursing through my chest was worse than any physical pain I'd ever endured. Even the concept of me possibly never having known Killian cut through me like a knife.

Killian's agony surged through our bond and nearly buckled my knees. He was in as much pain as I was but for a very different reason—he was about to learn what had happened to his family.

"What do you mean?" Annie asked. Even though she wasn't as impacted as the two of us, pain laced her voice.

"That night at the lake was set up by Saga, Azbogah... and Erin." Breena's shoulders sagged as if the weight of the secret were holding her down. "It was back when the council was debating opening Shadow City's gates so all could come and go. I was a teenager then and dealing with losing Mom and my priestess. I didn't know what happened until it was over, and Erin told me if I ever said a word, I'd lose her, too." A tear slid down Breena's cheek, and her chest heaved. "I'm so sorry. I never thought about the consequences until now. I finally put it together that it was *your* family that was involved."

"Tell me what happened," Killian rasped and clutched me. "I need to know. *Please.*"

I'd learned that getting answers didn't always bring you peace, but maybe not knowing was worse. Either way, I wouldn't dissuade him from hearing something he desperately wanted to know.

"Erin cloaked herself and Saga, and they left the city when one of the blood shipments arrived." Breena stared at her boots as if she couldn't look at us. "That night, Erin cast some spells around the lake to make the animals scatter while some bear shifters were swimming."

He swallowed hard. "That was who reported the strange noises."

"She knew your dad, being the type of alpha he was, would scout the area. They'd been planning for a while and had staged similar mild disturbances before, so it would have seemed like a routine check. People who had been there when she cast the spell could tell it wasn't something usual for the area and would alert the police, but whenever your dad or a policeman would follow up and check out the area, things wouldn't seem out of place or in any way threatening. The point was that he wouldn't be worried about checking out the area and bringing *you* along. Your sister and mother were collateral damage."

It made sense that Killian's dad would bring him. Since Killian was the future alpha, he'd want him along to do those alpha-like tasks.

Killian flinched, and I stepped forward, wanting to punch the witch. I hated what she was doing to him.

Don't, Killian linked. *She didn't say anything wrong. Just hard truths. That's why I blew off the threat and went to the school party. Olive tried to get me to come with her and swim, but we'd just been there a few weeks ago for the same reason, so I told her no. I wanted to hang out with my friends. They were going later that afternoon, a few hours after the bears reported it. They were supposed to arrive while the sun was still out. I didn't think anything of it.*

The time of day didn't matter. Wolves could see just as well at night as during the day. Dusk was when our vision was at its weakest but still better than any human's.

I hadn't realized that Breena had stopped talking until Annie cleared her throat. I focused on the witch and saw her irises darkening with concern.

"Dick and Saga found shifters to hang out at the lake, pretending to be there for a lazy swim in case backup was needed. Saga and Erin cloaked themselves in the woods, and Erin used malicious magic to kill them." Breena bit her bottom lip. "They had the execution planned so there would be no survivors. The point was to get rid of Griffin's father's outside allies and stop Shadow City from opening its gates. They had watched you enough to know you would carry on your father's legacy, so you both had to go."

His chest shook. "That's why we had no clue who was behind it. Erin covered up the entire attack, and we never suspected a witch was involved. We couldn't sense the magic, and there was no coven around, anyway."

Breena nodded as tears dripped down her chin onto her black shirt. "I'm so sorry. I didn't know. I only learned a few years later when Erin threatened that if I didn't follow along with their plans, I could meet a similar fate. If I had known *then*, I would've warned someone."

I snarled. Her apology didn't make any of this okay.

"It's not your fault, Breena," Annie said gently and

flicked her attention to me. "You were young, hurt, and manipulated."

Her words were a slap to the face. I understood being young and hurt. I'd left my pack behind when they'd needed me, and while I'd been away, horrible things had happened. My rage left me as quickly as it had risen. I was directing my anger at Breena because she was right here.

Erin was the problem.

She always had been.

"She's right," Killian agreed. His grief and agony swirled between us, but if I hadn't felt it, I wouldn't have known. He was standing strong. Only his beautiful chocolate brown eyes were haunted.

"I don't deserve your understanding." Breena clutched her pendant, and her eyes widened. "I've got to go. Erin is back and summoning Diana and me. If I don't get to the city quickly, she'll locate me."

The last thing we needed was for Erin to find Breena here with us, especially if she realized Rosemary's and Levi's blood was missing.

Between bringing us the blood and Breena telling Killian the truth about his family's death, I was pretty comfortable trusting her. "Be careful." Erin had been scheming and making her moves for who knew how long, and to win this war against her, we needed to stand on even ground.

"I'll come back or find a way to meet with Sterlyn tomorrow." Breena tugged on the sleeves of her black sweater and shivered. "Get rid of the blood as quickly as you can. Erin has the blood spelled, so she can easily track it whenever she finds it's gone." She hurried off, leaving Annie, Killian, and me alone in the yard.

The turmoil flowing from Killian dulled like he was in

shock or numb. I remembered experiencing that sensation after I'd learned what had happened to Dad. When the emotions came back, it would feel like he'd lost his family again.

"I've linked with Sterlyn, Cyrus, and Griffin," Annie informed us. She hurried over to the black cauldrons and sniffed, then gagged. "I don't know why I just did that. I hate the smell of blood, but it does smell just like Levi and Rosemary. I'll take a sample to Eliza and have them confirm it hasn't been spelled to smell that way."

Part of a supernatural's scent came from our blood since our magic ran through our veins. "That's a great idea," I said. I'd have offered to go with her, but when Killian crashed, I needed to be with him. "I'll get rid of the rest."

"I'll grab something to put it in and get our car. Be right back." Annie darted away, leaving Killian and me alone.

The numbness was still there, and I watched Killian stare off into the distance.

I wished that I could protect him from what was to come, but some things were impossible. All I could do was be here for him when he broke, whenever that might be. Given how long he'd waited for answers, I doubted it would take much time.

I wasn't sure how to proceed. I didn't want to hold him and cause him to break down, but I didn't want him to think I wasn't here for him. So I simply stood right next to him so he could smell and see me. I'd wait for him to take the lead.

The breeze held a chill that wasn't normal in these parts. The new moon didn't help matters, and the lack of light emphasized the cold. The only noise was the faint rush of the Tennessee River, but even the woodland animals had yet to return.

I didn't blame them.

Time lost all meaning until a gray Honda Pilot drove from the back of the neighborhood toward us.

Annie was back.

She pulled into our driveway and jumped from the SUV. She held two Tupperware containers she obviously planned to use for the blood. She poured a little blood from each cauldron into the clear plastic containers, then fastened the red lids. "I'll let you guys know the verdict as soon as Eliza does whatever the hell she does."

"Just be safe." I forced a smile...or I tried to. Considering how cold my face was and the numbness I felt through our bond, there was no telling if I'd actually managed it.

Her attention darted to Killian, who was still staring at the sky, and she frowned. It wasn't hard to predict what was coming.

She caught my gaze again, sympathy brimming in hers. Not saying anything else, she climbed into the car and drove away.

As her taillights faded, agony shot through our connection. "We should—" Killian started, but he stopped. His bottom lip quivered as he held his sadness at bay.

"I'll take care of it." I knew he was worried about the cauldrons. I picked them up and nodded to the front door. He was going to break down, and I knew he wouldn't want anyone to see. Not because he thought it was a weakness but because his pack needed us to keep up a show of strength with everything going on.

"Let's go inside," I said gently, hoping he'd oblige.

He didn't say a word but relented. The storm of emotions had to be taking all his energy to keep in check.

It was finally my turn to take care of him. He stopped in the living room, gazing at the family portrait, and I rushed to the guest bathroom and poured the blood into the toilet.

Then I flushed it down and quickly washed the cauldrons with soap in the tub. When I got them clean, I pulled out the bottle of bleach and wiped down the tub and the toilet. We couldn't leave a trace behind.

Now that the blood was settled, I got to do what any good mate would do. I helped him into the shower and climbed in, then washed both of us. Afterward, I dried us off then just held him in bed while he got to mourn the family he'd lost.

Over the next three days, panic ensued. More humans were coming to the Ridge and the Terrace instead of leaving, and Breena never showed up again like she'd promised, not even within the city.

The good news was that Breena *had* given us Rosemary's and Levi's blood. With the amount she'd dropped off and the amount that would've been used in the spell to make the demons visible, Erin shouldn't have much, if any, left.

As I dressed, the delicious smell of bacon drifted into the bedroom. Killian had gotten up a few minutes ago to cook breakfast.

Though the night he'd learned about his family's death had been hard, the next day had been much better. He'd needed a night to mourn, but in a way, he'd found peace and forgiveness within himself. He now knew he couldn't have done anything to save them.

Stomach grumbling, I strolled into the kitchen and found him wearing his cartoon fish pajama bottoms and no shirt. He stirred the eggs, causing his biceps to bulge and his abs to constrict just enough to make me drool.

The food smelled delicious, but I'd rather devour my mate.

He smiled crookedly and winked. "Keep that up, and I'll burn breakfast."

I wasn't even embarrassed. He was my mate, and I wanted him. He had nothing to be ashamed of. "I could get behind that plan as long as you're the one behind me."

He moaned. "I gotta say, I love brazen Jewel." He removed the pan from the hot eye and turned off the stove. "But let's make sure we don't set the house on fire."

I'd seen enough fires to last a lifetime. "Sounds good to me."

Stalking to me, he pulled me into his arms and kissed me. I opened my mouth, inviting his tongue inside. I wanted to taste him.

You put clothes on to come in here and seduce me, he teased as he slipped his hands under my shirt. *That's not very nice. But at least I get to unwrap you like a present.*

I snorted. *It's a good thing you already have me because that pickup line was pretty lame.*

He growled. *Damn right I have you.* He hoisted me up in his arms, and I wrapped my legs around his waist. I'd just grabbed the edge of my shirt to remove it when a loud pounding sounded at our front door.

Damn it.

"Go away!" he yelled, and I snickered.

It was likely Emmy. But then his eyes glowed, and he stilled.

Cyrus's voice came from the other side of the door. "I would, but Eliza called all of us over to the coven's location. She wants Lowe and Stephanie to join us."

Though my hunger for Killian hadn't been sated, it had been quashed enough for me to place both feet back on the floor. Eliza and her coven had been desperately working with the witches' network to keep other shifters from being kidnapped. As far as we knew, we were safe, and I suspected that was because we'd destroyed Erin's angel and demon blood. Hopefully, if they were requesting Stephanie's presence, that meant they'd found something positive that could aid her in finding the cure for the shifters.

"Sterlyn just informed me. We'll be right behind you." Killian scowled and pecked my lips. He nodded toward the kitchen. "Will you make us both a biscuit for the road while I get dressed? I'll link with Lowe and inform him of the request."

"Of course." This time, I booped him on the nose, then turned and headed to the stove.

Within minutes, Killian and I were climbing into his truck. I handed him his two biscuits and placed our coffees in the cupholders. I dug into my breakfast, rushing to eat it before it got cold.

We rode the entire way in comfortable silence, though I couldn't help but worry.

He turned onto the makeshift road that led to the hidden backup silver wolf location. The truck jerked as it rolled over the uneven ground. To anyone driving past, it would appear like we were off-roading.

We jerked and jarred for a while until the ground leveled out and turned to dirt. The houses came into view. The fifty modern, one-story homes were built strategically among the sizable oak trees so no one could spot them from overhead. Each one had a similar design, down to the size and dirt-brown color. They'd all been built with the same layout so construction could be done quickly.

The houses closest to the entrance were finished with

solar panels adorning each roof. The ones furthest away weren't completed, but it appeared that the packs staying in the woods had begun working on them again.

Annie's Pilot was parked at the first house on the left. Eliza, Aurora, Circe, Herne, Lux, and Aspen were gathered between the house and the vehicle. Eliza held Annie and Cyrus's baby boy, Arian, while Circe held his twin sister, Lizzy. They were already so loved, and Annie and Cyrus watched their newborns being loved on with adoration in their eyes.

"I swear, these eyes are just like yours and your father's, Cyrus." Eliza brushed a finger against the little boy's cheek. "And the dark hair makes them shine so much brighter."

A slight sting of pain in my heart caught me by surprise. I hadn't ever gotten to meet my uncle Arian, Cyrus and Sterlyn's father.

Though I already knew their color was identical, I glanced at Cyrus. He smiled sadly but looked at Arian with so much love.

My attention darted to the baby girl. She had the silver hair of a silver wolf alpha and dark purple eyes.

Both little ones were adorable, and they were easy to love without even knowing them.

My skin buzzed, even though Killian wasn't touching me, which meant he was watching me. I tore my eyes from the little ones to find him looking at *me* with adoration.

I can't wait until we have our own, he linked, and my heart warmed.

The sound of a vehicle purred behind us as wings fluttered overhead. As I turned toward the noise, Griffin's Navigator peeked through the leafless branches, and Rosemary and Levi landed next to the Pilot. Everyone was here, which hopefully meant we'd get some answers.

As soon as the Navigator parked and Ronnie, Alex, Griffin, and Sterlyn climbed out, Eliza walked toward us and handed Arian to me. Without thinking, I took him in my arms. His warm body heated my skin as I cradled him. His musky scent screamed *shifter*, but a cleanness clung to him that was all baby.

Killian beamed.

"We can go ahead and get started. I wanted to coordinate with Stephanie on where she is in her process with what we've learned. We didn't want to share this information with you anywhere else in case Erin was watching." Eliza kissed the baby's forehead and walked to the center of the group.

Ronnie hurried to my side to see the baby. "Any excuse I can get to leave the city and see my niece and nephew."

"As much as I wish this was a social visit, I requested you here for one reason." Eliza rubbed her hands together. "We think we have a solution to our problem."

"Which problem, exactly?" Levi squinted and wiggled his fingers. "There are several."

"Supernaturals having been exposed to humans," Circe clarified and walked past Annie to hand Lizzy to Sterlyn.

My heart stopped. I must have misunderstood because that sounded way too good to be true. "And how's that?"

"Remember when Breena told us that Erin used vampire blood to make that human forget about Tom and us?" Aurora's chestnut eyes brightened.

"Yes." Griffin lifted his hands in victory. "Did I pass the test?"

"Are you trying to take Sierra's place now that she's tied to Torak's hip?" Alex arched a brow. "Because I hate to say it—she's wittier than you. That was just appalling."

"Yet he's distracted us from the conversation, just like her." Rosemary placed a hand on her hip and glared.

Griffin kicked the ground. "That wasn't appalling."

"Dude." Killian shook his head. "It was."

"But we still love you," Annie said and gave him a thumbs-up.

"What about the amnesia spell?" Cyrus rolled his eyes, but he had a faint smile on his face.

"With the help of the network, we figured it out and cast smaller versions of it." Aurora clapped her hands. "With several covens around the globe, we feel confident we can cast the spell so all humans will forget that we exist."

Arian closed his eyes and nestled into my chest, and I hoped my racing heart didn't disturb him. But this most definitely sounded like *good* news.

Ronnie straightened. "So...you just perform the spell, and it's done? Humans go back to not knowing about us?"

"It isn't so simple." Eliza exhaled. "It has to be cast with vampire blood, the strongest around, and it has to be performed where the secret was revealed."

"There's the bad news." Alex sighed. "It was sounding way too good. There had to be a catch."

I must have missed something. "What do you mean?"

"He means Erin and her coven will know we're in Shadow Ridge, performing magic." Circe waved a hand at our group. "We'll need all of you to stop them from interfering while we perform the spell. Every one of our coven members will be needed to channel this volume of magic, along with the other witches worldwide."

Lovely. That sounded fun.

"Uh...I know I have Mother's demon sword to negate magic, but I can't protect all of us." Levi puffed out his chest. "I'm good, but believe it or not, I have limits."

"Many limits, in fact." Rosemary nodded. "But I still love him."

Killian chuckled as I grinned. She was so honest.

"Sadie's magic can help, and the dragons, if they're willing," Herne said as she stepped forward. "We've been spelling necklaces that will protect you from Erin's spells for some time, although they won't last too long. Erin and her coven will know you're wearing one pretty quickly. We just need you to hold her coven off long enough for us to complete the spell."

"Wait." Alex crossed his arms. "You said the strongest vampire blood around. What does that mean?"

"We'll need cauldrons of your blood and Ronnie's." Eliza tugged on the hem of her shirt. "Maybe even your sister, Gwen, since she's also a full-blooded vampire. But each of you will have to agree. After what happened with Rosemary and Levi—"

"Of course I'll do it. There's no question," Ronnie insisted.

"Wait. What about the demons?" Sterlyn leaned against the Pilot. "I hate to be the bearer of bad news, but that's a whole different issue. The demons might expose us again."

Circe nodded. "We've got a plan for that as well. The spell will be twofold, but we'll need the ruby from the artifact building. The one that you told us was among the stolen artifacts that were planted on Rosemary's mother before the demon war. Azbogah chose it for a reason. It amplifies power, which we'll need for both spells."

"I can get it," Griffin answered. "The guards won't deny me entry to the artifact warehouse with everything going on."

For once, we had a plan, and hopefully, one Erin

wouldn't anticipate. I asked the inevitable question: "When do we do this?"

The purr of the engine from another vehicle filled the air. Killian linked with Lowe and me, *Is that you two?*

Yes, it is. Sorry it took us a few minutes, but Stephanie was in the middle of something in the lab, he replied just as a white Ford Ranger appeared in the clearing.

Our group remained quiet as the Ranger pulled up behind the Navigator, and Lowe and Stephanie got out of the truck. Stephanie was lanky by shifter standards, and she wore her long caramel hair in a haphazard bun on top of her head. Her hunter green eyes shone brightly, and she had a smile plastered across her face. Even before she reached us, she exclaimed, "I think I figured out the antidote!"

Stomach fluttering, I exhaled a breath I hadn't realized I'd been holding. "The shifting control problems can be cured?"

She nodded enthusiastically as she hurried over. "Yes! I just need time to replicate the serum."

Lowe beamed as he took Stephanie's hand in his. "She's pretty damn amazing, and I don't care if I'm biased."

"That's great news." Eliza smiled, but worry still darkened her light green eyes. "But I asked you here for more than that. Do you and your friend have a plan to remove all the testing information from the facility?"

Blinking, Stephanie shook her head as if she were trying to change gears. "We have a plan, though I'm not sure if we can actually use it. Brittany got an IT person's ID and password so she can delete the medical files permanently from the server, but that will raise questions."

"How soon could she be ready to do that?" Eliza rubbed her hands together and leaned toward the shifter.

Stephanie shrugged. "At any time. Preferably during the night when there aren't as many lab techs on site, but—"

"Could she do it tonight?" Circe asked eagerly. "We have a plan to make humans forget all about supernaturals."

Nodding, Stephanie licked her bottom lip. "She can do that. We just need to tell her the time. I'll have her get ready and pack up in case she needs to rush to my parents' place if something goes wrong."

"Tell her all the information needs to be deleted at eleven-thirty tonight. Not a moment sooner or later." Eliza wagged a finger. "If she delays by even a minute, people's minds could be erased and someone logged on could find the folders and see the test results on accident, triggering those questions."

"Can you prepare all that before heading back to Shadow City?" Circe asked. "Tonight, before the humans have time to capture more supernaturals, would be ideal. Just make sure you make the phone calls outside the city."

Lowe tugged on Stephanie's hand. "Let's go. I'll drive farther from the city but somewhere you'll have a cell signal, then I'll get you back to the university so you can continue working on the serum."

"Okay." Stephanie waved as she hurried back to the vehicle, and before long, Lowe was pulling away.

"That settles it. Everything will happen tonight," Eliza answered simply. "Let's hurry."

A branch snapped, and we all turned toward the noise and froze.

CHAPTER TWENTY-EIGHT

WE'D BEEN careful on our way here, ensuring we hadn't been followed. I knew without a doubt that Cyrus and Sterlyn would've done the same. So how in the world had someone found us?

I shouldn't have been surprised, not with our luck.

"Our spells weren't tripped," Circe hissed through gritted teeth. "No one should be here."

Sterlyn and I shuffled into the middle of the group. We held precious cargo, and I couldn't allow Arian to get hurt while in my care. Everyone else crowded in front of us for the same reason.

A flash of blonde hair peeked through the branches, followed by dark brown.

"You've got to be *kidding* me," Sierra shouted from the spot where all the noise was coming from. "You're having a *group* meeting, and no one informed me?" She marched from between a cypress and redbud, yanking her shirt back into place. A twig stuck out of her usual ponytail, but her gray irises were bright with disbelief. "You all have some explaining to do."

Torak strolled out from the same spot, shirtless. With the musk wafting off them, they must have been on a run.

"Oh, no!" Aurora wagged a finger in front of her face. "Don't you dare get an attitude. I told you we might have something figured out, and you said, 'Cool. I'm going for a run.' Don't blame this on us."

Sierra paused a few feet in front of the group. "I didn't know it was 'call in the entire crew' level. That has to be specified."

With all the chaos, Sadie and her friends were staying here with the two newly released packs. Torak had wanted to remain here as well since he had many friends in the one pack. Of course, Sierra had remained by his side.

I wasn't sure why they hadn't completed their bond.

"Babe." Torak snickered, and she glanced over her shoulder.

Her jaw dropped, and she raced to stand in front of him. She growled, "Where is your shirt? It was out there with *your* pants. Thankfully, those aren't missing. 'Cause if they were, we would have some major *problems*."

"You shifted faster than Katherine can from dragon to vampire, which is saying something." Torak wrapped his arms around her so she was completely covering his chest. "And leaving my ass behind. If you don't want me shirtless, wait for me."

She glowered, but his touch worked its magic, and the anger smoothed from her face.

Oh, how I'd missed her since she'd started spending most of her time here. Not the rom-coms she made us watch, but her snark and big personality.

"We don't have time for this, Sierra." Killian's body relaxed as he turned to me. "We've got to prepare. It'll take everyone who can fight to get through tonight."

"That's very true." Cyrus pulled his keys from his pocket. "It would help if some vampires could assist as well."

"Of course we will." Alex puffed out his chest. "Have we not realized that this group is stronger when we work together?"

Ronnie kissed his cheek and murmured, "And that's why he's my husband. So loyal and delectable. Besides, Joshua has been dying to see Lillith."

Eliza scowled. "We've spelled a few more necklaces between planning and have a total of two hundred, but we can't spell more. We need to save our energy for tonight to do this quickly before more supernaturals are captured anywhere around the world."

Two hundred was better than I could've expected with everything they'd been doing to get the answer for tonight. "We'll make it work. We have to."

"We need to head back." Sterlyn pecked the top of Lizzy's head before handing her to Annie. "Erin is in hiding, but the other witches are not. They'll notice if we're gone too long, and we don't want them to suspect anything more than they already do."

Though it was still morning, night would come soon. We had our own pack to organize.

"Will someone catch me up so I can fill in my pack and Donovan and Sadie?" Torak asked as he placed his hands on Sierra's shoulders. "I know we'll all want to help."

"I can do that." Lux waggled her brows.

I suspected she was trying to get a rise out of Sierra rather than actually ogling Torak.

"Watch it," Sierra snarled as her eyes glowed. "We may be friends, but I will cut a bitch for looking at him."

And there it was. Lux beamed, confirming my suspicion.

Even though I didn't want to stop holding my baby cousin, I passed him to Cyrus. He took his son so gently, and his face held so much adoration. He loved his family like any good mate and alpha would.

Taking my hand, Killian tugged me back to the truck. "Sierra, link with Jewel and me when Torak and the others are ready to make plans."

Chest filling with love, I could have exploded. I adored the way Killian included me. "And we should reach out to Jeremiah." We'd only visited the older silver wolf neighborhood once during the past few days. PawPaw's pack was still worried about their shifting problems and sticking close to the hidden neighborhood, afraid to venture out, while Jeremiah's pack had stayed close by to reassure them. I supposed trauma had a way of bringing out the best and worst in people, and this was a fortunate occasion in which it was the best.

Surprisingly, the two packs had grown close, but Jeremiah's pack was still hoping for the situation to be resolved so they could go back to their actual home. This spell and Stephanie's serum could accomplish that.

"Let's get to work." Killian hurried over and opened the passenger door for me, and it wasn't long before we were all rushing off to prepare for the night.

A DAY HAD NEVER PASSED SO QUICKLY. Before I knew it, it was approaching eleven, and the spell-casting would soon be at hand. Sterlyn, Griffin, Rosemary, Levi, Alex, and Ronnie headed back to Shadow City. The witches were acting normal, but Diana, Breena, and Erin still hadn't been seen.

We'd learned that Erin's coven consisted of around seven hundred witches, though no one was certain about the exact number. Most of the witches kept to themselves. No one knew if that was because they weren't interested in knowing other people or because they couldn't leave. But seven hundred witches could channel a *lot* of power.

We'd managed to recruit four hundred and twenty allies to our side. Alex and Ronnie had sent fifty vampires, although they were still dealing with other vampires in their population who'd turned bloodthirsty. We had twenty-three members from the silver wolf pack since Mom and Chad couldn't shift correctly, one hundred wolves from Killian's and my pack, fifty wolves from Jeremiah's pack, fifty guards and police officers from Shadow City, eleven angels, ten demons, twenty dragons, Torak, Sadie, Donovan, Roxy, and Axel. For some reason, the human song "The Twelve Days of Christmas" popped into my head. The only thing we were missing was a partridge in a pear tree.

Unfortunately, we couldn't reach out to other kinds of shifters in Shadow Ridge, as we weren't sure who might be allied with Erin. We stuck with the people we knew we could trust.

We also didn't want too many cars driving in from Sadie's and Torak's packs. Though they were staying close to Eliza and Circe's coven, there was no telling where Erin might have eyes now that she knew we were working against her. Sierra hadn't completed her bond with Torak, so we would use her as the communication point to coordinate when they arrived.

The spell needed to be performed at the moon's peak, which was around eleven-thirty. On Eliza's signal, covens around the world would begin the spell at the same time, based on our time zone.

All the packs would be in wolf form. That was when our magic was strongest, and we needed that strength to fight Erin and her coven. Eliza had made that clear. As soon as Erin felt the immense magic being channeled, she would come.

Our group ran through the woods to the downtown area, where Billy was making sure all the humans were in their rooms. We'd instituted a curfew since the last demon attack, and we hoped that would keep the humans out of the way.

The silver wolf pack—minus Sterlyn, Chad, and Mila—my pack, and the vampires were heading to the spell site and would stick to the woods until it was time. Since we were on the front lines, we all wore a necklace so we could be protected long enough for our backup to arrive. The remaining twenty-six necklaces had been given to Sierra and Torak to hand out however they saw fit.

Sierra remained with Torak, the dragons, Sadie and her friends, and Jeremiah's pack members while our reinforcements in the city waited in their homes so they wouldn't raise any alarms. Everyone was on edge and eager for this to end.

If anything went wrong, our chance of making the world forget about us could be over. I linked with Killian, Lowe, and Sierra, *Stephanie has the cure ready and talked to her friend, Brittany, who is still working at the last facility.*

The plan is in place, and everyone knows their part, Lowe replied. *Stephanie is at the Shadow Ridge University lab, getting the cure in the appropriate doses.*

And the witches got the ruby? I asked. My anxiety swirled through our fated-mate bond.

Killian answered, *Roman, a trusted guard who works at the artifact building, handed the ruby over to Griffin. Kira, a fox shifter friend, got it to Bune, who sneaked it to our witches.*

Everything the witches needed had been secured.

The trees thinned as we got closer to the brick buildings of downtown. A few raccoons scurried through the woods, oblivious to what was about to go down.

The vampires moved quietly behind us, carrying firearms. They could've outrun us, but they were letting us take the lead on the Ridge side. Alex and Ronnie had provided us with their most trusted warriors, and they weren't trying to show off with us.

The plan was for the wolves to hold off the witches, hoping to distract them so the vampires could shoot and incapacitate them from afar. But we were all experienced enough to know that plans rarely went as expected.

My blood thrummed faintly with my angel magic. The waxing moon was slightly less than a quarter, enough for me to get a jolt in size and energy. The seventeen other silver wolves running in our large group would be feeling the same energy. The four regular wolves wouldn't feel any different since they were silver wolf mates, but Annie would have the biggest jolt of magic as a demon wolf whose powers were strongest when the moon was mostly dark. She was slightly less than double any other wolf's size.

Even though a battle was imminent, my wolf was happy to be free. As we drew closer to downtown, I pranced through the woods, enjoying these last few moments of freedom.

Through the branches, downtown came into view, the lone light midway through the town changing from red to green despite no traffic. Usually, this area was bustling, even at this late hour, with the bars, holiday decorations, and festivities, but not today. The silence was creepy.

My happy-go-lucky feeling vanished now that we were arriving.

Five police officers from our pack walked the street, making sure the curfew was being followed. They scanned the areas for cameras and cell phone video recorders. We couldn't chance the spell being livestreamed, especially not if it worked.

An owl hooted, and the breeze ruffled my fur. We spread out, waiting for our witches to arrive.

Killian linked with our packmates, *Remember to hold back the Shadow City witches, but be careful.*

I lifted my head, the urge to howl nearly overwhelming me. Killian was such an amazing man, and most importantly, mine. It was easy to believe that your own life was inconsequential in battle.

Our witches appeared in the streets of downtown as if from thin air. They must have used the spell Erin had once employed in front of me.

Eliza had said that all one hundred were coming, and the streets of downtown weren't so empty anymore. They all gathered in front of the building where Killian had been standing while he'd been interviewed on TV the very first time I'd seen him.

Had that been only a month ago? It felt like forever.

Circe, Aspen, Eliza, Lux, Hern, and Aurora stood in the center, and the other coven members circled around them. Circe held a small black cauldron that contained Alex's, Ronnie's, and Gwen's blood. Aspen, Eliza, Lux, Hern, and Aurora formed a tight circle around her, each one touching her shoulders or arms. The other coven members reached out, touching the person in front of them, forming a chain of bodies while grasping a black stone in their free hand.

I looked at the sky, noting that the moon was rising high.

The witches began chanting. "*Fac ut obliviscatur circa magica*." Though various voices could be heard, they merged into one. The effect was eerie and something I never would have imagined if I hadn't heard it.

Nothing happened.

Do we know what to expect? Lowe linked. *I don't sense anything.*

Wolves couldn't feel the magic from a spell since ours was an animal magic and not one of earth.

No, but we need to keep an eye out for the Shadow City coven, Killian replied. *Jewel and I will join the half stationed near the bridge they'll take to come here. We need to surprise them.*

My heart warmed. Out of everyone in our pack, my wolf was the strongest. Even Killian had admitted that. Between that and our training, he'd realized we both needed to be part of the first defense. I was also the alpha mate and couldn't expect my pack to do something I wasn't willing to do myself. Most important, we'd learned that the two of us were strongest together.

Killian huffed and linked, *Lowe, I'm counting on you to lead the pack on this side. Your dad is close by and will be here with you, too.*

Though I wasn't an alpha, I could feel the pride emanating from Lowe.

Determined to be beside him, I caught up quickly, and out of the corner of my eye, I watched as Cyrus and Annie led a few silver wolf pack members to us. Of course, Killian, Sterlyn, and Griffin would be communicating.

The river rushed louder beside us as Killian and I and a

few silver wolves ran together. The vampires knew to stay there and shoot if needed, so none of them followed us.

Erin's coven is moving, Killian linked with the pack. *Everyone hurry. They're at the gate, and the guards are opening it. Sterlyn and the others in the city are heading to the gate to slow them down.*

Heart pounding, I pushed my wolf legs harder. Our group panted, and I attempted to control my breathing. Getting lightheaded and out of breath wouldn't be good when the war hadn't officially started. I focused on our goal —the long, elegant gate that reminded me of the pictures I'd seen of the Golden Gate Bridge, with its immense towers that jutted toward the sky.

But when my attention landed on the gate, it was already open, with witches pouring from it. I blinked. *I thought Sterlyn's group was going to stall them inside.*

They're trying, but witches are attacking them. Sterlyn, Griffin, Alex, Ronnie, Gwen, Roman, Kira, and more guards and police officers can't get through the gate like they planned.

The witches in front would be the strongest, which was how they'd opened the gate so quickly.

They must be desperate. I was certain they didn't know what Eliza and the coven were doing, but they knew it couldn't be good.

Let's move! Killian shouted. *Someone send some vampires down here. We'll cut them off on the bridge.*

The closer Erin's coven got to our witches, the easier it would be for them to pool their magic together and stop the spell. Vampires firing in two locations might give them pause.

I'll tell the vampires, Billy linked. *I'm heading there now and haven't shifted.*

That worked.

Cyrus and Annie glanced at Killian and me, and as soon as Killian nodded, the four of us took off, our packs following behind.

We raced to the beginning of the bridge. I was closer now to Shadow City than I'd ever wanted to be, but this was war.

As we turned right, where the grass ended and the cement of the bridge met the ground, the coven was about a quarter of the way to us, with Erin leading the pack. Her scarlet-streaked black hair flew behind her, and her misty gray eyes could have been black.

When she saw us, she sneered and raised her hands, her lips already moving.

I braced myself for whatever spell she tossed at us.

CHAPTER TWENTY-NINE

SOMETHING SLAMMED into me and coated my skin like sludge. Though it was tugging me backward, I was able to continue my forward momentum.

Does it feel like oil is all over you? I asked Killian.

No, but we're being pushed back, he replied.

Interesting. Maybe I could feel the magic's negativity because I could sense its caster's essence. In a way, magic was part of someone's soul.

Erin's eyes widened as she pointed at us and glanced at a young woman beside her. The woman had long maroon hair and ebony eyes. A faintly malicious aura swirled around her.

I suspected that was Diana, Breena's sister. I searched the frontline for Breena, fearing she'd told Erin everything she knew about us, but she wasn't there.

I dug my paws into the cement, determined not to get pushed off the bridge. We had to give the vampires time to get into position.

Annie inched out in front of us, her extra strength and size giving her leverage.

The witch who must be Diana lifted her hands. Her lips moved, and the sludge across my skin thickened as her spell amplified Erin's.

Despite casting spells, the witches continued to hurry toward us, their faces set in grim determination. They were as resolute as we were in their goal to stop us.

More witches chanted, and the pressure and maliciousness became damn near unbearable.

But I refused to give up. I snarled as I pressed forward. Annie, Cyrus, and the rest of the silver wolves pulled ahead of the other wolves by a few feet. We had enough moon magic flowing in our veins to give us a slight edge.

The witches were halfway to us.

I wasn't sure how much longer we could fight the magic. As more witches came out of the gate, they joined the spell, adding to its potency.

Something dark caught my attention, and I tore my gaze from the witches to see ten demons floating out of the gates and over the witches' heads. Mocha eyes focused on me, confirming one of them was Levi. As he soared toward us, he removed his shadow sword from his side.

He was the only demon I'd ever seen with a sword that had a shadow form. He'd mentioned it had belonged to his mother.

Sword raised, he lowered himself to the bridge right in front of us. I had no clue what he was planning, but he was going to get hurt. I'd expected the demons to attack from overhead while the witches were distracted, not get in front of our group.

When he landed in front of us, the pressure against my body disappeared, and I stumbled forward. Fortunately, I righted myself as the shadow sword shimmered.

His sword was shielding us from the magic spell. I

wanted to watch in awe, but I'd have to marvel about it later.

All the wolves on the bridge lunged forward. Our claws tapped on the pavement like a battle cry before war.

"Auntie, what's happening?" Diana gasped, her eyes wide. She stretched out her hands, palms facing us, as if that would resolve the issue.

"It's that demon and the demon sword he's bonded to," Erin spat. She yelled over her shoulder, "Direct your magic to the side you're closest to, not the center."

She intended to go around Levi.

They were just a few feet in front of us, and I crouched to move faster.

Everyone, do the best you can, Killian linked as he kept pace a few steps behind me.

When I was close enough to reach her, I lunged at Erin.

She chanted, "*Fac ea volant retro*!" and lifted her hands toward me.

The force rammed into me, throwing me back several feet into Killian. We tumbled, and the wolves behind him stopped short.

Luckily, pain didn't explode between us, but I still had to check on my mate. *Are you okay?*

I'm fine. I'm just glad I cushioned your fall, he replied as he nudged his head into my fur.

"Why didn't she go back farther?" Erin said through gritted teeth, and raised her hands again.

A demon with icy black eyes—Zagan—darted down to Erin. He slammed into her, causing her to trip and crash into Diana. The other demons darted into action, attacking the front line.

This was our chance.

Everyone, move! I linked as I jumped onto my feet and closed the distance between Erin and me.

She lifted her palms, one toward the sky where Zagan was located and the other at me, and shouted, "*Mitterent flammas!*"

Flames shot from her palms toward Zagan and me. The demon was able to fly backward, avoiding the fire, but not me. My fur burned, and I whimpered as I tried to get away.

Her palm followed me, and the flames charred my chest. My skin smoked, and the smell of hot flesh had my stomach roiling. That was *me*.

Jewel, Killian linked. His terror caused my chest to tighten and increased my agony.

"Damn it!" Levi hissed, and soon, he was in front of me, his sword positioned before us. The flames licked his sword but didn't blow past. Erin's face twisted in anger.

The throbbing agony in my chest was bearable. That had to be due to the necklace Eliza had given me. If not for that, I was certain I'd have been debilitated. No wonder Eliza had mentioned that Erin would figure it out quickly. Her eyes narrowed, and her gaze locked onto my chest.

I glanced down to see that my fur had burned away, exposing the necklace.

Ugh. I'd hoped that our protection spell would remain undetected for a little longer. Now the witches would be determined to take them.

Head back, Killian linked. *You're injured.*

This time, his concern didn't annoy me. I had no doubt he had felt my pain, and he wasn't overbearing...just genuinely worried. *It's not bad. I promise. The necklace did its job.* I linked with the entire pack, *The witches know we have a protection spell, so be careful.*

"Hold off on your magic," Erin commanded. "Tell the

witches in the back. Until their necklaces are removed, we should conserve our energy."

So they wouldn't be spelling us any longer. I wasn't sure if I should be comforted or worried.

The witches rushed toward us, and with each one of their steps, we countered with two. Like last time, I ran around Levi and pounced on Erin. She didn't throw her palms out; instead, she removed a black-handled dagger. Its silver blade was crooked, reminding me of an ocean wave. The tip of the dagger was a sharp point.

She swung the dagger at me, but her hand was unsteady, indicating she wasn't comfortable with hand-to-hand combat. I ducked. The blade *swoosh*ed past my fur, and I noted her other hand reaching for me.

Determination fueled me, and I spun away. Her hand grabbed the air where my chest had been a second before.

Her mouth tilted down, and her nostrils flared. As she swung her arm at me again, she stumbled a few steps forward, nearly losing her balance in her black high-heeled shoes. Her low top crept lower, and I didn't know how her boobs didn't pop out.

In hand-to-hand combat, I had the edge.

The other wolves engaged in battle with the front line of witches as wings pounded from behind. Rosemary and Eleanor flew from the gates with nine angels I'd never seen before. They spread out, but the witches in the back shot spells at them. I'd expected them to ricochet off their wings like bullets, but that wasn't the case.

The witches used wind against the angels, but it didn't seem to impact our feathered allies. One witch decided to use fire. A dark-haired male angel flew backward to get out of the way, but the momentum shift was too much, and the flames hit his wings, singeing his feathers.

Unfortunately, the angels didn't have necklaces. The angel fell, and the witches changed their tactics to fire.

Out of the corner of my eye, I saw Erin swing at me, but I reacted too late. I'd been distracted.

Dark fur flashed in my peripheral vision, and before the dagger could connect, Killian had knocked her hand off course, keeping me safe.

"Auntie!" Diana exclaimed as she turned to Erin. "*Opprimer terram!*"

Killian snarled, and his body slowed as if he were fighting gravity. *I'm being pushed to the ground, and I can't move fast enough to fight it.*

Chuckling, Erin snatched the necklace from my mate's neck and rasped, "It's over for you." As she lifted her hand to perform a spell on him, I used every ounce of my strength to jump and bite her hand. Maybe if I injured it, that would level the playing field.

She groaned and swung the dagger at my neck. She was going for the kill. One of us would have to die.

Releasing my hold, I scooted back on all fours, her dagger just missing my head. Diana had expected the move and ripped the charm from my neck.

Now both Killian and I were exposed.

But giving up wasn't an option. I didn't hesitate and attacked.

"*Canite eam auferet!*" Erin chanted and pointed at me.

Something struck me, lifting my body high into the sky. I was thrown clear across the bridge, landing where the grass and cement connected.

My entire body jarred as I landed, and my head hurt as if my brain had been jostled. I blinked a few times, seeing double, and waited for the two bridges to become one. I didn't want to jump into the river when I thought I was running on cement.

Dark fur shot toward me, and I knew who it was.

Killian.

I wanted to soften his landing, but I wasn't sure where he'd fall.

Regardless, I had to help my mate. I stood, my legs nearly buckling, just as he crashed to the ground ten feet away.

His pain mixed with mine, but it didn't worsen my vision. I hurried to him, almost tripping over his body. I linked, *Killian!*

I didn't break anything, he replied. *Just a little pain. Yours feels worse.*

At least he hadn't said he was fine when he clearly wasn't.

The pain is ebbing. That wasn't technically a lie, but I wished it would fade faster.

I watched in horror as more wolves lost their pendants. The silver wolf pack had engaged in battle, with Cyrus and Annie taking my spot and Killian's with Erin and Diana. But now the witches knew our weakness.

When the pendant was off Darrell, a witch shot flames at him, engulfing his body in fire.

No! He was like a father to me, and I couldn't lose a second one. I raced toward him, desperate to reach him to save him.

He whimpered loudly, indicating pain I'd never seen him in before. My heart broke, even though I couldn't feel him via a pack link anymore. Lungs seizing, I tapped into what little angel magic I had to reach him faster.

I'm coming with you, Killian linked behind me, but I didn't wait for him. Someone I loved needed me.

The stench of burned meat blew back to me, and I nearly vomited.

Darrell stumbled backward as he tried to free himself from the flames, but the witch followed him, a sick smile spreading across her face.

Levi's shadow head turned, and his gaze latched onto Darrell. He hurried over to him, putting the sword between the witch and the wolf.

Thank gods!

The witch's focus was on hurting Darrell, so she didn't notice me. I leaped, and my teeth sank into her neck. Her warm blood spilled into my mouth, a hint of herbs mixed with copper. I jerked my head, thrashing her neck so there was no way she could survive.

A strangled cry came from my right, and I turned to find a male witch focused on me. I linked with Killian, *Get Darrell out of here.* This witch wouldn't let me leave. He was enraged about what I'd done.

No, I'm not leaving you. Killian replied.

Before I could respond, Emmy appeared beside her dad. She was taking care of him.

The male witch growled, "*Fac eam explodere in flammas.*"

My skin grew hot, and I whimpered. He was burning me alive.

Levi appeared before me, letting his sword take the brunt of the spell. "Get out of here. All of you," he commanded.

Sterlyn and the others are on the bridge, heading this way. It's slow, but they're fighting the weaker witches from the back, Killian informed us. *Levi wants us to retreat. Everyone, head back now.*

I wanted to tell him no, but we were completely

outnumbered. Pain sliced through my chest as a pack link cooled—someone had died.

Everyone, retreat, or we're going to be slaughtered, Killian commanded.

Normally, I would have argued, but there were hundreds of them compared to our forty, and the ache of the loss of a packmate nearly had me crumbling in front of everyone.

We pulled away, running toward the entrance to the bridge. The hair on the back of my neck stood tall. They could pick us off. Our only saving grace was the demons and angels who were keeping the witches occupied, but when I glanced over my shoulder, I could see only six angels. Five had flown off, gotten injured, or worse.

Dark laughter danced behind us.

"Let's end them all!" a woman cooed.

"No!" Erin exclaimed. "That's too easy. Let them run. We have to stop that spell. After it's over, we'll teach them what happens when you go against an enemy far stronger than you. It'll be the last lesson they'll ever receive, and they won't forget it, even in death."

They were taunting us, but worse, I was certain she meant it. She had such evil inside her that I wasn't sure she'd ever had humanity.

I had to believe we could find a way to get out of this mess. We had a lot more fighters waiting, and hopefully, the dragons were immune to their fire.

As we reached the bridge entrance, a sweet smell caught my attention.

The vampires were here. I scanned the area and found them hiding behind the bushes. They could slow the witches further.

Behind us, the witches ran, their feet pounding.

"Remember, the witches are our main focus. Get to them and end whatever spell they're casting!" Erin commanded. "Do not waste more energy than necessary until we end that spell."

That was why they weren't frying us. We needed to find a way to drain them dry. I linked with Killian, *Maybe it's time to bring out Sadie and the dragons.*

The closer they got to our witches, the easier it would be to use their magic against them. *And we should tell everyone to join us*, I added. *We didn't hold them off long enough. We can't let them reach Eliza and Circe.* I didn't want to give the orders; Killian did.

He huffed beside me, the pain of our lost pack member affecting everyone. We all wanted to mourn the loss, but that would have to come after.

He repeated the order, and Sierra linked, *It's about damn time!*

As we turned the corner toward downtown, our group ran far enough ahead that the vampires wouldn't have a hard time hitting the witches. Levi and the other demons had remained on the bridge, Levi protecting all the angels he could with his sword.

The battle was pure chaos.

Gunfire rang as the vampires aimed at Erin, Diana, and the others in front of the line. The witch next to Erin got shot in the arm and groaned.

Erin mashed her lips together and exclaimed, "*Aperi terram*!" The other witches jumped in, using the same line as they focused their spell on where the vampires were hiding. A witch close to the vampires got shot between the eyes and fell, but the witches chanted louder.

The ground shook under my feet, and my stomach

clenched tightly. I didn't have to be a witch to know they were commanding the earth.

Retreat! Killian linked.

Annie and Cyrus must have determined the same thing because the silver wolves were moving seconds before us. They were retreating from the shaking directly under our feet.

My body shook so hard that my teeth rattled. Roars echoed around us, and I wasn't sure if it was coming from underneath or above, that was how badly my body was shaking and my ears were ringing.

A long, faint crack opened in the earth, right in front of the vampires. They were so focused on taking down the witches that they didn't see the threat. They were going to get swallowed up if they didn't pay attention.

Fear hit me. I didn't know how we would survive this.

CHAPTER THIRTY

SOMETHING POUNDED ABOVE ME, and I diverted my attention to the sky, afraid that the witches were launching multiple attacks. My vision jarred from the shaking underneath me, but there was no denying what I saw.

Dragons.

The earth cracked. I had to do something to get the vampires' attention. I linked with Killian, *I'm heading over there.*

Killian's head swung toward me as I bolted past him. His fear wafted through our bond, but he didn't stop me. Instead, he linked with the rest of the pack, *Back up, and get out of the way.*

My back tingled, indicating that Killian was following me.

The earth split, the hole growing larger as the witches channeled magic toward the vampires and wolves.

As I ran toward the vampires, another crack appeared under the fescue grass. My stomach churned. *Killian, jump!* I leaped as far as I could toward the tree line. The fissure started where I'd been moments ago and trailed after me as if it had a brain of its own.

Damn witches.

As the fracture reached under my body once more, I howled to warn the vampires and rolled away from the witches and toward downtown.

The gunfire stopped.

My heartbeat hammered in my ears in time with my shaking body, making any other noise hard to hear. I glanced behind me to see Killian's lower body hanging into the crevice. His claws dug into the earth, but they were beginning to slide as dirt crumbled underneath him.

No!

I swallowed hard as I raced back to my mate. *Killian, I'm coming.*

Do not! he replied, and a lump formed in my throat at his concern.

He must have lost his mind if he thought I'd stand by while his life literally hung in the balance.

The dragons flew over us. Their scaly wingbeats were deafening over my internal battle. Heat swirled around me, removing the chill from the air as the strong scent of brimstone scorched my lungs.

I reached Killian as Cyrus and Annie led the wolves to the bushes, then raced toward the vampires. The dragons had caught the witches off guard, and they were attacking the new threat.

Cyrus hurried over as I placed my paws on top of Killian's to keep him steady. He had to get out before another witch struck us. I linked, *Climb up.*

I'm trying, he answered, determination radiating through our connection. *My claws keep cutting through the earth. I can't get leverage.*

Huffing, Cyrus pranced beside me to get someone's attention without making too much noise. I wished I could shift back into human form and pull him up with my hands, but I was afraid to remove my paws from his.

He dropped another inch, and I gritted my teeth, pressing down on his paws. I whimpered, unable to hide my heartbreak. I couldn't lose him.

Gunfire started again, and I damn near cried. The vampires didn't realize we needed help, and the angels were still fighting the witches on the bridge, trying to prevent more from reaching land.

I pushed down as hard as I could, desperate to keep Killian from falling, and when his eyes homed in on me, I stopped breathing.

If I don't make it out of this, I need you to move— Killian started.

Stop right there. My lungs started to move erratically. *We are* not *saying goodbye. I will not lose you.*

Something appeared beside me, and my chest tightened. I didn't have the ability to fight an enemy right now, so when I detected the sweet scent of a vampire and Joshua's face appeared before me, my eyes burned with unshed tears. I'd been so certain that Killian would die.

Joshua leaned into the opening and wrapped his arms around Killian's chest. Cyrus hurried over and lay on top of Joshua's legs to keep him anchored. Joshua lifted Killian out of the hole and set him down on solid ground.

Cyrus moved off Joshua's leg, allowing Joshua to release my mate. Joshua breathed heavily and sat up on his knees. Sweat beaded on his upper lip from his exertion, and his attention darted back to the witches.

I brushed my head against his arm, saying thank you the only way I could in animal form.

He must have understood because his eyes softened. "If it weren't for you two racing toward us and howling, I would've lost several fighters. So thank *you*."

Joshua stood. He removed a gun from his waistband, lifted it at the witches, and fired. "We can hold them off for a minute. Go regroup. We'll need everybody on hand."

Killian had already alerted our pack, and they should be getting closer. In theory, separating so multiple groups could attack was smart because Erin might not expect us to have more backup.

Needing to touch Killian, I nuzzled his neck. The buzz of our connection sprang to life, and some of the fear that had clutched my body receded. He was still alive.

We can see you, Lowe linked with the pack. *Those dragons are kicking the witches' asses.*

I turned back toward the witches to watch the battle. The witches used their magic and fire against the dragons, but they didn't seem impacted by it. I knew gunfire could hurt them the same as us, so hopefully, the witches wouldn't pick up on that.

Erin and Diana stood side by side, fighting the dragons, but the priestess kept glancing at us, and it wasn't hard to figure out why.

Static surged around us, growing more intense with each passing second. The warm feeling of our coven's spell had me on edge. If I hadn't trusted the coven, I'd have been terrified, so I understood Erin's reaction.

A witch farther from the vampires broke from the group and ran across the road. All the wolves had dispersed from that area, seeking shelter from the witches' spells, so there was no one there to track him.

Shit.

I pulled away from Killian, needing to get my head back

in the game. The slight pause was over, and the witches were gaining momentum. More witches joined the wind spell, forcing the dragons back, while a dozen more witches began spelling water from the Tennessee River to splash out their flames.

Our moment of having a slight upper hand was over. I shouldn't have been surprised. They had close to double our numbers.

A dozen dead witches were scattered over the ground, but the coven stepped over the bodies as if they didn't matter. Erin and the witches focused their magic, forcing the dragons back.

I hated that they could do it, but they had to be draining their magic.

I raced across the road, determined to stop the witch I'd seen. Killian tried to follow, but I heard him stumble to the ground. Faint pain swirled through the bond, and my stomach roiled. I wished I could come up with a way to get him out of here. I'd almost lost him, and I didn't want him to get hurt again.

Damn it, Jewel. I can't keep up. I injured my leg climbing out of that hole. He growled threateningly behind me. *Wait up.*

I'm just going to slow that witch down until someone else can break free and help me.

I'm heading that way, Lowe linked. *I see you running across the street.*

I wanted to tell him to stay back with the rest of the pack, but that would be foolish. The witch could kick my ass unless he was drained, but from the quick glance I'd gotten, he hadn't seemed tired. *Okay. Make sure no one else slips away.*

The more of an advantage they gained over us, the

easier it would be for more witches to sneak away to do who knew what. We couldn't follow every single one of them. There weren't enough of us.

The male witch sees you, Killian linked as my paws hit the sidewalk. I ran around the building where the witch had disappeared, not letting the update affect me. It didn't matter. I couldn't let him get away, nor could I let Lowe handle him alone. Lowe was coming to back me up.

As I turned the corner, the herbal scent grew stronger...like he'd be right in front of me at any second. I tried to remain quiet, and when I took the last step around the back of the building, the witch was standing at the tree line, ten feet away, with his palms extended at me.

He'd known I was coming.

"*Ventus audi mandatum meum,*" he said in a low, cold voice.

A gust of wind knocked into me, and I flew across the clearing and slammed into the large cypress tree right next to him. My head hit the trunk, and I was pinned against the tree as the wind rushed over me.

The pressure made it hard to inhale. I opened my mouth so I could breathe that way, but my tongue stuck to the roof of my mouth, making breathing even harder.

A grim smile stretched across his face, and he stepped eagerly toward me. He lowered one palm and removed a knife from his waist. He held it in front of his face, letting the faint stream of light from the slightly less than quarter moon glint off the edge. "I bet your angel-wolf blood can be used for something powerful."

Gods, I hoped not. A warning tingled in my stomach, but I couldn't escape.

He lowered the knife to my neck, watching my face

intently. I wouldn't give him any pleasure by showing distress.

Lowe ran around the other side of the building, and hope exploded in my chest. He moved quickly toward us, but I needed to keep the witch's eyes on me. So I played the part he wanted me to: I whimpered, though the wind felt like it stole my breath. The corner of his eyes squinched, confirming he'd heard my cry. He smiled widely, his teeth so blinding white they hurt my eyes.

"And they said your kind was so brave." He chuckled as he pressed the knife into my fur. With the knife's position, if I gasped too much, I'd injure myself worse.

The edge of the knife stung my skin, but it wasn't awful...yet. My lungs, however, desired to take a deep breath.

Lowe snarled, revealing his presence to the witch. I wanted to smack him. He should've attacked while the witch was focused on me.

The witch spun and swung his open palm toward Lowe while keeping the dagger on me.

I jerked my head to the right, away from the blade, and pounced on the witch's chest. His eyes bulged as my claws thrashed through his black shirt and cut into his flesh. I clamped my teeth onto his throat and ripped through skin and cartilage as quickly as possible. I didn't want to taste his blood any more than I had to.

As the witch fell to his knees, two quick intakes of breath behind me confirmed my worst fears.

More witches were coming.

Lowe ran past me and the body, leaping toward the newcomers.

"*Vocabo ignem*," a petite, ash-blonde witch shouted. Flames poured from her palms and slammed into Lowe.

Luckily, he had the pendant, but watching flames engulf his body was something that would haunt me for the rest of my life. I ran toward Ash Blonde and...Diana.

Diana wrinkled her nose and shouted, "*Opprimere eam in terram!*"

The gust that had pinned me to the cypress's trunk forced me onto my belly. Severe pressure pressed on my back, and my spine popped.

A familiar voice shouted, "Let them go!"

Sadie.

Sierra, Torak, and Donovan's pack had arrived.

The witches ignored the newcomers until a pink beam sliced across the clearing and into Ash Blonde's chest. The petite witch stumbled back, displaying a hole in her black cotton shirt from the impact.

Dark fur flashed into sight, and Killian steamrolled Diana from behind. She stumbled forward, using her hands to brace herself and releasing me from whatever hold she'd had on me.

Donovan and Axel sped across the clearing in their wolf forms, landing on the two witches, while Sadie, Roxy, Torak, and Sierra hurried past, racing to join the fight on the main street. Sadie, Torak, and Sierra had remained in their human forms.

April linked with the pack, *Erin got by the group stationed in front of Eliza and the coven.*

Cold fear doused my body, turning my blood to ice. *Killian, we've got to stop her. Can you tell Sterlyn so she can tell the silver wolf pack?*

Already on it, he rasped. *Sierra, if you can, tell Levi. We'll need his sword.*

Pride swirled through the bond. *Yes,* she linked, *I'll find him now.*

Just please *be careful*, Killian replied, his dread adding to my inner turmoil.

He hated putting Sierra in danger, believing she wasn't adequately trained. He'd acted the same way with me at first. I'd thought he didn't think I could hold my own in a fight, but now I understood he feared losing me like he had the rest of his family.

Trusting Donovan, Lowe, and Axel to handle the witches, Killian and I took off. He limped a little behind me, but I couldn't wait up. Not if Erin was close to Eliza.

I'm sorry, I started.

No, you need to go. But you'd better not get hurt!

The trust I'd needed from him from the very beginning had finally appeared.

My wolf surged forward as we ran toward the coven circle. The air was energized as if it had come alive and had a mind of its own. I wondered how long these spells would last. We'd been fighting for what felt like hours.

I stayed behind the buildings even after the woods gave way to more restaurants and various other brick buildings that surrounded the main strip of downtown. The area wasn't huge, and there wasn't much back here before civilization faded into woods and other neighborhoods close by. Shifters enjoyed being out in nature.

I cut over on the road that led to the town's lone traffic light. I should've outrun Erin by now.

As I raced forward, I saw Eliza and the coven to my right. Something red floated out of the black cauldron and disseminated into the air.

I ran onto the main road, about twenty feet ahead of Erin. Her face was bright red with anger as she crouched and raised a hand, aiming a spell at the cauldron.

Her lips moved, and I didn't have enough time to reach

her. I scampered to the spot that would put me right in front of her magic and stood on my hind legs. A horribly agonizing throb built inside my chest as if my heart might explode.

I tried to gasp, but the pain was intense. I'd been wrong before—I'd never experienced torture like *this*.

Jewel! Killian linked. *I'm almost there. Hold on.*

Erin released the spell, her eyes narrowing. "You stupid mutt. You just got what you deserved." She stepped sideways, lifting her hands again, but I crumpled. The agony wasn't receding, and my heart was beating erratically.

If I didn't stop her spell, my pain would have been for nothing. I tried to climb back onto all four legs, but she crouched again, taking aim.

After everything we'd done to protect our witches, she was going to ruin the spell. *Killian, I can't stop her.*

All I could do was witness the chaos. More witches rushed to aid Erin, the dragons chasing after the horde but not stopping enough of them. The witches' numbers were wearing our side down. A few silver wolves ran beside the witches to hold them off, but they were blasted by spell after spell.

This was it. Our Hail Mary hadn't worked.

I'm here. I see you, Killian linked, our bond surging with panic, increasing the discomfort in my chest.

Erin's lips moved, and my heart sped up as my shifter magic tried to heal me, but it wasn't enough.

Darkness floated across my vision.

It had to be death.

That seemed fitting in this moment, but I wouldn't die doing nothing. I'd vowed to protect until my last breath, and that was exactly what I'd do.

CHAPTER THIRTY-ONE

STRENGTH SURGED through the fated-mate bond into me, and I tried valiantly with my last few seconds on Earth to protect everyone I loved. Everyone who needed the humans to forget about them.

Though I moved, I wasn't fast enough. Erin's lips were moving as she cast the spell.

Stay down! Killian linked, his desperation choking me. The surge of his alpha power coursed through him as he readied to make me obey.

He wasn't being an asshole, but I also knew I didn't have to obey. I was stronger than him, but I *wanted* to follow him.

Erin smirked evilly as her mouth repeated the chant. She knew she was going to ruin the spell.

I crouched, the pressure in my chest intensifying. I braced to launch myself at her.

Her smile dropped, and her nostrils flared.

Pausing, I turned my head toward Eliza and the coven and realized what the darkness I'd seen was.

Levi.

He stood in front of the coven in shadow form, sword raised. Dark tendrils of magic swirled around the blade as it absorbed Erin's spell. He'd arrived in time to block her.

Red liquid shot into the air just as Erin snarled, "No!" She lifted her hands above her head and said, "*Ventus pulsate descendit sang*—"

Before she could finish her chant, Breena appeared beside me. She shouted quickly, "*Removere aere ab intus*!"

Erin's voice vanished, though her lips still moved, and her eyes bulged as she jerked her head toward the witch beside me.

Continuing the chant, Breena moved in front of me. Killian ran past Erin, his attention locked on me.

When he reached my side, he nuzzled me and linked, *Let's get you off the main road.*

Not yet. I settled back down on the cement, not wanting to leave until we knew our witches had achieved their goal. I also wasn't sure I could make it that far. My heart was pumping harder with each passing second, and I was beginning to wonder what spell she'd hit me with because I was certain my heart might burst from my chest.

Eliza and the others stopped chanting, and Eliza set down the black cauldron. They didn't look upset, though sweat covered their faces. Eliza removed a huge ruby from her dress pocket and opened her other palm to reveal a pointed smoky topaz before clasping the stones and her hands together.

They're starting the demon spell, Killian linked with our pack—and likely with Sterlyn and Griffin as well.

Some weight lifted from my shoulders, but things weren't officially over. As long as the malicious demons were around, our secret could be exposed again.

Someone, please find Rosemary, Killian continued. *Jewel isn't doing well.*

I'm actually close to her, Sierra replied. *She came to check on us. I'm telling her.*

I didn't want to dissuade him because I wanted to live, but I wasn't sure she would make it here in time.

Killian whimpered as he nuzzled my neck.

A tall, sienna-skinned man rushed to the front of the approaching witches. He lifted his arm, his mouth moving, and Breena flew backward. The spell that had been holding Erin lifted, and the priestess took in a large breath.

"You *dare* go against your priestess and your family?" Erin spat, quivering with unbridled rage.

The end was here, but we had to do something to stop the war. I tried again to climb to my feet, but my head spun, and I nearly toppled over. Whatever that spell had been had wreaked havoc on my body.

"End the spell while I deal with my *niece*," Erin commanded as she marched toward us, her attention on Breena.

Killian growled. *We've got to get you out of here.*

No, you have to fight. I wasn't foolish enough to think I would be much help. *We're outnumbered, and we've already lost one pack member. If you don't act, more will be lost.*

Fine, but I'm not leaving your side. Killian spun and lunged at a witch close to us.

The dragons flew overhead, but fifty witches kept their focus on them. They spelled one after another, switching between assaulting them with water so they had to fly down and attack and using wind against them to slow them down. Their best fighter was the small black dragon that could fly at double speed, but the witches could knock her down more easily because of her size.

Something ripped inside the pack link, causing me more agony. We'd lost another pack member, and we would likely lose more. I hadn't imagined such a travesty.

Breena rolled onto her back, readying to spell Erin again.

Erin beat her to the punch, rasping, "*Vocabo ignem!*"

A ring of fire blazed around Breena. She curled into the fetal position to protect herself.

"No," Diana gasped as she broke through a section of witches. Her attention homed in on Breena, who was trying to perform a spell but couldn't. "Erin, what are you doing?" Diana asked as she hurried beside Breena, right across from me.

"I told you she was a traitor, just like your *mother*," Erin spat as her face twisted in disgust. "And like her, Breena has to die."

"What you're doing is wrong! You aren't acting for the coven but for yourself!" Diana exclaimed. "I see that now!"

Breena reached her arm upward and whispered, "*Voco pluviam.*"

Raindrops fell from above her, but Erin chanted her spell again, and the flames rose higher. The flames evaporated the rain before it hit the ground.

"If the city is open, then I am protecting the coven by taking over the world." Erin stretched her fingers, and the flames inched closer to Breena. "Yet further proof that your life has to end."

I stood on four legs, my heart beating like a jackhammer. I couldn't let Breena die. This *couldn't* be her end.

Killian fought viciously beside me, attacking the man who was organizing the Shadow City coven.

To end this, Erin had to die. It would be my last act. Needing to ease my torture, I began to play Chopin's Prelude No. 7 in A Major in my head. After just a few notes, the pain ebbed enough that the world sharpened.

Diana's face paled, but she didn't move an inch to help her sister. Instead, she lifted her chin and shook her head. "Maybe we make her suffer instead."

"No. She'll try to leave like she did before. Clearly, she stayed close by to help *them*." Erin lifted her head skyward and began her chant again.

I had to act now. I moved forward and stumbled. Instead of her throat, as I'd intended, I bit her leg, but I prayed it was enough to buy more time. Her metallic herbal blood spilled into my mouth and down my chin, and I kept thrashing the skin. I had to hurt her enough to make her stop the spell.

But Erin didn't falter. She continued saying the last word, "*Ign—*" right as Diana said quickly, "*Terra fractura*."

The ground underneath Erin and me shook hard, harder than it had earlier. The movement was centralized under us.

"Diana!" Erin's voice vibrated. "What are you doing?"

The flames that surrounded Breena dissipated.

"Saving my sister," Diana answered, then shouted, "*Terra fractura*!" again.

The cement underneath me disappeared, and I dropped. I released Erin's leg as we fell into a dark abyss.

Wind blew around me, making it hard to breathe, and my mind grew foggy. As I was unable to focus on the sound of the song, agony swirled back around me. Nausea churned, and I knew it was over.

I love you, Killian, I linked. Those were the last words

I'd ever say. I needed him to know that in my last moments, he was the one person on my mind.

Jewel! His fear added to my grief and pain, and my stomach came close to emptying.

Strong arms wrapped around me, stopping my fall, and I struggled. Somehow, Erin had grabbed me from behind. But why? Maybe my blood would give her enough juice to get back up the fissure. I clawed at her arms, desperate to die without her on top of me.

"Stop it." Rosemary's voice filled my ears, and my body lurched from the abrupt stop of my descent. "You're going to make me drop you."

I whimpered as my heart seized. Even though she'd caught me, my time was coming to an end.

She hissed, which I'd never heard her do before.

Bright white light filled the dark hole, and her warm angel magic poured into me. The familiarity struck me once again, and I sensed her magic latching onto my heart. I wasn't sure how I sensed that, but my heart felt lighter despite the pain still there, and my body warmed.

Her wings flapped, and I felt her lifting us back to the top. We moved at a slow and steady pace where the wind didn't steal my breath.

Please tell me she got to you in time, Killian linked. *I can still feel you.*

She did, I replied. *And she's healing me.*

Joy and relief surged through our bond, further easing my plight. I played the prelude in my mind again, wanting to do everything possible to speed up the healing process. I'd seen the toll it had taken on Rosemary the night my grandparents' cabins had burned, when she'd had to heal so many people.

Moving her arms underneath my chest, she positioned

her hands closer to my heart. The thrum of the healing increased, and my heart settled into a steady rhythm.

"I don't know how it happened, but it was like someone enlarged your heart, and it had to continually pump harder," Rosemary murmured.

My guess was that Erin had tried to explode the cauldron, but the spell had hit my heart instead. I'd probably never truly know, but that didn't matter as long as I survived.

The earth was dark and jagged. Erin couldn't have survived the fall. I was so fortunate that I hadn't hit one of the sharp edges jutting out from the side.

The entire way to the top, Rosemary funneled her magic inside me. When she lifted me from the hole, I was surprised at the quiet. I'd expected to hear the sounds of the battle continuing.

She lay me down on all fours, and my heart felt normal again. She'd healed me, and though I was exhausted, I felt only a deep ache for the packmates we'd lost.

Thank gods, Killian linked as he raced over to me. He pressed his side into mine as he nuzzled my neck. *It's over*.

My mind struggled to register the words. I found the remaining conscious witches of Erin's coven frozen in place while the dragons, the wolves, Eliza and her coven, and the vampires all stared warily at one another.

Sterlyn stood in the middle of Erin's coven with Griffin flanking her side. Alex, Ronnie, a blonde vampire, a red fox, and a gorgeous black panther stood behind them with a small group of wolves in the very back of the group.

Annie, Cyrus, Theo, and Emmy, along with the rest of the silver wolf pack, were standing between the Shadow City coven and Eliza and Circe's coven, ready to defend our witches if it came to it. The vampires had their hands on their weapons, while the dragons, demons, and angels hovered overhead.

"The humans have forgotten about us, and the demons that chose evil are locked in Hell once more," Eliza said as she flapped the neckline of her silver dress. She was drenched in sweat. "We're safe, and we need to clean up the town and head home before the humans leave. They won't remember why they were stuck inside."

The sienna-skinned man looked at Breena. "You're the priestess now. Tell us what we should do."

Breena cleared her throat and tugged at her shirt. "Maybe Diana should—"

"No, big sister. This is all you," Diana replied as she squeezed Breena's shoulder.

Straightening her spine, Breena glanced at me, then at Eliza and Circe's coven. "We help clean up and ensure nothing like this ever happens again. We will ally with this coven and the other council members and stand united and strong, the way we always should have."

Several witches muttered among themselves, but no one spoke out against the plan.

I wasn't sure how much longer I could stand. The fight and injury had taken so much out of me.

Killian's eyes met mine. He linked with the pack, *I'm taking Jewel home so she can recover. She was in the front and severely injured. Fill me in on what gets done, and Jewel and I will be back in the morning to help.*

I wanted to argue, but my eyes were struggling to stay open.

When he nudged me to walk past the coven, I obliged, desperate to get home. He was right. I couldn't stay, and there was no point in asking him to because if he were the one in this state, I wouldn't.

You two go. We'll handle it from here, Billy linked. *We have people manning the hotel rooms to enforce the curfew while the humans sleep.*

That was all I needed to hear. I linked with Sierra, *Can you please tell Rosemary thank you?* I hated not being able to communicate with her in this form.

Will do, Sierra replied then linked Killian in. *Sterlyn, Griffin, Kira, Alex, and Ronnie are heading up front to handle things with Cyrus and Annie, now that they can get through the crowd.*

With everyone involved, I trusted they'd let us know if we were needed.

As we passed the witches, Eliza broke through the center and stepped in front of me. She touched the top of my head and smiled. "Thank you, Jewel. I saw what you did and what you risked. Your father would be so proud."

I licked her hand, unable to communicate my gratitude any other way.

As Killian and I slowly made our way home, tears of grief and pride spilled from my eyes.

EPILOGUE

ONE MONTH LATER

I'D NEVER THOUGHT I could embrace a normal life. Well, normal by wolf shifter standards. But here I was with Killian, finally enjoying something that he loved—fishing—with our growing family.

We stood next to each other at the slough he always used. It was a late February afternoon, and the air was chilly, but it was the warmest part of the day. The sun was descending, but it was still high enough for its rays to hit my body. The light reflected on the murky water, emphasizing the small trickles and eddies and lighting up the muddy color.

This was the very spot where Sterlyn had washed up on shore after her family's pack had been slaughtered. She'd somehow escaped with her life...and run into Killian.

In a way, it was like our stories had intertwined and come full circle.

"So...if it's a boy, I'd really like to name him Bart. And if we have a girl, I'd like to name her Olive." I rubbed my belly with my free hand. "If that's okay with you."

Killian turned his head toward me and beamed. "*That* is

more than okay with me. As long as our baby is healthy and we're together, that's all that matters, but still, there are no better names than those two."

The last month had been hard in unexpected ways. Apparently, Sierra had been waiting for the crisis to be over before completing her bond with Torak. Killian had been surprised, but not me. Sierra was very wise, but she hid it well, so most people didn't see it. She hadn't wanted to be cut off from our pack during the battle, but as soon as things settled and we'd mourned all our dead—three of our pack members, one silver wolf, ten vampires, and one angel—she and Torak had completed their bond, and she'd left to live with him.

In a way, it was like we'd lost four pack members, and though Sierra's loss was in the best way possible, I still felt a void deep inside.

While I'd been falling to my death, I'd missed the craziness of the demons being sucked away from Earth and into Hell. Eliza, Circe, and Breena had worked together to close the portal forever. Now that only malicious demons were in Hell, the portal could be closed without risking the balance.

With the evil demons gone, the number of vampires turning bloodthirsty and losing their humanity had drastically fallen. The demons had been preying on the vampires they'd made, and now Ronnie, Gwen, Alex, Joshua, and Lillith had things under control. Although we'd lost Sierra, we'd gained Lillith, because she and Joshua had discovered they were soulmates.

Even better, the lab tech, Stephanie, had cured all the wolf shifters who had been experimented on. The two packs we'd last rescued were back in their actual homes, while my grandparents' pack had decided to remain in Sterlyn's family neighborhood. PawPaw's pack homes were the only ones destroyed by fire, anyway, but he also wanted to stay close to Mom and me since the silver wolves didn't have to hide anymore. The only sad part was that Stephanie's human friend, Brittany, had forgotten all about her being a wolf shifter. The best friend she'd once been able to confide in had forgotten what made her and her family so unique. Stephanie was struggling with it, but after all we'd learned, she'd decided not to share that secret with Brittany again to keep her best friend as safe as possible. It also probably helped that since she and Lowe had completed their fated-mate bond, she had someone she could lean on to get through the hard times, and we'd gained a new pack member.

Mom and Emmy had been around daily, helping me move things out of Olive's room so we could convert it into a nursery for the baby. We were also making Killian's old room into a guest bedroom, but with the neutral color schemes Emmy and Mom were picking, I felt like we were getting his room ready for a second child, which might not be possible, given my silver wolf heritage. If I could have my way, I'd love to have as many babies as I could with Killian, so I wouldn't dissuade them.

Sterlyn, Griffin, Alex, Ronnie, Annie, and Cyrus were splitting their time between here and Shadow City. The silver wolf pack had merged with the Shadow City wolf pack, reducing a lot of tension, and a new council had been formed, one that ran more like the United States government, though less corrupt. Each supernatural race had a set number of spots, and an election would be held in the next month to choose the new leaders.

The angels and demons were bridging the divide between their kinds. Since the demons were now welcomed into Shadow City, many angels and demons were discovering they were preordained mates, including Zagan and Eleanor, who'd completed their bond.

Killian wrapped an arm around my waist, his hand settling on my stomach. He kissed my cheek and linked, *This might be the happiest I've ever been, fishing with my pregnant fated mate with nothing dire hanging over our heads. I have the two most important people in my life right here with me.*

I smiled so widely, my cheeks hurt. *I've got to say, I never enjoyed fishing until I came with you. Granted, every time Chad and Theo forced Emmy and me to go with them, they wound up throwing fish and worms at us.*

His eyebrows furrowed. *You were more like siblings than friends, weren't you?*

Yes. With a pack as small as ours, it was hard not to be that way. Dad's face popped into my mind. I remembered how he'd taught us to ride our bikes and build the perfect fort out of blankets, and the countless nights our pack had sat around playing cards. Those were memories I'd hang on to forever.

"I bet they didn't ever give you this." He untangled himself from me and hurried to his bag. He pulled out a clarinet and beamed. "I thought you'd like to take lessons, now that things have calmed down. I want our baby to love classical music the same way you do."

I'd always wanted to learn how to play the clarinet, but Dad hadn't wanted us to spend too much time with people outside our pack, so I'd never had the chance to learn. My heart almost burst as I realized that wasn't holding me back anymore, and of course, my mate would be the very person to help me realize it.

Something tugged at my line, and I almost lost my grip on the pole.

"Whoa." Killian chuckled as he hurried back to me and placed his hand over mine. "You've got to jerk and reel it in."

My skin buzzed at his touch, and I reveled in being this close to him. I didn't fight as he helped me reel in the fish.

Two sets of footsteps headed our way, and when the smallmouth bass I'd caught broke through the murky water, I heard Mom gasp.

"Killian, have you gone insane?" Mom clucked her tongue. "Jewel is *pregnant*."

Emmy stepped up beside Mom and crossed her arms. My best friend shook her head. "And fish can make her sick."

For a second, I thought they were kidding, but with the way they were glaring at us, I realized they were, in fact, disgruntled over this. "Eating certain fish is bad for pregnant women, but I'm not *eating* them. Just catching them."

"But the strain on your body could be too much." Mom placed a hand on her hip.

"From a small fish jerking on a line?" I'd fought witches, wolf shifters, and humans. "I've handled worse."

"A pregnant lady must relax and not put herself in stressful situations." Mom pointed at my stomach and growled, "And that's my grandbaby you're carrying."

They've lost their minds, I linked with Killian. *I thought that was supposed to be me.*

They care about us and our baby. Killian snickered as he took the fishing pole from my hands, the fish dangling from the hook. "Crisis averted, and the baby is still in there."

"Not funny." Emmy shook her head, but the corners of her mouth tipped upward. "And do you know how ridiculous this all looks with a clarinet in your hand?"

For that, you will have to make it up to me in bed tonight.

You turned on me, I scolded, but the thought of him naked had my body heating.

His desire warmed our bond, and I grew hotter. *Oh, don't worry. I'll make it up however many times you want.*

"Ew." Emmy waved a hand in front of her nose. "Her horniness is getting worse and worse."

"It's the pregnancy hormones." Mom nodded. "I was the same way with—"

"Stop." I lifted a hand, not wanting to imagine her and Dad that way. "You've made your point."

Mom broke into peals of laughter. "I had to get you back somehow. I don't want to smell you and Killian like that, either."

And somehow, in that moment, everything felt right. Killian and I were starting a family, I was growing close to my cousins, and a whole new chapter was here for everyone's taking. One with no wars, no bad guys, no political games. Just one huge found family that enjoyed one another's company while we dealt with our old demons...no pun intended.

For once, it didn't hurt to look ahead. I only wished we hadn't lost some loved ones along the way so they could be part of this new, exciting future.

But one thing was certain. Their lives hadn't been lost in vain, and we would carry their presence with us.

After all, love never ends. It's always with us.

ABOUT THE AUTHOR

Jen L. Grey is a *USA Today* Bestselling Author who writes Paranormal Romance, Urban Fantasy, and Fantasy genres.

Jen lives in Tennessee with her husband, two daughters, and two miniature Australian Shepherds. Before she began writing, she was an avid reader and enjoyed being involved in the indie community. Her love for books eventually led her to writing. For more information, please visit her website and sign up for her newsletter.

Check out her future projects and book signing events at her website.
www.jenlgrey.com

ALSO BY JEN L. GREY

The Marked Dragon Prince Trilogy

Ruthless Mate

Marked Dragon

Hidden Fate

Shadow City: Silver Wolf Trilogy

Broken Mate

Rising Darkness

Silver Moon

Shadow City: Royal Vampire Trilogy

Cursed Mate

Shadow Bitten

Demon Blood

Shadow City: Demon Wolf Trilogy

Ruined Mate

Shattered Curse

Fated Souls

Shadow City: Dark Angel Trilogy

Fallen Mate

Demon Marked

Dark Prince

Fatal Secrets

Shadow City: Silver Mate

Shattered Wolf

Fated Hearts

Ruthless Moon

The Wolf Born Trilogy

Hidden Mate

Blood Secrets

Awakened Magic

The Hidden King Trilogy

Dragon Mate

Dragon Heir

Dragon Queen

The Marked Wolf Trilogy

Moon Kissed

Chosen Wolf

Broken Curse

Wolf Moon Academy Trilogy

Shadow Mate

Blood Legacy

Rising Fate

The Royal Heir Trilogy

Wolves' Queen

Wolf Unleashed

Wolf's Claim

Bloodshed Academy Trilogy

Year One

Year Two

Year Three

The Half-Breed Prison Duology (Same World As Bloodshed Academy)

Hunted

Cursed

The Artifact Reaper Series

Reaper: The Beginning

Reaper of Earth

Reaper of Wings

Reaper of Flames

Reaper of Water

Stones of Amaria (Shared World)

Kingdom of Storms

Kingdom of Shadows

Kingdom of Ruins

Kingdom of Fire

The Pearson Prophecy

Dawning Ascent

Enlightened Ascent

Reigning Ascent

Stand Alones

Death's Angel

Rising Alpha

CPSIA information can be obtained
at www.ICGtesting.com
Printed in the USA
BVHW040306090623
665683BV00014B/48